WINTER DRAGON

SEASON'S WAR BOOK TWO

OLENA NIKITIN

ISBN: 978-1-9998861-3-4

Content warning:

Dear Reader, we appreciate that everyone has a different level of sensitivity and may be triggered by various topics. We leave it to your discretion whether you can handle the content in our books. The book is intended for a mature audience of particular interests and contains a certain amount of sexual scenes and sexual innuendo, as well as scenes of death, physical violence and torture. It is a work of fiction set in a world with different racial, cultural and social norms. Any resemblance to actual persons, living or dead, events or localities is entirely coincidental, and the names, characters and incidents portrayed in it are the work of the author's imagination.

Contents

Burge
Ty Mawr
Arknay
Dark Elves Land
Northern Kingdoms
Elaran
Dancik
Cadwaladr
Kion
Zaron
Bodowyr
Green Hills
Black Forest
Oakcross
Central
Wasteland
Osterad
Stone Halls
The Kingdom of Cornovii
Fareon
Liath
Madron
Loome
Riverbound
Stronghold
Carn Cuny
Men-al-tol
Warenna
Rouwa
Steppe Orcs
Alsia
Thorn
Southern Marchia
Ilarutan
Trethevy
High Elves
Steva
Verdante

CHAPTER ONE

The snow that Ina had so admired as she left Osterad was now getting on her nerves. They left two days after the palace battle, officially tasked with investigating attacks on the western border. However, Ina's priority was finding her dragon. It felt like all odds were against them. Since the first snowflake landed on her cheek, it had snowed continuously for two days, and now snow covered the road so completely there was no way to discern whether they were still on it. She was cold, miserable, and annoyed at leading this expedition. Looking down at her horse, she muttered something very unladylike as Woron stoically ignored the awful weather, his heavy body ploughing through the drifts, clearing the way for Ren's smaller horse.

Ina took one more look at their surroundings. She had to admit, she had no idea where they were, and suspected they had strayed from the road hours ago. With a gentle touch to his side, she brought the stallion to a halt and reflected on their situation. They were clearly lost. The night was upon them, and with the snow and wind getting heavier every minute, they had an excellent chance of ending up as a couple of frozen statues

'We need to find shelter,' she said, looking at Ren. 'Do you have any idea where we are?'

His features were pale, almost grey, when he appeared in front of her. 'We should be close to Three Willows, a village near the forest's edge.'

'What forest?' Ina struggled to see anything through the dense snow, despite Ren pointing directly ahead.

'It's a little further this way, so we should keep going. We'll die in this storm if we camp on an empty field. Let's go to the trees and use them to shelter us from the elements!' Ren had to shout to get past the now howling wind.

Ina, guiding Woron in the direction Ren had pointed, wrapped her cloak tighter around her body. Her thoughts dwelled on her cosy townhouse with its large fireplace and cat to warm her lap. *I am not a bloody hero*, she thought, and pictured ripping off Mar's head and sticking it where the sun didn't shine straight after she ensured he was safe in her arms and back in his human form. It was that bloody lizard's fault she was traipsing through the countryside in this damn weather, and Ina planned to show him how much she hated riding through it on horseback.

A line of trees appeared on the horizon with a flickering light breaking through the overwhelming white, and Woron hastened his pace without prompt. Ina felt sorry for the magnificent animal, but even the best horse had limits, and it looked like he was about to reach his. She noticed three hunched figures covered in snow gathered near a barely lit fire upon their arrival.

'May we join you?' Ren asked loudly. One figure waved their hand. 'I think that means yes?' He looked at Ina, waiting for her decision, but she was already on the ground. The camp appeared smaller when they brought the horses closer to the cart, but they weren't picky about the shelter in this weather. Ren added the last of the gathered wood to the fire, and in the revived firelight, they noticed their hosts were three dwarves. Their attire and nearby cart suggested they were merchants, but it was difficult to judge based on what was visible in the snow. Ren looked at Ina with concern in his hazel eyes.

'They are close to freezing to death, and we will share their fate soon if the storm continues. Are you able to do something about it?'

Ina was taken aback by his statement. 'With the weather? Ren, even the archmage could not calm this blizzard.' She knew he was right. Although she couldn't control the weather, she had to do something before the snow buried them alive, preserving their meat for the wolves. Ina touched her chest, feeling the steady pulse of her peridot. If the gem stored enough power, maybe she could hold off the snow from the camp till morning. Ina thought about the warning net she'd spread around her house. Could she change the spell and create a dome to ward off snow and wind from their tiny space?

'Ren, we need more wood, but don't go too far. I'll be set up soon.' She smiled at him, but it was more to give herself courage. 'We won't die in this blizzard, I promise.'

Ren nodded and went to the forest. She heard him break some branches, and she hoped whatever creature was guarding this glade would forgive them. Ina started walking around the camp, anchoring the dome spell. Golden strands touched the ground, melting the snow around them as Ina spun the remaining fibres into a thick mesh net.

'Ren, come back now. I'm ready!' she shouted into the night. When the tired warrior walked inside her barrier carrying some firewood on his back, it was time to close the last strand behind him. Ina picked the best spot to sit for the spell, placed a blanket near the fire, and settled herself down. She closed her eyes, concentrating on the matrix, and connected it to the stone. The spell elements focused on repelling the snow and blocking the wind, and after thinking for a moment, she added another layer, keeping in the warm air. The net shimmered, bending to her will with its golden pulse synchronising with her heartbeat.

'We are safe for now,' she said, looking at Ren feeding the fire, and soon the air began warming up, melting the snow underfoot. The dwarves stirred from their positions at the temperature change and helped around the campsite, caring for the horses and putting a kettle over the fire to boil up some water for a drink. Ina's heart sang as she sat there, observing the silent work.

She smiled at Ren, trying to mask her concern. This spell was complex and draining, and her friend already had enough to worry over. If she ever returned to Osterad, she would kiss Gruff on both cheeks and his scruffy hands for the peridot he gave her, but even with this precious gift, she was unsure its magic would last till the morning. The shadow that appeared in front of her made her raise her head. With a deep bow, the ancient-looking dwarf passed her a steaming cup.

'My lady, please,' he said, pushing the cup into her hands. 'Is this your doing?' He gestured to the net, now lightly covered in snow, which looked like a shimmering white roof over their heads.

Ina reached up, taking the cup gratefully. 'Yes, it is. Thank you for taking us in. We would have frozen if not for your fire.' The tea was so strong and sweet that Ina could almost chew on the drink. The dwarf's gaze lingered on her face longer than she was comfortable with before he spoke again.

'What is your name, my lady? We both know your magic saved us all, and Stone Hall's clan always pays their debts.' The elder stood, hands-on-hips, and Ina suspected he expected her to name her price. Stone Hall City was known for exquisite artwork and their mines, so having a friend there would be worth some theatrics. She bowed her head respectfully, remembering her Great aunt Nerissa's lessons.

'I'm Inanuan Zoria Thornsen, a judicial mage from Osterad, and I'm grateful to sit by your fire. There are no debts to pay but your name, so I can tell the king who saved his humble servant.'

Ren looked at her, his lips twitching, holding back a laugh, but the dwarf leader accepted her words. He bent slightly and spoke. 'I am Vorberg Stonemeir. We came from Stone Hall with a petition to the king, only to be stuck here in this damned blizzard.'

'Petition?' Ina's curiosity piqued. It was a stark reminder that the second reason for this bloody journey was investigating the Grey Mountains' unrest. Although Mar's safety was her priority, she could not miss the opportunity, especially if a man with answers was standing in front of her, stroking his beard.

'Those damn kobolds! They are attacking again, but not just the normal raids. Now they are ambushing merchants. Soon there will be no trade between Stone Hall and Cornovii.' The dwarf was visibly agitated, gesturing widely and almost hitting Ina in the face when he moved too close. 'The king has to secure the transportation tunnel.'

Nodding, she backed out of range. 'I'm sure King Rewan will send help. We simply need to survive this weather in order to tell him.' Exhaustion seeped into her bones from the constant use of magic, and Ina tried to hide a yawn as she spoke. 'I think we had all best get some sleep. This storm won't end tonight.'

Vorberg nodded, observing his younger kin getting ready to sleep, and the elder stroked his beard. 'We can survive it now, thanks to you. Your name will be known in the Stone Halls if you ever need help.' He muttered something under his breath and settled between his kin to preserve the heat.

Ren moved closer and wrapped his arm around Ina's waist, pulling her to his side. He saw her questioning look, so he pointed to the group. 'For heat, this is the best way to keep warm during a storm.'

The magical dome she created kept in most of the fire's heat, but there was still a chill in the air. Ina, allowing Ren to hold her close, leaned against his chest, trying to relax. It would be a long night, and she would need all her strength to keep them from freezing. A shiver ran down her spine, and the warrior pressed her closer. She felt the heat of his skin radiating even through their thick clothes. *Does he have a fever?* Guilt and concern flooded her mind. If not for her rushed departure, they could be at least better prepared for this journey. His hands were bare, and feeling she had to do something, Ina put them under her cloak without a second thought.

Ren sat there with a gentle smile on his face. She observed him with half-closed eyes, surprised that despite the circumstances, he appeared happy. Ina was glad to oblige if holding her close was the reason for that. She wrapped his hands close with only a shirt guarding her against his icy touch and rubbed them to help the circulation.

'I'm fine, my lady,' he whispered, pressing his cheek to her ear.

'No, you're not. We are both chilled to the bone, and I suspect you have a fever, so stop playing the knight in shining armour and just cuddle me tight,' she stated before adding with a smile to lessen his hesitation, 'I would wrap myself around Woron if not for the worry of getting kicked.'

Her open invitation unshackled whatever was holding him back. Ren rested his chin on her shoulder. His cold nose tickled her neck when he inhaled deeply.

'Mar was right. You smell of apples; so sweet I could take a bite.'

Ina stroked his hand but didn't answer. For some time, she had known Ren had feelings for her. In her heart, she loved him, and if not for her feelings for Mar, it would be easy to allow his steadfast affection to fill her days with joy. With the friendship that grew between them and the spell that connected them in the past, she wanted Ren in her life. Ina would even consider some unconventional solutions if her dragon were more flexible. Still, despite their friendship, Mar was unwilling to share, and Ina's heart had already chosen the dragon. *I'm so sorry, my friend. You deserve better, and I will be strong enough to let you go one day.* Ina's thoughts were interrupted by the dry cough that shook Ren's body, adding a worry about his health to the bad start of this journey.

The night progressed with an occasional shuffle of bodies changing position or snorting of horses. The howling wind subsided, but the snow still fell, dense and white, covering the world like a thick blanket. Ren dozed off, but he held her tight even in his sleep, and Ina was grateful for his support. Her awareness flickered; fatigue from the journey and constant focus to sustain the spell were taking a heavy toll on her body. She could not fall asleep, but it was more and more challenging to maintain the magic. Before dawn, she noticed the power in her stone was running low, and soon she would have to resort to drawing it from her body. There was no Chaos around that she could use. The small fire was almost gone, and the natural order of the winter weather could not fuel her magic.

A sharp tug in her chest and the flickering of the magical dome told her the stone was depleted. The spell siphoned her life force to sustain itself, and she could only pray to the gods to end the snow before the magic depletion would stop her heart. Not that she had any hope they would listen.

A loud, restless neigh from Woron woke Ren up. Half asleep, he looked around, but their camp was calm except for the stallion thrashing like a demon. Ren slid Ina aside to check on the horse, frowning in surprise that her limp frame did not resist the sudden movement. He shifted his gaze upon her face, and what he saw almost stopped his heart.

Ina's glassy eyes were barely focused, and her face was deathly pale, with a thin trickle of blood dribbling from her nose as she looked at him and muttered. 'I don't think I can…'

Her words stopped as her head lolled back, and the snow-covered dome above their heads came crashing down. Ren threw his cloak up at the last moment, saving them from the sudden shower, but the dwarves were brutally awakened by a mix of snow and icy cold water. Loudly cursing, they dug themselves out of it and looked around for the cause.

Ren stood up, lifting Ina, and uncovered her pale, blood-smeared face. He rushed to open her cloak with trembling hands, looking for a heartbeat, when Ina tried to swat his hand away.

'I'm fi—' she murmured before falling unconscious.

Ren held her tight as if his life depended on it. The failure of his duties burned deep inside him. He should have spotted her exhaustion, but he fell asleep like a novice. Ren tried to calm his rasping breath, burying his face in Ina's fur cloak and breathing in her scent.

Vorberg came closer and looked at the witch. 'Drained, hmm? I didn't believe she would last that long. You have a sturdy lass here, so don't worry. She is just exhausted. I've seen it before.' He gestured to his companions. 'Make a space on the cart. We are going back to Three Willows.'

Ren nodded, relieved by this scant reassurance, and when the cart was ready, he placed Ina on the furs. Woron objected to Ren harnessing him to the cart, but settled once they began their journey through the heavy snow. Even with his strength, it felt like forever until the little convoy reached the village.

The tavern, located at the edge of the settlement, welcomed them with the stench of stale beer and burnt porridge, but Ren was grateful for any shelter that could provide a bed. Unfriendly faces turned around when he entered the establishment. This reaction was not new to Ren. His exotic features always caused a stir, but now he needed food and a room to look after Ina.

'I'm not looking for trouble,' he announced and headed to the counter. The innkeeper gave him a hostile glare that stopped abruptly when a shiny gold coin rolled across the bar. Ren not only got the biggest and—as the inn wench assured him—the cleanest room, but also the proposal of her company for the night. Politely declining this *tempting* offer, the warrior quickly inspected the place before bringing Ina inside.

Ren had tried everything he could during the ride to wake Ina up, but she only murmured in protest. When he placed her on the small but sturdy bed, her eyes flickered open, only to close as she settled on the cot. After a few gentle shakes didn't bring any response, Ren, determined to wake her up, dared to slap Ina across the face.

'You are such an ass,' she slurred, quickly drifting away. The warrior felt helpless. The witch needed her sleep, but not in wet clothes, still chilled to the bone. After another coin changed hands, the inn's servant soon had a fire burning brightly and a warm plate of food in the room.

'My lady?' he tried once again, to no response.

Ren sat on the edge of the bed and looked at her still frame. Ina's soft snoring, barely audible, calmed his worry. As the dwarf elder said, she was just asleep. He'd never seen someone so unresponsive in their sleep, but he had also never seen anyone magically drained. Ren hoped he didn't break her trust when he undressed her. Her cloak and thick tunic were easy, but when he went up to undo the laces of her cincher, his hands trembled. Calming himself, he took a long, steady breath. It's not how he imagined undressing Ina for the first time. Ren shook his head at the irony of the situation. The precise and stable hands that could kill using nothing but a silver needle now trembled when they touched the laces. The gem she cherished so much was now dull and opaque, causing him to worry even more. *I have to know*, he thought, absolving himself, placing his hand on the soft skin of her neck. A strong heartbeat was still there, easing the tightness in his chest. He exhaled, feeling his heart synchronised to her rhythm, and the connection deep inside him flared up. Ren paused, his hand resting on her skin longer than he considered appropriate. The urge to kiss her almost erased the rational thoughts from his mind and twisted his lips in a bitter smile.

'Mar?' Ina whispered, breaking his focus.

Chastised by this simple whisper, he promptly finished the job and wrapped a blanket around her, with the witch only muttering incoherently without waking.

Finally, he sat down by the fire. It had not been the best beginning of the journey, and such a heavy blizzard was not typical this early in winter. If not for Ina's skills, they would be frozen statues on the side of the road. A long night with the woman he loved more than anything but could not touch was a daunting prospect. Since the day she cured him, the connection he felt remained a steady beat in his heart, easing his loneliness in this foreign land. Ren didn't know much about magic, yet he felt it every time he lay a hand on her skin. Despite his common sense and knowing she didn't love him the same way, he craved her presence and touch. A short, barking laugh followed by a bout of cough slipped out, breaking his silent musing. Ren was not a jealous man. He loved them both. For brief moments with her, he was willing to live in a dragon's shadow, but he knew his captain was made from a different clay, and to his sadness, even this path was blocked for him.

The fire roared behind him, filling the room with heat. Ren stripped his armour, laying his weapons nearby, and now with locked doors and windows, he slowly relaxed. Suddenly, Ina moaned in her sleep, kicking the covers to the floor. Without thinking, he was suddenly towering over her as her long shirt bunched up, showing much of her thigh. Ren's breath quickened when he picked up the light blanket to cover her, swaying when a bout of dizziness blurred his vision.

The short distance back to the chair felt like torture. Ren sat down heavily, hiding his face in his hands, determined to stay awake when the heat in his body intensified. He shook his head and reached for the poker to pull some logs from the fire, only to groan in agony when his hand missed the handle, and the white-hot iron caught on the flesh of his forearm, burning him intensely. The searing pain instantly cleared his mind, replacing it with a sharp, battlefield focus. Ren cursed silently, looking at the wound and focused on warding off the pain. The cold water from the jug brought temporary relief. Still, each movement sent waves of pain through his arm until Ren's eyes darkened, realising his clumsiness and exhaustion rendered him almost incapable of fighting when Ina needed him the most.

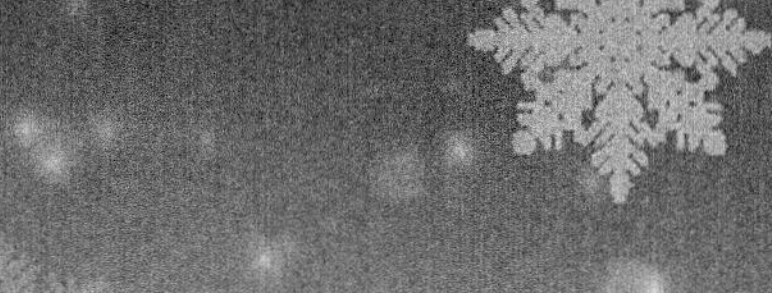

CHAPTER TWO

Several days earlier

The drow noble sat on the uncomfortable ebony chair and squirmed restlessly. This throne wasn't designed for a person of his height, but the kobolds loved their traditions and rituals, and he intended to use this until his goals were accomplished. Frightened underlings kneeled before him, shivering in fear as their report was likely bad news, or, more likely, they were just that scared of him now.

'Another tunnel collapsed, my liege,' started the first, his head pressed firmly to the floor. 'We will have to start anew.'

Frustration and anger burned through the noble as he looked at the cowering males. This incident should not have happened after he'd executed the eldest son of the chieftain and mounted his head on a pike at the mine entrance for insolence. 'This is the third time it has collapsed. Are you trying to tell me your miners are incompetent, or are they consciously sabotaging our efforts?'

The drow suspected the latter, and the thought of those acts of defiance brought a snarl to his lips.

'Am I not a kind master? You have plenty to eat and drink, and thanks to me, you finally have enough to survive the winter without starving. Are you telling me a simple tunnel is too much?'

The elder cringed, his ridged forehead scraping on the stone. 'You are kind, my liege, but the tunnel walls are unstable and likely cursed. I have no other explanation for this.' His metallic voice reverberated in the stone chamber.

The drow stood up angrily, looking down at the offending elder. He was often the tallest in any gathering at over six feet tall, and it always gave him a sense of superiority that could be wielded to great effect. His hand sported an intricately decorated ring topped with a glowing green gem, and as he trailed his fingers over the arm of the ebony throne, it brightened, causing the chair to ripple and change. Wood creaked and screamed as it moved and hardened into burnished steel. His smile grew bigger as the prostrate kobolds moaned in terror. The corruption of their ancient artefact would forever remind these weaklings of his power.

'I will give you another explanation. You and your kin are doing everything in your power to stop the exploration. Now let me promise you something. If the tunnel is not ready within the month, I will skin every single one of you alive and then throw your carcasses to my dogs.' He licked his lips, almost tasting the blood on the tip of his tongue. A wide grin uncovered sharp teeth, and those gathered in the room trembled. Everybody knew the drow lord had a taste for blood and cruel sports. Even his kin of noble birth had perished in his dungeons, their battered bodies often displayed as a warning.

The miner's head hit the floor as he looked back down. 'It will be done, my liege. I will make sure of it.'

'Oh, I know it will,' answered his lord. 'I heard you have a daughter. I will allow you a month. Give me a tunnel, or give me her body.'

The elder wailed in anguish as the guards dragged him out of the audience chamber. The drow's companions cheered and clapped, but quickly went quiet when their master focused his attention on them.

'K'yorl and Nalfeim, take a unit, go down, and find a village. We need more provisions if we're staying here for another month. And maybe bring back a girl or two. Those cave dwellers with their dirty faces have little to offer men like us. The rest of you make sure the transportation tunnel is secure. If I hear about another dwarf sneaking through to Cornovii, you will share the kobold's fate.'

His words were welcomed with more cheers, and two burly men rose and saluted their leader. 'It will be done. Are you interested in anything in particular?'

He waved them off. 'The one I'm interested in is still in Osterad, but I will have her eventually, as well as that jewel she carries. For now, just bring me someone clean to kill some time.'

He returned to his new throne as his men dispersed to carry out their orders. As he closed his eyes, he saw Ina dancing, surrounded by flames in the middle of the ballroom. It had taken a lot of effort and a powerful illusion spell to disguise himself, bribing that idiot Liander, but he'd attended the coronation ball. He'd gone there to confirm a rumour of Sowenna's regalia resurfacing, but tasting the raw Chaos the witch awakened with her dance was enthralling. After that dance, she had been the centre of everyone's attention, but he couldn't care less. His priorities had changed. He now desired both the gem and the magic she carried.

The woman herself was not to his liking. Her skin was too light and her manner too free, but he'd be willing to put up with that. The Chaos magic was his birthright. He deserved the power she wielded, and he would enjoy taming this wild mare and teaching her to eat from his hand. His eyes lost focus, and the image of Ina, wearing the complete set of the Chaos regalia, felt so real he reached out his hand to touch her.

So many things had happened since his mother's necromancer gave him the ring. That day he'd lost her patronage, but one look at the gem, and he knew what he had to do to restore himself. His goal was simple, and once he fulfilled it, there would be a new ruler of Arknay, but he had no intention of stopping there.

Unaware of their new leader's thoughts and world-changing plans, the miners toiled to excavate the tunnels. Grey-skinned men worked, shedding sweat and blood to fulfil his wishes—even at the cost of their lives—but the mountain no longer yielded its secrets to their tools. Reinforced tunnels collapsed or flooded with poisonous gas. Nothing seemed to go right, and the miners whispered that the Lord of the Mountain impeded their progress. Yet the display of their leader's power stopped any thought of rebellion.

After taking to the sky after the shocking end of the battle, Mar circled the palace in sheer panic, trying to understand what had happened. That word, *circle.* He'd never thought of it in this way before. Flying through the clear, crisp air of late autumn helped to calm his mind, allowing Mar to analyse the situation.

One moment he was fighting a horde of monsters, the next, he was one, and his men were attacking him! He knew it was connected to Ina's magic, and this thought provided some reassurance. That feeling before his transformation had happened before, and that time he'd returned from death's door to wake up in Ina's bed. This time, whatever she'd done, Mar felt whole, like two parts of his soul had finally fused, calming the inner discord he so often felt. If only he weren't now scaly, massive, and a dragon.

Regret filled him. Leaving Ina behind tore apart something in his chest, and Mar considered swooping down to snatch Ina away, only to see her surrounded by Chaos magic, magnificent in her anger, shaking her fist at the sky and cursing up a blue storm.

He watched her as he banked to the left, smiling, even as he worried about what to do next. He couldn't land in the city, as the guard and mages would defend the city against the threat he now posed. Could he land somewhere quiet and change back to being human? Was that even a possibility? The image of Ina, wonder in her eyes, reaching out to touch his face, not scared of him in the slightest, eased the pressure in his chest. Whenever fear threatened to cripple him, he reminded himself he was not alone and that where magic was involved, Ina would find a way. Their relationship was rocky, but he knew he would have one person who wouldn't abandon him to this fate.

The only question was, how? The only information he knew of dragons was from the tales his grandmother spun to get her unruly grandchild to sleep, which told of the turbulent relationship between Liath and Dragonkind.

I need to go home. Of all Cornovii, the people of Liath would be the least scared by the sudden appearance of a dragon. If I can express myself, they'll be able to alert Ina or Nerissa, and between them, they will find a solution.

These thoughts and the precise plan that came with them calmed the last worry. Mar turned his head and looked towards the Grey Mountains. His large wings effortlessly caught the evening currents as he headed towards home, oblivious to the screams of terror he caused in the towns and villages below when the shadow of a magnificent beast moved over the ground. His thoughts kept drifting back to Ina. He hoped she was safe. His little spitfire had outdone herself this time. His roaring laughter reverberated through the sky as Mar remembered her slight figure, shaking her fist at his retreating form.

A few hours later, as exhaustion weighed down his wings, the shadow of castle Liath appeared on the horizon. Mar flew lower, and uncertainty flashed in his mind for the second time since the change. He felt the previous excitement and joy of flying slowly disappear, and his usual pragmatism resurfaced. What if his family wouldn't accept him in his current state?

As he approached the castle, the sounds of screams and trumpets calling soldiers to arms cut through the quiet of the early evening, lights flaring to life the closer he got to the walls. The situation didn't look good, but Mar prepared to land, extending his rear legs and spreading his claws to grab onto the battlements. Suddenly, a sharp pain ripped through his right shoulder. Blinded by the setting sun's light, he had missed the massive arrow shot by a ballista.

His body was not flying anymore. It was tumbling, hurtling towards the ground. He struggled bravely to flap his wings to hold himself in the air. Shouts of men with a volley of arrows told him landing meant death. Mar had witnessed too many battles not to recognise the frenzied attacks of frightened soldiers. "Shoot now, question later" was their current state of mind, and he could not risk it. He could fight them off, but killing his father's men-at-arms for merely defending the castle was cowardly and pointless.

It took a massive effort to gain some height, and his injured shoulder pulsed in agony each time he beat his wings. While the massive arrow limited his movements, it also slowed the bleeding, but without a safe place to land, Mar knew it was a death sentence to go anywhere near the ground. The dragon remembered his grandmother's stories about the old ruins on Jagged Wing Peak. It was supposed to be a place where dragons lived long ago, and now stripped of choices, Mar headed towards the mountains.

Night fell over the land, and even with enhanced vision, Mar could barely distinguish between different shapes on the ground. Finally, he noticed a small clearing between sparse trees and jagged granite. Mar reduced his altitude, readying to land, but the arrow's shaft tore through his muscle, leaving the wing flapping uselessly by his side. With the other still fully open, he tumbled from the sky, crashing into the ground so hard he lost consciousness.

Awareness slowly returned, and the pain of his battered body came with it. The rocky ground was no substitute for a feather bed, but he didn't have the energy to move, feeling he could count every bone as he lifted his heavy head, noticing the sharp edges of a building. Mar blinked, confused, but the structure was still there. It looked as if it were carved from the rock itself, and even with the mark of time on its walls, its core was primarily intact.

Standing up was a study of endurance. The bruises and cuts from the impact warred with the crippling pain from his ballista wound, which, as he looked, was at least now empty of the large wooden projectile, though the gaping wound, dripping with reddish-gold blood, both worried and fascinated him.

What else would he have to learn about his body? Mar knew he had to stop the bleeding, but he didn't have the faintest idea of how whilst in this form. He tried imagining his human self and attempted to force the change, but nothing happened. The massive paw in front of him was still covered in scales. Mar tried again with the same result. He could not change. The panic gripped his heart, speeding his heartbeat, and blood pumped from the wound.

He had to do something quickly, and, as a last resort, Mar turned to old folk tales. Dragons were supposed to breathe fire, so, aiming for a crooked tree, Mar tensed all his stomach muscles, unsure what he was supposed to do, and burped heavily, instantly regretting it when acid flooded his mouth. As he started feeling dizzier and dizzier, the dragon thought of Ina, alone as he died in this desolate landscape. Still, at least she had Ren to protect her now. As his anger and regret ripped a roar from his throat, searing white fire followed his outburst, engulfing the tree. He rushed forward before impossible heat consumed the wood, grabbed a burning branch, and thrust it into his wound.

Immense agony ripped through his body, and the dragon passed out for the second time that day.

The light of the breaking dawn slowly woke the sleeping dragon, and despite the ground being covered in frost, the sun's weak rays chased away the strange dreams running through Mar's mind. The joy of flying through the winter sky, the magnificent dragon's body, and the flames erupting from his throat all felt so real to the warrior as he lay on the ground.

It was then that the memories flooded back. The battle at the palace, the pain of his forced transformation, even his escape and subsequent injury at Liath. The frightening truth left Mar scrambling to stand up, and, as he looked down, he came face to face with reality. Two large scaled and clawed hands. He was a dragon.

Blue-grey scales covered his body, and the occasional jagged flash of gold lightning across his chest and wings clad the powerful muscles that moved beneath the still supple scales. It was a magnificent body, but Mar would give anything to get his old form back.

Suddenly, the sound of rustling caught his attention. He hadn't expected there to be any living creatures here, except possibly a goat or two. Mar wanted to curse in frustration when the thought of animals made his stomach rumble. Yet another problem to tackle. How was he supposed to feed this enormous body? Turning to the source of the noise, he noticed a young woman walking out from the ruins. This incredible view left him stunned. Without even a hint of fear, she approached him and patted his muzzle.

'Oh good, you are awake. I thought you'd shut down to regenerate.'

She walked back into the building, and Mar slowly stood, trying to collect his jaw from the floor. A moment later, she came back, dragging a resistant goat behind her. The animal fought desperately, but the woman seemed to have more than enough strength to wrangle the struggling creature.

'Here, snack on this. You will need it to rebuild your muscles,' she said, throwing the terrified goat to his feet.

Mar acted on instinct, and before he realised what he was doing, his massive jaws snatched the animal up and tore it apart. Fresh blood flooded his throat, and Mar nearly gagged. Instead, the taste dragged a moan of pleasure from his throat.

'Who are you?' he tried to ask, but the only sound that came out was a weird groaning and roaring.

The woman walked closer and grabbed one of his horns.

'What is wrong with you? Did you hit your head or something?' With a sharp jerk, the female twisted his head around, trying to find the source of the injury. Mar tried to pull away, but she didn't let him. Her light blue eyes bore into his, and he shuddered, feeling ghostly fingers brushing through his thoughts.

'Strange,' she muttered. 'You consider yourself human, but why?' She attempted to continue her inspection, but Mar jerked back. This digging in his mind felt wrong, and he didn't intend to endure it, not even for another goat.

'Okay, okay….' The woman backed off. 'I'm sorry, but how else can I find out what's wrong?' She looked at him and paused for a moment, then approached him slowly, hands up in a gesture of goodwill. 'Let me help you. You want to talk, yes?'

When Mar nodded, she placed her hand on a slight bulge in his neck. 'Exhale through this. It takes conscious effort, but with a little practice, you'll be able to speak like a human, an elf, or any other sentient race, for that matter.'

Mar tried again. It took a few attempts, but he managed to growl out the question.

'Who are you?' The words, distorted, almost a hissing growl, surprised him, but the woman only laughed and nodded in appreciation.

'I see you are a quick study. I am Ayni, and who you might be?' She tilted her head and gifted him a beautiful smile.

Mar focused on his speech. This time, it was easier. 'I am Marcach of Liath. Why are you not afraid of me?'

Ayni burst out laughing. 'You must have hit your head harder than I thought if you don't know the answer to that. I'm a dragon like you. Why else would I be in Angrath Temple?'

Mar blinked and shifted forward, only to wince when he moved his injured limb. Instantly, the woman's attention focused on his injury. She approached him and, without hesitation, thrust her hand into the torn, burnt flesh that was once his shoulder.

The dragoness raised her eyebrows, seeing the amount of destruction. 'What the hell happened to you? Dragonfire caused this wound.'

'Ballista,' answered Mar sharply without giving her any details. His trick with the fire had stopped the bleeding, but passing out on the burning branch hadn't been the best of outcomes.

Ayni looked at him for a moment, but, seeing he had nothing more to add, she crouched next to a bag he hadn't noticed before. Moments later, she approached him with a jar full of grey, greasy ointment.

'This will have to do. I don't know what you are hiding from me, but a ballista didn't cause those burns. This ointment will help you heal, but it will take longer than usual, and you can't change, or you could end up crippled. Human flesh won't heal a wound from dragon fire.' She spread the greasy salve over the wound angrily, visibly annoyed he hadn't given her the whole story.

Mar endured her ministrations in silence. He knew he needed help, and rejecting it offhand would have been foolish. He blessed his luck and lack of knowledge that stopped his transformation. If this woman was right, he could have permanently damaged his dominant hand. While she tended to his wound, he scrutinised his rescuer. Slender and tall, with raven black hair and very light, almost transparent blue eyes, she was beautiful in a strange, ethereal way. Curiosity got the better of him, and despite his better judgment, he asked, 'What does your dragon look like?'

Ayni chuckled lightly at the question as she finished patching up his wound. 'Well, let me show you.'

Mar worried there wouldn't be enough space for two dragons, but this concern quickly disappeared as the woman moved away, and despite watching closely, her contours began blurring before his eyes. Between one breath and another, she disappeared, replaced by an exquisite dragon, aquamarine scales radiant in the morning sun, and Mar had to admit she was beautiful in both dragon and human form.

Ayni stretched under his watchful gaze, and he could hear her soft purr.

'Do you like what you see?' The playful note in her voice made him realise he was staring like a cadet at his first-ever breast. To cover his embarrassment, he laughed.

'Believe it or not, you are only the second dragon I've ever seen.' He avoided the question, but his statement was met with surprise.

'What do you mean, the second? Who was the first?' Her curiosity was palpable, and he felt her consciousness again attempting to invade his thoughts.

'Don't you dare,' he snapped, causing her to scowl, then answered voluntarily. 'The first one was me. I've not been like this for long.'

Ayni only shook her head. 'That is unusual. Maybe you have forgotten after the fall, but we will fix it with time.' She spread her wings and shot up into the air. 'I will bring some food. You must be starving.'

Mar was left alone as the pain in his shoulder subsided to a dull ache, and he used the time to think over what he'd learned. After seeing the woman changing her shape so quickly and without effort, he felt hopeful and, in some ways, a certain amount of relief. *Maybe I can keep it.* The thought of being able to maintain his dragon form was new, yet he had to admit that he liked this new body and finally felt complete. Now he knew what had happened to him in battle. That feeling, the sensation of power and strength when he fought, must have been the dragon taking over. Mar took a moment to think it over. It wasn't taking over exactly. It was more like he was connecting to that part of his soul, becoming the dragon. Still, there was the question of why he suddenly changed now and not during some other time in his life. He didn't think Ina's magic could be the only reason, but all his family were human as far as he knew.

Mar flexed his shoulder with a grimace, and after remembering his transformation, he started thinking about Ina. Although the battle for the palace had been a chaotic mess, he still remembered Ina's reaction to his new form. She had seemed enraptured and wanted to pet him, just like her cat. Mar's roar shook the peak when he laughed. His untamed witch. Could she pin him to the floor now? Sharp claws of desire pierced his heart. Mar knew he'd wanted her when he was just a human and had fallen in love with her during their time together. Her witty mind and untamed spirit had grown on him, especially since he learned that under the harsh words and brazen manners hid a woman who'd been hurt too many times to show her soft side, yet she readily sacrificed herself to save a stranger.

Since transforming, the pattern of his thoughts had changed, and now there were fewer doubts and more certainty in how he saw her. One thing stood out for him. He loved Ina more than he'd ever loved anyone else and knew he had to prove that to her. It would take time, and he would need the help of his strange new acquaintance, but he would find his way back to his human shape and Ina, and when he did, he would marry the hell out of her. Content, Mar closed his eyes and drifted to sleep, waiting for Ayni to return with provisions.

The dragoness circled the small clearing, looking down at the sleeping Mar. He was bigger than an ordinary male, but acted so innocent, like a cute, helpless hatchling. Since her last mate was killed, she had retreated to the isolated Angrath temple to grieve. The world had lost its shine after the war ended, and the elders had ordered their people to live as humans, hiding their true nature. Seeing Mar in his dragon form when she returned from the hunt, Ayni realised she hadn't seen her kin for far too long and was sure she wouldn't recognise another dragon in a crowd of humans, even if they bumped into each other.

The longing to be with her own kind tugged at her soul, and the dragoness smiled for the first time since she had hidden away. If fate sent her a new mate, she would take it. Ayni missed soaring over the land with nothing but the wind beneath her wings. She grinned, swooping over the rugged mountainside. She would heal him, and then they would fly together in the mating dance.

This thought thrilled her, and after another playful loop, Ayni headed to the nearest human settlement, hoping they had some spare livestock.

After spotting the tiny hamlet, she landed behind a rock outcrop just big enough to hide her form, honouring the rule that dragons should not be seen or heard. Ayni transformed into the shape she used most in this area, a middle-aged peasant, and went to the nearest building and knocked on the door. Although the farmer initially didn't want to sell his animals, a few silver coins convinced him to change his mind, and she took possession of an old heifer long past its milking days.

The obnoxious animal instinctively sensed she was a predator, struggling and moaning its distress. Ayni cursed up a blue storm, dragging the terrified cow back to the rocks. *Men! Feed them, heal them, and hope they will be grateful enough to show their appreciation.* Finally, after taking to the sky with the annoying cow in her claws, the dragoness lost her patience with the cow's cries and snapped its neck with one swift twist. *It's time to feed that fine specimen of dragon maleness. The sooner he heals, the sooner we can fly*, she thought, brushing off his lack of knowledge. It was amusing, and she felt good helping him. Ayni was determined to make him recall his lost memories, but later—after she'd had a little fun.

CHAPTER THREE

The sound of a busy kitchen woke Ina from her dreams of being helpless as an endless white avalanche buried her alive. The effort to open her eyes dragged a moan from deep inside her soul, and the confusion at the unfamiliar rough-hewn ceiling forced her brain to work. She remembered fighting overwhelming exhaustion while trying to keep the magical dome over the camp before everything went black.

'We survived then,' Ina mumbled, looking around as she sat up. The room was plain, but the clattering of dishes and hum of human voices from below suggested they'd made it to an inn or similar establishment. Ren was nowhere to be seen, and dragging herself off the bed, Ina noticed she was wearing only her long shirt, with the rest of her clothes scattered around the room, hanging from the furniture. It looked like Ren wanted to ensure everything would be dry by the time she woke up.

The morning chill made her shiver as soon as her bare feet touched the floor, and Ina hastily dressed. The half-burnt wood in the fireplace looked promising, but nothing happened when the witch attempted to cast a fire spell. She took a shallow, panicked breath and tried again, but nothing happened except a dull ache in her fingers. One glance at the gem on her chest revealed the uncomfortable truth. She had drained herself and her stone entirely, and it would take days to restore her magic.

A stray idea intruded. If she could find a natural source of Chaos, it would be easy to recharge her peridot. As soon as she had this thought, Ina put it aside. After the palace battle, she promised herself not to bathe in Chaos and yet, at the first obstacle, her desire to lose herself in the addictive power reared its ugly head. Instead, she opened the door and asked a passing maid to start the fire before walking to the window.

A flash of movement caught her attention. Next to the stables in the small courtyard, Ren danced with his sword. That was the only way she could describe his fluid, graceful movements as he glided around the small space. Relieved to see he'd recovered from their ordeal and fascinated by his technique, Ina grabbed the poker from the fire and clumsily followed his moves. Despite feeling embarrassed at her lack of skill, she followed the more straightforward combinations. *If I can't work my magic, it would be helpful to know a trick or two.*

Ina had never trained in combat, as her mother and great aunt wanted her to comport herself as a lady, and by the time she started university, enough people had belittled her inability to work any branch of Order magic that all confidence to try it was gone. The few attacks the witch could manage, she had learned from her mercenary friends in the tavern. Not that she would ever start a tavern brawl—not on purpose at least—but after getting caught up in two fights in Gruff's place, Janik, the bloody idiot, taught her how to disable any drunk man who saw a woman as an easy target. Ina pictured her former associate as she thrust the poker forward, pleased at how satisfying it felt.

'Die!' she shouted, preparing to kill the wardrobe when the door snapped open, and Ren charged into the room.

Despite his laboured breathing and heavy perspiration, the warrior's eyes were focused as he looked around the small room, sword drawn and ready to strike the enemy. As he noticed Ina, alone, her poker pointed towards the wardrobe, he stepped closer and turned to the potential danger.

'Ina? Move back. I'll deal with this,' Ren said slowly.

'But Ren—' she tried to say, but he raised his hand to silence her.

'Step away from the wardrobe,' he said, crossing the small room, not a single plank creaking beneath his feet.

Ina rolled her eyes and stepped aside. The warrior yanked the door open, revealing an empty interior and a few spiders running away from the sudden light. Still, it wasn't good enough. Ren poked and prodded the back panel before he turned around to Ina.

'My lady, who was attacking you?' he asked, and despite the calm tone of his voice, Ina noticed how on edge he was.

'Why does everyone always assume someone's trying to kill me?' She could not resist but answer his question with one of her own.

Ren just raised his eyebrow. 'I saw through the window you were stabbing something and heard a commotion in your room, and you shouted, "Die!" when I was running up here. Care to tell me who was it and where they are now?'

Putting it like that, Ren had a point, and now it was her turn to explain. Pink shades of embarrassment blossomed on her cheeks as she started. 'My magic is gone, for now. I can't even start a fire, and I don't know how long it will take to get it back. I saw you practising, and I wanted to learn.' Ina tried to hide the poker behind her back. 'That was what you saw in the window, and I may have tripped over the furniture a few times.'

Ren blinked several times, looking at her with disbelief. 'You're trying to tell me you practised Jian kata… with a poker?' Something broke in him, and the warrior doubled over, laughing. He struggled to calm down, and gasping between bouts of laughing intertwined with cough, Ren stuttered, 'But why, my lady?'

Ina huffed with exasperation. She was proud of her new moves, but Ren seemed to find it a joke. 'I wanted to learn how to defend myself when my magic is depleted or blocked. I would like to know other ways to fight instead of always relying on magic and my Chaos. Right now, even a simpleton with enough strength could take me down. I don't like it, Ren.'

Ren approached and reached behind her, taking the poker from her hand. 'I will teach you, if you'd like.' His eyes were smiling, and he behaved as if teaching her couldn't make him happier.

'Will you really?' She enthusiastically grabbed his forearm, only for him to wince in pain. Looking at the linen fabric of his shirt, damp from a seeping wound, it was her turn to look at Ren and frown.

'What happened?' she asked, pulling his sleeve up.

At the sight of the wound, Ina gasped. Its charred edges exposed the weeping flesh below, and as the sickly sweet smell hit her nostrils, the witch realised infection had already set in. All this when her magic was gone. She called to a servant for clean water and linen cloths, then turned to look at Ren, masking her worry with disapproval.

'Really? When were you going to mention you were hurt? When your arm turned rotten and fell off? What is wrong with men and their need to never ask for help?'

Ren looked down sheepishly and meekly sat in the chair for Ina to wash his injury. Without knowing how long she'd slept, the witch had no idea how much time they'd already lost, but they were going nowhere until this burn was healed. The guilt over the delay in finding Mar left Ina distracted as she scrubbed and cleaned away all the charred flesh until fresh blood flowed freely. He obediently drank the healing potion he was given and only hissed a little when she applied the burn cream to his wound. Ina bent over his arm, cooling the sting with a gentle breath, and the light breeze tickling his arm made him open his eyes. When she straightened up, blinking back unwanted tears, the defiance in his eyes told her he regretted nothing.

'It was just a minor wound, and you needed the rest.'

'Men, you're all the same. Ren, it would break my heart if something happened to you.' Ina placed her hand on his forehead before standing up. 'You are injured and running a fever right now, and I have no magic, so we'll stay here till you're recovered. That way, we won't head into another blizzard completely helpless.'

As Ina fussed over him, Ren could see the worry she tried to hide, so the warrior submitted to her care instead of arguing over his health. He would have more time to think before arriving in Liath, as he doubted Mar's family would warmly welcome the infamous witch and a strange warrior, especially when they informed them their precious firstborn was now a dragon. Ren knew Ina was unpredictable and chaotic, but he'd trusted her to have a strategy when he asked about her plans outside Osterad's gates. However, she just looked up at the falling snow, smiled, and uttered the words every soldier feared.

'We will go there and see what happens.'

So they went and saw, almost dying in the blizzard. Now it was time to plan out the rest of the journey. This injury was a good excuse to keep the witch at the inn a few days longer and recover from the cough that stole his breath during training. Ren took Ina's hand and kissed it gently.

'My lady, I'm sorry for causing you to worry, and I am grateful for your help. Mar knows this land, and I'm sure he will be fine for a day or two, even if he is a dragon.' Ren cupped her face when he noticed she was holding back tears. 'We will go as soon as we can, even if my injury isn't healed. Perhaps you should check on our companions? The dwarves should still be in the tavern, and if you want to practise the Jian sword style, I shall find you an appropriate blade. I fear a poker isn't suited for this work.'

Ina nodded vigorously and pulled on her cloak. 'You are a better friend than I deserve. I'm sorry for dragging you through such hardship.'

'Ina, he is also my friend, and I'm glad we can help him together.'

Ren didn't want to burden her with his unrequited love. He hadn't lied. Even if the witch had stayed home, his friendship with Mar would have compelled him to find the captain. Still, he couldn't deny being alone with her, and these moments of intimacy weighed heavily on his conscience, testing his resolve to hide his feelings.

Despite the name, the town of Three Willows didn't have a single willow, and the only trees around were dark-leafed pine that looked to be part of the nearby forest. With a blanket of snow that glowed in the morning sun, it looked like an idyllic place to live. Ina and Ren strolled along, looking for the local forge, hoping to purchase a decent blade for Ina to use. After the incident with the fire poker, Ren was determined to teach her how to fight. It didn't come from the goodness of his heart or the desire to be a teacher, but rather the knowledge that, left to her own devices, the witch would learn how to use it poorly, possibly hurting herself or those she fought alongside.

The blacksmith wasn't far away, and as Ren haggled with the smith over two large hunting knives, Ina wandered around, touching the various swords on display, imagining herself wielding them, her fiery vipers entwined with the blades, a natural extension of her magic, serving justice or vengeance as needed. However, as Ren clasped hands in agreement with the blacksmith, it looked like she'd be skinning rabbits instead of gloriously conquering evil.

Once they had finished at the forge and wandered through the rest of the village, Ren took her into the forest, far away from prying eyes, and asked her to attack him. When Ina protested and pointed out she wanted to learn how to use a sword—not hack and slash like a crazy fishwife—Ren only raised his eyebrow, then swished a thin, long twig through the air in front of her.

'If you want to learn, you will follow my commands.' The power in his voice demanded her obedience, surprising the contrary witch. Still, Ina had been raised by Nerissa, and, hearing this, she chuckled lightly.

'And if I don't?' she teased, knowing the answer, but again, Ren surprised her.

Approaching the witch, he smiled lightly. 'If you don't, we have two choices. I'll stop teaching you, or I can use this twig to discipline the unruly pupil.'

'You wouldn't...' she said, eyeing him suspiciously, backing off when Ren approached closer.

'Then try to stop me, my lady. I hope you are fast enough to do it before I smack your disobedient rear.'

The cold, predatory demeanour of the man she knew was offset by a wicked smile that quickened Ina's heart, her eyes tracking his movement as Ren slowly approached, giving her time to adjust. His lazy smirk showed he was toying with her like a cat with a mouse. Finally, a quick hit stung her bottom. Ina jumped away, hissing in pain, but Ren seemed to enjoy it.

Feeling like prey, she put the knife in front of her. 'Ren, please. I don't want to hurt you, but I won't let you hit me again.' Her statement should have made it clear, but instead, she watched his pupils dilate in anticipation when he snapped out.

'Then fight, Ina. Fight like your life depends on it.' Another hit seared her calf, and the witch snapped.

Before she could stop herself, the knife in her left hand swung wildly through the air, aimed towards his head, or at least where his head used to be, but Ren had already moved, adding another welt to her sore leg.

No matter how she tried to strike him, he was faster. Her body ached from the effort and the merciless whipping he rained down on her. If she only had her magic, she could end this instantly, but now, vulnerable and panting like a broken-down horse, she was close to tears.

Finally, he stopped, and Ina stood there shaking from exhaustion. Not a single attack she'd aimed at him drew blood. *This is hopeless. Why did I think I could be a fighter?* she wondered, lowering her head in defeat.

Ren approached her with a smile. 'Not bad for a beginner, my lady. Tomorrow we will practise more….' He cut off the rest of the sentence, seeing Ina's forlorn look. Uncertainty flashed through his face. He'd done it the right way, breaking the recruit, giving them a taste of their mortality and the pain that came with any fight, but now, seeing the woman barely holding back her tears, he doubted his judgement.

'Ina, I'm sorry,' he whispered, closing his arms around her. Not as tall as Mar, he still easily towered above her, and now, feeling her body tremble, he felt like scum. Teaching her the way of the blade was a silly idea. Lost in his thoughts, he felt her trying to push him away, and an icy shiver ran down his spine. What if she rejected him now? A few deep breaths helped calm the turmoil in his heart, but it took a moment before he realised she was talking.

'You are an asshole, Sa'Ren Gerel! Beating me when I have no magic? You wait. I will sear your pale arse soon. What was the point? I would listen to you when you teach me. I was just teasing. You will teach me properly tomorrow, or else… And I'm not crying—don't you dare think I'm crying—it is just exhaustion.' The incoherent stream of thought from the tired woman made Ren smile. One thing was clear. Ina intended to continue learning, so even if he had broken her body, he hadn't broken her spirit.

Ren gathered up the knives and wrapped them up, turning away to hide a painful coughing fit. 'Let's go back, we need food and rest. I promise I will be a better teacher, but Ina… I had to provoke you. With your character, you would never attack someone without good reason. Remember, I saw you during the palace battle, and whilst I understand, if you are in danger, it could cost you your life.' He sighed heavily, hoping she would understand. 'I don't want you to die just because you hesitate to stab some bastard.'

His explanation made sense, but the burning skin of her calves and buttocks disagreed with his training methods. As soon as her magic returned, she would give him a taste of his own medicine. Cheered by this thought, she followed him back to the tavern.

Evening came early, and with it, a fresh bout of snow. After checking on Woron, Ina returned to her room to sit by the fire and nurse her aching body, but a quiet knock on the door interrupted her ministrations.

'Enter,' she answered, not surprised when Ren entered her room. He looked somehow pensive, standing there with a bowl of hot water.

'How do you feel?' he asked, placing the bowl on the table, and Ina noticed him avoid looking directly at her.

'As expected. Everything aches, and I had to place a pillow on the sofa to cushion my bruised rear,' she said, noticing Ren's hand tremble a little. 'What is that for?' she asked, pointing to the bowl.

'Hot water can help ease the pain,' Ren answered, still avoiding her eyes.

She could not help but laugh, confusing him with her attitude. 'Ren, you're not offering to place hot compresses on my arse, are you?' She shook her head, stifling a giggle. 'It is just a pain, my friend, and it will disappear. There's no need to fuss about it. Now, come and join me. I need a distraction, and you are it.' She grinned, patting the space next to her. 'Sit, please.' When Ren sat down, she leaned her head against his shoulder and stared at the fire.

'I'm not mad. I know you had your reasons for treating me like that, and I trust your judgement, but I'm in pain and worrying about Mar. I need something to stop me from thinking about him alone and in danger. Please tell me about your homeland and why you came to Cornovii.'

Ren shifted uncomfortably in the chair, but eventually told Ina about his past.

The kingdom of Yanwo was a far distant land beyond Orc Steppe and the great desert, spoken of in whispers and mythical tales by the bards, a place Ina always dreamed of visiting. Ren's mother was one of many wives of the emperor, and Sa'Ren grew up in opulence, but no money, jade or silk could buy a happy childhood. His father believed in survival of the fittest, and as far back as he could remember, the young prince had been in a fight for his life with his many siblings. Slowly, with time, their numbers had dwindled through poison and war, until only he and his younger brother were left.

Ina looked at him and assumed the only plausible conclusion. 'So you lost the fight?'

Ren's sadness was overwhelming. 'No, my lady. I won.'

Ina raised her head and looked at him. 'I don't understand. If you won, why are you here?' she asked, confused by the turn of the story.

'I won the fight, but as I stood over my brother, looking at him so defenceless and hoping for a quick death, I couldn't do it. I could not murder him in cold blood for the dragon throne. Of all my siblings, he was the one who always understood me—

loved me, even—so instead of slitting his throat, I gave up my position and left, never to return.' As Ina looked into Ren's eyes, she smiled. That was the Ren she cared so deeply for, and she instinctively wrapped her arms around him and gave him a soft peck on his cheek.

'Well, I'm glad you stopped. If not for this, I would never have met you otherwise.' Ina saw his mood lighten, and he even flashed a half-smile when she poked his side.

'This won't do, Ren. I need more, so you have to tell me all. How was life there, and about food, and did you have a lover?' Suddenly, her eyes rounded, and Ina gasped. 'You mentioned the dragon throne. Do you have dragons as well?'

Ren felt warmth seep into his soul. He missed Yanwo, but seldom talked about it, remembering only the painful times. Ina's teasing and avid interest reminded Ren of those bright memories of childhood. Slowly stroking her hair, he told her about the colourful clothes, exotic animals, and the legends of the first emperors; noble warriors who rode dragons into battle, defeating all who defied them.

Ina chuckled, hearing how his siblings stole blossoms from the emperor's plum tree to show off their courage and, seeing her smile, Ren refrained from mentioning how the guards who protected that tree were killed for their failure. He also preferred to remember his homeland as the beautiful land of his youth, despite knowing that colourful magnificence masked the rigid law and cruelty of dragon lords who readily sacrificed their children for power and money.

Listening to his stories, Ina slowly drifted to sleep, and her body slipped down, gently guided by Ren. Now breathing quietly with Ina's head on his lap, Ren felt happy, wishing this moment could last forever. It was deep into the night when he gently carried her to bed. The quiet warrior could not force himself to return to his room, and sat there, watching her sleep, filled with a deep sense of peace. Ren didn't notice when his eyes closed, and he drifted into a land of chaotic dreams.

The sky was grey just before sunrise when he woke up, feeling his body burning and sweat soaking through his clothes. The cough that plagued him the last few days had finally become a dangerous fever. Thirsty, he reached for the water jug only to find it empty, so he quietly opened the window and gathered some snow from the windowsill, pressing it to his burning forehead for temporary relief. Suddenly dizzy, the warrior sat down with a thump, too weak to even get back to the chair.

CHAPTER FOUR

Ina woke up to the sound of a hacking cough. Still half asleep from waking suddenly, she looked around, noticing Ren curled up next to the window. She didn't mind him staying a night; he and Mar had some twisted ideas regarding her safety, and now it felt almost normal to wake with one or the other in her room. The cough sounded again, and the harsh rattle that accompanied it cleared the remaining stupor from Ina's mind as she realised Ren was the source of the awful noise.

'Ren? What is wrong?' she asked, dropping to her knees next to the sick warrior. As he tried to catch his breath, Ina checked his temperature.

'I'm fine, my lady. It is just a cold,' he said, attempting to sit up as the witch continued her examination.

'A-ha,' she said, placing her hand on his forehead. 'And that is why you are as hot as a furnace?' Her hand slid to grab the edge of his blanket, then yanked it from his body. Ren tried to resist, but it was futile. When worried, Ina channelled her inner

Nerissa, and now, with the decisiveness of an arch-healer, she pointed to her bed.

'To the bed, now.' When Ren protested, Ina tilted her head, observing his struggles with a sarcastic smile. 'I thought only Mar was stupid enough to argue with me when I worry. I won't let you suffer when a nice, warm bed is ready, and I won't take no for an answer. Bed. Now.'

She would have enjoyed scolding him if she wasn't so worried about his condition. Ren shuffled to the bed, trying to preserve the last of his dignity. She tucked him in, and her eyes softened when, despite his weak protests, she unbraided his long, raven hair. She looked at his face, remembering how he cared for her right after the fight in the underground, and gently stroked his burning skin.

'It is my turn to look after you, Sa'Ren. Please be a good patient. I would feel bad beating you into submission.'

Her little jest seemed to relax him, and Ina watched as his eyes closed and tight muscles softened under her touch. Ren gave in to her care and appeared almost happy, cocooned in the sheets warmed by her body. Ina looked at the jewel on her chest, but the stone barely showed any signs of life, and she doubted it had enough power for any magic, especially the "sacrifice"—the only healing spell she felt confident performing. Even if it was possible, the witch knew they would be bound more closely than they already were, and there was no way she could be that cruel to the two men who meant the world to her. Ina knew Ren had feelings for her, not just because of the spell, but the deep friendship that had developed during their adventures, and she didn't want to risk damaging their fellowship with the warped bond of the spell. *Gods forgive me for my greed, but I care for them both. I've chosen Mar, but must I lose my kinship with Ren?*

The thought of Ren's absence in her life was unbearable, and she was glad the choice was taken from her hands this time. Still, with no magical solution, the only hope was with her elixirs and potions. *You are the Master Alchemist, you stupid cow, and you could make the healing potion blindfolded, from horse piss and berries. They must have something in the kitchen I can use.* Ina scolded herself, equally amused and annoyed by how easily she forgot her primary education once she relied on her peridot and Chaos magic.

'Rest. I need to dig into my bags and the kitchen stores. We need something to heal you, and my magic is like a tavern bitch now, lying low and whining,' she said, turning around to open the wardrobe.

Her patient nodded, too tired to protest. Lying here in her bed and being cared for appeared to please him. His demeanour quickly changed when Ina returned with a handful of mugs. She gave him an apologetic look, sitting on the edge of the bed.

'Ren, before we start, I have to tell you I'm not good at cooking,' she said, passing him the first cup.

'Why are you telling me this?'

Before she answered, he drank the potion and instantly regretted it. The liquid was so repulsive that Ren scrambled to the back of the bed to escape the next drink she handed over.

'My lady… Ina, this doesn't smell right. Are you sure…?' he rasped, still gagging after the first.

'I am, and it will work miracles. I've just never managed to make it taste nice.' She tried to reassure him, mixing the contents of the following two cups before pushing it to his lips.

Ren was cornered. With the stone wall behind his back and the witch pressing another repulsive drink to his lips, he knew he couldn't escape. He took the clay vessel from her hand and gulped it down quickly before pushing it back while Ina patted the pillow.

'Lie down. It will be a tough night, but I promise it will work. The potion will force the sickness out, and I will be right here to look after you.'

Ren sighed, followed her instructions, and it wasn't long before he felt the first effects of Ina's concoction. His heart was pounding, and his skin burned as if dipped in molten metal. Ina sat beside him with a bowl of water and a towel, wiping the sweat from his body. Ren's muscles spasmed uncontrollably, and he prayed to all gods of Yanwo that his friend knew what she was doing as the pain overwhelmed his mind, and he descended into delirious dreams.

Ina kept looking at Ren with increasing concern. His body's reaction to the makeshift healing potion surprised her. The herbs she used should have caused some sweating and an uncomfortable night, but Ren drifted away, barely holding onto the threads of consciousness. When the water in the bowl turned warm from the heat of his body, Ina opened the window and gathered some snow to cool it down. With her hands stinging from the icy water, she continued wiping the sweat from the warrior's chest when Ren's eyes snapped open, pupils dilated, staring into the abyss caught by the ghosts of Nawia.

'Ren?' she called quietly. 'Ren, wake up.' Ina bit her lip, trying to contain her feelings at the lack of response, and hoped the sound of her voice would anchor his soul to this realm. She gasped as his eyes suddenly focused on her face, not noticing the wildness within them until too late as Ren grabbed her shoulders and pulled her into the bed. Trapped under his body, Ina struggled to escape, but he held her tight. His hand trailed over her face as he muttered words in a language she could not understand.

'Ren, please let me go,' she pleaded, trying to free her hands, fighting the rising panic. The Sa'Ren she knew and loved would never impose himself on her. It was her fault for feeding him a potion that caused hallucinations, so she didn't want to hurt him to escape his arms. Yet her words and struggles only encouraged his strange behaviour. Ina felt his hot, dry lips on her neck, feverish kisses marking her flesh. Whatever he saw in his delirium released a passion Ina never suspected he harboured, but even now, his strength didn't cause her any pain. This strange tenderness mixed with fiery desire awoke the reaction that surprised her.

Ina felt the impulse to give in to this moment, to surrender to Ren's love. He was an attractive man with a special place in her heart, and now she witnessed just how passionate he could be. She doubted Ren would even remember this encounter, judging his present state, but that would not be fair, and letting this continue would betray both men's trust. In a moment of distraction, she pushed the crazed warrior away and scrambled to the floor, watching his growing confusion change to anger.

She moved backwards till her shoulders hit the wall and gasped when Ren, fast as lightning, leapt forwards, imprisoning her in the cage of his arms, his entire attention focused on her eyes.

'Why can't you love me, Ina? What can I do to make you love me more than Mar?'

The pain and sincerity she heard in his voice made her blood run cold. It wasn't just infatuation induced by a spell. Quiet, calm Ren loved her with a passion that burned just as fiercely as her dragon's fire, while all she could offer was a loving friendship.

'Sa'Ren, *stop!*' She heard her voice issuing the command, resonating with magic, compelling obedience from the man in front of her. 'You will go back to bed, and you won't remember anything that happened tonight.' After her encounter with Liander, she hated and feared mind magic, but it was still better than her gentle friend feeling guilty and ashamed of his actions.

Ren's eyes lost their focus, and he returned to the bed. Ina joined him, sitting on the edge and looking down, tears shining in her eyes. The toll of using this tiniest piece of magic and the emotions that tore up her heart were released in the only way she couldn't control.

This is why she strayed away from love. The pain she caused to those she shared her heart with tore her. *I'm so sorry, my friend, I can't be what you want me to be. You deserve better than my awkward friendship.* Ina slowly pushed a tangled strand of hair off his face and tried not to think of the man they were here to save, but it was impossible to think of one without the other, and the image of that magnificent dragon burst into her mind. Firming her resolve, Ina clenched her fist. She had to think about Mar and turn him back, fix at least one of her mistakes, doing it without hurting this beautiful soul before her any more than she already had. As the tears finally stopped falling, this thought allowed the witch to lie down and fall into a deep, dreamless sleep.

Feeling the sun's rays on his face, Ren opened his eyes. He felt rested, his cough wasn't troubling him, and his body felt pleasantly relaxed. After a slow, languorous stretch, the warrior realised he was still in Ina's room, but his ward was nowhere to be seen. Ren sat up on the bed and looked at the small bundle curled up on the floor. Ina must have fallen asleep looking after him, but he couldn't remember anything that happened past the nasty potion she fed him. The bundle moved, and a redheaded bear emerged from under the blanket, grumbling about generosity and prices.

'Ahh, you're awake,' she said, sitting up with a wince and a curse. 'How do you feel?'

Ren lowered his feet to the cold floor and shivered slightly. 'Rested. In fact, my lady, I have never felt better. Your potions are indeed powerful.' He grinned, stretching his muscles.

'You have no idea,' Ina said, hissing painfully at the tight muscles in her back when she changed position, and Ren looked at her, frowning.

'How long was I asleep for?' he asked and, hearing it was almost a whole day since he succumbed to the fever, shook his head in disbelief. 'Did you stay here all that time? I will call for breakfast, and then we will train. You must move your cold muscles,' he said, leaving the room.

Ina considered cursing him with boils for being so happy when she felt every bone in her body after sleeping on the floor, but eventually, she gave this thought up. It had all ended well. They both survived the blizzard, his sickness, and he didn't remember his actions. If she were careful, this unfortunate situation wouldn't happen again.

After breakfast, Ren, as promised, taught her the basics of knife fighting. This time, he didn't beat her up. He simply demonstrated the moves and asked her to repeat them. It was no different to learning the dagger and sash dance she performed with Mar at the coronation ball, and Ina learned the movements quickly. She even surprised him sometimes by including some dance moves. The bright smile on Ren's face told her he was happy with her progress. It was clear he didn't remember last night's events, and Ina once more felt relaxed in his company. Suddenly, Ren commanded her to attack him with all she could. Deep down, Ina knew he was just too good for her to hurt him, but she still hesitated, until the moment Ren approached her and brutally pushed her into a snowdrift.

Screeching as the freezing powder slipped down her neck, Ina lashed out, slashing the dagger across her opponent's body, missing completely, but giving herself the time to stand up and attack properly. Cut, parry, stab, dodge—each movement speeding up till both fighters were a blur of motion. Just as the witch thought she would collapse, Ren slipped in a puddle of yellow liquid, thoughtfully provided by Woron moments previously, and landed face first in the snow.

The witch laughed herself hoarse, flopping down onto a bale of hay, and Ren soon joined her, chuckling and bumping shoulders in camaraderie.

'You have a gift, my lady. Once you push past your reservations, you are pretty good with a dagger.'

As her cheeks turned red with embarrassed pride, Ina looked at her friend and asked, 'So are you going to teach me how to use a sword soon?'

Ren placed his hand over hers. 'Not yet, my lady. We need to set on the road tomorrow to find Mar, but I promise we will practise daily on the way to Liath. Of course, if we find a sword small enough for you.'

'Are you sure you are ready? I want to go as soon as possible, but you barely recovered. You said Mar knows Liath better than any of us, and he is a bloody dragon. We will find him in the castle feasting on sheep with a little luck. I know it sounds cruel, but I'm trying to be rational, and risking your life to change him is not something he would want.'

'Ina, I'm fine!'

'No! You will be fine when I say you are. I will find Mar even if I have to walk these mountains barefoot, but I won't sacrifice you. End of discussion. And I'm not too short for a bloody sword!' Ina shouted the last words marching towards the tavern, followed by Ren's surprised stare. Slowly, a coy smile appeared on his lips, and he couldn't take his eyes off the disappearing woman.

Tar'eth Alean couldn't sleep. His campaign hadn't gone as planned, and he couldn't understand why. His army quickly subdued the kobolds, and the occasional demonstration of magic scared them into submission. The overseers assured him the miners spared no effort in getting to the heart of the mountain, yet every time he felt closer to his goal, something disrupted the work. Maybe it was the legendary Guardian of the Mountain or plain bad luck, but he was no closer to his goal than when he started, and his supplies were running short. He must get the circlet to succeed, but this damn thing felt ever more distant.

Tossing and turning in his bed, Tar'eth glimpsed the last flames flickering over the half-burnt logs. Memories of a fiery woman burned through his mind, and the way she pulled raw

Chaos to herself in the ballroom still made him shiver. After the recent troubles, maybe her magic combined with his ring would be enough. Perhaps he wouldn't need the circlet after all.

Tar'eth rose from his bed. He could not fall asleep, so he might as well use this time productively. As the chamber door opened, the guard blinked, trying to focus as his lord appeared in the gap. 'Bring me a woman, and make sure she has red hair.' The sharp command was barked out before the prince retreated and slammed the door closed.

The soldier snapped a salute at the closed door and hastened to fulfil the order, frowning deeply, but despite searching the living quarters and prisons, none of the women around had red hair. He knew coming back empty-handed was not an option. One woman—practically a girl—caught his eye, and he promptly pulled her out of the cells.

Throwing her into the arms of a prison guard, he commanded, 'Wash her and bring her to the lord. Don't let him wait, or we'll both regret it.'

The jailer prepared the girl as quickly as he could, and soon they stood before the heavy oak door as she cried. He lowered his head and knocked.

'Enter,' came from the other side of the doors, and gritting his teeth, the prison guard went in, pushing the pale prisoner forward. He didn't have the time to utter a word when another command turned him on his heel. 'Leave her and go back to your duties.'

Tar'eth's lips twitched as he watched the guard rush from the chamber, shoulders hunched in fear. His power over the lesser born always put him in a good mood, and his smile grew as the girl standing in the shadows caught his attention.

The shadows held no secrets to the drow, so he took his time to study her. She was young, barely a woman, emaciated rather than thin, and her pale skin highlighted the blonde of her hair, hair that was nothing like the red that haunted his every dream.

They dared to defy him? The snarl that left his lips was followed swiftly by the back of his hand striking across the woman's face, snapping her head back as she crashed to the floor.

The terrified female scrambled to her knees and rushed to the door, banging her fists on the solid wood of the door and screaming in panic.

'Help! Please, help!' Her wild grasping for the handle halted as Tar'eth strode forward and tore her away from her means of escape, his fingers cutting into the flesh of her neck as she was dragged into the centre of the room, sobbing.

Sobs that were met with pure disdain from the raving drow. 'She would not cry,' he hissed, hitting the girl again.

'Please, no! I am just a kitchen maid. Please stop. I am not her. Whoever she is, I promise to serve you, highness. Please, stop,' she begged, but the rabid prince hit her again and again.

'She would not beg!' Tar'eth screamed, inexplicable rage coursing through his body. Why was this woman here? She wasn't the witch. A horsewhip suddenly appeared in his hand, unnoticed, even as he used it to beat the helpless girl's body. The rough material sliced through her clothing and skin with ease, splattering blood across his face and into his open mouth. The metallic taste was intoxicating, and a red veil fell over his eyes. Reality bled into fantasy, and he saw the witch curled up on the floor before him. He grabbed a fistful of her hair with a smirk, lifting her bloodied face to the light.

'You can't hide from me forever,' he purred, pressing his lips to hers. 'You will be mine, and we will rule the world together.'

His kisses turned into bites as he savoured the blood and pitiful moans.

Sanity slowly returned as Tar'eth's rage bled away, and he threw the girl back to the floor. His mouth twisted in disgust, and he spat out the girl's blood.

'You are not Ina. How dare you defile her image?'

The woman's cries were broken and despairing as she lay there like a broken rag doll. Throwing the horsewhip into the corner, Tar'eth called the guard.

'Clean up this mess and throw the scraps to the dogs,' he commanded without looking back, and the guard gathered up the poor victim, unsurprised by his master's actions. Those close to the lord whispered about the tar-maladie, the illness of the mind, the obsessive madness the royal family was susceptible to, which made the bearer savage and prone to rage. Since descending into the kobold mines to look for the circlet, their lord showed more and more of its symptoms. There was little logic in the punishments he meted out so freely. Now, guards and close companions alike were afraid to contradict their leader.

The drow prince washed his hands while several servants mopped the blood off the floor. His victim had eased the madness temporarily, and he could think clearly again. Tomorrow, he would send more scouts to look for Ina and, if necessary, send his troops to Cornovii. This thought brought him surcease. When the room was finally quiet again, the drow lowered himself to the bed and sighed with relief. The metallic scent of blood still lingered, soothing his senses, and he felt able to sleep now. Soon his even breathing was the only sound that filled the room, and Tar'eth smiled in his dreams.

CHAPTER FIVE

A dull, wet thud preceded a spray of blood and guts in Mar's face. Spluttering with indignation, he reared up, cursing as pain ripped through his injured shoulder. As he shook the blood from his eyes, the surprised dragon looked around, zeroing in on the cackling laughter of Ayni, her feet digging into the ground as she landed gracefully, smirking at his reaction.

'What was that for?' roared Mar, still trying to shake the dripping blood from his muzzle.

'It's your dinner. A nice juicy cow, to be precise. I thought you would have known this already,' said Ayni, teasing him. 'Or are you feeling like an adolescent who needs a strong, beautiful female to provide for you?'

Mar shook his head again, but the smell of fresh blood called to him. The sweet, metallic taste lingered on his tongue as he licked his muzzle, and to his embarrassment, his stomach rumbled, demanding sustenance. The dragon in him wanted to finish the carcass in one gulp, but Mar felt repulsed by the thought. Not that he hadn't had raw meat before, war is war, and you eat what you have to, but here and now, in front of this other dragon, he felt the strongest desire to hold on to his humanity and resisted giving in to the primitive animalistic urge to devour the corpse.

Looking on from the side, Ayni watched the massive beast transfixed, staring at the cow with an unblinking gaze. The rumble in his stomach grew louder, his hunger apparent, but still, he didn't move.

'Is something wrong with the cow?' she asked hesitantly, worried now that she'd offended this male she so wanted to impress.

'No,' snapped Mar, without breaking eye contact with the carcass. Suddenly, he spewed out a large stream of fire, almost burning the animal to a crisp, then pounced on the still smoking cow and, snatching it up with his jaws, crunched the bones as he chewed the flesh with visible pleasure.

'What in the name of the dragon king was that?' she asked, surprised by his actions.

'It was raw, and I'm not a beast,' Mar said, pleased with himself for solving his existential dilemma.

'Not a beast? You are the king of beasts. You are a dragon! And you wasted so much of that cow that I should bite your ass for acting like a naughty hatchling.' Ayni's eyes narrowed, showing her displeasure, but Mar didn't care. The stubborn sucking hunger had subsided, and, with a satisfied burp, he circled a few times, preparing himself for a nap.

Ayni was faster, changing her shape in a blink of an eye, and, approaching Mar, she punched his snout. 'Not so fast. I need to tend to your wound, and then the two of us are having a conversation,' she said, and Mar just nodded, content with a full stomach, uncaring of what happened next as he fought the overwhelming desire to sleep.

Ayni went to the temple and brought back her bag. Mar stretched a little, allowing her to clean and treat his shoulder. The process was painful, but not as bad as the first time, and he noticed a freshly forming scar between his scales. The female was gentler this time, and he had to admit the feeling of her hands trailing over his scales was almost pleasant.

'You said a ballista hit you. Where did this happen?' Ayni said, finishing her ministrations.

'In Liath. I wanted to go home, but my home didn't want me back.' Mar barked out a short, bitter laugh that stopped when he noticed the woman's frown.

'You shouldn't have gone there,' she said, sitting next to him. 'We have hidden our true forms from the humans for over a hundred years. Going back to the wars and hunts from those years is something no one wants—human or dragon.'

Mar considered her words for a moment. As far as he knew, dragons disappeared nearly two hundred years ago, and everyone assumed they were extinct. A few societies still trained warriors to fight them, despite thinking they were gone for good. That training helped them kill whatever other monsters still lived near humans, with wyverns being the most popular target for noble sons wishing to earn their reputations as fighters and hunters.

'So what exactly happened, and when can you teach me to change shape? My shoulder has almost healed, and the quicker I become human, the quicker I can return to Liath.'

Ayni shrugged at his strange fixation on becoming human again, already mentioning this several times. Still, with his memory loss, he needed an explanation.

'After the losses from fighting the humans for so long and the slow birthrate for dragonkind, the surviving elders decided we would hide in plain sight. We still live amongst other sentient beings. We… just don't fly that often. It is mostly frowned upon unless it is night or in a particular location, such as this temple, where no other race has set foot in a hundred years.'

This information was a revelation to Mar. Of course, she had told him initially that there were more of their kind, but he struggled to believe dragons could live amongst others undetected. There was more to find out, but Mar was concerned with just one thing.

'Show me how to change back, or explain the process to me, as everything I thought to try failed miserably.' The cranky captain was back now that he had a task to do and a person who could help him execute his plan.

Ayni shrugged. His obsessive behaviour was tiring, but he'd need to change sooner rather than later. Focusing on her hand, she let the air shimmer until the translucent outline of a massive dragon claw appeared around it. She took a few steps back so he could see it clearly.

'I am a dragon. No matter what shape I wear, I will always be a dragon. All I did was move part of my mass to the Outer, leaving the part of me I see as human here.' She visibly struggled to explain a fundamental truth every dragon knew in their heart. Spoken out loud, the reality of the outer realm and the energy behind the veil sounded foolish and absurd.

Mar's face was blank. He hadn't the faintest idea what any of that speech meant, but something in the ghostly shape hovering over her hand touched a memory deep in his psyche. It wasn't anything he knew or had experienced in this life. Still, somehow, it felt as familiar and as natural as breathing.

Ayni saw his blank stare and sighed. 'Let's try something else,' she said. 'Imagine a heavy wall of mist. It looks impenetrable, yet as it swirls and moves, you see small gaps once in a while. Push your hand through one of them, widen it, feel your dragon flowing through the veil, and let it rest in the outer realm. Now imagine your other shape emerging and covering your soul like a suit of armour.'

'Ayni, that sounds utterly insane,' he said, not even attempting her method.

The dragoness rolled her eyes. 'Think what you want, you stubborn male, but try it anyway.'

Mar sighed. She sounded like Ina. It seemed he was destined to be pushed around by stubborn women. He closed his eyes and tried to imagine the veil. Initially, nothing happened. He tried again and again, but just as he was ready to give up, Mar glimpsed a wisp of grey mist in the corner of his eye. Focusing on the thin ribbon, he felt it grow and thicken until his entire vision was filled with a deep, swirling mist. Remember Ayni's instructions, Mar watched the swirling greyness, waiting impatiently till a gap appeared to the left. Once he noticed the first break in the fog, he saw more, and when one felt close enough to touch, he moved his hand inside and felt the desire to move through. Mar pushed hesitantly, imagining the gap widening, letting his dragon slip into the outer realm. As he let go of the last piece of his dragon, there was a touch, and then a shadowy form clasped his hand, slipping through the gap as he fell back from the veil. Mar's eyes flew open in fear, wondering what had grabbed him just as he fell to the ground, wearing his human shape.

A loud laugh reverberated through the small valley. Mar opened his eyes, and everything seemed bigger and less colourful. Ayni was still laughing, almost rolling around in her mirth. Between gasps of breath, she finally said, 'Mar, when I said you should wear it like a cloak… you know, it meant you could dress.'

'Hmm… what?' Mar felt the freezing wind gusts and bitterly cold snow under his feet. His gaze followed Ayni's finger down to where she pointed, and a heavy sigh burst from his lips.

He had transformed into his human body, a very naked human body, exposing his attributes to the woman openly looking at them. His hands instinctively drifted to his loins when he said, 'Teach me how to make clothes.'

Still laughing, Ayni just shook her head. 'All you have to do is form them in your mind as you touch the Outer. They are part of you and your magic. You can even make armour as hard as your dragon's skin.'

The relief Mar felt at that statement had him reaching for the Outer in record time. Initially, Mar's efforts left him looking ridiculous, but eventually, he recreated his regular clothes and stared at the woman with triumph in his eyes. Then he tried to take off his cloak, and a searing pain dropped him to his knees. The dragoness grinned widely, visibly amused by his struggles.

'Ah, this. I forgot to mention you can't remove your clothes if you dress that way. It is like chopping off your arm or leg, that's why I prefer normal clothes, and living around humans, you should always wear their clothing as they overreact when you make them suddenly disappear.' He knew she was having the time of her life, playing with his ignorance. Still, he would happily forgive her as each step brought him closer to his humanity and Ina.

Mar felt joy spreading through his chest as he thought of his spitfire. He was sure Ina would try to help him. She would blame herself for his transformation, and each time she took the blame for something, she would try to fix it. A mischievous thought flashed through his mind. Maybe he should come back as a dragon and let her try. The last time she had *fixed* him, he woke up almost naked in her bed, and sure as hell, this time, he would accept her offer to stay a little longer. His smile caught Ayni's attention.

'What are you thinking about?' she asked, observing the golden glow dancing in his eyes.

'My witch, Ina.' Mar stretched his arms, feeling his bones creak as usual. 'She would be thrilled seeing me like this.'

'Human mages are so easily amused.' The dragoness agreed, but her eyes lingered on him longer than needed, as if his mention of Ina's name gave her pause.

Mar practised transforming several times until he felt comfortable changing from human to dragon and back. Taking his dragon form one last time, he spread his wings and shot up into the air, only to crash back down, his wound sending searing pain through his chest, and he had to clench his teeth to stop roaring out in agony.

His companion approached him, rolling her eyes.

'It will take a day or two till you can fly. So take your time and rest here.' Trailing her hand over his wing, she pressed her body to his side. 'You know I can look after you.'

As Ayni's hand moved over the hard scales of his wing, Mar felt almost no sensation, but when her fingers stroked over the softer membrane between his limbs, his back arched in pleasure, melting under the gentle touch. Before he could stop her, the dragoness gave a coy, mischievous look and caressed the rest of his wing. He hadn't realised this part of his body was so sensitive.

While he enjoyed the sensation, it felt too intimate for a casual acquaintance, and Mar didn't feel comfortable with it. He folded his wings close to his body and moved away from Ayni, who seemed far too pleased with herself.

'You will probably be able to fly at some point tomorrow,' she said confidently. 'But first, I want to look at your wound, hopefully for the last time. With the salve, it is healing well, and your transformations have hastened the process.'

Mar reluctantly allowed her to touch him again. He was grateful for her help, but being at anyone's mercy always left him angry and frustrated. Adding to that, his need to get back to Liath made for one growly dragon. However, Ayni's nimble fingers were practised and quick, and he was soon curled up asleep, completely unaware the woman glanced over at him with a calculating look.

The morning felt almost glorious as Mar uncurled his body and stretched out his wings without the previous pain or stiffness. Ayni was there in her dragon form, and her eyes roamed over his body in appreciation before she caught his eye and spoke.

'How do you feel today? Ready for a flight?' She appeared happy for some reason, but Mar assumed it was simply due to the chance of flying with him. She soared skyward as soon as he nodded, disappearing into the clouds. More aware of his limits, especially after yesterday's misadventure, the captain gently spread his wings, letting them catch the first breeze of the mountain wind. Nothing hurt this time, not even when he tensed his muscles, preparing to launch himself into the heavens.

Mar crouched down and, with one powerful thrust of his legs, leapt into the sky, flapping his wings erratically as the unpredictable mountain winds gusted left and right, tossing him around like a child's toy. Hearing Ayni's mocking laughter over the noise of the savage currents, Mar fought harder to control his unstable flight.

With a twisting snap of his tail and another strong beat of his wings, Mar stabilised his body, gaining control of his movements and soaring upwards, finally catching sight of Ayni's aquamarine scales while heading towards her lazily circling form.

'I thought you would never get here. It would've helped if you used the wind to carry you up rather than fighting it. Come, let me show you how.'

Several hours passed as they flew up, down, twisting and circling through the air like children frolicking in a lake. Mar was happy, and it surprised him how carefree he felt as a dragon, almost as if the world was brighter and more colourful. As if his soul were part of something exceptional when he transformed.

Ayni came closer and slipped into his air stream. Her slender neck turned to face him, and she asked with unusual seriousness, 'Marcach of Liath, are you willing to dance in the skies with me?'

He was tired from the long flight, and Ayni's question didn't make sense, but he eagerly agreed, hoping to learn some new tricks.

'Of course, it would be my pleasure. Just show me what to do.' He hoped for a quick lesson as, truth to be told, he wanted to land already. His stomach was rumbling, and he planned to leave for Liath tomorrow.

His answer made Ayni happy for no apparent reason. The dragoness turned her head to the side and shouted, 'So be it!'

With a single beat of her wings, she shot forward, and her tail smacked him across the nose as she sped away.

With a roar of indignation, Mar strained to beat his wings faster, grinning as his greater wingspan compensated for his lack of skill. Despite that, Ayni seemed to toy with him, her movements effortless and beautiful as she spun and soared before diving back down just outside his reach, teasing and beguiling his senses with the elegance of her dance.

Mar felt his heart beat faster as the urge to capture this magnificent creature surged through his body. He pushed himself to greater and greater effort to speed his flight, closing the distance between them as his superior strength finally made a difference.

Ayni's laughter blinded his reason, and roaring his challenge to the heavens, he surged forward, snapping his jaws at the coiling tail dancing before him, and, just as she twisted into a dive to escape his teeth, Mar tucked his wings close to his body and plunged downwards, reaching out to lock his jaws onto the softer scales of her throat, bellowing his triumph before releasing her and heading back towards their camp.

'I think that is enough for today,' he called back, and a subdued Ayni followed him without a word of contradiction. After landing, Mar seamlessly changed shape, feeling the change came much easier now, almost without conscious thought.

With the beginnings of a snowstorm overtaking their camp, Mar headed over to the temple. Ayni followed quietly, and once inside, Mar stopped suddenly, stunned by the vivid paintings of dragons on the wall, especially the one picturing the human-looking figure riding a massive dragon over the structure he recognised as the Castle Liath.

Ayni slipped past his motionless form and gestured for him to follow her down a small passage. At the end of the corridor was a cosy chamber with stone furniture and a place for a fire. Mar looked at Ayni with a baffled expression, and she shrugged in answer. 'You weren't able to change.'

'Nevermind,' he said and looked around to find fuel for the fire.

'I will bring wood and something to eat,' said Ayni.

Initially intending to protest, Mar turned, but a flash of pain from his overworked muscles left him wincing. It would take some getting used to flying as a dragon. 'I'll wait here. Best not go too far. The wind is picking up, and we don't need much,' he said, trusting Ayni to know how to survive in the storm. With nothing better to do, Mar settled down in the corner to nap, hoping that would help his aching muscles.

He didn't know how long he was asleep, but the warmth of the fire and the scent of roasting meat called to his senses. The lips that pressed to his own awakened distant memories, and Mar smiled, returning the kiss. Ina's smile and yielding body felt real, but when he opened his eyes, there was raven hair instead of copper, and Mar pushed the woman aside.

'What the hell are you doing?' he asked, frowning at her confused expression.

'But Mar, we danced in the skies together.'

'I've danced with many women. That doesn't mean you get to help yourself to a kiss!' he snapped, disappointed and missing Ina. After being awoken by the unwelcome kiss, the craving for her intensified. Looking at Ayni withdrawing to the other side of the room, he couldn't help but compare them. Ayni, beautiful with her tall slim build, would be the envy of the court, whilst

Ina's voluptuous curves and fiery hair drew his eyes and mind as no one else could. And temperament? There wouldn't be a quiet retreat and petulant pout if he'd snapped at Ina the way he had done with Ayni. No, the power of her magical temper would have thrown his body through the nearest door, open or closed.

That damned kiss woke Mar up to the fact that Ayni found him attractive, so, changing the subject, Mar focused on the dragoness. 'I'm sorry. I know it was just a misunderstanding. Let's eat dinner.'

He didn't want to explain the strange complexity of his relationship with Ina, especially not when he was unsure where he stood after his transformation. He wanted to wed her if she would take him, but would she want a dragon? Did he even have the right to propose? His words appeared to calm Ayni down, and she sat by the fire to share the meal with him. Mar knew it was time to leave this shelter, but he didn't want to go without saying goodbye. After all, if Ayni hadn't helped him, he'd likely have been crippled or dead in this unforgiving environment.

'I'm going to Liath tomorrow,' he said, sharing his decision. 'I would like to thank you for all the help you've given me.' Mar bowed his head, expressing his gratitude, but Ayni just sat there and looked at him through the flames.

'We can make a start in the morning after the storm has passed. Though remember, we will have to be careful to arrive as humans,' she added, and Mar felt he'd missed something important.

'We?'

'Yes, we. I am going with you.' Ayni seemed determined, and Mar tried thinking of a way to discourage her. He didn't want to take her, but he had no means or power to stop her. He felt his father's reaction to one dragon would be extreme, but two would pose a significant problem.

There was a slight twist of his lips as an idea came to mind, invisible to anyone who didn't know him well. 'I won't be going to Liath as a human, Ayni. I am a dragon. Hiding that fact would be lying to my family, and I wouldn't want to put you in danger from overeager soldiers.'

The dragoness stiffened, her eyes narrowing as if weighing her decision. 'I'm going, anyway. Maybe it is time for change, for us to stop hiding. I have lived in this temple for too long and don't want to spend another long winter night alone. Not to mention I have to ensure you won't get yourself and dragonkind in trouble.' Once again, she withdrew to the far corner and refused to talk to him. Mar sat and watched Ayni, trying to understand her motivation until, finally, the warmth of the fire lulled him to sleep.

CHAPTER SIX

Despite Ina's initial objections, Ren convinced her he was recovered enough to travel, and the next day, they set out first thing in the morning. After days of being confined to the stables, the horses pranced in the snow like dancers, happy to be free. Wrapped in her fur linen coat, Ina smiled, enjoying their antics. Still, something was different about the countryside, and she couldn't shake the feeling something awful was about to happen or was already happening in the mountain province.

Even travelling, Ren made her exercise during the brief stops and gave her the daily knife fighting lessons, which she found invigorating, much to her surprise. At first, her body protested, but she soon became accustomed to the harsh routine and even started enjoying it. Safe to say, Ren didn't go easy on her, making sure his pupil could defend herself.

Ina got battered and bruised, thrown into snowdrifts and occasionally in horse manure until she learned to evade his attacks, but he also taught her close combat, which she valued the most. She still remembered feeling helpless, tied up in front of Liander as he callously threatened her, and she hoped to never again be in that situation. Her magic slowly returned, and with it, her confidence. *I'm coming for you, Mar. I'm sorry you had to wait so long, but my lack of planning almost turned Ren into a real ghost.* Ina shook her head, trying to shake off the feeling of failure, but faced with dwelling on her mistakes or moving forward to put them right, she decided to focus on helping Mar and, with that thought in mind, tried to remember her Aunt Nerissa's lessons on healing magic.

The further they travelled, the more she appreciated why the king was concerned about Liath. Cornovii was a peaceful country with a healthy tradition of trading with its neighbours rather than fighting. The exception to this was the western border. The mountains of the west were a harsh environment, home to kobolds, shifters, and other creatures. So the stronghold of Liath became the military centre for Cornovii, with its garrisons arrayed against the many dangers that came down looking for an easy meal, and Mar's family kept them all at bay.

However, they noticed the increase of refugees headed towards Osterad. The grim expressions, half-starved bodies and desperate determination were alarming, and Ina tried to question the weary families. She ignored the suspicious looks and frightened flinching, but an unsettling picture began emerging, one of looting and pillaging of the countryside. The loss of faith in the house of Liath shocked and worried Ina, spurring her to hurry their horses towards their destination.

Luck, it seemed, was conspiring against them as they arrived at the ferry town of Stary Bod and were greeted with the news the ferry had already left on its last journey of the day and that all rooms at the inn were full, with even the stables rented out to desperate refugees. Ina's mood soured at the news, but she didn't want to fight the needy for a place to sleep so redolent of horses.

With a concerned look at Ina, Ren moved abreast of Woron and nodded back towards the village. 'The fear here is almost overwhelming. There is more going on than people will talk about, but I learned there is a camp near the ferry. We can wait the night there.'

With the village so full of fear, Ina hoped staying between others would be safer than sleeping in the open, as there were bound to be brigands and creatures preying on anyone unlucky enough to be caught outside alone.

The camp was larger than they expected. The human instinct to flock together for safety had created an encampment nearly as big as the village, and the refugees had used their carts to form a rudimentary barricade to discourage any overly curious animals. Near the encampment was a firepit with a wild pig roasting over a sizable fire. Relaxed conversation and an abundance of cheerful laughter drifted over as Ina and Ren dismounted before politely asking if they could join the group. A small gang of intoxicated males climbed to their feet, belligerent and loud, attempting to force them out, but an elderly man armed with a cane stepped forward and started bashing heads, forcing them to retreat to their seats.

'Everyone's welcome,' he said, catching his breath before returning to his seat.

Ren and Ina exchanged amused glances. The last thing they'd expected was an unsteady senior with a cane coming to their defence. It took them a moment to organise themselves, and as soon as they sat down, the playful children approached Ren.

Initially, they only stared at him as he tended to his blade, but fear was quickly overcome by curiosity, and the boldest child spoke.

'Are you a kobold?' he asked, and a few adults sucked their breath in shock. To anger a stranger with a sword was never a good idea.

Ren smirked. 'No, why would you think that?'

'Because you look funny, and if you were a kobold, I could kill you and become a knight.' The child struck a heroic pose as he eyed the warrior with suspicion. 'I wish you were a dragon. There was a dragon in Liath, but they shot him. I want to shoot a dragon too.'

Ina snapped around and grabbed the child's hand. 'Who shot a dragon?' The ferocity of her actions made the child's chin tremble, and he pulled at his arm, trying to free himself. A woman leapt from the crowd, rushing to gather the child into her embrace.

'Please let my child go, my lady. He's just repeating what he heard from the older children. All we know is a dragon flew over Liath a few days ago, and the castle guards shot him. That's all, my lady, I promise,' she said, repeatedly bowing her head. The rich clothes and regal horses intimidated these simple people, but Ina was not the one to underestimate the power of a mother worried for her child, so she let the boy go as he buried his head in her skirts, clutching at her legs.

'Did he fall? Was the dragon killed?' Ina asked quietly, trying to calm her fluttering heart, unsure if she wanted to hear the answer.

'No!' shouted the boy courageously, now that he had his mother's protection. 'He flew to the mountains, and I will hunt him down.'

Ina released the breath she didn't realise she was holding and smiled at the boy. 'Why would you hunt the dragon? They are beautiful and valiant, and they help people,' she exclaimed, and the child looked at her with round eyes as if she'd spewed out heresy.

'The dragon is a monster, like the one that attacked Osterad. We need to kill them all,' he explained, and the witch could only roll her eyes. Suddenly, an idea popped into her head.

'Really? But the dragon I saw defended Osterad from the monsters, didn't you know? He even saved the king.' She placed her hand over her heart in a theatric gesture. 'I was there. It was terrifying.'

At Ina's words, the boy's eyes grew bigger, and the rest of the children returned, gathering around to listen. The adults pretended not to hear, but she noticed hands stilled, and heads turned in her direction.

'Please, share the story, my lady,' asked the elderly man, and Ina smiled. Her prey was on the hook, and she was ready to weave a tale they would never forget.

'Ren, could you play a tune from your homeland?' she asked, nodding encouragement when he raised an eyebrow. Ren's flute replaced the sword in his hands, and a haunting melody filled the air as he raised it to his lips, eyes closing as he remembered the battle and let the memories shape his play. Ina paused for a moment to feel the emotion in the music before she reached for her magic and a fiery diorama of the capital blossomed into existence. The gasps from her audience brought a smile to her lips as she shared the story of the battle for Osterad.

Her voice rose and fell as she wove the tale of the beautiful but evil princess and the king who tried to rescue his subjects. She told them about the monsters that spewed forth from tunnels beneath the city and attacked the innocent people of Osterad, of the heroic battle between the brave captain and the warped troll, conveniently skipping her part in the melee.

Ina noticed almost everyone in the camp had come to the fire and watched in awe as she brought to life the titanic battle.

The monsters attacked the palace, flaming maws gaping open, claws ripping defenders apart, and the king bravely commanding his army to save the citizens. At that moment, the monsters breached the palace gardens, overwhelming the lone orc warrior and his lover, the beautiful Valkyrie mage. Suddenly, a massive dragon landed on the battlefield. His claws tore the attackers apart, his fiery breath burning them to a cinder, saving the servants and children from the senseless slaughter.

Ina had the time of her life using her magic to illustrate the heroic struggles of the men and women from the palace. When the dragon smashed the evil army, there were women weeping and men cheering. Even a few men brushed tears from their cheeks after the evil princess was captured, and the noble beast bowed to the king and flew off to the mountains.

Ina wouldn't be herself if she didn't take revenge for her former friend's betrayal. She told them how her sinister deeds twisted the princess's face till it reflected the evil of her soul and how the righteous King Rewan wept during the execution of his beloved sister.

After she finished, and the strains of Ren's flute faded to silence, someone brought them wine, whilst others carved up the roast boar, sharing it with the crowd. Strangers came to them, asking more questions and carefully expressing their admiration for the king, the guards, and the magnificent dragon. When Ina turned her face to Ren, she grinned, noticing his amused look.

'What was that?' he chuckled. 'Your tale couldn't be further from the truth if you tried, and you completely omitted the contribution of the fiery witch in the conflict.'

Ina laughed, raising her hands in protest. 'I've had my fair share of fame. Look at them. They needed hope. They needed a fearless warrior defending their way of life, and now they have one, and hopefully, with time, their belief in the king will grow as well.' She grabbed a bottle of wine and gulped it down, stopping only to catch her breath. 'Besides, I'm more walking accident than hero, and once you become a saviour, everybody has expectations, and you have to behave, well… you know; that's not the life for me.'

Ren looked around. The camp atmosphere was much livelier and far from sober, with hope shining from hearts previously tired from travelling. He wished her story were true and that Osterad would welcome them with open arms, but he suspected they would just add to the hoard of homeless already on the capital's outskirts.

After he finished rolling out their makeshift bed on the frozen ground, Ren turned to Ina. 'My lady, it is time to sleep. We have a long journey tomorrow.'

Ina sighed in response. Ren had done his best, but sleeping on blankets laid over the bare ground? And after the day of bumping around in the saddle? No, that was not appealing, but he looked at her, waiting, and reluctantly, she lowered herself to the bedding. The cold seeped through almost instantly. They didn't have enough fur and fabric to protect them from the frozen ground, and soon Ina was shivering despite the fire. When her teeth began chattering, she decided it was time to try a spell, any spell that would give them a bit of warmth, but Ren's arm wrapped around her, pulling her close to his chest.

'Sleep, my lady. You need it,' he muttered in her ear, adding his blankets to those already covering her. Guilt swept over her, but Ren only tightened his grip when she tried to pull away. 'Please, let me help you.'

It wasn't the first time he had comforted her like this, but she knew it wasn't just consideration and friendship this time. Still, she couldn't pull away without hurting his feelings and telling him what had happened during the fateful night. Immobilised and warmed by his body, she began drifting asleep when a rustling on the riverbank caught her attention. Ina held her breath, listening for a moment, but it didn't happen again. She was about to blame rats, but something in Ren's unnaturally still pose worried her.

'I heard—' she started, but he placed a hand over her mouth.

'I know, get ready.' His voice was barely audible as he whispered in her ear.

Slowly sliding to the side and untangling herself from the covers, she slid her hands to her thighs. Ina had initially objected to wearing long dresses slit on both sides, but Ren had been right about how useful there were. Now, grasping the hilts of her knives, she was grateful for his suggestion. Before she could draw them, a large group descended on the camp.

Ren leapt into action. His voice broke the silence in a strident call to arms, waking the surrounding refugees. The confusion of half-drunk men grabbing the nearest weapon, often the tools of their trade, slowed the attackers' advance, but didn't stop them, and, as the first blood was spilt, Ina was staggered by the sudden influx of Chaos magic. As the attackers hurt more people in the melee, the influx of Chaos fed Ina's magic, overwhelming her senses. It took her a moment, but gritting her teeth, she cut herself off from it.

In front of her eyes, an armed man ripped a screaming woman's halter and tore away a small purse hidden between her breasts whilst her husband lay bleeding on the ground.

Ina held back her Chaos magic, but didn't bother to rein in her anger. The frustration from the long, tiresome journey finally found the perfect release. Her knives struck forward, sinking into the man's sides, searching for his kidneys, and the fierce joy of the act shocked her. The rescued woman's eyes widened, but Ina rushed past towards the next opponent, and, as she passed the fire, made a dangerous decision.

Linking to her peridot, she called forth the flames from the blaze and wrapped the element over her blades. *It is just simple elemental magic to defend myself.* She rationalised, but deep down, knew she just loved her fire vipers and the feeling of being a deadly warrior.

Her next opponent lunged unsteadily, the ground treacherous from the snow and blood, and, thanks to Ren's hard training, Ina dodged to the side with ease. Her left hand was aglow as she sliced it across the man's throat, laughing in jubilation even as blood sprayed across her face and the man's body caught fire from the magic covering her blade.

The smile on her lips still lingered as she caught sight of Ren gliding through his enemies effortlessly. His silver blade reflected the moon's light, and, with the speed of his actions, it looked as if he killed his opponents with the moonlight itself. The same man who sacrificed his comfort to keep her warm just moments ago was now death incarnate, and the duality and beauty of his nature took her breath away.

Where Mar was a roaring inferno, Ren was a winter blizzard. His face expressed little, if any, emotion, his expression almost one of boredom. Suddenly, he looked at her, and his eyes widened in dismay. Whilst she stood there, staring at him with doe eyes, lost in the beauty of his swordplay, the last bandit had snuck up behind her and prepared to attack. Instinctively reacting to Ren's fear, Ina dived to the ground, and the blade slashing through the air only cut a shallow slice across her arm instead of removing her head.

Fear battled with embarrassment as Ina lay there looking up at her assailant. Ogling Ren and pride in her fighting skills had nearly caused her death, and now she was at the mercy of this filthy brigand.

The roar of fury that erupted from Ren when he saw Ina hurt left her gasping in shock, and the formerly icy warrior crashed into her attacker, his sword smashing against the bandit's sword with uncontrolled ferocity.

As the brigand fell back from the onslaught, Ren's face was no longer the calm mask of the Ghost. Instead, a terrifying visage of hate faced the lone thug, wielding the moonlight in a dance of death. Suddenly his blade licked out, scoring deeply across his opponent's forehead. Another crushing blow to the frightened man's sword, and Ren spun, his blade whistling through the air and cutting the muscles of the bandit's left arm. On and on it went. Ren could easily extinguish his life, but each time he cut his opponent, it was a minor wound intended to hurt but not kill.

Her attacker screamed and bled, and Ren made sure the man bled a lot. Ina squeezed her arm, trying to stem the wound, but it didn't prevent Ren from delighting in chopping the brigand to pieces. The man stopped trying to defend himself and dropped to the ground, begging for mercy, but Ren had none to offer, and Ina understood it was up to her to end it.

'Stop toying with him. Kill him, or let him go. His screams are giving me a headache,' she said, and it was partly true. The lack of sleep, holding back her Chaos magic, and stupidly missing the man's attack made her head throb, and now she just wanted it all to end.

'As you wish, my lady,' Ren said, stomping on the man's chest and slowly drawing his blade across the brigand's throat, smiling as he watched the life drain from the man's eyes.

The frightened gasp from the remaining defenders showed they'd seen Ren's fury, but Ina only raised an eyebrow at his actions.

'Was that really necessary? Why didn't you just kill him from the start? All this mess, and now we can't interrogate him.'

Ren cleaned his sword on the dead man's clothing before looking up from his task, scrutinising Ina's expression before calmly explaining. 'He hurt you. The death of the thousand cuts was the least he deserved. Besides, he is just a common bandit. There is nothing of value he could tell us.'

The emotionless mask of the Ghost that Ren showed the world didn't scare Ina. She noticed the tightening of his lips and stepped closer, placing her hand gently on his cheek.

'You are right, and I made a stupid mistake, forcing your hand, so I apologise. I promise to pay attention next time, and I hope you'll continue to teach me to be better,' she whispered, watching as Ren closed his eyes, savouring her touch. Finally, he turned his head, kissing her palm gently.

'I will, my lady. I will teach you all I know, but….' His voice faltered as if worried that his cruelty would repulse her. He resumed after taking a deep breath. 'But please don't condemn me for my actions. It is difficult for me to see you injured.'

This last statement didn't surprise her, but seeing him subdued was heartbreaking. *I wish I could let you see yourself through my eyes, my moonlight guardian*, she thought. Ignoring common sense and her better judgement, Ina stood on tiptoe and kissed his cheek. 'You never have to justify your actions to me. I trust you with all I am.'

Her words seemed to loosen the tight knot squeezing his heart, and Ren smiled before looking up and noticing the silent circle of peasants, eyes filled with a mixture of fear and hope. There were several seriously injured people, but most were just bruised and scared, and like a scared herd, they turned to the strongest amongst them, needing a leader.

After they persuaded the old man with the cane to take control, Ina and Ren helped reorganise the camp, offering to heal those who could be healed and transporting those too injured to the village for assistance. After removing the dead bodies and sharing supplies between the survivors, people headed to their beds.

Ren picked a few able-bodied men and set up guard posts around the camp before returning to Ina with the biggest grin she'd ever seen him wear.

'What is going on? Why are you grinning like a madman?' The suspicion in Ina's voice was unmistakable, but Ren said nothing for a moment, settling himself close before turning towards her.

'They are singing songs about you. They called you *Fiery Vengeance*. I was touched by their praise of your bravery, self-sacrifice, and ability to heal the dying.' He couldn't hold back any longer and laughed so hard it bent him in half, with Ina moaning plaintively at the injustice.

'Oh no, not again… I know everyone is grateful, and I'd be happy with wine or a meal. I would even be happy with a goat, but no, it's always a badly written song.' She stopped and sighed. 'The god of drunken bards has cursed me, you know. That's the only explanation.'

'Why a goat?' Her last remark confused Ren.

'To feed the dragon, of course,' Ina said, confident that dragging a stubborn animal through a frozen Liath would be preferable to hearing another song about her deeds.

Settling into the pile of furs the grateful survivors had brought for them, Ina looked at the dawn sky where the rising sun painted the first pink hue above the horizon. Looking at the soft glow, Ina thought about Mar and Ren and how their fates were entangled.

'It's like all my wishes came true, just not the way I wanted.'

Ren looked at her with interest. 'What do you mean?'

Ina's mouth twitched in a bitter smile. 'I wanted to be a powerful mage, and I have Chaos that can devastate a city. I wanted a man I couldn't intimidate for a lover, and I have a fucking dragon. I wanted to travel and visit the world, and here I am, freezing my arse off in the middle of nowhere, fending off robbers.'

Ren smiled and reached for her hand. 'I see this differently. You are a powerful mage who saved the kingdom, you have a dragon who loves you, and you travel the world helping those who would otherwise fall prey to evil. It is a blessing.' And when

Ina smiled, ready to thank him for his kindness, Ren added, 'And you are the hero of many unforgettable ballads.'

'Oh, bite my arse with your ballads.' She snorted, rolling her eyes.

'With pleasure, my lady, just point your humble guardian to where you would enjoy it most.'

Ina tried to pout, but it was hard not to laugh, and after a moment of furious blinking, she gave in to uncontrollable laughter. Ren joined her till they were both out of breath, grinning at each other like fools, and with a gentle kiss on her forehead, he pulled the witch into his arms, wrapping a blanket around her.

'Sleep. We still have an hour or two left till the ferry arrives, and it is better to be rested, ready for the road.'

Ina was almost asleep when Ren moved her head to his chest, stroking his fingers lightly over her hair. The sound of the warrior's heartbeat calmed the wild thoughts racing her mind, and the witch felt soft lips gently press against the top of her head. The magical link that still bound them briefly flared to life, and Ina bit her lip, worrying. After all, Ren was a part of her life, and there was no sense in denying it. She just needed to find a way for them to be friends because, despite his comforting touch, all she wanted was Mar's arms holding her that close.

Unaware of her thoughts, Ren gazed at the slowly setting moon. His mother used to call him *Moonlight*, and the quiet warrior felt he understood why as he lay there, feeling as if he'd disappear with the sunrise. As the last curve of the moon vanished, Ren looked at the fiery redhead in his arms. Perhaps Ina was the morning star, a celestial body who seemed so close but would forever be out of reach.

Tomorrow they would arrive at Castle Liath, but Ina was safe in his arms tonight, and no one could take that away from him. No matter what happened when they found Mar, Ren knew he would keep this moment in his heart forever.

He pressed his lips to her forehead and whispered the words of love, '*Bi chamd hairtai*[1],' accepting fate and whatever it might bring.

After a few refreshing hours of sleep, Ina was woken by the sound of the ferry pulling up to the docks. With a quick peek from the furs, the mage realised she was alone, that Ren had already packed up their belongings and was now saddling the horses. Only she and the makeshift bed were left in disarray.

'You should have woken me up. I would have helped with the packing,' she said, feeling guilty he did everything himself, but Ren only smiled.

'You looked so peaceful. How could I do that to you?' He looked at her with an intensity that made her shiver. Ina realised how messy she must look and brushed her hair with her fingers.

'My comb is in the bags, somewhere,' she explained while braiding her hair. 'I'm sorry for last night. I heard you complain about my hair. It is difficult to keep it tied up.'

Ren looked at her, completely confused. 'I said what?'

'You said something about my hair. You should have just pushed it aside,' Ina clarified, unsure why he suddenly burst out laughing and headed for the horses.

'Come, my lady. We can't be late.' He chuckled, amused that she thought the Yanwo words were a complaint about her hair. The irony of this situation was almost overwhelming, but he had other worries for now. He had seen how packed the ferry was as it

1 *Bi chamd hairtai – I love you (Yanwo)*

docked. Whatever caused the people to flee their homes was still a problem. Ina was difficult to protect on the best of days, but now it felt as though they were headed recklessly into a fire, and he feared it would turn into an inferno with Ina around.

CHAPTER SEVEN

Rewan rubbed his temples, trying to ease the headache creeping up on him with each report and polite refusal from the provincial lords. Their rejection of deeper cooperation with each other and the capital could be felt in each honeyed insult on the pages he'd read as they made sure to repay him for the damage his sister had wrought in their regions.

Of course, that hadn't stopped them from asking for his help to solve their problems, and if it weren't so serious, it would be laughable how with one breath, they praised his new laws, then the next demanded those same laws excluded this, or that trade deal when it involved lining their coffers.

After his father's years of neglect and his sister's active stripping of their resources, it was no surprise many of them felt they didn't need Osterad anymore, and he was running out of ideas on how to bring them back to the fold.

His immediate solution was to make them realise they must rely on each other. The western mountainous region was a stronghold of military power, used to defend against the monsters, kobolds and shifter clans who raided the province regularly but had little to no farming capability. The southern region, rich in fertile soil, had no real military, so it relied on trade for its prosperity, making them vulnerable if its neighbours became belligerent with Verdante and the Southern March lords, always ready to exploit a defenceless neighbour. The north already considered themselves free cities. Their pirate ancestry had given them a fierce, independent spirit, and the only things that held them, even loosely to Cornovii, were the plentiful merchandise, both produce and crafted goods that earned them copious amounts of gold across the sea.

The only region Rewan didn't worry about was the east, but that was the Black Forest, home to woodland gods, fantastical creatures, and the humans who lived there were reclusive and self-reliant, but that meant, even as king, Rewan was reluctant to enforce his rule there and would always tread carefully and respectfully in the realm of the Leshy. Above all these problems was the Magic council. An august body that gave the enemies of Cornovii pause but insisted that only they had the right to rule over other magic users.

At the centre of these bickering and truculent provinces sat the king, trying to keep them from each other's throats whilst hoping he wasn't too successful, and they banded together to remove him from power. Rewan finally understood why his father drank so much. As he reached for a glass of his favourite beverage, the doors crashed open, and Kaian strode through with a flourish, snapping his fingers and dismissing the loitering servants. When the doors closed, the silver-haired advisor moved behind Rewan's chair and placed his hands on the king's temples. The gentle pressure from Kaian's long fingers eased his liege lord's pain, making Rewan sigh with relief. The trust shown by this act showed how close the two men had become this past year, and the scion of the Water Horse clan had more than just the king's ear at his disposal.

'You should leave your office more often,' said Kaian, kissing the top of Rewan's head. 'Some funny stories are doing the rounds in the taverns and meeting houses that you'd probably enjoy.'

Rewan chuckled. 'You're supposed to be a master assassin, not a gossip maid. You've been visiting Gruff too often.'

'So you don't want to listen? Such a shame. Besides, what's wrong with mixing work with a little pleasure?'

'Just tell me, you tease.' Rewan couldn't stop smiling at this blatant provocation. Whatever his assassin had to say, it would be worth taking the time to listen.

Kaian took the opposite chair and poured himself a generous measure of wine. After he'd finished, Rewan was openmouthed in shock. Apparently, the most recent influx of refugees were telling stories of a ghostly, pitiless warrior and the blazing sorceress saving the defenceless town of Stary Bod.

Rewan knew sending Ina and Ren to the west would end in trouble, and it seemed his gambit was already bearing fruit. What shocked him speechless were the stories of the dragon who saved the kingdom, with the just and merciful King Rewan commanding the battle like some hero of legend.

The story was so popular that every bard in the capital regaled the taverns several times a night, even hiring students from the magical university to spin fiery illusions depicting the battle.

Kaian, laughing so hard he choked on his wine, revealed the story's author, and Rewan almost fell off his chair.

'Ina did that…?' He still could not believe it, but now some of the most recent reports made sense. The mood of the citizens of Osterad was much more welcoming of the starving refugees lately, and the local merchants had even offered goods and services to those camped outside the city.

Kaian grinned at the kaleidoscope of expressions that rushed over the king's face. 'I told you she was extraordinary. It was a smart move to get her on your side.'

Rewan's mood improved significantly, and he teased his partner in a moment of good humour. 'Maybe I should force her to marry me after all,' he said, and Kaian burst out laughing.

'We would all have fun nights then, as Ina seems to like, let's say, a friendly triangle?'

Seeing that his hook didn't catch, Rewan let the subject go and focused on a more pressing matter.

'Talk to Gruff, and make sure this song or tale is sung on every street corner, and maybe we should send some bards to the provinces. Also, we need a more refined version for the nobles. The illusion idea is perfect for that. See to it, please, and suppose, for a moment, our little witch tames her dragon. I want him back as a captain or field marshal if that happens. Whatever military position he wants is his, but I want to have that dragon in my ranks and the witch in my court.'

Kaian rose from his chair and offered the king a deep bow. Rewan's intelligence was refreshing, and he loved watching those tiny gears in his head work so impressively.

'I will make sure it happens. I assume you will be too busy to see me tonight with all this work?' he asked, knowing the answer already.

'I'm never too busy for you. Oh, and bring a discrete young lady with you. Let's see how this triangle would work,' said Rewan, and then added with a grin, 'It doesn't need to be a redhead, but that would be a bonus.'

Kaian shook his head, closing the doors as he left. A plan formed in his head. There was a redhead in his ranks, and placing her in the king's bed would benefit all involved. With that settled, he quickened his steps with a smile, heading to the *Drunken Wizard.*

It took them almost a whole day's ride, but despite her tiredness, Ina couldn't stop herself from enjoying the city as soon as they walked through the gates. All the buildings were made of stone from the mountain; each a stronghold in its own right. There were no frivolous embellishments, yet the city was beautiful with a proud spirit.

When they arrived at the castle, they were politely but firmly told to dismount and, soon after, led to the Duke's chambers. Their arrival had already been announced, and as they walked in, Ina almost stumbled at the sight of Mar's father. The resemblance was uncanny, and if not for the amount of grey in his ashen blond hair, she would have thought it was Mar himself. Expecting the Duke to break the silence, Ina was again surprised when the Duchess was the first to speak.

'Where is my son?' she asked so suddenly that Ina automatically answered.

'I believe you shot him down.' As soon as those words left her mouth, she cursed herself. Once again, her diplomacy was more "punch in the face" than sympathy and flowery words.

The lady paled, but her husband rose from his chair and towered above her with a deep scowl. He looked at Ren, and recognition sparked in his eyes.

'You were with my son. Where is he? And what is this damn woman talking about?'

The *damn woman* released an exasperated sigh and pushed herself forward. As someone said, like father like son, and it appeared her first encounters with the men of Liath were destined to be frustrating.

'My lord, I'm the lady Inanuan of Thorn, a judicial mage of His Majesty, King Rewan,' she said, lifting her head to face him and giving him a moment to absorb the information. 'You will address me, not my companion. I have returned your son's horse and possess the latest news from the capital. I'm also tired, hungry, and on the brink of turning this beautiful chamber into rubble. I will kindly ask you to show us some hospitality.' She looked directly at the man, pronouncing every word with a dignity that would make Nerissa proud. It must have worked, as his anger deflated, as much as his posture.

'My apologies. We are desperate to hear about our Marcach, especially after your revelation, but you are right. I will ask the servants to prepare a meal and your rooms. In the meantime, could you please tell me at least if he is alive?'

Ina sighed and sat on the nearby chair. 'That, unfortunately, I do not know, but the dragon your guards shot at was Mar. Long story short, your son transformed during the palace battle, and I'm here to help him back to his humanity.'

The reactions of Mar's parents couldn't be more different. His father laughed with disbelief, looking at Ina like she had just grown a second head, but his mother covered her face in her hands and cried. Eventually, the lord of Liath noticed his wife's distress.

'Why are you crying? That can't be true. The ancestry of Liath is just a legend,' he said, scanning her face anxiously, but when she finally looked up, he fell back in shock, and disbelief crept into his voice. 'Lorraine, this can't be true.'

The lady shook her head, fighting tears when she answered. 'The things your mother told me… about your bloodline. There is… something. Not a legend, or a rumour. I don't know the details, but she claimed the dragon of Liath is not just an empty symbol and to look for golden eyes in our children. She said if I spot them, to kill the child before it becomes a dragon. I thought it was just the words of a madwoman, not something real.'

Ina stood there, forgotten during this entire exchange, but hearing the last sentence, she blew up. 'No one is killing my dragon.' Her statement reverberated with magic as her anger slipped her control, and everyone turned to stare in alarm.

'Your dragon? How did my son become your dragon?' asked the noble, approaching her. The initial shock from his wife's confession was quickly forgotten as he focused on a problem he thought he might deal with easily.

'That is another long story, my lord, but trust me, your son is my friend, and I will transform him back to human, or die trying.'

A quick nod was the only reply to her statement as a servant arrived, loudly announcing that both food and accommodation were ready, and the lord of Liath dismissed them from his presence.

'Have some rest, my lady. We will talk more tomorrow. For now, I have to talk to my wife and I… I need some time to digest this information. Please be ready for more questions during breakfast. You and your companion will be expected to attend.'

The atmosphere during breakfast was grim. The lord and lady of Liath appeared tired and bleary-eyed, but had accepted the uncomfortable truth that their oldest son was a dragon. Now they wanted to know how it happened. Ina had to give a detailed description of recent events in the capital. Mar's father ground his teeth in frustration, listening to the story of monsters attacking the city and the princess's betrayal. Ren took over the report about the last battle and delivered a detailed military description of the palace's defence and Mar's fight. Ina saw the old noble's face brighten with pride and joy, nodding as he listened to each detail.

Lorraine, Mar's mother, focused on Ina, enquiring about his life in the capital and trying to discover Ina's involvement with Mar. Sitting there, trying to preserve a modicum of decorum, the witch dutifully answered all her questions whilst avoiding exposing her relationship with the couple's son.

'How do you intend to turn my son back to human?' Lorraine asked, but before Ina could answer, they heard shouts of alarm from outside.

Mar's father hit his fist on the table, shouting at the servants. 'One of you check what is going on there, and be quick!' he said without even an attempt to hide his anger.

A moment later, the panting footman ran into the dining room.

'My lord, the dragons… they are attacking.'

With the sudden thud of a falling heavy chair, Ina stood up and ran outside. She didn't know where to go, but instinct led her towards the commotion. After running through the maze of the castle corridors, Ina stood on the wall, looking at the approaching dragons. She felt a familiar tightness in her chest and instinctively reached for Ren's hand when she saw Mar's blue-steel colouring.

'He is here. And alive,' she said, fighting back the tears, but her joy was short-lived as a loud thwump announced the first ballista volley. Her heart almost stopped as she watched the dragons swerving to avoid the black, lethal arrows. When she could finally breathe again, her rage flared up. Ren was already halfway to the tower to command ceasefire when she turned on her heel and unleashed pure Chaos.

'Nobody is killing my fucking dragon!' she shouted as power erupted from her fingertips.

Her aim was never so precise. Two streams of raw magic hit the ballistae, obliterating the wood and iron, leaving nothing but a cloud of dust that quickly dispersed in the bitter wind. Soldiers shouted and scattered, unsure who the enemy was before their lord took command. Ina, surrounded by swirling Chaos, looked for more targets when she heard Mar's voice booming behind her.

'Ina, are you out of your mind? That was an expensive weapon.'

Even distorted by the inhuman throat, it was Mar, and Ina turned around, looking up. Almost in front of her, hovering in the air was her dragon, as magnificent as she remembered him. The morning sun highlighted the membranes of his wings, creating a surreal tableau, and Ina gasped in pure bliss as she savoured the beauty of the creature before her. It only lasted for a moment before her temper kicked in, and the air turned blue with obscenities.

'You bloody moron, how could you take off like that, leaving me alone? What the hell were you thinking? You could at least take me with you. Instead, I froze my arse off to get to you, and now here you are, flying around and preening like an overgrown cockerel.'

Mar's roar shook the castle wall as he burst out laughing. The simple happiness he felt at finding Ina still treated him the same was overwhelming. His little firefly was not scared of the vicious dragon, but angry like a bag of badgers for being left alone.

'I missed you, too. Now come down to the courtyard for a proper welcome.' Mar twisted to the side and flew down to wait.

Ina's emotions were in so much turmoil that she barely registered the other dragon. Her guilt for transforming Mar, and the worry for his safety that had been bottled up for so long, came back with a vengeance, leaving her chaotic nature bare to the world. If Mar thought their conversation was finished, he was sorely mistaken. So, with a defiant shrug, Ina headed for the stairs. On her way down, she heard the cries of soldiers battling the powerful gusts of wind. It must be caused by the dragons landing in the courtyard. Ina pushed aside the thought of the second dragon as she ran down the slippery stairs. Ren was already standing there, sheltering his eyes from flying debris.

Both dragons landed gracefully, folding their large wings before their contours blurred and changed. Ina slowed down, thinking her eyes were playing tricks on her. In the blink of an eye, in the place of a dragon, stood Mar dressed in leather armour matching his dragon scales. *What? How? Why didn't he return to Osterad if he was back to his old self?* She halted her steps when the flood of questions overwhelmed her mind. Still, the burden of guilt she was carrying since the battle suddenly disappeared, replaced by pure unbridled joy. Unwanted tears distorted her vision, and Ina wiped them away quickly. The last thing she needed was this oaf to make fun of her.

Her resolve to be firm with him was short-lived when Mar looked at her with concern growing in his golden eyes.

'What happened, my spitfire? You are not happy to see me?'

The hope and uncertainty mixed in his voice sent her flying into his arms. Mar caught her in a tight embrace, crushing her body so hard she could feel his heartbeat through his armour. His warmth and the scent of his body broke something in her, and despite her best efforts, Ina started crying, pounding his chest.

'You hairy cretin! How could you just fly off, especially if you knew you could change back?' she said, pounding his torso. 'Why didn't you take me with you? Ren fell ill when we dragged our arses through the snow to find you because you couldn't keep yours on the ground.'

Mar buried his face in her hair, inhaling her aroma. His transformation had heightened his senses, and he noticed without all the perfumes masking her natural scent, Ina smelled like apple pie. A mouthwatering apple pie.

'You should never use perfume again,' he said, stopping her tirade.

'What the—' she managed before Mar, led by his yearning, grabbed a handful of hair and captured her lips. His kiss radiated longing and joy, and Ina yielded to his desire, savouring his taste, oblivious to the world.

Strong hands unexpectedly pulled her back, and confused, Ina turned to the culprit. She expected Ren, but in front of her stood an inhumanly beautiful woman, so perfect she almost resembled a doll. Ina blinked and smiled at the stranger, suddenly remembering two dragons had landed.

Her smile faltered when the strange woman looked at her with disdain and said, 'Get your hands off my mate.'

'What?' Her words made no sense, and Ina blinked rapidly, trying to process their meaning.

'Get your hands off my mate. Or, as you humans say, get your hands off my husband.'

The wave of magic that rolled off Ina rattled the cobblestones and the castle's foundations. The witch slowly turned to Mar, the certainly in the woman's voice erasing any rational thought from her mind. All she knew was he could easily shapeshift, yet instead of going back to Osterad, he brought the most beautiful woman she'd ever seen to his family nest.

'I see you brought your *wife* to introduce her to your parents. My apologies for imposing my affections upon you,' she said, her voice calm despite her body trembling with the anger of betrayal.

'I have no idea what's happening, but I'm not married,' he answered, stepping towards Ina, but she took a step back, contempt written all over her face. Mar looked at Ayni, who smiled with poorly hidden triumph and repeated, barely restraining his anger. 'We are not married, and you shouldn't lie to my betrothed.'

Ayni smirked, appearing to enjoy the commotion, and answered. 'Oh, but we are. You accepted my food and shared my fire, and when I asked if you would join me in the Dance of the Sky, you agreed. Dragons know no ceremonies other than that dance, and I must admit, you performed splendidly by catching your bride.'

One look at Ina's pale face and Mar cursed the gods that allowed him, in his ignorance, to accept the help of a woman who intended to trap him in a marriage he'd not agreed to or wanted. 'I'm also a human, and I would never consent to your help if I knew the price you intended for it. I will not be tied to a woman who tricked me into a custom I was unaware even existed. You are not my wife, Ayni, and you never will be.'

Mar turned to Ina to explain, apologise or beg if it would fix the damage his foolishness had caused, but his gaze was met with icy fury. The disgust in her voice cut him deeply as she spoke.

'Every thief would claim innocence when caught. Would I even know about it if I didn't come all the way here to beg your forgiveness for the transformation and offer help you clearly didn't need? Should I believe you were ignorant when it takes a conscious effort to *catch* your new bride?'

There was no reason or logic left, just a maelstrom of crushed hopes, dreams, and the sudden realisation that next to this magnificent dragoness, she was nothing but a witch from a dirty hut in the forest. Ina looked at his stunned expression, the pain of her words visible in his eyes, then looked at the dragoness, who possessively placed her hand on his shoulder. Her fists clenched, and Ina straightened her spine, holding to her pride—the only emotion keeping back the tears.

'You don't have to deny your actions to placate me. I won't turn your home into rubble. I'm no crazed mage. No, I understand. You were injured, and she was there, sophisticated and regal, happy to heal your wounds and share your burden, just as I was in the forest. There seems to be a pattern, Sir Marcach, don't you think? I was clearly not good enough in my care to even be mentioned in a letter to your parents, but worry not. You were a good lover, and I enjoyed it while it lasted. I wish you the best of luck, and I won't stand in the way of your happiness.'

Almost choking on the last few words, Ina turned and fled into the castle. It all felt too surreal to comprehend, and it took all her focus to push down the torrent of emotions threatening to unleash the Chaos raging in her soul. Nerissa would have been proud of how she handled herself. Ina had retained her dignity and still managed to put that cheating dragon in his place. She never thought that after expressing his love so passionately, he would cast her aside so quickly, and so soon after she realised her feelings were just as strong. Her emotions surged uncontrollably till all were burned away by anger, and Ina promised herself she would never let any man fool her again.

Ina's speech took Mar by surprise, and when she ran back to the castle, he leapt forward to chase her, but Ren's grip on his arm stopped him in his tracks.

'No, let her calm down. Trying to explain anything now will end in more pain, and I doubt it would just be hers.' Mar yanked his arm from his friend's hold, determined to go. 'I said stop. I may believe you, but she won't, not right now. Her words came from a broken heart. If you push her more, she will break this castle. Is that what you want?'

Ren's words felt too true for comfort, and Mar growled, focusing his anger on Ayni. He approached the dragoness with a feral snarl.

'Whatever thoughts are in your head, we are not married. There is only one woman I will grow old with, and it's not you,' he said, articulating every word, but Ayni simply shrugged.

'I thought you came to the Temple mating grounds to find a partner, and I asked for your consent, remember? And you answered my mating call in the sky, you might have injured your head, but your dragon knew what you were doing.' She looked up at him, visibly irritated. 'I simply wanted a dragon mate this time. One that won't die so quickly. What is so hard to believe? Besides, I saved your life. A bit of civility and gratitude would be welcome,' she added, hammering in the last nail to his coffin.

After observing the scene, Mar's father came forward and embraced his son brusquely.

'I'm pleased to see you safe, Marcach. Let me organise a room for your friend in the guest wing to show our gratitude. Then we can sit down together and talk.'

After the servants escorted Ayni to her room, Mar found himself under the watchful eye of his father. The latter demanded a full report on recent events, and the captain dutifully recounted everything that had happened since the infamous palace battle. Ren added his observations of the journey from the capital, and the three men exchanged concerned looks.

Mar's father changed the subject to relieve the sudden tension. 'Now, care to tell me how my overly careful son entangled himself with two women?'

'It's complicated,' said Mar, making his father laugh.

'I could see that, my boy. But your complications were quite damaging to my castle, so maybe ask your lady friend, preferably both of them, to not take their anger out on our defences,' he said, pointing to the crumbled ring of rubble where Ina had stood before. 'And sort it out before your mother decides on taking this problem into her capable hands.'

Mar felt utterly stupid. Only his father could scold him in such a calm way and make him feel so foolish. Despite his better judgment, he answered. 'Then get used to some shaking, as Ina would say. I just need to explain this whole mess to her.' Mar noticed Ren's deep frown and the amused looks his father gave him, but before they could speak further, a female voice from above called out.

'Alleron, how long will you keep my child away from me?'

Mar's father embraced him and pushed him towards the castle entrance.

'Come, my son, time to face the music. Now you have to explain it all to your mother,' he said with a hint of pity in his voice, as the real interrogation was about to begin.

CHAPTER EIGHT

Mar hadn't seen his mother for far too long, and whilst she looked as regal as ever, he couldn't help but notice the little signs of fragility in her movements.

Lady Lorraine welcomed him into the dining room with a quick peck on the cheek, pushing him towards the chair in front of a meal large enough to feed five. Mar didn't even look around for Ayni, knowing his mother would have arranged for her to settle into the guest quarters, wanting to speak to him with no one overhearing their conversation.

For the next hour, he recounted the last few weeks' adventures, adding more detail each time Lorraine asked.

When he came to the battle of Osterad, his mother's face paled, but she honed in on his description of Ina's involvement, asking for more details each time he mentioned her name.

Finally, he told her about his transformation and the long flight to Liath, including the incident with the ballista and the help provided by Ayni.

Mar hadn't noticed his father's presence until Lorraine looked over to her husband, exchanging a worried glance, but with that silent communication, Mar knew something was going on.

Mar, already impatient and desperate to ease the pain in his lady's eyes, nearly stormed out at the silent communication between his parents.

With an apology ready, the agitated warrior gripped the table to leave. Food was the last thing on his mind, with his firefly hurt over his apparent betrayal. The thought of her seeking solace elsewhere had him nearly ripping the table to pieces in the desire to see her.

He knew Ren's feelings, but he'd also noticed the change in his friend's behaviour, and he didn't like it. Ren's attitude today challenged him in many ways, especially after seeing how comfortable Ina was with him.

Only half-listening to his mother's words, he almost missed the question she asked about Ayni.

'The woman you brought with you claimed to be your wife. Is it true?'

A flicker of disgust escaped his control, and Mar hoped his mother had missed it. He suspected Lorraine had seen their arrival from her balcony, and she would have realised something was profoundly wrong. His mother had an intuition that had caught his mischief too often as a child, so she probed further, not letting him remain silent on the matter.

'So, is she your wife?' she asked again, flinching when he slammed his hands on the table.

'She is not my wife. Ayni helped me when I was injured and stuck as a dragon, that's all,' he answered, trying to tame his anger. 'I made some mistakes, unaware of dragon customs, possibly misleading her, but there is nothing between us except a debt of gratitude. The only woman I want is now sitting alone in her room. Or at least I hope she is alone.' Mar stood up and turned to the doors. 'I'm sorry. We will have more time to talk, but now I need to find Ina and explain this mess before any doors go flying.'

With this brief explanation, he exited the room, leaving his parents looking at each other, confused.

'What doors?' Lorraine was the first to ask.

'It doesn't matter, my dear. I think we have a bigger problem,' said Alleron, tightening his lips. 'We have a dragon, a crown mage, and Marcach trapped between them. The one he wants won't even look at him, taking refuge in her room, while the other is acting like he's a treasure to be added to her hoard.'

The lord of the house rubbed his temples and looked up when the slamming of doors reverberated through the castle.

'What should we do?' Lorraine looked up, brushing the dust from the ceiling beams off her shoulder.

'Frankly, my dear, I don't know. I saw Marcach and the mage kiss… Love that strong has destroyed empires. Now, that mage feels betrayed.' Alleron shook his head before looking towards the guest wing. 'For now, all we can do is step back, hope he gets his foot out of whichever orifice it's stuck in, and proves his love is true. If the gods allow, we will still have a castle to live in after they're finished.'

Another loud thud made them turn around and look at each other.

'Will you open this fucking door? We need to talk. Ina! I will break it into kindling in a moment. Please let me in.'

The corridors and halls echoed with Mar's voice, and Alleron looked at his wife, smiling. 'Flying doors? It seems our son, the battering ram, has finally met his match,' he said. Lorraine snapped him a look of distaste.

'He is a noble and should behave as such,' she said, trying to avoid her husband's embrace as he moved in close.

'He is a man in love, my darling. We both know the men in this family lose all sense when this madness descends upon us.' He kissed the top of her head and grabbed a wine bottle that wobbled on the table. Soon, more thuds and the splintering of wood told them Mar was as determined as his father said in regard to matters of the heart.

Ren made his way to Ina's room, bearing gifts. After the shock of seeing such an enchanting woman appear next to Mar had worn off, the warrior found himself reminiscing about his homeland and the beautiful murals of dragons that adorned the palace. The exquisite aquamarine dragon would have taken pride of place there if ever an artist could capture such fierce beauty. However, that brief fascination could never erase from his mind the haunted look on Ina's face when she retreated into the castle. Ren knew Mar would spend some time with his parents, reporting on recent events and catching up with them.

After giving Ina some time alone, Ren knocked politely, only to be asked just as politely to leave her be. He congratulated himself when a mixture of persuasion and the honey cakes he'd stolen from the kitchen enticed her into opening the door. His smile quickly faded when he saw her, so unnaturally calm for her nature, with puffy eyes and red cheeks that told him she'd been crying, hiding like a wounded animal.

Ina broke the silence first. 'I'm fine. There's no need to worry. I lost my temper outside, and I will apologise to our hosts later.' Taking the tray of food, she sat on the windowsill. Ren watched as Ina trailed her finger over the frosted window and melted ice trickled down, forming the pattern of the Leshy's tree, causing more tears to fill her eyes.

Ren approached her, unsure of what to do. Ayni's earlier declaration, whether true or false, offered a new opportunity for him. But now, seeing Ina so sad, he wished he could find the right words to cheer her up or for him to be the one she wanted by her side.

'What are you going to do?' he asked, combing a stray lock of hair back before it became glued to the sticky cakes.

Ina was silent for a moment, mulling over his question. 'I think we should pack and go back to Osterad. We came here to help Mar, and his transformation is no longer a problem. The rest he can sort himself. It's too late to leave today, but I will go tomorrow. That would be enough time to get to the ferry before nightfall.'

Ren gently placed his hands on her shoulders and turned Ina to face him. 'We will do as you wish. Just tell me what to do to dispel this sadness. Should I challenge Mar and kick his arse? Or'—he hesitated, unsure about bringing it up—'remove that woman from his side?'

His last statement made the witch gasp. 'Don't. Things between Mar and I were complicated, even back in Osterad. I just imagined more than I should have after that damned ball. And this dragoness… Ren, she is exquisite. And so ladylike. She is more suited to being the wife of a scion of Liath than I would ever be. He was free to seek his happiness elsewhere after the way

I treated him, and let's not forget who transformed him into a dragon. He is not a problem here. In my arrogance, I assumed he would wait for me forever. And the ironic thing is I still don't know how I feel about him.'

Ina stopped for a moment, remembering their night in the garden. She told Mar she didn't believe in everlasting love and didn't want commitment. For her, love was an ephemeral firefly, beautiful when alive, but fading too quickly when faced with the harsh reality of life. Ina's lips twisted into bitterness as her words that night cut into her soul. That reality came quicker than she expected.

'I didn't realise it would hurt this much, but I will get over it soon. I always do,' she said, and, as if on command, she heard Mar's voice from the other side of the door.

'Ina, can I come in?'

Ina shuddered, casting her hands forward, instinctively sealing the doors with a snap of power and reinforcing the locks. Her heart pounded so heavily that it drowned out the rest of the world. Within that rhythm, another heartbeat pulsed, and the golden light of Mar's magic called to her senses, but Ina was firm in her resolve. The connection between them was too distracting, and the less she saw him, the better for them both.

'Please leave. We have nothing to discuss. You should entertain the *wife* you brought to your parent's castle. I will be gone tomorrow, so please don't trouble yourself with my presence.'

Ina's words were a deliberate attempt to antagonise and drive him away, but Mar hit the wood harder, making the oak planks bend beneath his hands.

'You are not going anywhere. I don't have a fucking wife. How many times must I tell you? Let me in,' he said in an anguished voice, and she felt the pressure on the other side of the doors intensify, filling the air with the metallic scent of an irritated dragon. Ren sensed the threat and moved forward, drawing his sword and taking a defensive stance in front of her. The situation was getting out of control, and Ina took a deep breath. Mar was not going away, and all she could do was try to prevent bloodshed.

'No, Ren, we will not do it that way.'

The door bent inwards and was about to break when Ina released the spell. Mar burst in, and the golden glow of his eyes almost lit the room as he focused on Ina and Ren.

'Ren, leave,' he snapped, voice raw and commanding, but Ren didn't yield. 'Sheath your sword and leave. There will be no bloodshed between us, brother, but I will talk to Ina.'

Ren still didn't move, and seeing this impasse, Ina placed her hand on his shoulder.

'Please give me some time with him, or nothing will be resolved,' she said, nodding towards the door.

Ren kissed her fingertips and moved to the exit. Once abreast of Mar, he stopped. 'Today was hard enough for her. I will take your heart if you cause her any more grief.' He said it casually, as if wishing him a pleasant evening.

'If I hurt her, I will give it to you myself,' the captain replied with iron certainty.

Mar waited till the door closed and hesitantly moved forward, his previous boldness replaced with uncertainty. What could he say now to make her listen? He'd only thought about seeing her again, and words failed him now that he was here.

Standing in the middle of the room, he felt like a fool, and it tore him apart to see Ina looking so small and vulnerable. He could see she'd been crying, and the realisation that he was the reason behind her tears stung worse than being shot by the ballista.

Mar took another step forward, reaching out to gather his love into his arms, but Ina stopped him with a shake of her head.

'Say what you came here for and leave my room, please.'

There was no emotion in her voice, and Mar felt lost while the woman holding the key to his salvation firmed her heart, seemingly indifferent to his feelings.

'Why are you acting so distant? I swear on my honour that I didn't betray you. I'm as confused as you are by all this.'

'No, you didn't betray me,' she said when his voice faltered. 'But that revelation hurt more than I expected, and I can't help how I feel about it.'

Mar growled, and she smiled bitterly, not at all surprised by his reaction. 'Mar, I'm not mad. Maybe I was initially because it all crashed down on me at such an unexpected moment, but I'm no longer angry. We are still friends, and if you give me time, I will adjust to this new arrangement.'

This new cold and reasonable Ina was infuriating, and Mar couldn't take it any longer. She was in his arms moments later, and he lifted her chin to look into her eyes.

'Stop it. Just… stop it. I was confused and injured when I landed in the mountains. I had to accept Ayni's help or die in the snow. Why can't you believe that's all it was?'

Lost in the softness of his voice, Ina touched his chest. 'I'm sorry, Mar, I didn't want things to be like this. I didn't want to change you. I know it must be difficult for you, and I wish I could turn back time.'

Mar looked into her eyes, and the world stopped for him. He needed her happy and loved. His feelings before the change, now amplified, drove his lips to hers, seeking the comfort of her embrace.

'I have no regrets. I love you whether I'm human or dragon. Only you.'

Ina tasted better than he remembered. Sweet apples and cinnamon spice tingled on his tongue as he explored her mouth, feeling her melting against his touch. The dragon inside reared its head. This woman belonged to him, but Mar sensed the storm within her and fought the possessiveness threatening to obliterate his sanity.

Betrayed by her own body, Ina did nothing to stop the kiss. Her lips parted, letting him in, and fire engulfed her skin where his hands touched her. Their bond blazed to life, and the pressure in her chest intensified, demanding more of him. But before she lost herself, Ayni's beautiful face flashed through her mind, fuelling her doubts. What if these feelings he spoke of were just the aftereffects of the forbidden spell? Why did this man suddenly change her entire outlook on life? It took all of her strength to push him away, and the raw pain she saw in his eyes almost broke her resolve.

'I'm sorry, Mar. I will treasure the time we had, but there is no future for us. The spell I performed in the forest tied the three of us together, which was wrong of me, but I promise it will fade with time and distance, and I think Ayni's presence here is evidence only distance was needed,' she said, unsure who she was trying to convince.

'Ina, I know what I feel. It is not the spell. I love you. No one else but you. How many times do I have to tell you this?' Mar almost roared the last words and crushed her to his chest. He couldn't believe how such an intelligent woman could be so blind. He knew about the spell. It was the first thing he'd asked Jorge about. There was a bond between them, but when examining it, the judicial mage had shaken his head and said whatever connected them, magic had very little to do with it, refusing to disclose more.

Trapped against his hard body, Ina drew a sharp breath, unable to stop the tumultuous thoughts rushing through her head. She was trying to be reasonable to let him go, to be with his own kind, but Mar claimed to love only her. Why did he bring another woman to his parent's castle if that was true?

'Let me go. I have to think about it.' She pushed against his solid chest. There were too many ifs and buts, and she couldn't think straight at the moment, and the only solution she could think about was a bit of distance to decide what to do.

'Think about what? Which of us you want in your bed? Should I call Ren back so you can ask him for permission to have feelings for me? You seemed to become very close when I was away. We are both under the same spell, and I saw how he looks at you, but I never questioned your feelings for him.' Mar was desperate and at his wit's end. Ina's resistance and his inability to convince her of the sincerity of his feelings were tearing him apart, but as soon as those veiled suspicions left his mouth, he knew he'd made a colossal mistake. Ina's eyes widened, her uncertainty burnt away by fury.

'You have your pretty little dragon. I have Ren, and it is none of your business how I feel about him. Now get the fuck out of my room.'

The sudden blast of her magic threw him through the door. He was ready, yet he could not resist a raging Ina, not even with his dragon's strength. Mar scrambled to his feet, watching her take a long, calming breath, trying to tame the vortex of magic around her, and just as he was about to return to the room, Ren appeared on the stairs.

'I heard Ina call my name, so if you've finished trying to demolish the castle, I think you should leave and change for dinner. Lady Lorraine has invited everyone for a meal in the family suite.'

Mar clenched his fists, looking like he would rip his friend to piccces, but Ina heard and nodded.

'Thank you, Ren. Mar was just leaving. If you could close the door, I will change and join you shortly.'

After quietly easing the door shut, Ren turned to Mar and shook his head. 'You're making her miserable again. I told you to give her time, yet you push her to yield when your dragoness is still in the castle. I feel like I don't know you anymore.'

Mar turned his now glowing eyes towards Ina's room, remembering the vulnerable expression that felt like a dagger to his heart. With a snarl and curse, he turned to Ren. 'I love that damn witch, and I did nothing wrong, so save this horse shit for someone else. I'll see you both at dinner.' With that, Mar stalked off, cursing red-haired women and lovestruck mooncalves.

As he passed the door to Ayni's chamber, he paused. Ren was right. He had no chance to smooth things over with Ina if he didn't sort out the issue with Ayni. This farce had to end, and, without knocking, he pushed in, only to be confronted by the beautiful woman's features lighting up with happiness at his presence.

'I'm glad you came—' she said, but he slashed a hand through the air and interrupted her.

'I don't know what game you're playing here, but dragon custom be damned, I will not be coerced into marriage. Ayni, I owe you a debt of honour, but don't mistake my gratitude and friendship for love. I never want to hear mention of our marriage again.' He spat out the last words and saw the flash of anger run over her face.

'Oh, and you have no blame to shoulder? You ate the food I provided, and then you danced with me. I asked openly, you accepted, and you caught your prize as a true dragon would.'

Ayni knew what she was saying was not precisely the truth. She misjudged his presence in the temple, and her loneliness made her act recklessly, but he was interesting and fun to be around, and she'd grown to like him. Coming here, she hoped that once his worry was eased, they would complete the mating ritual started with the dance. Seeing this human woman kissing the man Ayni already considered her mate made her blurt out her claim, and now it was too late to retract her statement. Not to mention hearing his loud discussion with the other woman and its rather destructive ending had given her an idea. *Maybe with enough time, he would reconsider?*

Mar ground his teeth as he stifled the desire to rip the dragoness to pieces, but before he lost control, Ayni said, 'I won't mention our mating dance, but I want to stay here for a while. I find it pleasant that I don't have to hide, and if you allow it, I promise to behave.'

Her mischievous smile contradicted the contrite words, but Mar was out of ideas and, ready to grab any chance, nodded curtly and stormed out of the room.

Ina barely had time to dress when a servant appeared, asking her to come downstairs. She entered the dining room, pausing as she suddenly felt everyone's attention. Their assessing stares told her that everybody in the castle likely heard the ending of her *intimate* discussion with Mar. Ina straightened her shoulders with a frustrated sigh and strode into the room, but her mood soured further as she saw the dragoness sitting next to Mar, as if she belonged there, looking stunning in a royal blue dress and gold jewellery, the colours enhancing her already ephemeral beauty. The contrast between them was highlighted by Ina's grey dress, made from good quality wool for comfort and durability, not courtly life. She would give anything to have a stunning gown and feel less like a servant next to such beautiful ladies.

Ren stood up and led her to the table, she felt his thumb stroking the inside of her wrist to give her courage, and she smiled at him gratefully for this little gesture of comfort. It was just dinner, and she had survived worse situations. Besides, she didn't even have to talk much.

The smile didn't escape Mar's notice, who watched Ina like a hawk. She looked casually beautiful. He would love to sit with her by the fire, playing with her long hair like they had in Osterad. Instead, he had been placed next to Ayni, and the dragoness, albeit polite, radiated the confidence of a noblewoman, and he constantly had to pay attention to avoid her casual yet affectionate touch.

'I'm glad we can sit together, especially now my son has returned. Please, eat, and later I will share the news I received from the king.' Alleron gestured to the guests, filling his plate enthusiastically.

They followed his example, and Mar's mother kept small talk going with a mastery that made Ina envious. Suddenly, she heard her name.

'Lady Thorn, what are your plans now that your mission is complete? The weather is worsening with heavy snow on the way, and travelling will be very dangerous.' Lorraine's formality made Ina look at her, curious why Mar's mother used her title.

'I was going to return to Osterad, my lady. I have obligations I need to fulfil.'

'What obligations? Your cat is missing you?' Mar's angry question drew everyone's attention before his mother could say a word.

Ina turned to him, and her eyebrows lowered when she saw Ayni's hand drift to his shoulder, but Mar seemed not to notice or care.

'At least my cat misses me enough to not jump into another owner's lap.'

Ayni snorted a brief laugh, and Mar's father interjected.

'About this, my lady mage. While you were in discourse with my son, I received a message from the king. He congratulated you on your latest fascinating ballad but wanted to remind you that entertaining the peasants is only part of your duties. With the recent influx of refugees, he asked you to investigate the cause for this as soon as possible.'

'Oh, what an asshole.' Ina leaned back in the chair when reminded of her conveniently forgotten mission.

Ina's unladylike response made Lorraine gasp, and Alleron looked at her with a frown. As a military commander, he didn't allow such words regarding the king, at least not whilst sober.

'Lady Ina, Rewan is our king now, and we should show him some respect.' A slight twitch of his lips betrayed his hidden smile, but the witch just shrugged.

'If he wanted my utmost respect, he should stop visiting me in the middle of the night.'

'What!' Mar and Ren shouted in unison, then turned towards each other.

'Did you know about this?' Mar's voice filled with ice-cold fury.

'I'm not following every step she makes, contrary to what you might think,' answered Ren, who took Ina's hand, pressing it harder than intended. 'Tell me what happened?'

The tension in his voice was apparent, but Ina was looking at Mar, and something inside her just wanted to make him jealous.

'Well, nothing happened. Rewan came, then left… after a while.'

Mar's face paled, and she saw the vein on his neck repeatedly pulsing, much to her satisfaction. His jealousy felt good, yet she soon had to avert her gaze when Ayni elegantly poured wine into Mar's glass. Again, he didn't stop her when she held his hand much longer than needed.

Ina looked at Alleron, who observed his son with growing concern, and asked, 'Is there any other message from his majesty for me?'

The older man tightened his lips, visibly annoyed at the situation. 'No, only the request that you should focus on investigating the attacks. I would also like to petition your aid for this matter.'

'In that case, I will leave as soon as it is safe to leave. Now, please excuse me. It has been a long day.'

Mar's gaze followed Ina as she exited the room, only now he noticed Ayni was still holding his hand. He freed it with an annoyed sigh, but when his eyes met Ren's, the silent judgement in them only raised his anger.

'Tell me what happened after I left,' demanded Mar and, with growing discomfort, heard the story of the battle's ending and the confrontation in the throne room. When Ren got to the part where the king asked Ina to marry him in front of so many witnesses, Ayni burst out laughing.

'Why would your king want to marry her? She is nothing special.'

Mar turned to the dragoness, and with a vicious smile, he answered, 'Now there, my lady, you are mistaken. Ina is a pure Chaos mage, and the only reason Rewan still has a throne to sit on.' When Ayni's eyes widened in shock, he couldn't resist adding, 'She is the most dangerous person on this side of the mountains. I would be careful with your words and deeds, Ayni. Ina is not known for her mild disposition and showed incredible restraint dealing with your antics.'

Ayni lowered her head, her mind racing. Pure Chaos mages should not exist. She knew the Magical Council had done everything in their power to eradicate them. Yet, here she was, under the same roof as a waking horror.

By the time they finished the uncomfortable gathering, the moon was high in the sky, and the company dispersed to their rooms. Ren asked several servants, but Ina hadn't been seen since excusing herself from the meal, and for the second time today, he went to check her room. When a quiet 'Come in' followed his knocking, he entered, and a cold draught cut him to the bone. Ina was sitting on the windowsill, with the casement open to the elements, letting in snow flurries that lightly dusted the oblivious woman's clothing. Without comment, he walked over and wrapped a blanket over her shoulders, watching their frozen breath mingle in the frigid air.

'That's enough, my lady,' he said, and Ina didn't resist when he closed the window and led her to the sofa. After starting the fire, he joined her and blinked in surprise when Ina laid her head on his shoulder. Her hands were icy despite him rubbing them, and, after a moment of hesitation, he slid them under his shirt, shivering when they connected with his bare skin. This selfless move brought a bitter chuckle.

'Why are you always sacrificing yourself for me? I don't deserve it,' she asked in a strange voice, making Ren look down at her.

'I'm not. You are freezing, and I don't want you to become ill.'

Silence followed his answer, and he felt Ina's eyes studying his face. Her hands moved up, embracing his neck, making his heart skip a beat. He didn't know what was happening, but suddenly, Ina twisted around and sat on his lap.

'I know you love me… For once, I want to know how that feels. I want to feel your touch tonight.'

Her quiet, hesitant plea tore apart the restraint he imposed on himself, and when she pulled his head down to kiss him, Ren descended on her like a bird of prey, savouring this long-awaited kiss. Words failed him. Instead, he worshipped her with his touch, his lips moving hungrily over her jawline and the delicate curve of her neck. Ren felt Ina's body move against his in desperate desire, and with trembling hands, he reached for the laces of her dress, cursing out at his clumsiness, as usually skilful fingers struggled to untangle the simple bow as they trembled violently. When her dress finally slid to her waist, Ren's breath caught in his throat as he stared enraptured before lowering his starving lips to the pale flesh, hands stroking upwards till they gathered her breasts and pressed her hardening nipples to his mouth.

Ina's back arched, and the fateful words slipped from her lips as she moaned with pleasure. 'Mar… please.'

Time stopped as her eyes flew open. Her hands covered her mouth when she saw the raw pain he tried to hide. She knew how deeply she had hurt him, but she truly wanted to give them a chance. During dinner, seeing Ayni with Mar again, Ina felt angry at herself. She rejected the selfless love for a man who, despite his flowery words, so easily replaced her with a more refined and beautiful version. However, despite her deep connection with Ren, even at the height of passion, she couldn't erase Mar's face from her mind. There was only one reason for this, her feelings for Mar were not spellbound, at least not anymore.

A stray tear dropped on her cheek, and Ren smiled bitterly, pulling up her dress.

'Don't cry, please. I understand.'

His words broke her heart. He was the best man she knew and deserved better than a witch who always made the wrong choices.

'I'm so sorry. I never intended to hurt you. Please forgive me. I truly wish we could be more than friends. I love you, Ren, but against my better judgement, I love him more.' She hid her face in her hands, unable to control her tears. Ren took her hands off and kissed her fingertips before cuddling her to his chest.

'Don't cry, *Minii Khair*[2]. Just promise me that your heart will choose me in the next lifetime, and in this one, you will let me be by your side as a friend and guardian.'

He held her, rocking her softly till she calmed down. When she fell asleep in his arms, Ren carried her to bed. Deep inside, he knew he would never take Mar's place in her heart, yet when

[2] *Minii Khair* – My love (Yanwoo)

she turned to him, he followed her passion, unable to resist his longing for her touch. He knew what caused all this, and Mar needed a lesson about jealousy because his thoughtless behaviour let Ayni push Ina tonight, leading to more heartache.

The sofa gave him an idea, and stripping some of his clothes, he threw them carelessly on the floor for the servants to find later and took a nap on the soft couch. When the first light of dawn tinted the room, he called the maid. He knew the gossip would sprcad likc wildfire when he exited the room, barely dressed, leaving the poor girl to look after Ina. That should be enough to give Mar a taste of his own medicine. Slowly exhaling, he walked down the stairs, reflecting on the irony of using Yanwo's palace schemes in his new life in Cornovii.

Chapter Nine

With a deep yawn, Ina woke up and stretched out, feeling well-rested. Memories of the previous night slowly seeped into her consciousness, and the shame at her actions left the witch groaning, cheeks burning red in embarrassment. Dinner with Mar's family right after an explosive encounter with the dragon and his *bride* had thrown her off balance, and even the day she called the old king a limp dick in front of the entire court could not compare to the previous day's madness.

The sense of abandonment, being forced to sit through an evening of the stunning dragoness demonstrating how close she was to Mar, and the insufferable man's temper, had Ina turning to the only man she knew loved her. Their attraction may have started because of the sacrifice spell, but soon she learned to respect and care for this quiet, kind warrior for who he was, and if not for Mar, she knew it could easily grow into something more. Ren calmed her in a way Mar never could, and last night she desperately needed some peace, but her big mouth proved her heart had chosen the dragon's passionate inferno over Ghost's soothing cool water.

Ina brushed her hair and tried to plan her next steps. Anger at her own actions, which hurt her dearest friend's feelings and complicated the already strained relations between the three of them, grew into a desperate need to break something, and Ina decided to ask Ren for training right after breakfast. She needed time with him alone to apologise, and if he beat her to a pulp and threw her in horse manure, she would take it without a word of complaint because gods knew she deserved it. With that thought, Ina tied her hair in a war maiden braid and headed down to eat.

The servant girl's knowing smile at breakfast caught her attention, and although it was slightly confusing, Ina shrugged it off and headed to an empty seat. Her arrival resulted in raised eyebrows, and Ayni smiled facetiously before asking, 'Are you heading to battle?'

'No, just for training. Ren, do you have time to help me this morning?' she asked casually, taking a seat next to him, hoping he wouldn't mention last night. His hand stroked over hers, giving it a reassuring squeeze, and when she looked at his face, she was greeted by his usual gentle smile.

'I always have time for you, my lady. We can train next to the barracks if our hosts allow.'

'I can train you.' Mar's tense voice and rigid posture told Ina he'd noticed Ren's gesture, but this wasn't about the dragon's jealousy. She wanted Ren to know how sorry she was and hopefully repair the damage caused by her lack of restraint.

'Ren's training methods suit me better,' she said, knowing that was only half the truth. Mar's presence clouded her judgement, and she wanted to let off some steam, not increase the pressure she felt inside.

'Have you decided what you plan to do, Lady Inanuan?' Alleron asked to break the awkward silence that followed her words.

'As per the king's order, I will investigate the attacks, and for that, I need to ask a favour. Since I've returned Woron to his home, would you be so kind as to sell me a decent horse? I don't want to wander the mountains on foot,' she said, and Mar's father agreed enthusiastically, welcoming the change of the subject.

'We will see to this tomorrow. Today, please rest and make your preparations. My castellan will make sure you have everything you need.'

'I'm going with you.' Mar's stubborn tone made her look at him.

'And what if I don't want to take you?'

Mar was a sizable asset to any expedition with his fighting skills and local knowledge, but she wasn't sure if she wanted to have him around. She needed to focus on the task instead of being distracted by the uncertainty of her feelings and the craving for his masculine body. Plus, the audacity of forcing himself into her life was irritating and no, she wasn't smiling at the reminder of the oafish captain of King's Guard who had wormed his way into her heart.

Mar spread out on the chair and looked at Ina, tapping his finger on the table. His calculating stare lingered on her face as he assessed how much trouble she would make for him before he answered with a smirk, 'Then I will fly above or walk behind you, my spitfire, and you'll have to explain a roaring dragon to the terrified peasants. I'm afraid you have no choice, my love. You will suffer my company, whether or not you want it.'

Mar's parents exchanged concerned glances as she huffed in annoyance, rising angrily from her seat. Her magic hummed in response to his oafish statement, but deep down, something inside warmed at being called his love in front of so many witnesses. Ren joined her, but Mar's attempt at following them was interrupted by his father.

'Please join me in the office, Marcach. There are certain things we need to talk about.'

It was a request Mar knew he couldn't refuse, so, after one lingering look at Ina's retreating rear, he followed his father.

The discussion went as expected. Alleron brought him up to date on the local situation in his brusque, commanding style, highlighting the most recent attacks and the area's defensive capabilities. Most of the province's population was now sheltering in Liath or other major towns, with farms and small villages raided and pillaged, leaving the crops stolen or rotting in the awful weather.

All in all, it painted a bleak picture. With half of their supplies gone, destroyed or stolen, it would be challenging to survive the harsh winter.

A laugh from below caught Mar's attention. Ren and Ina were exchanging blows, and, contrary to his feelings, he had to congratulate Ren on how well he had trained her. The captain could see the legendary Ghost's artistry in Ina's movements and a marked improvement in her stamina.

With one last flurry of blows, they stepped back and bowed before Ina approached Ren, gesticulating wildly, clearly begging for something. His standing made it obvious he didn't want to give in to the witch's pleading. Mar chuckled under his breath, knowing just how persistent she could be and openly laughed as Ren threw his arms in the air in defeat, shouting a command that earned him a kiss on the cheek and Ina's hilarious, happy dance.

Moments later, a squire ran over with two short swords, handing them to Ren with a respectful bow. Mar watched in disbelief as his friend gave a sword to Ina and slid his arm around her waist, adjusting the position of her body into a low and robust sword stance.

Without realising his father still spoke, Mar growled, watching the happy pair until a firm hand came down hard on his shoulder, breaking his stream of thought.

'Are you sure this is the one you want? She doesn't seem to be interested in you.'

'Ren and Ina are friends. She saved his life the same way she saved mine, and the spell she used created a special connection,' said Mar, feeling the need to find an excuse for their behaviour.

'I heard the rumours she used the sacrifice spell, my son. I will always be grateful she saved you, but that doesn't explain why Ren spent the night in her room and left almost naked in the morning. All the servants are gossiping about it.'

The jealous rage that burned through his mind left Mar staggered, looking down at scaled fists and the stone ledge in pieces on the floor. The urge to complete his change nearly overwhelmed him until his father's fear-tinged command pulled him back from the edge.

'Control yourself, Marcach of Liath. Do not shame your family name.'

Without looking back, Mar ran downstairs.

Outside, Ina was having the time of her life. Ren stopped her apology mid-sentence, saying they both bore responsibility for yesterday evening, and it was more enlightening than painful. He behaved as if nothing had happened, and when she pestered him relentlessly, he finally taught her sword work. Of course, she couldn't resist enhancing her performance. It only took a little of her magic to create the fire vipers, and she grinned when several soldiers gasped as they wrapped around her arms and sword. The training grounds were open to all, and soldiers were already watching their practice, not to mention the dragoness who, like a bad coin, turned up everywhere Ina wished she wasn't.

Ina attacked Ren slowly, ensuring he could fend off her whips. She purposefully made it more of an illusion than actual flames, and Ren's throaty laugh told her he enjoyed her creativity.

'Upping your game, my lady. Is that why you wanted the sword?' He defended her attacks with ease, visibly thrilled by the new challenge. Several times he disarmed her despite her best efforts, but she learned something new each time, and finally, when she distracted him with her sword, her viper went for his leg.

The movement was rapid, and she would have succeeded if she didn't trip on something hidden under the snow, falling face-first into the snowdrift. The crowd burst out laughing as Ren's attempt to rescue her left them both sprawled out in the drift, and Ina's bright laugh joined in with the general hilarity.

'I'm a great warrior. I brought the mighty Ghost warrior down!' she shouted, trying to stand up, but Ren only pushed her back.

'In your dreams. Now stay in the snow to cool off.'

Their banter was stopped short by a deafening roar.

'Ren, you go too far.'

Mar ran across the field and, in one powerful movement, pulled her from the snow and pressed her to his side. After an initial moment of confusion, Ina tried to push him away, but this mountain of a man didn't even notice her attempt. His focused stare bore into Ren's face.

'How could you do this? I thought you were my friend. I know your feelings for Ina, but using her anger and our misunderstanding was a low blow.'

Ina didn't know what he was talking about and writhed in his grasp. 'What the hell is wrong with you? Stop acting like an oaf. We were only practising. '

Again, Mar barely paid attention to her, but to her displeasure, so did Ren. The two men were standing there, all puffed up like giant roosters, ready to strike.

'What if it wasn't just anger? What if Ina wanted this?' Ren smirked, suspecting his morning theatrics were a reason for this behaviour.

Ina was utterly confused. *What the hell were they talking about now?* She tried to protest, but Mar turned her to face him, searching for something she didn't understand, looking like a wounded animal. She didn't know what triggered this, and the need to soothe his pain was overwhelming in its intensity. Ina raised her hand to touch his cheek, but suddenly he crushed her lips in a long possessive kiss and pushed her back into the snowdrift with a snarl.

'You are mine!'

In a blink, he was charging at Ren, who met the attack with a satisfied smile as if he'd expected this.

Mar's thoughts were a maelstrom of confused need, anger, betrayal, and love. The anger, though, seemed to overwhelm everything else as he launched himself at his brother-in-arms, weaponless and artless in his fury.

Ren met his unbridled rage with an elegant riposte that flowed around him, and the sharp pain to the back of his head from the flat of a sword sent a flash of stars across his vision.

With a low, smug chuckle, Ren waited and shook his head. 'I thought this would be a challenge. How does it feel, Mar, to be taught a lesson? It's just a shame it won't be as much fun teaching it.'

Slowly standing up, Mar took a measured step to the side. The Chaos inside condensed into controlled focus. 'I should thank you, brother, for reminding me who I am fighting.' A glance down to his hands and that focus forced the flesh to change. Scales covered his arms in a shivering wave, and his fingers lengthened into clawed weapons. Mar smiled as he returned Ren's nod. 'Yes, I really should thank you.' He sped forward, his movements fluid and controlled as he attacked.

Eyes widening briefly in shock, Ren raised his short sword, parrying Mar's attack with the flat of the blade, unsure if the scales would stop a sword's edge. The discordant clang vibrated up his arm as, sliding to the left, Ren watched Mar's claws sweep past his face. Both men grinned at learning the scales were as strong as steel, and Mar punched out with his other hand, catching the Ghost on his hip as he drifted to the side.

Ina struggled out of the snow as the two men fought, indignation warring with awe as she watched, spellbound at the beautiful ferocity of their fight. She lost herself briefly in these well-matched warriors' deadly dance until blood was drawn and spattered over her tunic. She looked in disbelief at the red stain on the snow, and anger tightened her lips. Whatever was going on in these blockheads' minds had to stop now. Taking her stance on the icy path, she shouted.

'That's enough! Stop the fight.'

But it felt like she was shouting at the void. The warriors didn't pay any attention to her words, and the gathered crowd was now clapping and cheering the fighters, encouraging them to more bloodshed. Ina placed her hand on her peridot and used her ire to awaken Chaos magic. She would make them listen. Her stone glowed with an eerie light as she drew from it, filling her body with magic.

'I said enough!' Amplified by magic, her voice thundered through the air as she thrust her hand forward, and a blast of freezing air shot between the fighters. Ren tumbled into the snow at the sheer power of her spell, but Mar withstood it. Still, its force pushed him back and brought him to his knees.

'Stay out of this, Ina,' he said, digging his claws in the ground, but Ina wouldn't listen. Instead, she created a fiery viper and shot it forward, wrapping its head around his scaled arm and giving it a sharp tug, but Mar held on and slowly pulled back despite its power.

'This is between Ren and me, and a little witch has no part in a fight between grown men.' Mar taunted her, and she didn't even know why, but one thing was clear: he wanted her to feel his pain.

'I will show you a little witch, you idiot,' Ina said, clenching her teeth and lunging at him, blade raised just like Ren had taught her.

As Ina attacked, the memory of the last time they'd been bound like this flashed in his mind's eye, and Mar grinned, letting his feet move into the steps of the dance. 'Oh, my beautiful spitfire, the bond will not be cut by my hand this time. You are connected to me for as long as I live.' The clash of steel and scale shrieked as Mar parried the lunge and swept past Ina, pulling on the burning whip to spin her around to face him again.

Stripped of choice, Ina followed him, attacking as he parried every attack. Their coordination was unnerving, and the gathered audience gasped at every cut and thrust, admiring their efforts. Ina's anger drained away as she found strange euphoria in the dance. But one involuntary glance to the side and her ire returned when she saw Ren staggering near the fence, holding his bloodied hip.

It was time to set her priorities right. Ina stopped and turned to Mar, releasing her magic. 'Why did you attack him? What was so wrong in our training that you had to injure your best friend?' she said, fighting the angry tears. Mar stepped towards her and grabbed her wrist. The weapon fell into the snow when he pried it from her hand.

'My best friend wouldn't sleep with the woman I love. Yesterday was difficult for you… for us all, but I didn't expect he would use your pain as a chance to get into your bed,' Mar said, finally verbalising his feelings, and her mouth snapped open.

'Are you out of your mind, you dumb fuck? I never slept with Ren. Is that what this is all about, your jealousy and groundless suspicions?'

Ina could not believe her ears. All this mess was because he thought she'd slept with Ren? A flash of guilt swept over her as she realised his suspicion was not entirely unfounded, but after bringing this *bride* to his parent's castle, what she did in her bedroom was none of his business. She raised her eyes and looked at him when he pulled her close and leaned in. Again, she saw this haunted look in his eyes as he visibly calmed himself and spoke softly.

'Yes, Ina, my jealousy. You've been in my thoughts since the day I met you, and if you say that fucking healing spell is to blame one more time, I swear I'll spank your ass here and now. This isn't some spell-driven obsession. I see you, woman, and you are magnificent. You are strong and clever, and you fight with all you are for what you believe. You are passion, vulnerability, and sheer bloody-minded power who never forces others to be lesser. How could you think I'd ever look at another woman when you're in the world? If that's what you believe, you are sadly mistaken, and I will fight for you every moment I exist.'

That was a lot of words for one oafish captain, and Ina was taken aback by his flowery statement. To make it worse, he looked like he believed every word, and she felt she desperately wanted to believe him too. That was messed up on a whole new level, and Ren was the casualty of their misshapen romance. Ina looked at him, weighing her thoughts. *If I accept his love, would things be better or worse? Do I want to take this risk?* Her thoughts were racing, and his touch didn't help in making a rational decision.

'Mar, this has to end. Your words are… beautiful, but you can't just attack any man I'm close to,' she said, pausing when he grabbed her shoulders with a vicious snarl, looking like she had just pushed him off the edge.

'You won't touch any other man. Haven't you heard a single word I said, woman? Then let me rephrase it simply for you. I love you, you are mine, and no one else will touch you.' Mar had

had enough of this. It was about time she understood, and if he was making a mistake, so be it.

The icy blast that followed his words took his breath away and thrust him away from her. Ina stood tall, panting, looking directly into his eyes.

'It takes more than poetry or some unfounded claim to earn my love. I'm not yours to command, and if I choose, I will touch whoever I want.'

Suddenly, she turned around and grabbed a young soldier whose curiosity brought him too close to her. The storm she felt inside gave her a boost of strength as she pulled the young man's head down, whose eyes widened in shock when she kissed him hard. Finishing this assault, Ina pushed the boy away, pointing at him as she stared at Mar, who watched the soldier scramble up and run away from him with pure terror plastered over his face.

'What now? Will you fight him too, Mar? After all, he touched me without your permission?' she jeered.

Mar looked up at her, and she could see the distress in his eyes. He approached and touched her cheek, exhaling slowly in defeat. 'No, Ina. I just want you to know that this oaf loves only you.' His gaze drifted to Ren as Ayni helped him staunch his wound. The guilt washed over his face, and he averted his eyes, looking ashamed and strangely vulnerable, but before she could say anything, he said, 'No matter what anyone else says, I'd never lie to you.' His contours blurred, and the majestic dragon leapt into the sky.

CHAPTER TEN

Ina looked around the training yard, worried by the amount of blood on the ground and annoyed at the motionless soldiers staring wide-eyed at the retreating dragon. She took a deep breath and approached Ren. Ayni was staunching the wound, and the blood flow had almost stopped. She knew Ayni was helping, but Ina couldn't help herself.

'Shouldn't you chase your mate?' she asked, but the other woman simply shrugged.

'I think he wants to be alone now. It's not every day you declare your love for all the world the hear only to be rejected.' Ayni's answer stung, and Ina flinched at her words, second-guessing her actions. Maybe she was too harsh on Mar, but love or not, she wouldn't let anyone command her like that. Pushing thoughts of the annoying dragon aside, she knelt down and addressed her friend.

'Ren, can you walk? We need to get you to the castle so I can dress your wound.'

'He can,' said Ayni, and Ina's head snapped in her direction.

'I'm sure Ren can speak for himself. We are grateful for your help, but it's no longer needed,' she said, readying herself to support Ren's injured side.

'As you said, he can speak for himself, and I will stay till he tells me to leave.' Ayni threw Ina's words back in her face, and the witch felt her blood boiling. This bloody woman had broken her relationship with Mar, and now she was trying her charm on Ren. Before another fight started, Ren interrupted.

'I can walk, and I will go by myself. We've seen enough bloodshed for today.' He stood up slowly and hobbled away to the castle, the two women following in his steps, staring daggers at each other every step of the way.

Ren's wound looked much worse than it was. The warrior's leather armour had protected his body remarkably well, and the only damage was a deep gash in the skin. Ren wasn't happy to be stripped and hid his modesty behind a towel, and the situation didn't improve when Ina and Ayni began quarrelling over his treatment. He wished he had Mar's ability to fly away and leave this mess behind. Instead, he became a wounded pet under the care of two insane women.

Ayni cleaned his wound whilst Ina ran to her room, retrieving her entire collection of mixtures and potions. Ren tried desperately to downplay his injury, knowing how awful the concoctions would taste, but this was ruined as Ayni's ministrations forced him to hiss in pain.

'Be careful. You are hurting him,' said Ina, scolding the dragoness.

'You should have tried being careful before your behaviour started this mess,' said Ayni, not letting Ina get the upper hand.

'I didn't cause their fight or even start any rumours. It was your absurd claim that started all this. Why didn't you stop Mar from storming onto the training ground? I would if he was my husband.'

Ayni threw the cloth into the bucket, splashing the bloodied water everywhere. 'Oh, of course, now I'm his nanny. How am I supposed to stop him if he chooses to chase after you like a love-sick puppy? Gods! I wish I never flew the sky dance with him.'

Ina pursed her lips. 'Well, you wouldn't need to regret it if you'd checked the groom was single before marrying him.'

Ren sighed and rolled his eyes in exasperation. He was paying a hefty price for this morning's caper. The goal was supposed to be for Mar to realise how Ina felt when she saw her lover with Ayni. Instead, Ren ended up with torn clothes, a wounded side, and two women bickering as he sat there bleeding.

'My ladies, please leave my room. I can handle the rest myself.'

Ina smiled and turned to Ayni. 'You heard him, go. We can handle this.'

He saw the dragoness scowl, and trying to prevent more trouble, Ren took Ina's hand and brushed a chase kiss upon it. 'You too, my lady. I'm tired and wish to be alone.'

Ina was about to protest when he pressed her palm to his cheek and smiled. Biting her lip, she gave up and placed two vials on the table instead.

'Please drink it, and I will ask the kitchen to send some food up for you. If you need me for anything, please let me know.'

Ren turned to Ayni. 'Thank you for your help, my lady. It is truly appreciated.'

The dragoness flashed him a beautiful smile. 'You are a strange man, Ren, but I think I like you.'

Ina ground her teeth and pushed the other woman through the door. 'Oh, for fuck's sake, have I wronged you somehow? Less than a day, and now you want Ren as well?'

Ayni laughed. 'Oh, you are a delightful little witch, but you should decide who you truly want, as you can't have both of them in your bed.' The dragoness took a lot of pleasure from teasing this stubborn human. She saw Ren leaving Ina's bedroom early in the morning, and it was clear nothing had happened between them, but for some reason, the eastern warrior left the servants thinking something had. This ploy was obviously aimed at upsetting Mar, and this, along with his general demeanour, intrigued her. Watching Ren fight had only added to his appeal and left Ayni wishing he had been the dragon who'd landed at the mountain temple.

'He would make a magnificent dragon.'

The colour drained from Ina's face at this remark, and Ayni, seeing a fist flying in her direction, ducked and ran down the stairs. Her laugh echoed down the corridor for a very long time.

❄❄❄

Mar flew aimlessly over the city, letting his body's instincts catch the thermals. The freedom and solitude of flight cleared his head, but that meant he had to face the hard truth of his actions. He attacked Ren based on some unproven gossip, and if not for Ina's intervention, Mar was unsure what would have happened under the influence of his jealousy.

The only good thing that came out of it was Ina stating she hadn't shared her bed with his best friend, and he knew the witch well enough to know if she had, she wouldn't hesitate to tell him to his face. The servants had jumped to conclusions about the close relationship between the two friends—a close relationship he envied—and he'd believed every word.

Mar couldn't stop thinking about Ina's words. They were harsh, but the dragon knew she was right. His claim to her was based on his feelings, but she had not once claimed to love him back. Since the night they were together, he hadn't talked to her properly, but her actions and the connection he felt deep inside left him assuming she felt the same.

Mar had never needed to court a woman before. His mother arranged the marriage to his late wife, and the ladies who sometimes frequented his bed, those who weren't paid, found their way there without his help. So now, when it truly mattered, he didn't even know where to start.

A flash of red on the ground caught his attention, and Mar lowered his altitude to see Ina fighting through the heavy snow towards the gardens. He smiled as he imagined her cursing everything in her way. Finally, she stopped next to the frozen lake and disappeared under the crown of a willow tree.

He landed, trying not to cause a disturbance, and transformed, approaching slowly, wondering why she'd walked to the garden alone when dusk was almost upon them. The closer he got, the clearer her voice became, and finally, he saw her standing there, eyes closed, forehead pressed to the rough tree trunk. Ina's quiet words shocked him.

'I wish you could be here, Leshy, although I suspect you would just laugh at me. Why, from all the men alive, did I fall for a dragon? Have I done something wrong, and gods are punishing me?'

Mar's heart was beating so loud he was surprised she couldn't hear it. He was right about her feelings. His stubborn woman loved him, even if she had hidden it so deep that she could only confess to the trees. He knew Ina protected her heart, avoiding any relationships. She was explicit when she told him her opinion of love at the palace ball. He also learned that much when he researched her past during the Osterad investigation, but finding out how deeply she cared eased the pain that had become a constant companion since Ayni's claim in front of Ina had forced her to harden her defences against him.

Mar cursed his stupidity, realising his actions had worsened the sorrow she felt at his apparent betrayal, and for that, he deserved her anger. Feeling his frustration bubbling over, Mar took a deep breath, reining it back in. He wished he could take away all of her pain but knew that to have a future with Ina, first, he would have to stop being the one hurting her.

With a nod to himself, Mar slipped further away, and then, making as much noise as possible, he entered the garden, heading towards the willow and openly cursing the snow for freezing his family jewels.

'Mar?' Ina called out as she noticed him, and he made a show of being surprised by her presence. She stood still with her cheek cuddled to the freezing bark, grey fur cloak merging with the frosty tree, tears slowly freezing on her eyelashes. A stab in the gut couldn't have hurt him more than seeing her cry.

'I'm sorry if I'm disturbing you. I didn't know you were here,' he said, approaching slowly. He took the soft smile Ina offered him as an invitation to come closer and stood beside her, looking out across the frozen lake.

'You didn't disturb me. I simply missed the forest,' she said. 'Everything was much easier there.'

Mar stood in silence. Too many times, his hasty words turned her against him. He knew what he wanted to say, but facing her left him at a loss for words.

'I'm sorry, for today, for Ren's injury, for my words. I know you belong to no man. It was foolish of me to claim you.' The bitter notes in his voice caught her attention. Ina raised her eyes and studied his expression as she accepted his apology.

'We've all done stupid things lately. I was told today that sometimes mistakes aren't one-sided, and I trust that person's judgement more than my own.'

There was a resignation in her voice, but before he could reply, she noticed the snowflakes in his beard, and, giving him one of her mischievous smiles, she brushed them away.

'You look like a grumpy snowman, Mar.'

Mar reached for her hand and held it against his cheek. His breath warmed her palm, and he closed his eyes, giving himself a moment to savour her touch.

'Why don't you believe me when I say I love you?' he asked and wished he could have mind magic to see her thoughts as Ina's face displayed a kaleidoscope of emotions. He didn't like when she took her hand away and hugged her body as a protective gesture.

'I did, in Osterad. I had my worries and hopes, but after this wedding dance they forced us to do, we stood in the palace garden, and you said I was your wife in your heart. Not that I wanted this, but I believed you.' Ina hesitated, but after a steadying breath, she continued. 'I thought we had plenty of time, that I could learn to accept my feelings, but then there was a battle, and I changed you into a dragon. So I came here to find you, only to find out you performed a wedding dance with another woman.'

Mar felt the desire to grab her and shake some sense into her. Instead, he forced himself to stay calm.

'We both know I'm not married. I may be a clueless fool, but I made no advances to Ayni or even looked at her with a hint of desire. We both know I have many flaws, but I would never lie to you.'

Ina lowered her head, avoiding his eyes. Mar wasn't behaving as usual. He was pleading for understanding as if her decision could make or break him, and whilst she wanted to console him, all she could offer was the truth, even if it meant disclosing her fears.

'I believe you, but something inside me broke when Ayni announced your marriage in the courtyard. I believe you think you love me, but if this fades or you have a change of heart… I don't want to feel like this again. You know what I think of love. I'm a Chaos mage whose magic is driven by her emotions. Do you think having my heart broken once I'm completely committed to you won't end badly? Perhaps ending it now is for the best so we can move forwards as friends. You, me, and Ren, like we were in Osterad.'

Her statement was met with a short, bitter laugh. 'Ina, I am your friend, the kind who loves you. I promise to prove you can trust me, and not worry I'll make things worse.'

When she looked up, he was still there, and the tenderness she saw in him forced her to avert her eyes again. She followed the movement of his hand as it stroked and played with her hair, feeling his body so close to hers that her breathing shuddered with unexpected desire. Ina bit her lip and cast around for a distraction before grabbing a snow-laden branch and shaking it over Mar's head.

'You're saying I'm a difficult woman?'

She miscalculated, and the heavy snow fell not only onto Mar's head but her own as well, cascading down into the open collar of the formerly warm tunic, making her squeak. Mar was now openly laughing and lifted her up, swinging them both around and into the soft snow of a nearby snowdrift. With another squeal that put the last one to shame, the freezing witch squirmed and fought, but it was Mar who rolled over till he lay beneath her, hands holding her still. His face radiated such happiness that Ina surrendered to the moment and smiled back.

'You are a menace. I'm cold and wet now. What got into you?'

Mar looked at her, his eyes full of joy, and kissed the tip of her nose.

'You, my spitfire. You get into me, and now we both have to bear this burden.'

Ina pushed his head into the snow. 'Now you call me a bloody burden?' Her reaction made Mar laugh harder until he noticed Ina looking at him with a pondering expression. His joy turned into uncertainty the longer she stayed silent.

Biting his lip, he blurted out, 'Would you like to see my dragon?'

Mar didn't know why he proposed this, but something inside wanted to see the wonder shine in her eyes again, just as it had on his first transformation. When Ina clasped her hands together and nodded with a big grin, he smiled and focused on his other form. A moment later, a majestic dragon stood before her, with wings stretched out to the heavens.

He shivered in anticipation, seeing her eyes widen as she approached him. Ina removed her gloves, reached up, and caressed his neck with her still warm hands. Mar realised he was holding his breath, nervous about her reaction. The hesitancy of her touch fuelled the longing in his soul, and when she stopped stroking and embraced his neck, Mar slowly released his breath, trying not to frighten her. When she started wriggling, he tried, unsuccessfully, to see what his little witch was up to, and when a gentle touch brushed over the sensitive skin of his wing, the dragon curled around her, throat vibrating in a purr that startled her into letting go.

'Did I hurt you? I'm sorry,' she stuttered, unsure of what had happened.

'No, but it was very… intimate,' Mar said, trying to find the right words to express his feelings and spreading his wing, hoping she would do it again.

'Oooh…' Ina's lips parted, and her breath quickened when his forked tongue touched her neck. Her scent was intoxicating, assaulting his senses with its crisp, delicious aroma. Lost in the sensation, he didn't notice she'd ducked under his wing until it was too late. Suddenly, a dragon's roar shook the garden when her fingers tickled the soft folds of his wings. Mar grabbed the giggling witch by the coat, pulling her out.

'For god's sake, Ina, I could have trampled you.'

The gleeful woman was too happy to listen and stuck her tongue at him. Her unremorseful stance made him shake his head, especially when Ina poked his shoulder, still laughing. Mar changed back to human form, briefly shivering in the cold air.

'I found your weakness, and I'm going to use it when I need to subdue your grumpy arse.'

He pulled her closer, locking her body in his tight embrace, holding both hands behind her back. Mar pondered today's events. He'd made a fool of himself on the training ground and injured his best friend, but after he let her voice her worries and play with his dragon form, it was like their disagreement had never happened. Mar raised his eyes to the moon. There was no way he would ever understand women. Especially this one.

'You are my only weakness, my spitfire. I will do my utmost to earn your trust again,' he whispered as he lost himself in her eyes, still unsure where he stood in her thoughts.

Deep inside the mountain range, Tar'eth Al'Ean paced restlessly in his office. The scouts still hadn't returned from their mission, and now there were rumours that dragons had returned to the mountains. When he'd first come to this region, his army had quickly subdued the kobolds, and his psychic magic kept them docile. Thanks to his ancestry, and a touch of Chaos magic, he controlled or obliterated those who stepped out of line. There was a time when he wondered why the necromancer gave him one of the Chaos regalia. Such a powerful artefact should be treasured, not given away to a second prince, even with the hint of Chaos in his bloodline. He initially suspected it was one of his mother's schemes, but those thoughts quickly faded, replaced by the pure joy of manipulating magic that, till now, he thought was unavailable.

The drow prince looked at his ring and stroked its green gem. When the torture sessions in the dungeons could no longer supply enough Chaos for his needs, he decided it was time to gather every piece of the regalia. The original plan had been so simple. Subdue the kobolds, use them to find the tomb of Sowenna, the last drow empress, and recover her circlet. However, since a chance encounter in Osterad, the only image in his mind was the redheaded Chaos mage whose magic blazed like the sun.

This obsession felt like the onset of tal-maladie, the ancient madness that plagued the drow royal family. The mission to regain the Chaos regalia faded into insignificance when compared to controlling that woman and her wellspring of pure, unfettered magic.

Tar'eth stared at the mirror, seeing a slender face with high cheekbones and faded ebony skin that contrasted with his white hair and piercing blue eyes. He smiled, and the mirror image mimicked his gesture, revealing sharp teeth. *Will she like me? Ha, why would I care if she likes me, I will make her worship me,* he thought, turning at the light knock on the door.

'Enter.' At his command, a soldier, eyes downcast, entered his room.

'My lord, the scouts have returned.'

'Then bring them in.' Tar'eth felt his mood improve. He sat on the chair and poured himself a generous measure of wine, waiting for the report.

When two rugged drow entered the room, he didn't even notice how tired they both looked. Instead, he immediately began their interrogation.

'Tell me, what is going on in Liath? Were there any more sightings of dragons?'

The men exchanged a look, and finally, the taller of the two started talking.

'Two dragons landed in the castle of Liath and disappeared. We have no access there to investigate further.'

Tar'eth stood up from his chair and approached the man with malicious intent. He did not welcome this message, not trusting the sudden appearance of the dragon race. Humans considered them extinct, but his kin knew they were living amongst the humans. So why the sudden reappearance? He noticed the soldier step back, raising his hands defensively.

'My lord, the witch has left Osterad.' He shouted out the words that could save his skin.

Tar'eth stopped and tilted his head. 'Go on,' he commanded.

The soldier sighed with relief and retold the skirmish of Three Willows, focusing mainly on Ina's achievements. Then he mentioned she appeared to head to Castle Liath, and Tar'eth felt his troubled mind clear. He poured more wine into his glass and handed it to the soldier.

'Drink and have a rest. That is your reward for such good news.'

All this time, he'd been working on plans to extract his prize from Osterad, only to learn she was already travelling through his domain. Still, Liath Castle posed a problem. The old duke would be a formidable opponent with military experience, honed by a life on the borderlands. Add to that the power of a mage, and the outcome of any battle would be catastrophic. Somehow Tar'eth would need to capture the woman before attacking the castle. After dismissing the scouts, the drow prince sat at his desk and wrote a letter. His mother held Arknay, the drow's capital city, with an iron fist. If he handled this well, she would send him an army to capture Liath. It would take some time for them to arrive, and in the meantime, he could concentrate on sending out patrols to kidnap the mage.

He scribbled a quick command for all the patrols and scouts.

Look for the red-haired mage. Deliver her to the kobold's lair unharmed in body and mind. Kill any who accompany her.
Tar'eth Al'Ean, Second of Arknay

A shiver of anticipation ran down his spine, and a faint light in the peridot ring flickered to his hastened heartbeat. With her power, controlling the province would be child's play, leaving Cornovii impotent. This move would leave his mother no choice but to name him the heir to the throne.

Tar'eth called in his servant, handing over the letter and the orders for the soldiers. He could feel the touch of night, even this deep inside the mountain, and headed out of the tunnels. The drow stopped at the exit and took a deep breath, savouring the crisp night air and the clear sky filled with brightly shining stars, serenely looking down from the heavens. This was the first time Tar'eth had felt calm in months, and he lost himself in the moment, swaying with euphoria till the freezing conditions left him shivering. With a snap of his fingers, he once more summoned his attendant.

'Find me a woman, small with red or brown hair, scrub her well and… make her wear the mask.'

His request was met with confusion, but one look at the prince's face and the servant tripped over his feet to follow the order. Tar'eth turned to look at the snowy peaks and exhaled. Tonight he needed companionship, someone to warm his bed, someone who could be *her* and a woman he could bend to his will. Soon, Ina would yield to him, hopefully not without a fight. Tar'eth stretched and smiled at his thoughts, impatient for the challenge ahead, but before he had her on her knees craving to fulfil all his desires, he would have some fun with a new plaything.

He turned and headed to his bedroom, readying himself for a little fun as servants set out dinner. Then, as he specified, a woman arrived, shaking like a leaf. She was wearing a porcelain mask covering the upper part of her face, and in the candlelight, her shape and flowing auburn hair could almost fool the eye into believing it was Ina who stood before him. He regarded the terrified woman for a moment, enjoying her discomfort before he pointed to the empty chair at the table.

'Please sit, my dear. I won't bite.' His voice, a low, pleasant baritone, caught her attention. The woman shuffled to the chair and sat meekly, quivering like a terrified rabbit.

'Please, help yourself to some food.' He gestured to the feast between them, and when she didn't move, he used a hint of compulsion. 'I insist.'

He studied the effect his words had upon her. His lips twitched when she filled her plate with food. Except for her eyes and trembling chin, most of her face was covered with porcelain, and he had to admit he liked it. Tar'eth stood and approached the female. He couldn't mould her body, his Chaos magic wasn't sufficient, not even with the ring, but he could transform her mask. He filled her ears with soothing words while his hands lay over her face, changing the smooth surface into the image of his desire.

'That looks better, don't you think? You will never take this mask off, my dear, because this mask is who you are now, my Volte, and your only desire shall be to serve me.' Tar'eth drew deeper on his magic and used a stronger compulsion, linking with her consciousness, entwining his will with the defenceless woman's mind.

When her eyes turned glassy, and the enchanted female nodded dreamily, the drow prince dug into her memories. She was a simple peasant girl with no magical talent who had been captured during a raid. He entered the core of her existence, filling it with his recollection of Ina's movements and gestures. As a masterstroke of his mind's manipulation, he implemented a pattern of love and desire.

Tar'eth studied her face as the look in her eyes changed. When she gracefully stood up and her hands wrapped around his neck, seeking a kiss, he eagerly leaned down to taste her. Tonight would be for pleasure, pain, and experimentation. He had never been intimate with a human before, considering it below his rank. They were known to be good sport, but they died quickly, and Ina, with all her power, was still human. Tar'eth needed to learn to have fun with this plaything without breaking it. Otherwise, he wouldn't get to enjoy the mage whilst still having access to her magic, and this puppet would stave off his obsession till the redhead belonged to him.

CHAPTER ELEVEN

Unable to sleep, Ina kept thinking about her conversation with Mar. Lying together underneath that frozen tree, she realised she loved him. That love could never be described as normal, as she had an independent streak so strong it drove most ordinary men away. It was time to admit she was using the spell as an excuse and that it had nothing to do with how she felt. The problem was, Ina knew she wasn't ready for a relationship.

Just look at my reaction to Ayni, her announcement, and poor Mar's attempts to explain it. Within seconds, I had accepted the stranger's words over the man I trusted with my life. Time to be honest, Striga, you used her as an excuse to run away again, Ina thought, and a bitter grimace twisted her lips. Her ability to avoid serious relationships had been both well known and a running joke during her university years, and Nerissa had given her many the lecture on ending up alone with a herd of cats. Now here she was, a proud cat lover, alone except for a dragon who didn't have the sense to leave and a man she hurt with her inability to return his affection.

It was painful to admit she should be grateful to Ayni. If not for that bloody dragoness and her attempt at marrying Mar, Ina would never have realised her feelings and why she was sabotaging her relationship. Much to her relief, Mar seemed to accept her for the difficult woman she was, giving her time and space, but still allowing her to enjoy his company. Ina closed her eyes. The memory of his metallic scent and powerful arms embracing her was overwhelming, and sliding her hands down, she let her imagination conjure more lurid images, but despite releasing some tension, she still couldn't calm her racing thoughts.

After catching her breath, Ina decided to use her time constructively and sat at the desk to write a letter. As she recorded the journey's details, she warned Jorge that the wave of refugees would continue to grow and that she had yet to find the cause. Next came the letters for Nerissa and Velka, updating them on her adventures and giving her friend more explicit details, especially regarding yesterday's fight. After a moment's consideration, she added a brief letter to Marika, wishing her a speedy recovery and asking about her cat, Boruta. She still felt guilty for leaving him behind, missing his furry presence in her bed and the soothing purr that cleansed her thoughts.

When the first blush of dawn lit the sky, she heard a quiet knock on her door. Ina raised an eyebrow, wondering who had a death wish to disturb her so early. Not that she was sleeping, but she couldn't allow this to become a regular occurrence.

'Ina, are you awake?'

It was Alleron's voice, and the witch blinked, utterly confused. What could the old warrior want from her so early?

'Yes, my lord. What is the matter?'

'Good. Please dress for a ride. I will be waiting for you in the yard,' he said, and she heard his footsteps slowly fade away as he left.

After a long forlorn look at the empty bed, Ina dressed quickly before heading down, leaving her letters with the still sleepy chamberlain to send to the capital. Alleron was waiting outside, sitting on a majestic horse that could be the twin to Woron. Next to him was a smaller brown mare saddled but without a rider.

'Is this the horse you want to sell to me?' Ina asked, looking at the mare with appreciation.

'No, but she will take you to the fields where you'll choose your mount.'

Now she knew where Mar got his ability to irk her with a simple answer. She took a deep breath and stopped herself from telling Mar's father where he could shove his morning mystery. After all, you shouldn't look a gift horse in the mouth, no matter where this horse was.

'Thank you, Lord Alleron,' she said, feeling this would be sufficient for the morning's conversation.

The road was reasonably clear, but a light fog forced them to ride slowly in the frosty conditions. The wind that nipped at Ina's cheeks, freezing the moisture of her breath, discouraged her from speaking. Suddenly, Alleron reined in his horse.

'There is someone ahead of us. Stay here. I will make sure it's safe.'

The intimidating scowl directed towards her told Ina he expected instant obedience. Instead, Ina urged her horse forward. She didn't go far before the old warrior caught up with her and grabbed the reins.

'I told you to stay.'

'Oh yes, I heard.' His snappy tone and angry grimace were amusing and so reminiscent of Mar that Ina couldn't help but grin before turning towards the figure struggling on the path. With breath wheezing and hunched posture, the wanderer was anything but threatening. The bulky pile of deadwood he carried looked heavy enough for two, and when Ina noticed his grey beard and wrinkled face, she immediately slid off her horse and approached the stranger.

'Do you live nearby, grandfather? You should not be dragging all this wood alone on such a frosty day,' she said, but her initial smile disappeared when she noticed cataracts covering his eyes. Ina had wanted to help him by simply casting the feather spell to ease his burden, but, seeing his blind eyes, she decided to escort him home. *No good deed goes unpunished,* she thought, preparing herself for a long journey.

'Don't bother yourself, my dear. My home is close by, just behind this hill,' the old man said with a husky voice, broken by a frequent cough.

'Well then, even better, now we can have you safe at home much sooner,' Ina said, dragging the wood off the old man's back despite his muffled protests. 'That way, you will sit by the fire without feeling so tired. Here, let the kind-hearted lord carry it for you.' She thrust the wood into Alleron's hands, who stared at her, completely lost for words.

'Me?' Alleron's expression nearly had Ina giggling, and she quickly suppressed the urge before replying.

'You expect the delicate lady to do it?' Ina said, slightly offended by his question. She took the old man's hand and placed it on her shoulder.

'Let's go, grandfather. We will get you home in no time.'

The elder looked worried but didn't protest. Soon they were marching at a good pace towards the hill with the Lord of Liath plodding behind them with a thoughtful, stormy expression, leading two unsettled horses burdened with a pile of deadwood.

When they arrived, the old man's house reminded her of her old hovel, and Ina quickly lit the fire.

'There. I would leave some elixirs for your cough, but they are all in the castle. I will see later if I can send you some. Be well, grandfather, and don't wander around on frosty days,' she said and turned to leave, acutely aware she had wasted enough of Alleron's time. She was about to close the door when she heard the old man call out.

'Come here, child. Let me see you.'

The witch frowned in confusion but returned to his side. It was an interesting choice of words coming from him. Ina shivered when he placed his gnarled fingers on her face and trailed them slowly over her features.

'The blessing of the mountains will be with you, autumn child, so never be afraid to follow your heart,' he said, with a voice much clearer than before and his unsettling blind gaze locked on her face.

Ina opened her mouth to ask what he meant, but Alleron grabbed her by the hood and dragged her out of the cottage.

'Not a word. On the horse, now,' he commanded, and the alarm in his voice forced Ina to listen. He knew those mountains well, and whatever caused his change to war leader must have been a severe threat.

When their mounts finally returned to the main road, Alleron turned his grim visage to Ina.

'There has never been a cottage on that hill. Whatever we encountered was not human.'

'Ohhh…' Ina's mouth opened in shock, but after a moment, she sent him an apologetic look. 'I'm sorry, but I couldn't leave a blind old man to freeze to death on the roadside.'

Alleron exhaled, shook his head, and urged his horse into a trot. 'Come on, *autumn child*, we lost enough time on your trifles. Hopefully, this encounter won't cause us any bad luck.'

The rest of the journey was uneventful, and soon they arrived at a large, open field near a pine forest. Ina noticed a herd of horses huddled together for warmth. Despite the different markings, they were the same build as Alleron's mount.

'You want to sell me one of Liath's famous warhorses?' she asked, shocked to the core. This steadfast and loyal breed was prized even beyond the borders of Cornovii, and she doubted she would ever need a horse trained for battle.

'Sell? I want to give you one of our warhorses. You saved my son's life, and whilst I can never repay this debt, I can at least provide you with something worthy of your sacrifice.'

'My sacrifice?' the witch asked with caution in her voice.

Alleron's mouth twisted in bitter amusement. 'How else would you describe it? My son is obsessed with you, and so is Ren. I've fought on many battlefields, so yes, I know about this spell, but the healers would never dare use it. I can see why now.'

'It wasn't exactly the sacrifice spell I used on them,' Ina answered, suddenly feeling the need to defend Mar's behaviour. 'I don't think it's all because of the spell.'

'But you don't love them, and while I can't speak for Ren, I can assure you my son loves you.'

'What? Who said I….' Ina said in protest, but stopped herself, noticing Alleron's sly smile. 'Anyway, we came here for a horse, so let's get one,' she finished and slid off her mount.

Ina felt his gaze on her back and knew Alleron studied her closely, as her avoidance of his statement didn't escape his attention. When she was in the middle of the field, he said, 'Stop there. Let them see you, and your horse will come to you.'

Ina looked at him, taken aback by his words. It was the strangest way of getting a horse she had ever encountered, but it was still better than discussing her affairs. The herd in front of her milled about in a tight circle, a grey fog swirling around their bodies. The sight was mesmerising, and just as Ina began swaying to an unknown song, the mist parted, and a tall, proud mare stepped out, heading towards the spellbound mage. Almost at tall as Woron, her dappled grey coat seemed part of the mist itself. She stopped before Ina and gently laid her head on the mage's shoulder. It was love at first sight, and Ina threw her arms around the beautiful mare's neck and held on tight.

'Please tell me she's mine?' Ina pleaded, looking at Alleron with doe eyes and fluttering lashes.

Before he could answer, the mare swung her head, hitting Ina's midriff and sending her tumbling into the snow. The Lord of Liath gasped and nudged his horse forward. Before they could move, Ina was back on her feet and stood in front of the unruly horse, giving her the evil eye whilst trying to hold back her laughter, as the mare tilted her head and snorted straight in Ina's face.

'Are you laughing at me?' asked Ina, poking the horse's head. She turned to Alleron. 'Is she laughing at me? What kind of horse is this?'

The old warrior appeared as confused as she was, but when Ina marched towards him, the grey mare followed her, nipping at her hood.

'Go away. Why do I have to be saddled with you when there are so many normal horses around?' Ina turned and asked the animal, who continued nibbling at her clothes.

Alleron, who was holding his breath watching their antics, laughed. 'Ina, you are talking to a horse.'

'And?' She shrugged.

'It's a horse. It won't understand,' he insisted, watching Ina's failed attempts to mount the brown horse she'd arrived on as the grey mare interfered with her endeavours. Ina grumbled something under her breath, trying to jump up, but the grey mare was insistent and blocked her way.

'Fine, I will ride you,' Ina conceded, tired of circling the animals. The grey horse finally stood still, and, removing the saddle and tack from the brown mare, the mage slowly approached her new gift, expecting a fight, but much to her surprise, the grey didn't struggle as she was saddled and mounted. Ina urged her forward only to be given an amused look, and the horse didn't move.

With an exasperated sigh, she addressed the horse. 'Could you be so kind as to shift your equine arse and listen to my directions? I will not fight you every step of the way.'

Ina could swear the horse rolled her eyes, but she moved as directed, and now, with a brown mare in tow, they headed back to the castle.

Alleron looked at them both with a thoughtful expression. When Ina turned around and sent him a questioning look, he spoke. 'Mar told me things seemed to just happen around you, but I thought he was exaggerating.'

'And what exactly is happening now?' Ina asked, unsure where this all was heading.

'It's not that you are talking with the horse, but the fact she seems to understand that is disturbing. I'm not sure this horse came from my herd,' he said carefully. Ina's laughter caught him off guard.

'The old man wasn't human, the house was not there, and now the horse is weird. What else, my lord?' She was still laughing when she turned to the horse, patting its slender neck. 'I will call you Zjawa. It means *apparition* in old alchemy scrolls. That was the first thing I thought when you appeared from the mist.'

The horse only twitched her ears, but when Ina called her by the new name, the mare looked over her shoulder in annoyance. Alleron remained lost in thought for the rest of the journey back, and Ina was grateful when the castle walls finally appeared in front of them.

The midday sun shone weakly overhead as Ina and Alleron returned to Liath. Their arrival went almost unnoticed, with only the sentries in attendance nodding respectfully to their lord as he passed, the rest of the guards now practising their trade in the training yard. The witch directed Zjawa towards the unmistakable sound of clashing steel, hoping to show off her new friend. The gait of her new mount was so smooth that it felt like riding on a cloud. The witch had never felt so rested after riding.

On arrival at the training grounds, Ina realised the noise of clashing steel wasn't practising soldiers, but Mar and Ren fighting each other again. It was easy to see that both men were masters in the art of duelling as Ren glided with the fluidity of a mountain stream, avoiding Mar's precise and powerful attacks with ease, but for once, Ina wasn't hypnotised by their skill. She was incandescent with rage. Did they not have enough fighting yesterday? Whatever the cause of this quarrel, it had to stop now, especially since Ren hadn't even healed from the last wound.

Zjawa followed her command, and they charged onto the field, shoving the two men apart. Ina leapt off the horse's back and turned on the panting combatants as they stood there, shocked at the sudden interruption, her fists clenched and ready for violence.

'Really? I thought this was finished yesterday. Do I have to break up your fights every morning? Stop behaving like petulant toddlers. You are friends and are brothers-in-arms, so for fuck's sake, stop fighting over yesterday's misunderstanding.'

Ina's scolding was barely warming up, but something in the warrior's postures gave her pause, and when the two men looked at each other and slowly started laughing, she knew she'd misread the situation.

Mar reacted first, offering an explanation. 'We were practising. That's what soldiers do.'

Then Ren bowed his head and added. 'However, we apologise for making you worry.'

Ina felt her cheeks burning red when she realised her mistake. She wished the ground would open up and swallow her whole when it came to her notice that not only were half the garrison watching, but so were Alleron and a sniggering Ayni. The witch raised her head and exhaled.

'I'm sorry for disturbing your training.'

Well, it serves me right for charging like a white knight on an empty field, she thought.

Ina hated making a fool of herself, so she took a deep breath, bowed to Mar and Ren, and turned to walk back to the castle, gathering the tatters of her dignity close to her chest. As the assembled men started clapping and cheering her performance, she felt Mar's arms slip around her shoulders and his beard tickling her cheek as he leaned down and whispered into her ear.

'Care to join us? It would be helpful to learn to fight as a team.'

The surprise Ina felt showed clearly on her face as she looked into his fierce blue eyes. Mar returned her gaze with a soft smile and inclined his head towards Ren, who gestured to the space in front of him, encouraging her to join them. Were they not upset at the tirade she'd unleashed?

'What the hell happened when I was away?' Ina muttered to herself, and hearing this, Mar whispered in her ear again.

'Nothing, my love. As you said, we are friends, so we sat down to talk like we should have from the start. Now please join us. You need to learn how to fight alongside us.'

Mar's voice was deceptively calm when he asked her to practice with them, but Ina could feel a strange tension thrumming through his body as a thumb slowly caressed her neck.

'You smell like sweet apples, my delicious morsel.'

As he spoke, the purr in his voice befuddled her mind, and she missed the squire clearing his throat as he stood to the side, holding out a short sword. With a chuckle that sounded like pure sin, Mar gave her a gentle shake, and Ina blushed crimson as she turned and hastily grabbed the weapon.

'Ina, your enemy won't take turns waiting for you. You will need to be aware of everything around you.'

Before Mar finished those words, the warriors both charged at her. They moved much slower than earlier, but even so, Ina struggled to react in time and, acting on instinct, blasted them with a burst of pure magic, sending both men several steps back.

'Good,' said Mar, 'but if we were fighting in a battle, you could distract your allies, try something else.'

They charged again, but Ina was prepared, and she released her vipers, one wrapping around her sword, another coiling around her, acting as a shield. Mar and Ren exchanged grins and attacked. The clash of steel from Ina's sword parrying Mar's attack was a sharp counterpoint to the hiss of magic as Ren's strike was repelled by the viper protecting her body. Her protagonists instinctively controlled their assault, allowing Ina to learn how to fight, but she was soon sweating and panting from wielding both magic and sword in combat. Too proud to stop, Ina fought on, despite waves of dizziness and nausea, barely hearing the cheers from their audience. Just on the brink of fainting, a sudden commotion interrupted the sparring.

'My chickens! A beast is eating my chickens!'

A serf from the household ran onto the training field and pleaded with Alleron.

'My lord, help us. A beast is eating the chickens.'

Ina was trying to catch her breath, and the servant's words made little sense, but she followed everyone as they followed the lord of Liath and the distraught woman.

As they arrived at the kitchen garden, Ina skidded to a halt, eyes wide in shock at the sight of her horse, perched on the poultry house like an animated gargoyle, watching the panicked chickens run around, occasionally snatching one when it came too close, consuming it messily and with great enthusiasm. Before she could collect her thoughts, two soldiers approached the horse and tried to grab its reins, but with a disdainful shake of her head, Zjawa twisted around and leapt over their heads, trotting happily over to Ina to beg for a cuddle.

Ina looked at her 'horse', who dropped a half-eaten chicken at her feet, shook her mane, and whinnied happily. The witch sighed deeply and looked down. As her gaze rested on Zjawa's feet, Ina frowned, perplexed, watching her mount pawing at the ground. Her horse had five toes where a hoof should be, each ending with a sharp talon that easily tore through the grass underneath. Ina looked at the other feet, studying the bunched fingers, their claws almost like a normal hoof.

'What the hell are you?' the witch asked, looking at the horse, her question met with an amused animal stare.

'She is an orein.' Ina heard Alleron's mournful voice behind her and turned around to look at him. The witch noticed Ayni heading in their direction with an unreadable facial expression.

The dragon nodded respectfully to the horse, taking a long look at the mare before turning to Ina.

'Care to tell us how a mere human earned the blessing of the mountains?' Ina's head snapped up at those words, and a chill ran down her spine when her gaze met the assessing stare of the dragoness.

CHAPTER TWELVE

Ina sat by the large fire listening to Alleron regale those gathered with their morning adventure. She didn't miss Lorraine's perplexed scrutiny, and the knowing smirks Ren shared with Mar as if they expected nothing else from her. However, Ayni's unblinking stare unnerved her the most, and Ina finally snapped.

'I just wanted to help an old blind man. How was I to know he was a mountain spirit?' she exclaimed as soon as Alleron stopped talking. 'And what the hell is an orein?'

The Lord of Liath looked at her, and Ina sat down under his quelling gaze. He so resembled her great aunt Nerissa at this moment that Ina quietened and pursed her lips.

'First, you should have listened to me when I asked you to stay put,' Alleron started, then abruptly stopped as Mar's brief laugh interrupted his lecture.

'I'm sorry, father, I should have warned you, but at least she didn't drug you…'

'Anyway, what is done is done, and as for the orein, we don't know precisely what, or even who, it is. We know it is an intelligent being that takes on a horse's appearance, is as agile as a mountain goat, and has the appetite of a lynx. It is a spirit that comes to those in need if the Grey Mountains find them worthy.'

'And it likes chickens,' Ina added more to herself, but Alleron nodded.

'Yes, and it likes chickens. And now we know it also likes you.' Alleron turned to Mar. 'I've prepared everything for your journey. Horses and provisions are ready if you want to head out in the morning.'

Ina tilted her head and looked at Alleron, who seemed happy planning the journey without consulting her.

'What if I want to go this afternoon?' she said, and suddenly, all eyes were on her, but Ina only lifted her head, slightly raising her eyebrow. 'You, my lord, are discussing the journey with your son, but you seem to forget I was tasked with this investigation.'

Her annoyance didn't escape Mar's attention, and Ina gave a little twist to her barb as she added, 'If you would be so kind as to show me a map with all the raid locations, it will spare me from meandering, and I'm sure you would want to save the little woman from getting lost in the big scary world?' She noticed Mar sigh deeply, sending his father an apologetic look, and that act of men's solidarity irked her even more.

When Alleron's lips tightened, Mar stood up and reached out to her. 'Come, my spitfire, let us all go to the map room. I had enough of your style of investigation after our expedition in the tunnels.'

The map room was larger than she expected. A massive table took up most of the space with a diorama of the territory of Liath. The detail of the terrain was so precise she felt like a bird flying high above the land. Alleron waited till everyone gathered in and pointed to the structure in the centre.

'For those who don't know the area, this is where we are. We have been attacked all over the province, but most raids were to towns surrounding the Dwarven tunnels. As they lead to the neighbouring country of Zaron, we assume they are bandits who escaped or possibly an army preparing to attack Cornovii. The second option is unlikely as the drow queen has only recently ended the succession war, but you never know with that species.'

Ina knew the general geography of Liath, but now, seeing its vastness, she couldn't help but gasp. As she looked at the tunnel, it reminded her of the encounter with the dwarves.

'We met some dwarven merchants on the way here. They mentioned sending a petition to the king regarding the defence of the trading route.'

'What exactly did they tell you?' asked Alleron.

'If Cornovii doesn't send troops soon, there will be no trade between our country and the Stone Halls,' Ina said, observing a bitter smile twisting Alleron's lips

'Well, too late for that,' said the lord of Liath. 'Kobolds have already overrun the tunnel and taken control of most of the mines. We don't have enough troops to retake them and barely enough to protect the larger towns. I've been asking for supplies for months, but the bloody princess and that senile chancellor denied it every time.'

Mar studied the map with a frown, and Ina wished she knew what he was thinking. Suddenly, he broke his silence, pointing to a tight cluster of flags.

'We need to go to this area. These villages may be close to each other, but the terrain makes moving between them difficult, so I'll bet their base is close by, and they were raided at different times. Also, I don't think the kobolds are solely responsible for this. They are an honourable race and wouldn't break the pact. Something or someone else must be behind it.'

Ina didn't realise she was smiling until he smiled back at her. There was something unexpectedly enticing observing him, employing his military mind in planning. She noticed him watching her, waiting for any sign that she agreed with the plan, and that tempted her to tease him a little.

'Well, that perfectly summarises my "let's go and see" policy. We shall leave tomorrow morning. We have a sizable distance to cover, especially now the days are shorter.'

Ayni stood in the background, feeling like a silent witness to a great discussion, and she had never felt so irrelevant. The dragoness blinked slowly, wondering what made this woman so unique that a mountain spirit deemed her worthy and two powerful warriors followed her blindly.

Her gaze moved to Ren, who filled the space with his quiet presence. A faint blush tinted her cheeks when he caught her observing him. Although she came here with Mar, this calm man more and more dragged her attention, and Ayni snuck a glance in his direction, licking her suddenly dry lips. Why did he move her in ways Mar never did? He was not even a dragon, yet last night, she dreamed he trailed his slender fingers along her neck when she flew with him through the night sky, treating her with the same gentleness and respect he treated the witch. Impossible. It was centuries since she had desired to have a rider. This idea was so unsettling that Ayni shook her head to banish the unwanted thoughts and said, 'We can always fly there.'

'No, we can't,' Mar said, much to Ina's relief. 'We don't want the raiders to know the direction we're going, and we don't want to scare the locals who are still taught to fear dragons. We will all remain human, even if drawn into battle.'

'You could always stay here,' Ina baited the dragoness.

'The mountains are my home. Do you think I will sit down and let war lay waste to this region? Besides, I have to keep an eye on you. You can't be trusted around men,' Ayni said mockingly, hiding the real reason she wanted to join the expedition.

'Enough!' Mar's voice stopped their bickering when he came between them. 'Ina, we need healing potions and whatever you might find helpful in keeping us alive without using your unique skills.'

When she opened her mouth to protest his interruption, he smiled and put his calloused palm on her cheek. 'I don't know if I can take any more rivals, so no special healing, just old-fashioned Nerissa-approved methods. I'm asking you because no one else knows how to do it.'

He was right, and being contrary would not just be petty, but also pointless. Still, she didn't have to like it. Ina nodded and attempted to walk away with a shrug, but Mar's hand slid to her waist and pressed her to his side when he turned to Ayni.

'My lady, if you insist on joining us, please keep in mind Lady Inanuan is in charge of this expedition. If you want to be useful, find my mother and make sure we have our provisions ready and plenty.'

Ina watched Ayni's gaze trail between her and Mar as she did her best not to smile smugly. The way Mar distanced himself from

Ayni felt nice, but the way he supported her felt even better, and Ina involuntarily pressed herself harder to his side. Ayni smirked, giving them a quick nod before walking out of the room, and taking a deep breath, Ina slid from Mar's embrace.

'I will go too. Pillaging your mother's infirmary will take some time.'

The remaining men looked at each other when the doors closed behind her, and Alleron shook his head, placing a hand on Mar's shoulder.

'I don't envy you this task. Those women fight like cats, hissing and biting at each opportunity.'

Mar's lips twitched when he looked at his father. 'You are right, but despite causing trouble, Ayni saved my life. Also, she is the only source of knowledge, and I still need to learn about being a dragon. Besides, I don't believe she's a bad person, and Ina will see it once she gets past her anger.'

His father nodded, and although Mar still saw the doubt in his eyes, the old lord refrained from commenting on the subject. Instead, he tapped his fingers over the table, lost in thought.

'Just say what is bothering you,' Mar said, knowing his frowning expression all too well.

'As you said, something is behind those attacks. Some victims mentioned seeing dark elves dressed like drow soldiers in the fighting. I fear the other side of the mountains may be involved in this struggle. We have no power to resist an army of dark elves led by pure blood drows.'

Mar shifted uncomfortably and looked at Ren. The dark elves were a well-known race, albeit a little insular. Between them, a small contingent calling themselves the drow believed in racial purity with fanatical zeal. Those zealots had, for millennia, lived in the dark forest and caves of Arknay. Although not inherently evil, their deeds were rarely noble, and their fighting skills, combined with blood magic, were infamous throughout the known world.

'We must train with Ina daily for everyone's benefit, ensuring she can control her magic. That way, we'll all know what to expect in a battle. I will see to the horses now. Ren? Please find a suitable weapon for Ina. Oh, and Ayni too. See if she knows how to use a blade, that troublesome woman may not be familiar with them.' Mar rubbed his temples. It should be a simple mission, but he felt something was missing. He turned to his father.

'Write to the king, he has to know what is going on here, and I will write to Daro and see if there are any guards he could spare. One more thing, I know you won't like it, but inform the provost of battle mages about the issue, and maybe Lady Nerissa, as we could use a few healers.'

'You're expecting a war?' asked his father.

Mar smiled bitterly. 'Perhaps, but it's better to be prepared than caught off-guard.'

The discussion ended soon after that grim thought was voiced. Mar strode from the castle into the fresh air of the courtyard feeling unsettled and frustrated. He couldn't pinpoint the source, but it felt like the calm before the storm. He knew something was coming, and he had no idea how to protect those he loved against it. A loud welcoming whicker scattered the dark thoughts, and the smile that blossomed on his lips was a balm to a troubled soul. Woron dug his hoof in the hay, snorted, and leaned his massive black head on Mar's shoulder, and the relief that his faithful steed welcomed him brought a tear to his eye.

The captain took a horse brush and groomed his mount, using this simple activity to bring peace to his troubled mind, and he lost himself in the slow strokes until interrupted by a voice behind him.

'Why can't you act like a dragon? Riding horses to the mountains and letting a mage decide what we're doing? I didn't expect this of you.'

It was Ayni. She stood behind him, hands on her hips, ready to tear him to pieces. He looked at her in silence till she grew uneasy under his stare.

'I'm not a dragon, I may take that form, but I am still Marcach of Liath, Captain of the King's Guards. Liath and Cornovii are my home, and the safety of the people here is important to me, but you are free to go. Why do you stay here and trouble yourself with human affairs? If you need a reward for helping me, then name your price, anything except giving up Ina, and I will pay it.'

He watched as Ayni stalked forward, attempting to catch his hand, and he moved back. When her lips tightened in a thin line, he almost smiled. It looked like the beautiful Ayni was not used to rejection.

'I found an unexpected reason to stay here. Isn't it funny how things turned out? You were supposed to be my prize, yet you prefer the human mage over your own species. What does Ina have that I'm lacking, Mar?'

'You are lacking nothing, my lady. You are intelligent, fierce and beautiful, but Ina is… Ina.' Mar smiled at his thoughts, trying to describe the elusive charm of the witch. Ayni still didn't look convinced, and Mar didn't blame her. So far, the dragon had only met with a sharp edge of the witch's tongue.

Suddenly he heard himself saying, 'Ina is brave, loyal, and fair. You've seen her angry, betrayed and hurt, yet she stood up to the Lord of Liath to help an old blind man just because it was the right thing to do.'

Ayni raised her eyebrow, her head tilted to the side as she thought over his words.

'You didn't call her beautiful.'

Mar burst out laughing, startling the horses, and he took a moment to calm them down. In the end, he said, 'I'm past the age I would joust for a pretty face. For me, she is the most beautiful woman in Cornovii. However, even if her beauty fades, she still will be my magnificent Ina.'

He saw Ayni's face close down, determination in her eyes. When she kicked a stray rock that ricocheted from the stable doors, he patted Woron's back, hoping he won't have to protect the horses from a raging dragon.

'Fine! But why didn't you tell me this in the temple? We could have avoided making fools of ourselves.' Ayni paused for a moment. Mar felt as if the emotionless mask had fallen from her features when she looked back at him. 'I'm sorry for causing you trouble. All I wanted was some company, but I should have known better. Let me help you now. If we need to escape, you can carry your witch, and I can carry Ren. Besides, I want to see what is happening in the mountains, and the time I've spent in your company has been interesting.'

He heard the slight tremble in her voice when she mentioned flying with Ren, but the relief he felt, seeing the crisis averted, distracted him from paying attention to her tone. He felt a glimmer of hope that without Ayni constantly getting in his way, he could make some progress with his stubborn woman. After their conversation in the garden, she seemed less hostile towards his attempts at reconciliation and very receptive to his touch. He nodded to the dragoness.

'If you wish, Ayni. Just remember, we are travelling as humans, no shape changing even during battle if we can avoid it. There is too much gossip about dragons in Liath already.'

Ayni burst laughing, 'Oh, that is a shame. I so enjoyed the sight of you parading naked in the snow.'

Mar recalled his first change when he didn't know how to create clothes and joined her in laughing. 'It was a strange experience for me, too.'

Suddenly, he heard Ina's cold condemnation coming from open stable doors.

'I'm glad you both have such fond memories of your time together, but I would prefer you focus on the preparations for the journey, or are Ren and I the only ones with any sense of responsibility here? Once you finish, find me. I want a brief plan of where we are going. I also want to depart early in the morning.'

Mar closed his eyes and rested his head on Woron's neck as Ina turned on her heel and walked from the stables with her head high. His *let's go and see* Ina talking about responsibility and preparation showed her anger. Not that he liked her being jealous, but he liked that she cared enough to be.

'It must feel nice when someone cares so much.'

Ayni's soft voice caught his attention. And Mar tilted his head, looking at her with a question in his eyes.

'She came here with steaming mugs of tea. After all this, she still cares for you.'

Mar sighed. He hadn't noticed the cup or even her entrance, and once again, she only heard part of their conversation. Still, she gave him an excuse to see her later; this time, he intended to bring a hot drink.

CHAPTER THIRTEEN

The morning was bright and crisp as everyone gathered in the yard. Mar and Ina tried to hide their yawns, and although both looked like they had a sleepless night, Mar radiated contentment while Ina looked like a thundercloud. Unable to resist, the warrior frequently found himself looking at the witch's face, and each time, he felt the warmth spreading inside. When Ina had overheard the end of his discussion with Ayni, he'd braced himself for frustrating explanations and angry words, but, once again, she surprised him.

It was pretty late after he finished brushing Woron and went to Ina's chamber. As expected, the doors were locked, and his woman using her talent with colourful language, told the grizzled warrior what she thought about the timing of his arrival, but he was ready for this. Mar sat against her door, blew steam from a herbal tea through the gap and vividly described the taste of the warm apple pie in his other hand. The silence on the other side told him he'd struck the right chord, and soon the doors opened, and Ina's tussled head appeared in the gap.

'It took you long to come here, and no, I don't want to know what you have been doing. Just tell me where we are going tomorrow, and give me that damned plate.'

He was let in, and while Ina enjoyed his gifts, he briefed her about their route and provisions. With a thoughtful expression, she asked him about the terrain they would traverse and what sort of attacks he was expecting. When she ran out of questions, she curled up on the chair and stared into the fire.

'Thank you and goodnight, Mar. I will see you tomorrow.'

'Why haven't you asked me about my time with Ayni?' he said softly, approaching her chair.

'Because I don't want to know. It will change nothing, so why bring up things that can cause more pain?'

'Because I want to tell you. I want to share this experience with you… my friend.'

When she didn't answer, Mar sat on the floor by her chair and reminisced about the shocking end to the battle at the palace, telling Ina how overwhelmed it left him and how he'd decided the only way to prevent his friends from being harmed was for him to go. The warrior continued, expressing the joy of his first flight, returning home, and the feeling of betrayal when the ballista shot him. Then, hesitantly, Mar told Ina of the fear he'd felt the realisation that he could die without seeing her again. When he felt her hand trailing in his hair, he continued, telling her about his encounter with Ayni, including the failed attempts at transforming, how the dragoness had treated his wound, and how she taught him to return to his human shape.

As his words trailed off, Mar turned to study Ina's expression, but as he moved, he bounced the table, knocking a small jar onto his lap. He touched the spots of green substance on his tunic, sniffed the residue coating his fingers, and looked at Ina with a question in his eyes. She looked mortified, yet her lips twitched as she restrained her laughter, making him instantly suspicious.

'What is this, my spitfire?'

'Nothing…'

'Ina, it smells like a swamp. You're not trying to poison anyone, are you?'

'Mar, why do you always have to assume the worst? Just leave it be, go away, and I will see you tomorrow.'

'My love, I still remember how you drugged me to get what you wanted. Is it for Ayni?'

'Oh, for goddess' sake Mar, it is not poison! I'm not twenty anymore and can't smooth my skin like some bloody dragons. It is just face ointment. Now, will you go away?'

His roaring laugh earned him a magic punch that threw him into the wall, but he couldn't be more pleased. This newly discovered vanity made him feel closer to his woman. After returning to his room, his gaze fell on a piece of mahogany, and it occurred to him that he had the perfect way to bring her radiant smile to life.

During breakfast, Mar could not resist teasing Ina a little. He intercepted her when she came down, gently stroking her cheek. 'Your skin is so smooth today. It looks like you had a good night, my spitfire.'

'You are digging your own grave, you overgrown lizard,' she said, and he leaned in close, tickling her ear with his beard.

'Maybe, but this silky smoothness is well worth it.' He evaded her attempt to punch him and spent the rest of the morning smiling each time he caught her angry scowl. After checking their weapons and supplies alongside Ren, Mar mounted Woron with a spry hop and gave the order to move out.

Ina kicked the orein, and Zjawa turned her head, giving her a reproachful look and a quelling bite on the leg. The witch sighed mournfully and reached for a small potion to ease her headache. Throwing it back with a wince at the taste, she leaned down and apologised to her mount.

Last night had been intense. After overhearing Mar's conversation, she wanted to blast the dragoness through the stable walls, but instead, she just walked away to process her anger alone. When Mar turned up, much later than expected, she was prepared for pleading and angry words. Instead, he shared his feelings about his transformation and subsequent adventures. She couldn't help but feel guilty for his trials and accepted that the annoying Ayni deserved some gratitude for helping save Mar's life and teaching him about his magic.

When the clumsy oaf managed to knock over her face cream and then laugh about it afterwards, all sympathy went out the window. *I should have done more than just kick him out. He must think I'm a vain airhead now,* she thought. Just then, Mar called out, interrupting her musings.

'Ina?' he asked, his thigh rubbing against hers as he came alongside.

'Yes?' Even on horseback, she had to tilt her head to look at him, and as she did, the warrior seemed to loom above even more as he reached over, holding out a small object in his hand.

'I have something for you. I hope you like it.'

She looked down and took his gift, studying it closely. It was a crude hairpin made of mahogany, carved in the form of a viper's head. Surprised that Mar would buy something so simple, Ina looked up and, catching the uncertainty in his eyes, realised that he had made this for her. She bowed slightly to express her gratitude, almost glowing with the tenderness that filled her heart.

'It is a beautiful gift. Thank you. Please tell the maker I love his work.' She twisted her hair into a simple knot and tied it up with the pin. 'How do I look?'

Ina saw Mar's eyes soften as the tension fell from his shoulders.

'You look beautiful.' There was a coarseness to his voice, and, avoiding her eyes, he spurred his horse forward, taking the lead of their small group.

Ina adjusted the hairpin, a smile teasing at the edges of her mouth. Mar was full of surprises. A bag of cat treats and the small charm for the ball were easy to acquire, but taking the time to make a hairpin? That grumpy dragon and his thoughtful gifts touched her heart more than she cared to admit.

Her smile grew wry at her thoughts, and Ina focused on her surroundings. Since they'd left Liath, the road had been steadily climbing, and the wildness of the rolling hills eased something inside the witch's chest. Fields with scattered flocks of sheep and cows were interspersed with thickets of pine and rugged granite boulders thrusting out of the ground. The lack of wagons surprised her at first, till they encountered those brave enough to transport their produce, each group surrounded by rough-looking guards who bristled as they came close to their party. Ina, saddened by the sight, closed her eyes and allowed Zjawa to pick her way over the frosty terrain, trusting her extraordinary mount to keep her safe.

'What did he give you?' Ayni's voice disturbed the silence. Ina opened her eyes and looked at the dragoness, who didn't look at all comfortable on horseback, which Ina enjoyed seeing far too much.

'A hairpin.' A short answer felt most suitable. She might be grateful to Ayni for helping Mar, but that didn't mean she intended to share their complicated relationship with some stranger. They rode along in silence till Ayni spoke again.

'We are not married. We never finished the ritual. I hoped he would in time, but now I know it will never happen.'

Ina's head snapped in Ayni's direction, focusing sharply on the woman.

'Why are you telling me this? After causing all this grief, why now? What is your agenda?'

Ayni smirked and inclined her head to Ren, who rode behind, guarding the back.

'I guess my priorities changed.'

Ina reined in the orein so hard that the mare reared back angrily as she turned to Ayni. Chaos vibrated in the air, filling the air between them with static electricity.

'Be careful with your words and deeds, dragon. He is not a toy to play with or a consolation prize. If you are doing this to spite me, I will break you.' Her quiet voice was charged with menace, and Ayni's eyes widened when she sensed the magic. She struggled to tame her terrified horse as it danced to the side.

'I just like him, you demented harridan, so calm the fuck down,' the dragon said when the horse bucked beneath her.

'Ina!' Mar was first to react, galloping towards them, Ren joined him half a beat later, and now both men looked at them in complete confusion. 'What is going on? Why do you reach for Chaos?' Mar asked, looking around.

Ina blushed as she watched both men circling, hands on the hilts of their swords, eyes scanning the area, looking for danger. She was taken aback by Ayni's sudden shift of interest that. Like a village idiot, she overreacted to her words. To avoid embarrassing explanations, she flashed Mar an apologetic smile.

'It was nothing, Mar. Nothing happened. I just thought I saw something.' Ina realised he intended to ask more questions, so she urged her mount to set off at a fast canter, Zjawa whickering happily at the increase in pace. Mar rolled his eyes and turned to Ren.

'Stay with Ayni and meet me in the village. I need to find out what she saw before it comes and bites us in the arse,' he said before turning Woron round and chasing after the disappearing witch.

❄❄❄

After an exhilarating ride, Ina came to a shocked halt in the middle of a burnt-out village. No curtains moved in the gaping windows at her arrival. Most houses didn't even have windows, their charred shells forlorn and empty. She slid off Zjawa and led her mare to the well when Mar charged in. In a blink, he was off his horse, holding her close, and Ina lowered her head, pretending not to see his concerned stare.

'We are alone here, so please tell me what happened. What triggered your need for Chaos? Did that bloody dragoness mention the wedding again, or did you see something?'

Mar's hand rested under her chin, tilting it up to look at him, but Ina flinched. Still, as much as it embarrassed her, he deserved the explanation.

'Yes, she mentioned the wedding, or rather, the lack of it. She also mentioned that the only reason she was telling the truth now was because of her sudden interest in Ren, and I snapped. I'm sorry, I shouldn't have, but I don't trust her and can't stand some dragon toying with Ren's feelings. He deserves better than that.'

Mar exhaled and pulled her close. 'You mean, he deserves you?'

'What? No! That's not what I meant. I'm with you….' As soon as these words left her mouth, Ina bit her tongue and corrected herself. 'I mean, I don't want to see him hurt because some scorned dragon is trying to prove a point.'

Mar nodded. 'I know you two are close, but Ren wants more than friendship from you. He told me once that he would love you whether you returned his feeling or not. So you have to ask yourself, do you really want him to live his life alone, yearning for you? Give them a chance to sort this out themselves. We both know Ren is too loyal to even look at a woman unless she earns your approval, and if he isn't interested, he will make it clear. I've never seen him have any trouble avoiding unwanted attention.'

'Since when did you become such a fount of wisdom?' she said, and Mar laughed.

'Since you taught me the hard way to put my jealousy aside and trust your heart,' he answered and locked her in a tight embrace.

It pained her to admit he was right, but something inside her deeply opposed this idea. She pushed him away, grumbling. 'Fine, but if she breaks his heart, you can be the one to console him, as you were the one who brought this overly amorous dragon here.'

Mar let her go and looked around. He'd completely neglected their safety in his need to catch up with the runaway witch. After all, according to his father's words, this was a village so plagued with raids that the occupants had fled to Liath. Still, he saw at least one or two cottages with an intact roof, and that was better than sleeping in an empty field during the winter.

'Ina, Ren and Ayni should arrive soon. What do you want to do?'

'I should look after the horses since I ran them ragged. Please check the cottages for a safe place to stay tonight.'

She pointed to the best-looking house and turned, leading both horses to a small patch of grass, removing their tack, and giving them a brisk rub-down. Mar took a moment to watch her before he entered the almost intact cottage. The view that welcomed him left him cursing under his breath. Broken furniture and the remains of household articles lay scattered around the room. Even the bed was broken, but a small cast-iron stove appeared intact, and the house looked solid enough to retain the heat. Suddenly, a piece of broken crockery flew out of nowhere, hitting him on the forehead, its sharp edge cutting the skin.

Mar drew his sword and turned to his attacker in one smooth motion. A small, hairy, ancient man looked at him from behind the stove.

'Get out! Get out of my house,' he said, aiming another broken vessel at his head.

Mar easily avoided the missile and went to grab the unruly host of this house when Ina opened the door.

'Mar, no.' Her quick command stopped him in place. He watched Ina closely as she slowly walked into the cottage and faced the strange, scruffy old man. Her next move surprised him. Ina bowed low in front of their host.

'Forgive us for intruding. I call upon the law of hospitality. Please allow us to rest here for the night.'

Mar followed her example, and they bowed to the man as if he were the king. The protracted silence became uncomfortable, and Mar was about to straighten his back and call upon the ancient law of the fist when the man spoke.

'Hospitality is granted to you and yours, little witch.' And as if nothing happened, he shuffled to the attic, leaving Mar standing with a baffled expression.

'Ina, care to tell me what just happened?' he asked, slowly wiping the blood from the cut on his forehead.

'It was a domowik. I suspect the only reason this house still stands is its guardian spirit's care. They are touchy when someone enters their home, but now we can sleep here, and he will also guard us.' She gestured for him to sit on the windowsill. 'Let me see your cut. We can't allow it to spoil your manly beauty.'

While she was cleaning his wound, Mar closed his eyes and inhaled her scent. His hands reached for her, resting on her hips. Ina's cough brought him back to reality.

'What are you doing?' Her voice filled with amusement.

'I'm enjoying the moment while it lasts,' he said with a smile and looked through the window. 'Ren and Ayni are here. We need to get ready for the night.'

'Well, send your dragon friend in, and we'll bond over the cleaning as we wait for the hunters to provide for us.' Ina waved him off and stepped away.

The next hour was a blur of activity, with the women removing the broken furniture and men looking after the horses, security of the building, and starting the fire, which came in useful as dusk came quickly, bringing with it a light dusting of snow. Ren caught a rabbit, and Ina prepared a delicious stew using the various unidentified herbs in her pack. The smell of food and the warmth of fire tempted the domowik to reappear, a feral snarl on his lips till Ina offered him a bowl of stew with an inviting smile.

'Please, share food with us. We are grateful for your hospitality, grandfather.'

Her offer was accepted with a broad smile, and several blankets fell from the attic soon after. Ina hastily grabbed them and spread them on the floor in front of the fireplace.

'We will sleep like kings now.' She started humming a folk song that fit the situation. The makeshift beds were small, but close to the fire and successfully shielded against the cold floor. Ina was the first to kick off her boots and scurry into the warm blankets.

'How can you spend some much time on your horses?' she said, addressing the men. 'My ass gets completely flat from bouncing on the saddle.'

Mar snorted a short laugh, almost choking on the stew, and Ren looked at her with amusement playing in his dark eyes. 'I don't think your backside is any different, my lady.'

Mar finally contained his coughing fit and approached Ren, playfully punching his friend's shoulder.

'Lie down. I will take the first watch. I will wake you in a few hours.'

When he donned his fur cloak and walked out, Ina sighed gently. She didn't even think about it, but guarding the camp was second nature to these warriors. Ren nodded to Mar and followed Ina's example, taking off his boots and stretching out on the blankets. That left Ayni, who was now eyeing them with irritation.

'Are you waiting for a special invitation, dragon? Join us unless you prefer to stand there like a maypole.'

Ina tried to be nice but struggled to move past the previous incidents. She felt like the dragoness had encroached on her territory and realised she was as protective as Mar when it came to her friends. Ina watched with half-closed eyes as Ayni settled down next to Ren, blushing slightly when he smiled at her and, summoning all her self-control, Ina turned her back to them. She heard the whispered conversation behind her, but exhaustion quickly pulled her into a deep sleep.

Later, the scent of leather and iron seeped through her dreams, and the warmth of the massive body next to her called to her senses. Her hand found its way to the source of the sensation, and after a brief fight with some stubborn obstacles, she could stroke the majestic fur. Her dreams turned more explicit, and Ina sighed with pleasure, wrapping herself around the source of the heat.

Mar finished his watch, chilled to the bone. The snow had finally stopped, and only a few snowflakes danced in the air. The night was calm and bright, with a full moon high in the sky, and he had no trouble seeing when he entered the cottage.

Ina was on her belly with tangled copper hair covering her face, and Ren opened his eyes as soon as he entered the house. Ayni was sleeping next to him with her hand across Ren's chest. Gently, he moved it to the side and stood up as Mar prepared himself for bed, lying down in the nice, warm space vacated by his friend, when suddenly, Ina turned and faced him. Mar was about to say something when he noticed she was still deeply asleep, but as he settled down, she yanked his shirt up and slid her hand over his chest. Her leg followed, wrapping itself around his hips, and she squeezed him tightly, purring in his ear.

'My majestic fur....'

She stroked his chest, and a soft, delightful smile danced on her lips, making Mar want to be in her head to know what his woman was dreaming.

This commotion woke Ayni, who looked at them with an unreadable expression before standing up.

'I will go outside,' she said, quickly dressing before joining Ren.

Mar nodded, wrapping his arms around Ina. Despite the dangers of the road ahead, he felt happy. She was the piece of his soul he hadn't realised was missing. Careful not to wake her, he gently kissed her. His body responded as she ground her hips over his groin, and Mar groaned with frustration. He tried to push her away, battling the need to give in to his desire, but no matter what he tried, she continued to press herself to his side. Her hand landed on his cock at some point, and Mar moaned in desperation.

'Gods help me, I want you so much.' As if in answer to his prayer, Ayni ran into the house, shouting.

'Wake up! Ren said attackers are coming!'

Mar was on his feet in a blink, spilling Ina unceremoniously to the bare floor. It wasn't how he imagined the gods would answer his prayer, but he didn't have time to think about it. He looked at Ina, still groggy, as he pulled on his boots.

'Be careful with your Chaos. Ren and I will try to give you some space,' he said, running outside with a sword in his hand.

CHAPTER FOURTEEN

As Ina finished pulling on her boots and lacing them, she looked around, realising she was alone in the cottage. She'd had such a pleasant dream interrupted by this commotion that she needed a minute to gather her thoughts. She shuddered when something landed on her shoulder, but it was only the domowik holding out her short sword and pointing to the door.

'Help them, autumn witch. They need your magic.'

She didn't need any more encouragement and bolted out, only to be confronted by a raging battle. Several attackers challenged Mar, who seemed oddly pleased to be outnumbered. Ren moved around the skirmish so swiftly that no one came close to stopping him, whilst Ayni wielded her borrowed sword with impressive skill, holding back the men trying to cut their way through her defences. Even the horses fought, Woron kicking and trampling their assailants and Zjawa tearing into anyone she caught in her impressive fangs.

The odds, however, were not in their favour. The enemy that outnumbered them was heavily armed and obviously well-trained. Ina reached for her peridot, tapping into its stored energy, and her fire vipers burst into life, drawing the attention of everyone on the battlefield. As if by an unspoken command, the soldiers abandoned their opponents and ran straight towards her.

'Oh fuck,' she said, bracing herself for the attack. Fear weakened her control, and red tendrils of Chaos entangled her vipers. When she lashed out at the first attacker, the fire seared his skin, but it was the coils of raw Chaos that ripped the blood-curdling scream from his lips as it unravelled his being, leaving behind a dry, withered corpse. Ina barely noticed, fighting for her life, trying to use Ren's lessons to weave around the next attack as she sliced her sword across the man's throat, her assailants attempting to subdue her overwhelming numbers. Mar's words from the training field were at the forefront of her mind as she defended herself from both sides, back pressed to the cottage wall.

Mar and Ren fell upon the unprotected backs of her opponents, swords felling the distracted enemy, but as Ina's body wearied, her control began slipping, and any who came too close dropped to the ground, dead. With a final pained gasp, Ina looked up and saw Mar lose grip on his dragon. His body coated itself in scales and talons, becoming death incarnate as he tore into the remaining attackers until those still alive broke and ran, leaving the witch to slowly collapse, fighting the Chaos magic trying to escape her control.

Ren and Ayni pursued the fleeing soldiers whilst Ina knelt, detached, watching the swirls of magic curl around her hands, while a strange smile curled the edges of her lips until her mind focused on the trembling fingers in her lap. With the last of her energy, she forced her hand into a fist and shut down the terrifying power.

Ina felt no anguish for taking the enemy's lives. They had it coming when they raised a hand against them, but the way she did it… *It felt so good, so easy to just take it,* she thought, lowering her eyes on the desiccated corpses that looked at the sky with milky eyes, their mouths screaming in silent torment.

Previously, Ina had only gathered Chaos from natural destruction or monsters already corrupted beyond recovery. Today she had stripped the magic from ordinary living beings, from the very source of life, and now as she looked at Mar, she could feel the threads of Chaos calling to her, begging to join with her magic. She felt sick, an abomination, worse than any she fought in Osterad.

'No!' This one word carried all her conviction. *I will not become the bane of this world like the striga, stealing life that isn't mine.* The witch dug her fingers into the frozen ground and purged the magic that came from death straight into the dirt, and her foes' corpses slowly collapsed to the ground as her magic released them to their final rest.

Mar had already approached her when she finished, and his massive muzzle touched her chest. It was strangely comforting, and she embraced him, inhaling his metallic scent.

'I tried not to resort to Chaos. I promise, I'm not a monster,' she said, taking a deep breath. She felt the shape under her hands change, and after a moment, she was standing there, embraced by very human arms.

'Why would you even think that, my love?' Mar's voice was soft, albeit a bit surprised. He slowly stroked her back, and her trembling subsided under his touch.

'You saw what I did. I lost control of my magic and unleashed Chaos.'

'Are you sure you had no control? I saw a formidable mage who used her magic and stopped when it was no longer needed.' His hand drifted under her chin, tilting up her head. 'If it makes it better, I lost control, too. I shouldn't have transformed, there was no need for it in that skirmish, but the dragon inside me doesn't like to see you in danger.'

Ina cuddled her cheek to his large calloused hand. His words calmed the turmoil she felt inside, bringing her the needed peace. 'I love your dragon, and I know you didn't ask for this, but somehow you seem more content this way. Like a puppy that finally grew into a big dog. Less barking, more biting, but only when needed.'

She observed Mar fighting a losing battle as he unravelled her comparison. He tightened his lips, trying to look offended, but burst out laughing at the end. 'Your mind is a wondrous place, my lady. Confusing and strange, but still amazing. Now I'm a big dog to you… with majestic fur.'

'Hmm… what fur?' The last part didn't make sense to her, but Mar had already released her from his embrace.

'Come, we need to find the others, and if we are lucky, we will also have someone's tongue to pull for information.'

❄❄❄

The path Ren and Ayni disappeared down led towards a small pine glade near a rugged cliff. Mar heard the faint clash of steel, a dragon's roar, and then deafening silence. He hoped they were not heading into another skirmish. The group that attacked them in the village had been larger than Mar expected for a scouting party. He'd counted at least thirty attackers, which would have overwhelmed any normal group their size. However, they were no match for two dragons, a master swordsman and one very vicious witch.

Mar smiled, thinking about Ina's fighting style. She was a flexible fighter and wielded both sword and magic without combat experience, making her simultaneously vulnerable and deadly. They would need to practise as soon as possible, but he was already impressed at how she'd held her ground when the whole horde attacked.

Remembering that moment, Mar frowned. *What had caused the sudden change in tactics? Why did they all charge a mage who was wielding fire?* They would need to find the answer to those questions.

A glance at Ina reassured him she was feeling better, and the captain wondered what more there was to her distress. *Did my spitfire really think she was a monster?* Ina had never struck him as a frail wallflower to mourn people who tried to kill her, yet she'd looked so anguished after the battle. Her sudden mood change after he'd comforted her baffled him and forced a laugh from his lips.

'Why are you laughing?' Ina looked at him suspiciously.

'For no reason at all.' His lips twitched harder when he noticed her eyes narrow, her suspicion deepening. But before Ina could interrogate him, he saw Ayni's cloak and the light of a fire flicker between the trees. He took Ina's hand and pulled her into the clearing.

Ren crouched next to a drow male, and Ayni held her dagger against a kobold's throat. The rest of the attackers were scattered on the ground, dead from Ren's merciless blade.

'Did anyone escape?' Mar asked, hoping for a negative answer. They could do without reinforcements catching them out in the open.

'No, Ayni was very effective in preventing their escape.' Ren's compliment brought a beautiful smile to Ayni's face, especially as he looked at her with appreciation. Ina frowned slightly, but it was short-lived, and Mar was grateful for this small mercy.

He approached the kobold. The warrior sat there with an unreadable expression, but when Mar came closer, the man clenched his fist and hit his chest, bowing deeply in front of him despite the press of Ayni's dagger.

'Marcach of Liath, we broke our oath. The tatters of my honour beg for death by your hand.'

'Cave scum, you can die with your oaths and worthless customs,' the drow spat out, but Ren's fist in the face quickly silenced him.

'How do you know me?' asked Mar, surprised by this sudden recognition.

'I was there when you defeated our chieftain. I was a witness to the oath.'

Mar's eyes clouded as he recalled that fateful day when he became the unwilling hero, which led to his unhappy marriage. They had been fighting a losing battle, and when their captain had perished under a kobolds sword, the inexperienced Mar suddenly became the leader of the decimated squadron. He had made a pact with the kobold's chieftain, knowing the kobolds would honour their word. Their adherence to vows and customs was legendary and a weakness he exploited. If he were to win, the kobold army would never return to this region. If he had lost, his unit would become the kobolds' winter provisions. It was a desperate move, but somehow, he pulled it off.

At age twenty, Mar had fought in several battles. Still, he had been outmatched and unprepared for his opponent's vicious savagery. The chieftain had toyed with him, and they both knew it. That, however, ended up saving his life, as the kobold warrior had bled him so heavily that the ground became a slippery, red slush. As Mar aimed for the enemy's chest, he slipped on the blood-soaked earth, and his sword had pierced just above his opponent's chest plate with one clumsy, lucky blow, severing the chieftain's artery. Mar shook his head to dispel the unwanted images, as that day, he became a hero, leading to ten dark years in Osterad as the king's trophy champion.

'I don't want your life. I want information on why you are here attacking the villages, despite the oath.' Mar had little hope of getting the answer, but it was worth trying. He stepped back and cursed when the kobold warrior's face contorted. The man opened his mouth to speak, but his body jerked and twisted, with only a shuddering pained gasp leaving his lips. Yet the kobold kept trying, despite the apparent torment.

Mar stumbled as Ina pushed him aside, rushing towards the gasping male.

'He is under a geas,' she said in a tense voice, and magic swirled around her.

Mar only knew that a geas was a magical gag put on those sworn to secrecy, but he'd never seen it in action. He saw Ina place her hand on the kobold's forehead and murmur something under her breath. The jerking stopped, but the male was obviously still in unbelievable pain.

'You will never break my lord's geas,' the drow said, laughing at Ina's frantic efforts to break the spell.

'Ren, shut him up.' Mar felt utterly helpless as he stood by, watching the kobold struggle, and clenched his fist in frustration when he heard desperation roughen Ina's voice as she addressed the soldier.

'Stop trying to speak. I will find another way to break it. I just need a little time.'

Mar saw her breathing quicken when a dark and ominous cloud formed around the kobold's body. The thought she might be in danger herself hit him like a hammer.

'Ina, no!' Mar rushed forward, but his reaction was enough to break the witch's focus.

Once again, the kobold's eyes locked on him, and the warrior, choking on his own blood, said, 'The drow prince took over the mines. Our chieftain is dead. Guard your mage.'

Three short sentences and he was gone. Mar looked at Ina sitting next to the body, looking utterly bereft. When she raised her eyes to him, he saw a solitary tear running down her cheek.

'I'm sorry, Mar. An archmage made this geas….' She stopped and exhaled, looking at the dead warrior. 'He died with honour. I felt his pain. This spell tore his soul apart, but he still managed to speak.'

Mar nodded, too disturbed to say a word, and looked at the drow, who was laughing like a madman. He felt raw, cold fury overtaking him. Ren moved away when Mar's hand grabbed the drow by his throat, lifting him in the air.

'Who is your master?'

The drow struggled despite Mar's inhuman strength, but he stilled, eyes widening as scales appeared over his interrogator's skin.

'Who is your master?' Mar repeated the question, looking at the man, his gaze unyielding. 'And what you are doing here? The Arknay drow has no business this side of the Grey Mountains.'

The enemy attempted to spit in his face, but Mar squeezed his neck tighter, stopping him with casual brutality, more concerned about the greed in the soldier's eyes as he looked towards Ina. As his gaze followed the drow's, Ayni gasped, shocked as Ina began using her Chaos magic. Red mist coated the kobold as she dismantled his body's matrix. Small red flames danced over the dead soldier, turning the flesh into a delicate wisp of smoke. When she noticed Mar's questioning stare, she answered bitterly.

'I don't know their customs, but he tried to help and doesn't deserve to be food for scavengers.'

Mar nodded, shifting his attention back to the drow, who suddenly jerked in his grasp, oblivious to the pain, reaching for Ina. Greed, desire and madness lit up his eyes, a demented snarl uncovering sharp teeth.

'My beautiful terror, soon you and your Chaos will sing for me.'

The drow's voice sounded strange and distorted as if someone else spoke through his lips, and Ina's eyes widened at the unsettling threat. Mar frowned when the soldier began scanning their surroundings, and, as if on command, Ren hit the man in the temple, knocking him out cold.

Mar dropped the now limp body to the ground and turned to Ina. She approached him, placing a hand on his chest and, noticing a slight tremor to her touch, the captain covered her hand with his own.

'Mar, the person who placed the geas on the kobold just looked at us through this one's eyes. He may know where we are now,' Ina said, biting her lip.

'How certain you are?' Ren asked, guessing Mar's thoughts.

'Certain enough to not feel safe staying here. I felt his presence when I tried to break the spell and again when he spoke to me.'

Ren nodded, and Mar looked up, seeing the first light of dawn in the sky.

'We need to go back to the burnt-out village. Then, we can decide what to do afterwards. Ren, I will need your… skills to interrogate this one.'

He noticed Ina's probing gaze when she looked between him and Ren, but she refrained from asking questions. With the drow hung over his shoulder like a sack of turnips, Mar led the group back to the cottage, hoping their belongings were still there.

It was a quiet, tense journey, and the winter sun had fully risen by the time they arrived. The abandoned buildings were eerily peaceful as they returned to their camp. Ina noticed the horses were cleaned and fed with an overly amorous Woron showing Zjawa a little too much attention for the orein's liking. The domowik had a fire going in the cottage, and the smell of a freshly cooked breakfast drifted in the breeze.

When Ina smiled at him and bowed her head, thanking the spirit for looking after their animals and belongings, the old guardian flashed her a toothless grin and disappeared back to the attic.

'He likes you.' Ina heard Ayni's voice behind her back and turned to look at the dragoness. Ayni stood there, hands on her hips, giving her a calculating stare. Ina felt she had been weighed and measured the last few days, but she didn't care if Ayni found her worthy or not.

'You say that as if it surprises you,' Ina said. She had much more to say but caught Ren observing their exchange and, mindful of Mar's words, tried to be on her best behaviour. 'Can you help me find something we can use to serve breakfast unless you prefer to eat porridge straight from the pot?'

Ayni looked at her, and Ina could almost see the tiny gears turning in her head. 'I suppose I can help,' she said, and both women started searching the hut.

Ina wanted to use the excuse of breakfast to sneak over to the shed Mar had locked the prisoner in, especially when he'd stopped her following Ren inside earlier.

'Please trust me this time. We will handle this.'

She knew walking away was a bad idea, but the look in Mar's eyes was so compelling. Now cursing herself for falling into the trap of his blue eyes, she marched to the shed under the pretext of searching for a bowl. As a visceral scream of agony tore apart the morning silence, Ina broke into a run, only to bounce off the locked door of the small building.

She saw Ren bend over the prisoner through a gap in the wall, and a gasp escaped as she caught the flash of his dagger slicing into the drow's body. Strong hands grabbed Ina from behind, spinning her around and pressing her face into warm fur, causing a numbing fear until the familiar rumbling voice soothed her jangling nerves.

'Please don't. Ren wouldn't want you to see him this way, and I had to ask him to interrogate the prisoner. We need to know what we are facing.' She knew Mar was trying to reason with her, but the fact he was trying to keep her away from an essential part of the task was irritating.

'You think I can't handle a little blood?'

'I know you can. I'm trying to protect Ren, not you. He hates this part of himself and would never forgive me if you saw it.'

More screams and cries echoed through the silent town, interspersed with muffled words. When Ren finally emerged from the shed, grabbing a handful of snow to wipe the blood off his hands, he flinched as he noticed her standing there. Ina muttered a silent curse and approached him, placing a hand on his shoulder.

'Come, breakfast is ready thanks to our host's kindness, and we don't want to offend him.' She wiped the droplet of blood from his cheek as if it was water.

His body relaxed slightly under her touch, and Ren nodded, but his eyes remained dark. 'We need to talk, then leave straight after the meal.'

Ayni gave Ina an icy stare when they entered the cottage, but she handed them three cracked bowls filled with porridge.

'What did you learn?' asked Mar.

Ren sighed and put his food aside like he'd lost his appetite. 'I didn't learn much, but enough to get me worried. First, the kobold was right. The drow leader, the deposed prince, took over the mines. He was looking for something, a tomb containing a powerful artefact, but this soldier didn't know its purpose. He knew, however, that their priorities had changed, and several drow patrols are all searching the mountains for you, Ina.'

The clatter of the witch's spoon following his words felt jarring in the sudden silence.

'Why? What would this asshole want with me?' she said, trying to brush the scattered porridge from her tunic.

'I don't know, Ina, but the soldier mentioned tal-maladie.' Ren's voice sounded grim, making her put her bowl down, her appetite lost at the worrying words.

'The obsessive madness? You think I've become the prince's latest obsession?' Ina tapped her chin, thinking loud. 'He is a mind mage, or rather archmage if he could project at such a distance, but what could a drow prince want from a Chaos mage?'

'The last drow empress, Sowenna, was a Chaos archmage, and she was buried in these mountains.' Ayni's casual remark caused a collective gasp.

'The Sowenna who re-shaped the continent in the Mage Wars? I didn't know she was a Chaos archmage,' Ina said, stunned by this revelation.

Ayni only smirked. 'It was a very long time ago, but yes, she was, and a formidable one.' She gave Ina another all-knowing smirk, and the witch barely restrained herself from punching her in the face, especially after Ayni added, 'I saw what you did at the castle with Mar and Ren, and let's not forget that the orein chose you. I think you are well on the way to becoming one yourself.'

Ina felt thankful she was sitting on the floor as the world spun around her, and breathing suddenly became difficult. She felt Mar's hand on her shoulder, steadying her.

'Ina?' His concern calmed her, and the dizziness faded.

'I won't go insane and destroy the world,' she said through clenched teeth when she could breathe again. Visions of barren lands and red dust swirling through the air haunted her dreams since Nerissa had revealed the true nature of her magic, and after Ayni's remark, they felt more like prophetic visions than dreams. 'I've never craved power,' she said, seeking understanding in his eyes, but her dragon looked troubled.

'A bane or not, only time will tell.' Ayni shrugged, and now all the silent judgement of the last few days made sense to Ina. Before she could say anything, Ren continued his report.

'That's not all. The madness that drives the drow prince has escalated. He sent messengers to the capital, Arknay, promising them the return of the Chaos empress if they helped him to take Liath. A substantial drow army may be marching towards the mountain tunnel if the current ruler believes in his vision.'

Ina felt Mar's breath quicken against her back, and guilt flooded her. Because of her magic, his home could be overrun with drow soldiers and their kobold slaves. 'I will go to the mountain caves to find this tomb. Whatever he was looking for must be connected to Chaos, and we need to keep it out of his hands and destroy it, if possible.'

'It's too dangerous, my love. You would be practically offering yourself on a silver platter. As much as I hate to think of you as a weapon, you are one, and if they use you against us, all would be lost.' Mar's sombre words reminded her of her place in this world.

'Only if they can catch me, and the last place they will search for me is on their own doorstep. If this artefact is anything like my necklace, we must ensure he doesn't get it. Mar, I can turn your father's castle into rubble with this little gem. Can we afford to risk not looking for it?'

Mar, visibly irritated, turned to Ren. 'I will go with her, or she will drug us or do something utterly stupid to get what she wants. I want you to go back to Liath. Fuck, we need all the help we can get. We will need reinforcements from the capital. See if you can draft some battle mages and healers as well. Tell my father to enlist help from the non-human races, mercenaries, and whoever else will fight for us.'

'I will go with Ren.' Ayni's quiet words were met with curious stares, and the dragon lady shrugged, seeing this. 'I'm not much help here, but maybe I can help Liath. The castle could always use a big, scary dragon.'

Ina freed herself from Mar's embrace and approached the other woman, examining her face as if looking for signs of ill intentions.

'Look after Ren, please. He means more to me than I can ever express. I may not return, and I want you to promise to make sure he is safe… and happy.'

Ayni grunted, surprised, but she whispered a quiet promise while the men exchanged embarrassed looks over their heads.

'My lady… Ina, I can look after myself.' A soft blush blossomed on Ren's cheeks as he spoke, but Ina looked at him with determination.

'I have my dragon, so now you have yours. Maybe that's our fate in this lifetime, so humour me one last time and accept her help, and if I don't come back from this journey, I want you to be happy, no matter what. Promise me you will try.'

His eyes told her he understood the message she tried to convey. It felt like her heart fragmented when she spoke, but it felt right. Ina hoped she made the right choice trusting the dragoness, but she couldn't let him live a miserable life of unrequited love chasing her ghost if she could prevent it. Ren smiled tenderly when he answered.

'If you promise to come back safely. I promise… I will try.'

Chapter Fifteen

After saying goodbye, Ina knew part of her heart would always belong to Ren. Ever since that fateful spell, there had been a bond between them, but more than that, she truly cherished and respected the warrior and cared for him deeply. If her feelings for Mar hadn't eclipsed it, then maybe it would be different, but Ina knew she couldn't have them both. It was time to let him go, even if Ayni was the one taking an interest in the reserved swordsman.

She looked at them, slowly disappearing into the distance, and sniffled, blinking away unwanted tears. She felt Mar's hand rest on her shoulder, and he leaned towards her, brushing his beard over her neck.

'I still don't like this reckless idea of going to the caverns, but letting Ren go was the right thing to do.'

Maybe, she thought, but it still left a bad taste in her mouth. It would be easy to turn and lose herself in Mar's embrace, but this wasn't the time to show weakness. With a sigh, she stepped away and turned to face him.

'Do you know the best way to the caverns?' she asked, as Mar's smile turned into a smirk at her words.

'I could lead you back to the castle, and you wouldn't even know,' he said teasingly.

'Maybe, but once I found out, would you want to face my anger?'

Ina's confidence had grown since she'd learned more about her magic. Whilst it had been difficult accepting that Chaos was not as worthless as she'd been taught, her recent adventures had given her a new appreciation for who she was and the mage she was becoming. Ina headed to the horses, unaware of the pride shining in Mar's eyes.

The small pasture behind the burnt-out barn revealed Woron digging for grass from under the snow, but Zjawa was nowhere to be found. Ina gathered up Woron's reins and led him to the cottage, tying him to a post before heading off to search for the missing orein. She found her mount in the orchard, trying to climb up an apple tree for the last winter apple. Ina rubbed her temples, marvelling at the sight, unsure if she should laugh or cry. This was more interesting than expected.

'Zjawa, come down, you bloody nuisance,' she called, but the orein just looked at her with an amused expression and grasped an even higher branch, the creaking of the limb ominous in the quiet field. Ina rolled her eyes and moved closer, just as Zjawa stretched and snatched the prize, then jumped down and trotted back to Ina, playfully nipping at her clothes, soaking her blouse with fruity drool in the process. The witch couldn't help but smile, and taking the bridle, she led the unruly mare back to the cottage. Mar raised an eyebrow at their late return but refrained from commenting and saddled both horses before turning back to Ina.

'Are you sure you want to do this, my spitfire? It won't be an easy ride. We'll have to avoid the main roads, following roads that are little more than goat trails through rocky terrain. I know where to access the mines the humans made, but I don't know the kobold passages.' She knew he was trying to discourage her from being impetuous—his tactician's mind ever cautious—but ever since Ayni mentioned the tomb of the Chaos archmage, she couldn't shake the feeling she had to go there. Ina recalled her great-aunt's favourite saying, '*The darkest place was always beneath the candle*,' and knew that to be safe, she would need to be close to that tomb when it was found.

'I know you're right, but we need to know what's going on there and either stop them or destroy the artefact before the enemy gets their hands on it. Also, bringing war to Liath when the castle is unprepared would be the worst way to repay your father's hospitality. I'm hoping Ren can muster enough soldiers to help fortify the town while the drow chases us around those mountains.'

'I still don't like it.'

'I know, but we will go anyway.'

She tried to soften her words with a smile, but his eyes flashed gold in response. She saw his jaw muscle working when Mar approached her and, placing his hand on her neck, bent down and pressed his lips to hers. She could taste his worry and anger, but soon a growl of pleasure rumbled through his chest when she nipped at his lip, openly teasing him. His mouth grew feverish and hungry, awakening her desire. She didn't understand what triggered the kiss, but she decided to enjoy it. Maybe it would be their last chance, but when his hands gripped her clothes, threatening to rip them off her, Ina pressed on Mar's chest, pushing him away while he looked at her with a sudden frown.

'Why did you stop?' he said with a golden glow still visible in his eyes.

The witch pointed to the sun that was high in the sky. 'We need to go. The drow army should chase, not catch us.'

Mar clenched his fists and slowly exhaled with closed eyes. 'So why tease me? You must know how much I need you?'

Ina smiled mischievously. 'You started it, so you are not pinning this strange punishment on me.' She finished half laughing, gasping when Mar closed the space between them and seized her waist, lifting her onto the orein.

'Yes, we need to go,' he said shortly and jumped on Woron, flicking his reins and making the stallion rear. Mar turned him to face her when the mount settled and bowed slightly. 'I apologise, my lady. I didn't mean to impose myself on you....' He stopped and took a deep breath. The helpless expression touched something deep inside her when he said, 'I just crave your touch so much.'

Mar nudged Woron forward, and they galloped down the trail, forcing Ina to rush to catch up. Zjawa's steps were light, and sitting comfortably on her back took little riding skill. Despite being a troublesome chicken-eating mountain spirit, the orein was a true blessing for someone like her, and the mare kept pace with Woron effortlessly, allowing Ina to relax.

After last night's events, she decided to give their fledgling relationship a chance. It might be a mistake, but she felt that despite the inferno of their passion, Mar kept her grounded, and for this and his touch, she was ready to give up a bit of her independence. Maybe that's why she didn't try stopping Ren from leaving with Ayni. Knowing the dragoness seemed genuinely interested in him eased the part of Ina's heart clinging to their connection. She could stop worrying about her feelings and focus on finding out why the drow prince craved Chaos magic.

The witch snapped out of her introspection and looked around. Mar was leading them up a very steep path, and she instantly regretted giving up her daydream. The path's edge was so close that even Woron trembled, but her orein had simply opened out her strange feet and continued walking, as nimble as a mountain lion, so that was probably why Ina hadn't noticed how high they were.

'Mar? When will this end?' Ina asked, flattening herself on the orein's back.

'What?' Mar said, and she could hear the tension in his voice. He didn't even look back at her, focusing on guiding Woron.

'This path, when will it end? I don't feel too confident with heights,' she said, hoping her voice did not convey too much of her terror.

'Soon. I warned you we couldn't use the regular trail, but we should arrive at a small hidden valley soon. We will rest there for the night before we enter the mines, hold on a little longer,' he said, and she could only nod.

His "soon" lasted another hour, and by the time they arrived, Ina was shivering from the cold sweat soaking through her clothes. The valley was beautiful, despite its small size, as if the gods tried to fit the prettiest things nature offered in one place. Surrounded by the high mountain walls from three sides, it had a copse of pine trees beside a small hot spring. It must have been breathtaking when the meadow flowers bloomed. Still, it left an unforgettable impression even at the beginning of winter. The ground near the water was steaming and bare, and that's where Mar led their horses. Without waiting, the captain unpacked the blankets from the saddlebags and spread them on the ground as she dismounted.

'We will stop here. This place is as safe as you could be in the mountains,' he said with a smile, amused at her awkward gymnastics.

'Stop? It's barely the afternoon.' She felt like they were wasting their time, but Mar shook his head.

'The next part is even steeper, the night falls early in the winter, and we can't let darkness surprise us when still on the trail as one slippery step will end this journey with us at the bottom of this mountain. It will be a hike, my love. We must leave the horses here and ensure they are safe while they wait. I thought we could use the remaining daylight to train if you'd like? You have learnt a lot from Ren, but I have a trick or two that might suit you.'

A hike?! Why does it have to be a hike?. Why does everything have to be so high here? Her thoughts rushed, and Ina eagerly accepted this explanation to delay the climbing, not to mention Mar threw in fighting practice as a bonus, and that was hard to resist. Sword practice was an enjoyable part of the day and would give her the perfect excuse to soak herself in the hot spring afterwards.

'Mar, is it truly safe? I mean, safe enough to have a bath?' Ina pointed at the small pond and noticed Mar's lips twitch under his beard.

'It is safe. Unless an attack comes from above, there is no chance we could miss it, and the pathway both in and out is so narrow that only one warrior could attack, so yes, you can have your bath after we finish training.'

That was enough for her. The thought of her plans for the evening put a spring in her step. She hummed cheerful tavern songs while unpacking her bags and anchored detection spells around the valley to ease her mind.

When Mar came over with two swords, rolling up his sleeves, Ina could barely focus, but when he looked at her with disappointment, she began concentrating on the fight and fought as Ren had taught her. Mar's technique was so different from the Jian kata style that it took her a moment to adjust. In short, Mar played dirty, and Ina had to admit she liked it. She was reminded of the tavern brawls with Janik. It didn't matter what you did as long as you won the fight. Ina kicked, punched, swung her sword, and attacked him with magic. Her hearty laugh echoed in the valley when, in a moment of inspiration, she turned the now muddy ground into ice, and Mar landed on his arse with a loud thud. She pointed her sword at his throat, grinning in smug satisfaction.

'You lost, dragon. Now you are mine to command,' Ina said in jest, observing how the blue colour of his irises changed, and Mar grabbed the blade of the sword, yanking her forward. She immediately released her grip on the hilt not to hurt him, but the force of his move pushed her on till she kneeled on his lap. Mar pushed his face into her midriff, inhaling her scent.

'You have no idea, you delicious woman.'

She could feel his desire and wanted him to do more, but Mar seemed frozen, holding her so tight, like his life depended on it. Ina combed her fingers through his hair, pleasantly surprised at its softness, but her encouragement brought adverse effects.

'Ina... stop.' His breath shuddered when she caressed his earlobe, and the hoarse timbre of his voice halted her movements.

'Are you all right? I didn't hurt you, did I?' she asked, but his sexy laugh reassured her.

'No, I am perfectly healthy. I'm trying hard not to rip off your clothes and take you in the snow like a brute, that's all. Holding you in my arms isn't helping.' He pushed her off his lap and stood up. 'That's all for today's training. Have your soak, and I will guard us.'

Just like that, he turned, leaving her in the middle of the valley. *I don't mind the brute,* she thought when anger from his sudden retreat turned into a plan. Ina slowly disrobed until she stood in only her thin undergarments. With a deep breath, she closed her eyes and let the valley's peace seep into her other senses, feeling an unusual amount of Chaos magic in the air, swirling around like the wind, concentrated around the golden presence of Mar's dragon. Ina licked her lips, stretching out her arms, the act pulling the thin chemise tight against her body.

She was aware that Mar watched her movements out of the corner of his eye, his restless squirming adding a slight frisson to the air as she unbraided her hair, tossing back her head with a satisfying sigh. Finally, she pulled off the chemise and tossed it aside, chuckling quietly as Mar nearly fell over openly gawking at her, but the bloody man still didn't react to this obvious invitation.

Instead, he stood there as stiff as his sword. *I want to feel how much you want me. I want my brute.* Still, he stood there, and with no other idea, Ina pulled out the heavy weapon of womankind and… she squeaked.

Mar had struggled all day to keep himself away from Ina. Last night was good and bad for many reasons. Yes, they were attacked, but they also gained valuable insight into the situation, and now he could plan their next steps. He also felt the barrier that Ina used to keep her distance had disappeared and that she was much more receptive to his love, but that opened a whole new pit of vipers.

Mar's mind drifted whilst watching her. Would he live as long as Ayni? His scattered discussions with the dragoness led him to believe it, and although he knew he would stay with her, Ina might have other plans. Mar was not sure he could face life without her if she left him.

Since becoming a dragon, his body had changed, even in his human form. He had enhanced strength and stamina, could see better during the night, and to his embarrassment, he was constantly aroused in her presence. The only way he controlled his urges was to throw himself into battle or plan for war, but now his woman welcomed him with an inviting smile and responded to his caresses, and to his peril, there were no distractions in this idyllic valley.

He knew she was undressing and tried not to look, but caught himself glancing over despite his best intentions. The pressure in his britches intensified, and Mar prayed to the mountain guardian to throw a rock on his head to stop the thoughts rushing through his mind before he acted on them and did something he would later regret. However, the mountains had no mercy for him, his muscles rigid, feeling the sweat pooling under his collar.

Ina's squeak hit him like a bullwhip, and Mar turned around, sprinting to her in a blur of golden light, sword held high and ready for mayhem. Naked and beautiful, she looked at him with a satisfied smile on her lips, confusing him completely.

'What happened?' he asked, gripping his sword to restrain his urge to have her.

'Nothing. The water is hot, that's all.'

'Ina...' He tried to close his eyes, but the image of her body was still in his head.

'Why don't you join me? I set up shields on the two paths, and you told me we are safe here,' she said, and he dared to open his eyes. She was trailing her hand over her breasts, and Mar felt all reason tumble to the floor alongside his sword. He had never undressed as quickly as he did at that moment, and while standing there naked under her appreciative gaze, he growled out the last warning.

'Are you sure? For me, this is more than a brief moment of passion, Ina. I want more. Not just your body, but all of you.' It wasn't their first time, but as their previous encounters had ended in misunderstandings and hurt feelings, he felt he had to hear her say it out loud. He didn't want to go through rejection and heartache again.

'Does a lady really have to say?' She was still teasing him, and Mar was at his wit's end. He looked at her, feeling the long nights of craving fill his eyes till finally, she took mercy on him and opened her arms.

'Yes, Mar, this means I am ready for more. Now, will you come to me, or should I wax lyrical about how much I want your touch?'

He purred in pleasure at her squeak as he gathered her into his arms and jumped into the hot spring. Mar thrust his fingers into her wild red hair and pulled Ina into a savage kiss, swallowing her groan of desire before biting, nipping and kissing his way down to her collarbone. He knew he might not have a chance to tell her again, but leaving a small mark on her skin, the dragon in his soul whispered, 'Mine.'

That one word eased the turmoil in Mar's heart and released the passion he'd held back since their reunion. He felt Ina's hands in his hair, pulling him back to her lips, his spitfire unwilling to be passive in her desire. She slid her hand between their bodies and caressed him firmly, and Mar, already struggling with control, grasped her rear, crushing their bodies together to stop the sensation.

'Ina… I'm trying not to….' It was difficult for him. He had been abstinent since their last encounter, and now just a little touch made him close to release. But how could he tell her?

'Hmm, if you grant me a second round, I don't mind.'

Her mischievous smile and hand guiding him to her entrance broke his resistance. He buckled, entering her. Ina wrapped her hands over his neck and followed his movement. He knew she was studying him and that it was too soon for her to climax, but she granted him the privilege, and he intended to pay his debt later.

'You are incredible,' she said, kissing him deeply when, after a few strokes, he grabbed her hips and slammed her hard against his cock, exploding inside her.

When the waves of pleasure faded to a reasonable level and he could think clearly again, he flashed her a sheepish smile. 'My apologies. I have never neglected a lady's needs so much.'

Ina stroked his neck and chest, playing with the soft hair, yet somehow, she looked very content.

'I liked it,' she said, looking deep into Mar's eyes and cupping his face in her hand. 'It is very flattering when a man desires you so much he loses control. It makes you feel irresistible.' She embraced his neck and moved her mouth to his earlobe, nipping it. 'But it doesn't mean I won't collect my debt.' She rocked her hips, making him laugh.

'Oh, you are most assuredly irresistible, and I am an honourable man, so lay down and take it like a lady,' he said, wrapping his arms around her and carrying his lady to the blankets.

Mar felt impossibly happy, and as he expected, Ina tried to sit up, mischief dancing in her eyes, saying, 'Is that so?'

He nuzzled her neck, gently forcing her back onto the blankets and kneeled between her legs. 'Now, my lady, time for you to submit to the true power of the Lord of Liath,' he jested, diving between her thighs. Her surprised gasp turned to moans of pleasure, and he smiled with pride. Ina's hips rocked under his touch, and her soft moans grew louder when he intensified his thrusts. Her pleasure excited him, and Mar realised how true her words were. Seeing Ina lost in her desire for his touch drove him wild. Hard as the surrounding rocks, he slowed, watching the first waves of climax course through her body before thrusting hard into her still pulsating sheath, Ina gasping and tearing his skin with her nails.

A soft growl reverberated through his body as Mar slid deeper inside her, and Ina's eyes snapped open as she lost control, her magic diving deep into his chest. Mar felt an oddly familiar sensation as the tendrils of Chaos wrapped around his soul, bleeding into the golden heart of his dragon. He could feel Ina's passion and the pleasure he gave her, and he revelled in it, but the love he felt buried in the depth of her soul drove him to the edge. This tiny but undeniable thread tied them together with a strength that astounded him.

Mar barely held on when Ina wrapped her arms around his neck and pulled him down. Wild in her passion, she looked deeply into his eyes.

'Mine,' she said, and the possessiveness in her voice sent shivers down his spine. Mar couldn't hold back any longer and gave up all restraint.

When he could think again, he rolled off her body, pulling her to his side. Mar tried to hide the triumphant smile. Ina claimed him, which was more than he could have wished to happen. He stroked her hair as she lay on his chest until she raised her head, looking at him with a sleepy smile.

'That was… nice. We need to do it again, soon.' When Mar tried to comprehend how she could call his passionate lovemaking *nice,* Ina yawned and rubbed over him like a cat.

Mar lay back and laughed, promising himself he would do more *nice* things to her, again and again, till he turned this tiny thread of love into the strongest silken rope. Until then, *nice* would be good enough for him. Holding this thought, he embraced her, getting ready for sleep.

'Mar, it is cold.'

'I will bring more blankets.' He hadn't even noticed when the wind changed direction, and it was now blowing the hot spring's warmth away from them, but when he tried to leave, Ina grabbed his hand.

'I don't need blankets. I need a dragon.'

'What?' he said, confused at this bizarre request.

'Your body is so hot when you are in dragon form.' It was Ina's turn to flash a sheepish smile. 'Please, can I have my dragon?'

His heavy sigh followed her words, but deep inside, Mar felt joy that she so eagerly accepted his other form. He moved away to a suitable distance, looking at Ina dressing in tunic and trousers, and changed his shape. The witch came to him and nodded with appreciation.

'Now sit and curl up,' she ordered, and he rolled his eyes.

'I'm not a dog.' His deep voice made her raise her head, and Ina looked at him so intensely that he followed her request with a grumpy, 'Fine.'

As soon as he was curled up, Ina grabbed a blanket, nestled herself into the bend of his foreleg, and sighed happily.

'This is perfect. Your dragon is perfect and hot like a furnace.'

Mar coiled around her body, inhaling her scent. She smelled of him, and he realised he liked this strange arrangement. Soon she drifted off, and he knew she was deeply asleep when a soft snore disturbed the night's peace. Mar stretched out his wing when snow began falling, sheltering her from the elements. He didn't feel tired, and he could guard her forever for just one smile. His forked tongue slid out and gently touched the sleeping woman's cheek as he once again whispered, 'Mine.'

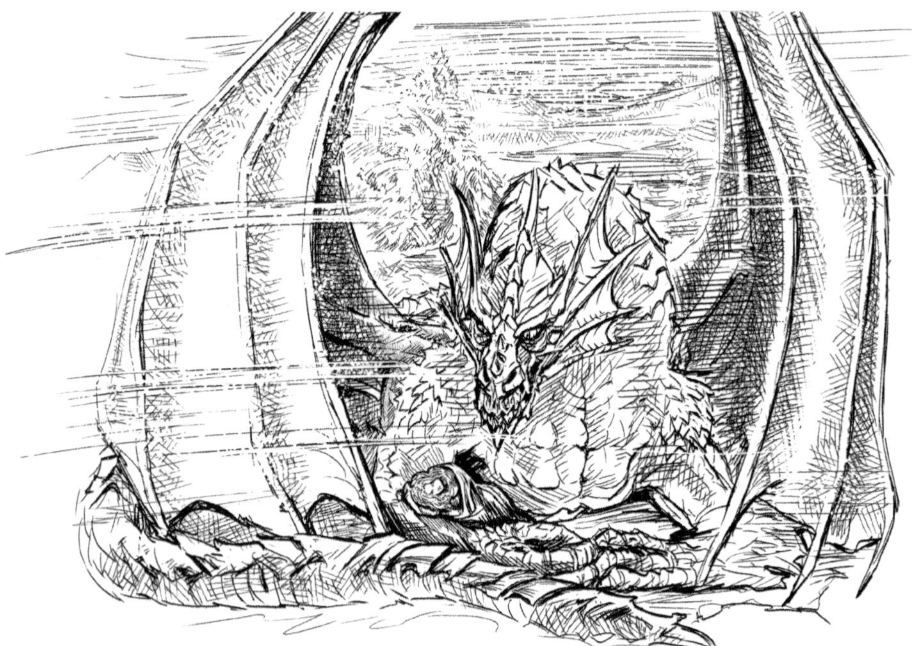

CHAPTER SIXTEEN

Tar'eth didn't feel the freezing touch of the wind as it lashed against the stone balcony. He looked at the vast open space below. A kingdom he had conquered using his wits and brutality, so despite his brother's manipulations forcing him to come here and "secure the tunnel", he had succeeded and discovered a whole new opportunity. One he grasped with both hands, and, forcing the kobolds to work for him, Tar'eth had imposed a hefty tax on the use of the route under the mountains, which meant the dwarves of the Stone Halls now paid handsomely not to lose their livelihood.

Ord'eth thought he'd secured a glorious victory by arranging the loss of his title, but he hadn't counted on Tar'eth's schemes. After a confidant mentioned hearing of a reference to a powerful artefact, he'd spent countless hours in the royal library and had discovered the whereabouts of a treasure beyond imagination.

Empress Sowenna, the creator of the Chaos regalia, was buried in these mountains. Tar'eth looked at his ring and smiled. It was the weakest of the set, given to him by his friend, though the necromancer never said where he found it. Still, that didn't matter. Soon he would possess the remaining pieces, and then they would see who deserved to rule Arknay.

Now, looking down, he had no regrets about his circumstances. In this almost desolate landscape, there was no one to command him, and further down the mountain below was the woman who would be his queen. He would have her, and she would become the perfect weapon after he moulded her mind to his liking.

He still struggled to believe the words written about the raw power of Chaos and its bearers. Mages who could connect with the very source of life and use its magic were rare gems. However, in their stupidity, humans called them abominations, and now Tar'eth had another opportunity, one that would leave him in control of a Chaos mage before she discovered the true extent of her power.

His hands gripped the stone railing as he closed his eyes, recalling the alluring touch of her soul when she wrestled with the geas placed in the kobold's mind. Ina had been magnificent, nearly breaking through his magic, and if not for his reinforcing the spell through his servant, she would have freed the unfortunate soldier's psyche.

Tar'eth took a deep breath, the icy air almost searing his lungs. He revelled in the memory of the witch's immense power. She was untrained, acting mainly on impulse, and it didn't help that he was distracted by the sheer beauty of her magic.

I must grasp her mind before she sees me and lashes out, Tar'eth thought, his mind racing with excitement as he planned Ina's capture. It wouldn't be a problem if he could get close enough, but how would he do that when her guard dogs surrounded her?

At that thought, Tar'eth remembered his new pet and turned to the woman standing silently in her porcelain mask.

'Call my guards, girl.' He knew she would fulfil his order. Since the night he'd invaded her mind, he had total control over her actions. He filled her with love and awe for her new master, and his little doll tried anticipating his every wish, fulfilling it even before he said a word.

There were no boundaries she wouldn't cross for a scrap of his affection, and Tar'eth wondered if it would be the same with Ina. He congratulated himself on the success of his experiment, and it was gratifying to have someone who worshipped him like a god.

He looked down, and a smug smile crawled over his lips. It was not just about Ina, but also about hunting her lover. There hadn't been a dragon hunt in centuries, and he would hang the beast's head in his halls. Tar'eth wouldn't be satisfied with anything less.

'You wished to see me, my lord?' asked the guard who entered his chambers. The woman took her post next to the wall, and the prince gestured for the guard to join him, surprising the young drow at the familiarity.

'Prepare my personal troop and my horse. We are going on a hunt.' Tar'eth's lazy smile widened as he stretched, bones creaking and stiff muscles protesting the movement. Sentient prey was a challenge he gladly welcomed, and it gave him a chance to escape the gloomy halls of the kobold's underground citadel. Gods knew he needed it. He was getting out of shape, sitting on that misshapen throne.

The guard saluted and left to fulfil his order, and the prince felt a soft female hand on his forearm. His pet was looking at him, tilting her head, and Tar'eth, feeling generous, patted her hand.

'No, you are staying here. Get everything ready for your new mistress to ensure she receives the best care.'

With his fiery witch beside him, he could return to Arknay as the first male ruler in centuries. He smiled viciously, his mind turning eastward. Or were his goals too small? With enough soldiers and Ina as his most potent weapon, why should he limit himself to the land on one side of the mountains? Perhaps it was time there was only one ruler of Warenga, a true emperor of the land.

Tar'eth turned around and quickened his step, arriving in the map room at breakneck speed. He unwrapped ancient scrolls and his latest maps, tracing the passages through the mountains. He had to admit, the kobolds charts were very precise. Tar'eth located the shortest route between the citadel and the village. His troops had pillaged the area so many times there were no defences left, so if he rushed there, he could catch the witch and her company before they were ready to depart. *What if they had already escaped?* This thought gave him pause, and looking again, Tar'eth marked down places for a suitable camp. *I need to leave a small group there with sentinels to alert me on the sight of her or the dragon. You are not escaping me, my beautiful Chaos, not now, not when I have you so close.*

The prince ran from the room and down the stairs two steps at a time towards the citadel's only exit. His horse was there, a slender brown stallion, its sides covered with scars from his whip. As Tar'eth patted the animal's head, it flinched but didn't step away. The guards weren't ready yet, but the excitement of the upcoming hunt and the proximity of his prize made him reckless. Tar'eth jumped on the horse, throwing the marked map to the surprised guard and snapped out a command.

'Catch up with me on the way, and don't dawdle too much.' He kicked his mount's sides and galloped into the black entrance of the gates, leaving his soldiers scrambling to catch up.

Ina stretched languorously and slid her hand over warm, scaled skin. The heat of Mar's body felt so decadent she wanted to wrap herself up in his embrace for the entire day.

Their night together had been one to remember, and the gentle throbbing in her nether region reminded her of Mar's eagerness to pay his debt. *Who knew his beard could be used in such an exciting way?* She smiled, stroking his scales and delaying the inevitable moment she would have to open her eyes and face the troubles ahead. *I know I'm a difficult woman, and you are insane for sticking around, but you do, and I'm so grateful I don't have to face it all alone.* It had taken her a long time to accept her feelings, but she didn't want to feel miserable and alone any longer. Ina sighed, simply happy with this man and surprised that, for the first time, she didn't feel her usual need to run away with the first rays of the sun, leaving her lover questioning the night's events.

Slowly opening her eyes, she gasped, staring straight into the glowing eyes of the dragon. Mar blinked when she yawned again, and his forked tongue trailed on the naked skin of her calf. Ina could swear he was grinning mischievously when she snatched her leg away.

'Don't give me ideas, or this witch will renounce any responsibility for her future actions,' she jested before standing up and walking to the hot springs, acutely aware he was still watching her. She washed quickly, knowing she wouldn't get another chance anytime soon. After turning back, she saw Mar was in his human shape, displaying his shapely naked buttocks to the world as he headed towards the horses.

'For fuck's sake, dress yourself, you shameless lizard.' She grabbed a handful of snow and threw the snowball, aiming for his rear end.

Bloody tease is doing this on purpose, Ina thought, refusing to look away. Sulking as he wiped away the wet snow, Mar huffed.

'I was going to grab a clean shirt, but please, be my guest if you like me smelly.' He spread his arms, showing off his massive body, and started walking in her direction with a threatening expression.

'Oh no, you don't.' She flicked her wrist and, with a magical push, forced him into the hot water, smiling when he burst into laughter and started washing.

If I'm going to fight for Liath, at least I will be fighting for someone I care for, she thought, looking at him. He smiled more often lately, and their interactions felt so natural that she could not believe he was the same grumpy oaf left half dead at her hut in the forest. Or maybe she had changed, had softened around the edges?

Unaware of her thoughts, Mar kissed the top of her head and went to the horses. Ina watched as he stripped off their bridles. He must have noticed her curious gaze, because he immediately explained.

'Just in case, Woron will find the way to the castle if needed. That way, at least someone will know there was trouble.'

She felt they were both delaying their departure, attempting to prolong the last moment of happiness before descending into the mines in search of an unknown artefact. Ina suspected Mar also thought they might not return from this impossible mission she'd dragged him into so thoughtlessly.

'I don't want you to go. Liath needs you, and if you think we may…' Ina stopped, biting her lip, unsure how to ask him to return home. She didn't want him to endanger his life, even though she felt she had to go.

'No.' Mar approached and placed his hands on her shoulders. 'I'm going, and don't even think about trying to antagonise me into leaving. It won't work anymore, Ina. Not after I finally got to know you.'

'I would never—' she started, full of righteous indignation, but Mar just laughed.

'Oh, you would. If you thought it would work, you would drug me, make me angry, or send me flying through a door. You only worry that my enticing body or dragon's roar will attract unwanted attention. I know you and your methods to remove obstacles when you think you are right.' Mar shook his head, amused by her stormy expression, then playfully swatted her backside.

'Enough procrastinating, my spitfire. We need to go. There is some climbing ahead, and I don't want to do it after dark.'

Ina was going to argue, but changed her mind and shrugged, muttering under her breath. 'He gives me a few hours of pleasure, and now he thinks he can tell me what to do. Men!' She packed a few necessary items and soon stood next to him at the entrance to the second path. When Mar passed her a rope, she looked at him sceptically.

'I told you, we will have to climb. I want you to secure yourself to me. There's a good chance I'll need to pull you up if you slip. I don't want to reveal my dragon unless we have to.'

‘So why don’t we fly there?’ she asked and frowned when he raised his eyebrow.

‘I just told you. Because I’m an enormous, very conspicuous dragon, and we are trying to be stealthy.’ Noticing her slight frown, he pointed to the valley. ‘My eyesight is better now, and although it is difficult to see, there are patrols spread all over the burnt village and the valley below like ants. If they spot the direction of our flight, we will have them at our throats in no time, and I don’t want to compete with kobolds and drows to see who fights better in the mines. Our only chance is to enter the mine, pretend to be human slaves if detected, and hope that whatever pushed you to make this insane journey will send you to the right place.’

Ina felt a blush warming her cheeks. She’d asked a stupid question and deserved that answer. She lowered her eyes to the rope and focused on tying it around her waist. Mar came closer and checked the knots before heading up the steep path. She felt dizzy and confused when he asked her to go first, but she trusted his judgement. Once he demonstrated how to grip the rock, Ina followed his example. For the next hour, they shuffled step by step, face to the granite wall on a ledge that was so narrow it took her breath away to even think about it. Mar’s hand gripped her shoulder just as she felt she couldn’t take it anymore.

‘Hold on a little longer. The path should widen soon, and the route will be easier.’ His words helped, but only until Ina’s hands grew numb from gripping the rock face. Her mind drifted, and she felt strangely warm despite the weather worsening. Her foot slipped, and she would have fallen without the firm hand that grabbed her coat. Ina looked at Mar, who pushed her forward with an unyielding expression.

When the path finally widened enough to relax, Ina was swiftly gathered into the warm arms of her dragon, his hot breath breathing life back into her frozen fingers.

'I'm fine,' she said, fighting to control her chattering teeth.

'No, you are not, and I'm the idiot who allowed this to happen. You are already half-frozen and losing your focus. Get on my back, Ina. We need to get to the cave.'

'No need, I'm fine,' she argued, but Mar leaned down and lifted her into his arms, ignoring the squeal of terror she made as her feet left the floor.

'Ina, I'm a fucking dragon. I'm stronger than I was, and you are lighter than a feather, so one more word and I will change and fly you back to Liath, understood?'

She mumbled obscenities into Mar's chest, eyes squeezed shut, embarrassed at the noise she'd made when her feet left the ground, before nodding her acquiescence. After taking a moment to be sure his woman wasn't going to argue, the captain swept his cloak over her body and set off once more along the path.

'I'm sorry.' Mar's words stunned her, and Ina looked up, intrigued, wondering what would come next. After a moment's silence, his steps never faltering, he finally said, 'I shouldn't snap at you, but I can't stand the thought of you being hurt, and I end up being the one who hurts you with my stupid temper.'

His tightened jaw amused her. The Mar she knew changed so much and now offered an apology for a few harsh words? No, she better set this straight right now before he started apologising for every little squabble. She was far too comfortable in his arms, and the view was also good.

'Don't appologise, I know you care for me. Besides, if you make me angry, I can always throw you on your butt with my magic, but you are cute when you get overprotective. Like a wrathful god with a bushy beard and golden eyes. Lately, I find it very appealing.' She teased him, stroking his neck, and the initial disbelief in his eyes turned into amusement. Mar shook his head, chuckling softly and kissing her hair.

'You are impossible. I should toss you on your arse,' he said when she pulled his ear.

'You should,' Ina agreed, 'but I'm too much of a catch to throw away, and once we are safe in Liath, I want to show you what one very skilful elf taught me to do with my tongue.'

A growling purr rumbled in his chest till he breathlessly said, 'You have no sense of timing, woman, but I will hold you to that.'

The entrance to the cavern stood before them like the gaping mouth of a giant, and Ina couldn't stop looking at it, her heart full of foreboding. Mar finally lowered her legs to the ground as they approached the dark tunnel, and Ina rubbed her numb limbs, clearing her throat in trepidation.

'Are you sure this is the entrance?' she asked, but the strange pull and warmth radiating from her peridot already told her they had found the right place.

'I'm not sure of anything. I saw a map long ago in the outpost I was guarding, but even then, those places were marked as unstable. I don't know any other way except the main tunnels and this. Somewhere in this cavern is a shaft that leads to the kobold mines. That's all I know.'

'Wonderful, the perfect way to discover new fears.' Ina tried to be enthusiastic despite the fear of being buried alive under the mountain. Her exclamation caused Mar to frown, placing his hand over her mouth.

'We need to be quiet until we know if it's guarded. Please stay here and watch the road below while I check the entrance.' Anticipating her protest, he added, 'I see better in the dark now, and your magic works better out in the open. Let's take advantage of it.'

Soon after, Mar disappeared into the cave's depths, and with nothing better to do, Ina crouched down, looking at the valley below. Twilight was upon them, and she didn't need to strain her eyes to see the flickering light of torches moving erratically at the bottom of the trail. Ina ducked down, lying on the frozen ground till Mar returned from his reconnaissance, and, pointing down the track, she asked, 'What do you think?'

'They are set on hunting you. The drow made his intentions clear,' Mar said and pulled her from the edge. 'Come. The tunnel is clear, and we need to get out of the open, especially now when the wind is blowing towards them. We will be easy prey if they have dogs.'

Ina followed Mar, but he still sensed the shudder she gave crossing the threshold of the cave.

'Are you cold?' he asked, wrapping his cloak around her without waiting for her answer.

'No, but I have this strange sensation, not to mention I just don't like the idea of an entire mountain over my head. Is it safe to create a small light?' Her answer made him smile, and he reached for her hand.

'Wait a little longer to avoid anyone outside seeing it. We'll make camp once we're further down the tunnel.'

After she tripped for the third time on the uneven ground, Mar took Ina into his arms and guided her down the sloping cavern. The keen-eyed dragon kept sheltering her head when she almost hit it on the protruding rocks. After a short time, he stopped and whispered in her ear.

'You can light your pulsar now.'

Ina immediately obliged, and a small orb revealed a stone chamber with remains of the rotten table and similarly decayed chair. Initially blinded by the light, it took her a moment to notice another dark entrance on the opposite side, and the witch sighed deeply. Something here was calling to her, not that she could identify the source or nature of the call, but she felt the need to go forward. Taking a few unsteady steps forward, she was surprised by Mar's grasp on her forearm, stopping her movement.

'Ina? What are you doing?'

His concern was palpable, but she didn't know how to answer this simple question. The call intensified, and Ina moved forward again, still held by her burly protector.

'What's wrong, my love?'

'I don't know. Something is there, and it is… mine? Or wants to be mine,' she said, stuttering when she tried to find the right words, eyes unfocused and distracted. Mar pulled her closer, shaking her gently.

'I don't like this. From the beginning, the idea of coming here was insane. It felt like something was manipulating us—me to choose this direction. A moment ago, you were enchanted. As if you looked upon the lands of Nawia. We will go home tomorrow. We just need to wait till the search party leaves the valley.' His concern sharpened her focus and broke whatever was enthralling her. Ina buried her face in his chest and inhaled deeply, instantly regretting it. Mar's unique scent, which she could only describe as hot iron, was still there, but deeply buried under the pungent aroma of sweaty clothes, soot, and blood. Ina pushed him away with a pitiful moan.

'Gods, Mar, you stink like a pack mule.'

Mar raised an eyebrow. 'You mean a pack mule who carried you here? Now, don't change the subject. We are going home tomorrow,' he said, but she noticed he tried to sniff his clothes discreetly. Quietly, she agreed with him but didn't want to express the fear that they'd been led here like puppets on a string. She had to distract herself, and teasing Mar was the easiest way. Mind magic of any sort terrified her, and she could still feel the strange pull, even if now it sat in the back of her mind, leaving her free to focus on setting up a small camp for them. She glanced at Mar, but he didn't notice her worry.

I still need to find what is hidden here, but will I be able to control it, or will it control me? The more she thought about it, the more terrifying the prospect became in her mind. Soon, Ina felt she had to focus her attention elsewhere, or she would start screaming They sat on the floor with only a blanket protecting them from the cold floor, and the dragon wrapped his cloak around her shoulders.

'Do you think Ren and Ayni are safe?' she asked, voicing the burning anxiety she had felt since she noticed the search party in the valley.

'It is difficult to catch the Ghost, so I'm sure they are halfway to Liath by now. Or are you worried Ayni will take advantage of him in the bushes?' She knew Mar had noticed her trepidation and was teasing her as a distraction, but somehow, the idea of her gentle warrior with the other woman made her unreasonably angry.

'Both. I worry about both. I don't want Ren to suffer,' she said and turned her face away from him before adding quietly, 'I don't want to lose my friend.'

Mar sighed heavily and pressed her back to his chest, and against her better judgment, she said, 'I know it is irrational, but it feels odd not to have him around.' She was silent for a moment, enjoying his touch, but the more she thought about Ren, the more she felt she must confess to Mar.

'I know Ren loves me, and it is not just because of the spell,' she said, and Mar nodded. Slightly offended by the lack of a more intense reaction, Ina added, 'The night you fought with him. We were in my bed, and… well, we went pretty far before we stopped.' She could feel Mar's arms tighten around her before he put his chin on her shoulder.

'I know. Ren told me the day you went to get your horse. I'm not happy about it, but I can't blame you or him. I knew he loved you even when we were in Osterad, and I turned up with a woman claiming to be my wife. The ugly truth is, I would've done the same, or more, if you had chosen Ren, and I had a chance at changing your mind.'

Ina smiled and drew a small circle on his skin. 'Would you really?'

He nodded, and she placed a small kiss on his cheek. 'That is a strange turn of events comparing to a day you called me a whore.'

Mar winced at the reminder of their first meeting and replied with a cheeky smile. 'I barely came back from the dead that day, what did you expect? But I'm still considering removing all the doors from our home,' Mar said, and Ina's back straightened instantly, with tendrils of Chaos reaching to the walls.

'Our what?' she asked, her voice suddenly panicked when the shadow of a burly man appeared in the faint light of the pulsar and the tunnel roof came crashing down.

CHAPTER SEVENTEEN

Ren felt Ina watching him as they left the abandoned village. His heart yearned to go with her and Mar, but he knew Liath would be overwhelmed if they weren't warned and reinforced. He didn't understand this sudden obsession to search for an unnamed treasure when the threat of war was at hand, but he had learned that Ina and her intuition were not to be argued with, so it was up to him to carry the burden of protecting his friend's home.

There was no getting past the bittersweet taste of their parting. Ina, despite her apparent sadness, had made it obvious she wanted him to move on from his yearning for her, even going so far as pushing him towards Ayni, and Ren admitted to himself that the dragoness was an extraordinary woman; beautiful, clever and, despite the coldness between herself and his friend, Ayni was more than warm when her eyes turned his way. With a shake of his head, Ren sighed. It felt wrong to think of another woman when Ina was lodged firmly in his heart. Still, he would wait and see. The thought brought a smile to his lips. It seemed Ina's attitude towards problems had rubbed off on him.

'You are smiling.' Ayni's voice woke him from his musing. 'Care to share your thoughts?'

'I was thinking of Ina and her unique way of dealing with problems,' he said, observing Ayni's brows knit together and then her back as she urged her horse into a trot. It took him a few moments to catch up with her.

'Why don't you like Ina? Is it because of Mar?' He knew he shouldn't ask, but curiosity got the better of him. Her response took him aback.

'It's not that I don't like her, but I don't like how you and Mar look at her. Like she has no flaws, just pure perfection that no other woman can compare to.' The snap answer made him shake his head in disbelief. The two women were similar in many aspects, but Ayni was oblivious to it, much to his amusement.

'Ina has many flaws, but she also has a heart in the right place. She saved our lives, at substantial risk to her own, with no interest in reward. Especially not with me.'

Ayni hung her head, and for a moment, they rode in silence while he pondered on Ina's goodbye. He promised her he would try to be happy, and so far, he was not trying very hard.

'It must be challenging to live as a dragon around humans,' he said, trying to build a connection, giving her a shy smile when Ayni turned around to look at him.

'It's not too bad, not now anyway. You might even brush shoulders with a dragon without realising it. Still, there aren't many of us, as we are good at hiding, and it gets lonely when you can't share what you truly are,' she said, and Ren nodded. He understood all too well. Before Ina, there had only been Mar,

Senad, and occasionally, Daro who he could open up to, but even with them, Ren rarely mentioned the longing for his home in Yanwo. The warrior supposed that was why Ayni had fought so hard for Mar. Life must feel less lonely when you find someone who was the same as you.

'Forgive me asking, but you don't seem upset now that Mar is gone. Do you love him?'

'No, I never did. I thought maybe I would, given time. I felt lonely and wanted a partner, and I made a mistake. He is a fine man and an even better dragon. Dragon males are arrogant and possessive. With him, it was different. It was fun to teach him instead of competing for dominance, and I thought, why not? Later, it was just my pride.' Ayni laughed bitterly, and Ren instinctively moved his horse closer. 'I'm not used to a mere human taking a man from me, but I'm old enough to know better. Still, it was very vexing.'

The corner of Ren's lips twitched as he restrained his laugh. 'I have to agree with you there. Ina can be very vexing, primarily to Mar, but she is not selective in this matter.'

Ayni raised her eyebrow, seeing his half-smile. 'Now, your turn to answer. Do you love her?'

'I do, but it is unrequited.' Ren's face was frozen in an unreadable expression. Still, he had started this conversation, and with Ayni answering openly, it was only fair he did the same.

'So why did you let her go with Mar? Why didn't you fight for her?' Ayni appeared intrigued, and he deeply regretted his initial curiosity. As much as he would like to avoid this answer, there was no turning back without hurt feelings.

'I did, and I lost. Ina loves me, in a way, but her feelings for Mar are a blazing inferno that burns so bright everything else lives in the shadows. I could keep trying, but that would only hurt everyone, or I could step aside, letting the people I cherish most be happy. It may be a pale consolation, but it will be enough.' He heard the sadness seeping into his voice and lowered his head. The last thing he wanted was her pity. Ren couldn't see, but to his side, Ayni's eyes lost their youthful veneer and shone with the look of someone much older and wiser, their depths filled with astonishment and compassion. It took a moment for Ren to compose himself, but when he raised his head, his face was calm and peaceful—the mask of the Ghost.

'We need to rest somewhere for the night. If I remember the map, there should be a forester's camp somewhere nearby, and in the morning, we will head off to Liath.'

For the next few hours, they pushed their horses through the drifted snow, only occasionally exchanging a word or two about their surroundings. Dusk was creeping upon them when they found the camp with a solid, well-maintained shack. Ren scouted around, but apart from a few signs of recent habitation, he couldn't find anything suspicious, and they headed inside.

Ren looked after the horses while Ayni unpacked their food and started the fire. The building warmed up quickly, and after eating a small meal, Ren took a pouch from his belt, pouring a small measure of dried leaves into a small pot before adding the water Ayni had boiled over the fire. Each movement made by the warrior gave the impression of a personal ritual, all carried out in silence before he poured a pale liquid into two cups he'd produced from gods knew where. After handing the dragoness a cup, Ren touched his forehead with the remaining cup before taking a sip of the liquid, then started preparing his bed for the night, placing his blanket next to the entrance, intending to guard them through the night. Ayni cocked her head, curious about her companion's actions, but decided against disturbing the silence, readying her bed and sipping the pale drink only to moan in pleasure at the delicate flavour. Ren looked over with a sly smile before nodding and lying down to sleep.

Exhausted by their journey through the challenging conditions, the travellers were soon asleep, but Ren's dreams were plagued by fangs and claws flashing in front of his eyes despite the relaxing tea they'd drunk. With a jolt, his eyes flew open, and it seemed as if his dream was suddenly made flesh as the teeth of a snarling beast confronted him. Ren instinctively reached for his sword, finding nothing but empty space. He cursed himself for his failure and leapt to his feet, ready to fight barehanded to protect Ayni.

'What the hell are you doing in my home?'

Ren stood still, not making any unnecessary movements to avoid provoking an attack. He noticed Ayni's eyes open, and she looked at him with a visibly tense posture. He gestured for her to stay still and bowed his head lightly to the massive werewolf.

'My apologies. We were looking for shelter, and this shack looked empty. I thought all the settlers in this region had left due to the kobold attacks.'

The werewolf looked at him and huffed in disdain. 'Humans left. My clan still controls these lands, and you are trespassing.'

Ren began gathering their belongings from the floor, but the werewolf stopped him. 'What are you doing? Do you think I'm an animal to disregard the laws of hospitality? Share your names, and I will grant you grace for the night. Tomorrow is early enough for you to leave our territory.'

Ghost thought luck must be on their side and looked at their host, who disappeared behind a curtain, only to emerge as a very shaggy-looking human.

'Have you eaten?'

'Yes, we came with our own supplies,' Ren said, unsure whether their host was offering to feed them.

The man huffed and sat at the table with a large portion of smoked ham.

'So what are you doing here? Travellers are not common in my lands, even during more peaceful times.'

'You are right,' Ren said, and following his instinct, he added, 'War is headed here soon, not just the raiding by the kobolds, but a drow army that will overwhelm your people. It would be better to seek shelter in Liath, and they could use your strength to defend their walls.'

The man looked at him with bitter amusement in his eyes. 'And who are you to issue an invitation to the high castle? Shifter clans aren't welcome in human cities unless collared as slaves.'

'I am Sa'Ren Gerel, second in command under Marcach, the scion of Liath.' Ren knew he was exaggerating his position, but having powerful shifters defend the city was too tempting. They were vicious fighters, and Liath needed all the help they could muster. 'You and your clan, or any others who join the defenders, are welcome. Times are changing, and if Liath falls, do you want to live under the dominion of the drow? We both know they will hunt your kin for sport and use them in their arenas.'

The man scratched his neck, not bothering to hide his scepticism, but after a moment of pondering, the werewolf answered.

'I will share your offer with my people and show you a quicker route to the castle tomorrow, but if we decide to join you, we will fight as equals, not as fodder for the battlefield.'

Ren reached out his arm, and after a moment of hesitation, the werewolf clasped it in his massive grip. 'We will welcome you as equals, on my honour,' Ren said, and the burly man nodded and pointed to his blankets.

'Sleep now, it will be a hard journey tomorrow, but you will get to the castle before the afternoon.' His gaze fell on Ayni, who stood up from the cot, approached Ren, and pointed to his makeshift bed.

'Do you mind? I don't want to take someone's place, especially after we invaded his home.'

That was an awkward solution, but the hut was too small for another bedding. With no reason to protest, Ren lay down on the blankets, resigning himself to a restless night next to Ayni's softly feminine presence. Before sleep gathered him into its warm embrace, he felt Ayni's hand drift down and gently touch his fingers in a coy gesture so unexpected of a mischievous dragoness.

As the werewolf promised, it only took half a day to get to Liath. The horses were at the end of their stamina, trying to keep up with the agile beast who led them, but Ren didn't slow down.

As they arrived at the castle, Ren was surprised by how quiet it was, with nothing but the usual street activity. No soldiers patrolled the area, and no extra soldiers guarded the walls.

Ren knew he would have a challenging conversation with the old duke. With limited resources, the defences looked sparse, and he had no ready solution on how to fix it. On top of that, Ren had returned for the second time without his son. The werewolf had left them some time ago, but Ren had at least a promise of consideration, and he hoped the shifter clans would take advantage of his offer of cooperation.

He sent Ayni off with a smile, nodded an acknowledgement to the guards, and entered Alleron's office. As expected, the lord of Liath sat there with a deep frown. When he saw Ren, he sighed and massaged his temples.

'Did you lose my son again, Sa'Ren?'

Ren bowed deeply, taking this moment to compose himself before delivering the information that would upset the man in front of him.

'After an encounter in an abandoned village near the mountain, Mar and Ina went to investigate the kobold mines looking for an artefact we learned about from a prisoner we captured. Ina believes it was the main reason they were here and something that would allow the drow army to overwhelm any army they faced.'

Alleron stood up from his chair and started pacing around the room. Ren observed his movement, noticing the old noble growing increasingly agitated. A hollow thud shook the room when he slammed his fists on the desk.

'That bloody fool going into this viper's pit, and for what? To please the woman who doesn't even want him by her side?' Turning towards Ren, his narrowed eyes almost made the warrior flinch. 'You brought her here. You should have gone with her, not my son.'

The fear and concern in the old man's voice were palpable, and Ren didn't hold his outburst against him. Instead, he answered calmly.

'I would if they had let me, but wherever they are now is beyond anyone's control, so let's focus on why Mar sent me here.' He gave Alleron a moment to contain his emotions. When the cold military commander replaced the concerned father, Ren said, 'We captured a drow soldier. It appears the kobolds are just tools in the hands of a drow prince. He wants an artefact hidden under the mountains, Liath, and Ina's magic. As we speak, they are gathering an army along with mages, and since they took over the trade tunnel, there is nothing to prevent reinforcements from Arknay.'

Alleron rubbed the bridge of his nose and inhaled deeply. 'And my idiot of a son will deliver him the Chaos mage on the silver platter instead of bringing her to Liath.' He looked at Ren, his eyes sharpening like an old hawk. 'You will stand in as his proxy and help me organise the defences. We need to prepare for a siege, and if the drow turns Ina against us, then I hope the gods have mercy on us all, as I do not know how to fight her magic.'

Ren saluted. 'I will do my best and… please trust them. What they're looking for is important.'

The next several hours they spent discussing the castle defences and its garrison, and it was painfully clear that years under Sophia's governance had depleted the once-powerful army of Liath. Lack of supplies had prevented keeping a large-scale force. The quality of the armour and weapons were no longer the standard suitable for elite fighters. As his last letter didn't bring them the expected resources, thankfully, Alleron welcomed Ren's attempt to recruit shifter clans to join their defences.

'We need more, Ren, to withstand a winter siege. I wrote to the king once, but I will ask you to do it again. If he doesn't have soldiers, maybe we could have money, so we can at least enlist the free companies.' The old man slumped in his chair, and Ren approached him.

'I know we discussed this before, and I'm sure you tried this as well, but I will write to the Mages Council. They must be able to send us some assistance, and there are guards in the palace, if Daro can spare them.' Ren felt something important was fleeing his memory before recalling the dwarves they saved in the blizzard. 'This is probably a slim chance, but the Stone Halls have a life debt with Ina. If we could get a message to Vorberg Stonemeir… they may choose to offer some help.'

Alleron looked at him like he had suddenly grown a pair of horns. 'How did this mage earn a life debt from a dwarf elder? Are you sure of it?'

Ren smirked. 'Ina has many gifts, and somehow getting people to owe her their life is one of them. I owe her mine, and so do your son and the king.'

Alleron looked at him for a moment, then burst out laughing. 'I will leave you to it. I will see to the regular army and leave you to deal with our colourful reinforcements. Now go. I have letters to write and ledgers to check.'

Ren felt relief exiting the room. The meeting, whilst challenging, ended much more positively than expected. Heading upstairs, he thought about all the little coincidences around Ina that eventually led to unexpected opportunities. The quiet warrior grabbed a passing servant and ordered food and drinks to be delivered to his room. Later, sitting at his desk with a small quill, he wrote an official letter to the king and the Magical Council detailing the current dangers and asking for reinforcements. Similarly, the second letter was sent to the Stone Halls, asking for any help they felt appropriate and could deliver. Ren just hoped they could get the letter to the isolated dwarves.

With those two sent, he penned a heartfelt letter to Daro. He didn't hide anything. His friend would be responsible for the defence of Osterad if Liath fell, and after a moment's hesitation, he wrote to Nerissa, the old healer who'd helped them in the past and deserved to know the situation.

The moon was high as Ren finished the last letter and stood up, stretching his muscles. The cold air that blew into his face when he opened the window gave him goosebumps, but the view was worth it. Covered in a thick layer of snow, the castle garden looked so peaceful and ethereal that Ren wanted to immerse himself in its serenity. He grabbed his coat and flute and walked out as quietly as possible to not awaken the sleeping residents. Snow crunched under his feet, and Ren savoured the crisp air, moonlight guiding his footsteps. It took a moment to find the perfect spot, a tall granite rock, that he leaned against before placing the flute to his lips.

A light melody filled the air, and he let his fingers slide over the instrument, changing the original song. His feelings seeped into the tune, and a lonely, longing note glided over the frozen lake. Ren closed his eyes and reflected on his past. Yanwo's beauty and his exile were entwined with Ina's unconditional acceptance, her tender touch, and Mar's brotherhood. The decisions he made that led to this moment left him burdened with so much responsibility and no one to share the struggle with, and now Ren felt so lonely and close to breaking.

Cold, slender fingers touched his cheek, taking him by surprise. The melody faltered, and Ren opened his eyes to see Ayni standing in front of him, wrapped in a heavy fur coat, with tears in her eyes.

'It's so beautiful and so heartbreaking. I wish things could be different for you,' she said, and he felt tingles of warmth spreading through his chest. An embarrassed smile blossomed on his lips when he spoke.

'I'm sorry to wake you, my lady. I couldn't sleep, but I thought I was far enough away from the castle not to wake anyone up.'

Ayni inhaled, blinking her unwanted tears away, and chuckled softly. 'Well, you woke up the dogs and me. Dragons have very sharp hearing, and when I heard your melody, I had to come. Would you play some more for me?'

The overwhelming loneliness eased with her touch, and when he continued his tune, the soft notes washed over the small courtyard. Ayni sat beside him, leaning her shoulder gently against his. The touch of her hand on his chest as he missed a note calmed him, and Ren smiled as he carried on playing. The warmth radiating from the dragon was so comforting that he stopped feeling the night's chill and played till the stars faded from the night sky. When he finally put down his flute and turned to Ayni, her head rested on his shoulder as she slept.

She looked serene, and he felt bewildered that this beautiful creature willingly sought out his company, comforting him with her presence. Ren leaned down and gently stroked the hair from her face.

'It's time to return to the castle, my lady,' he said, squeezing her shoulder, and the woman opened her eyes. She looked up, half asleep, and placed her hand on his cheek.

'You are such a beautiful soul with the heart of a dragon.' Her quiet voice stunned him, but she drifted into her dreams again, and Ren shook her harder.

'My lady, we need to go.'

Ayni stretched and yawned, giving him a slightly annoyed look.

'Yes, yes, I'm sorry. It was the best night's rest I've had in centuries. Thank you.' She gave him her hand, and Ren helped her up, feeling the gentle tremor of her slender fingers. He might have given her a good sleep, but she gave him a more precious gift: appreciation and company when he needed them the most. When the dragoness headed to the castle, the warrior followed her, feeling strangely content from last night's encounter. The pleasure and warmth didn't fade, even when it came time to face the military crisis in Liath.

CHAPTER EIGHTEEN

The complete darkness made Ina wonder if she was awake or still locked in the nightmare of falling rocks. With growing awareness of several sharp objects pressing hard against her body, the confusion soon cleared, and she struggled to move away from the crushing pain. The last thing she remembered was Mar wanting to go back, then casually mentioning living together, some shadowy figure she glimpsed, and the thunderous tunnel collapse. Her worst fears had come true, and now she was stuck in this gods-forsaken place.

Where is Mar? I have to find him. What if he is injured or under the rocks? Her thoughts were racing as panic took over. Ina jerked hard to gain some freedom, scraping her skin on the unmoving stone. Her leg kicked out as she thrashed, connecting with something soft, and a pained curse broke the silence.

'Stop kicking me in the bollocks, woman.' The weight on her body eased slightly, but Ina reached up and instantly pulled it back.

'Mar, you are alive! I thought… Don't you ever dare to die on me, ever! Wait, what are you doing on top of me?!' Her panicked words provoked his exasperated sigh.

'I thought I was saving you from the falling rocks, but your well-aimed kick made me rethink any future knightly outbursts.'

Her kiss stopped his complaints, and Ina lost herself in his embrace, relieved they were both alive. This feeling was short-lived when she summoned a weak light and discovered the truth of their situation. Although the small chamber was mainly preserved, which saved their lives, the tunnel to the outside world was lost, with several smaller rocks and debris covering their bodies. Ina ran fingers through her hair, brushing off the rubble, and found warm dampness. When she brought her hand to the light, the red coating was a silent testimony of how close she'd been to death, but the pulsating pain left behind wasn't entirely reassuring.

Mar looked at her, and she saw the tightened muscles of his jaw working hard as he controlled his anger.

'We have to go. I don't trust these walls,' he said, displacing the rocks with an impressive display of strength before helping her to stand up. Uncomfortable with the prospect of going deeper into the mountain, Ina looked at the rubble that blocked their exit.

'Why did it collapse only at the entrance? Maybe I could try to blast it open?'

Mar grabbed her hand, shaking his head. 'No, the walls are unstable, and most likely, we would be buried alive, and if we aren't killed, the hunters on the other side will jump at the opportunity to catch us as soon as we leave. The only way is to go forward, just like we planned.'

He was right, but how could Ina explain how the strange call she felt frightened her? That impulse that pulled at her soul to claim… Gods knew what. Ina shook her head, coughing as the dust dislodged from her hair and clenched her fists. She hated being told what to do, but it was time to grab this beast by its horns and put this problem to rest together with the strange figure who she suspected caused the collapse.

'Let's go then,' she said, grabbing Mar's hand and heading towards the other tunnel. She sent her pulsar ahead to light the path, but it only made more shadows. Frustrated, she released Mar and tried to create another light source, but he grabbed her tight.

'Oh no, my lady, we will not repeat the mishap from the Osterad tunnels.'

Ina knew what Mar referred to, but this solid rock was unlikely to hide trap doors and hidden chambers.

'I just want to make more light,' she said, hoping it would dispel his worries.

'Just no, Ina. Humour me for once.'

Mar was making things difficult, and she could only roll her eyes, huffing under her breath about stupid, stubborn dragons while trying to avoid the obstacles his shadow obscured as they walked along.

'I can hear you, and I don't care. Holding hands is the safest option.' Mar didn't let her go, but Ina stopped paying attention, focusing mainly on the way forward. The tunnel walls narrowed as they continued, and she struggled to breathe in the warm, stale air of the mine. The stories about miners who fell asleep and never woke up haunted her as they pushed forward. Ina felt her heart racing, her neck covered in sweat, and the world spun around, making her almost fall on an uneven path. Suddenly, she felt Mar's hand on her shoulder.

'We will be fine. Just breathe slowly. This tunnel must have an exit, and we will find it.'

Ina rubbed her cheek over the back of his hand. Suddenly, the stench of sweat and stone dust wasn't that bad. It was Mar, and, concentrating on it, she resumed her journey.

The next hour felt like torture. Ina fought her fear of the granite walls closing around her and the suspicion they would be stuck here, unable to move anymore. She heard Mar grunt as he squeezed through the tight passage, and she felt sorry for her dragon. Her skin was scraped and bruised, and she could only imagine what the jagged rocks were doing to his much bigger frame.

When a faint light appeared ahead, she wanted to scream with joy and somehow pushed herself forward to get to it. She barely felt Mar's hand slipping from her embrace until his voice stopped her.

'Ina, wait, for fuck's sake. I should be at the front,' he said, voice full of worry. Still, she was already ahead and racing towards the light as if it held their salvation.

'It is too late for this, you can't squeeze past me, and we need to get out. I can't take much more. Everything is so tight I can barely breathe.'

She could hear him cursing silently and twisted her head to send him a reassuring smile. 'All will be fine. It's not like there is anyone else here. You told me yourself it is an abandoned mine.'

Muted cursing followed her words, but she ignored it, pressing onwards until she finally stepped out into the open. Only then did she look around for potential enemies, but the space was empty, and the view was breathtaking, taking her by surprise. When she gasped in awe, the sound was followed by Mar frantically smashing his way through the tunnel. Ina ignored it, enchanted by the beautiful, multicoloured crystals covering the cavern walls and reflecting the eerie flickering light produced by a strange, silvery moss. The soft, spongy vegetation covered the chamber floor, and as the witch stepped forward, it released mysterious, glittering spores into the air. Tears began falling from Ina's eyes as she lost herself in the unparallel beauty before her.

'If you are done destroying the tunnel, look at this. It's so beautiful.' Ina grabbed Mar's hand as he emerged and pulled him deeper into the cave. There, Ina raised her face and inhaled deeply. She could feel fresh air flowing from above, and the sound of dripping water caught her attention. Moving in its direction, Ina discovered another marvel. In the corner, sculpted by centuries of erosion, was a small pool of crystal clear water that showed her reflection staring back in wonder when she looked into its depths.

'You are so beautiful, my spitfire.' Mar's voice and the gentle touch of his hand diverted her attention, and she noticed Mar's mischievous smile. 'You looked so youthful, sweet, and innocent with stars in your eyes. Not to spoil the moment, but let's camp here. I'm tired, and we have water and fresh air here.'

Ina sighed as Mar reminded her of the aches and pains of their journey. She was exhausted from resisting the strange call, battered from pushing herself through the tight passage, and her head still throbbed from the cave-in. With its beautiful lights, this peaceful cavern was the perfect resting place. Without waiting for further instruction, Ina took off her coat and spread it next to the small pond. Her blouse was dirty and ripped, but the witch didn't dare pollute the clear water with her filth. Instead, she removed a small piece of fabric and poured the water on it before placing the wet rag on her forehead. She watched Mar walking around the chamber before coming back.

'There is another exit. We'll go that way after having a rest.' Ina nodded and noticed him looking at her with concern in his golden eyes. It was fascinating to see how their colour changed with his mood, revealing which side of his personality was more in control. 'Your head is hurting,' he said, and she sniggered, instantly regretting it as her headache increased.

'How did you guess? It's not every day you get hit by a rockslide, blackout, and have to scrape your way past jagged walls.' She closed her eyes and felt Mar take the rag from her hands, wiping her face gently. He had no qualms about dipping the dirty rag in the cold water to wipe the dry, crusted blood and dirt off her before washing her face. Ina protested weakly, but in the end, she closed her eyes, enjoying his care. They quietly quarrelled about him polluting the water until an amused voice behind Mar's back shocked them into silence.

'What an extraordinary view. Shouldn't the lady dress the knight's wounds?' With the sudden shift of air, Ina's eyes snapped open and saw an old man with Mar's dagger next to his throat, smiling at her and completely ignoring the sharp blade tickling his skin.

'Who the fuck are you?' Steel coated the rage in Mar's voice, but the elder didn't appear threatening. There was something oddly familiar about him, and instinctively she reached out for his mind. The stranger swatted away her efforts, but she could see his eyes glinting, delighted at her attempt.

'Now, now autumn girl, that was rude. You should have just asked,' he said, but she could feel his amusement despite the scolding tone. She also felt for Mar. He was confused about the exchange and shifted his eyes between her and the stranger's, looking as clueless as his father for a moment. Then sudden recognition hit her.

'It's you. The man I help on the road, but… how?' She was trying to wrap her head around this. Alleron had mentioned something about the Guardian of the Mountain, but why would that spirit appear now?

'Because I wanted to see you for myself. So, did you like my gift?' He answered her unspoken question, and Ina gasped, gesturing to Mar to lower his blade. He followed her request and moved over, shielding her with his body. The old man laughed. 'And you, hatchling, answering your question. My name is Skarbnik, and I wouldn't hurt my brother's champion.'

It was Ina's turn to look dumbstruck. 'Champion? But… never mind, and thank you for the orein. Please join us, erm… by the pond.' Ina desperately tried to recall what she remembered about the sovereign and protector of the mountain.

Skarbnik looked at her, and it disturbed her that such an ancient being appeared so cheerful.

'I'm too old to sit on the floor, autumn girl, but I'm grateful for your invitation.' He raised his hand. On that command, rocks sprouted and grew into a throne. The guardian sat down and nodded his head.

'Now, care to tell me what brought you to my home?'

It was time for her to decide whether to tell her secret to this strange man or make up a believable excuse. She looked at Mar, but he stood there focused on Skarbnik like he was trying to bore a hole through the old man's head. Ina bit her lip and took a deep breath, hoping she didn't make a mistake.

'We are looking for an artefact in a tomb. I know you are aware of the drow. I'm here to make sure their leader doesn't get it. Do you know what it is?' As soon as she finished, Skarbnik and Mar's gazes turned to her.

'Oh, I know about the drow. You can thank me later for ensuring those pests didn't get you in the old mine entrance. Now tell me, why are you actually looking for it, child?' Skarbnik's voice was severe for the first time, and she felt a twinge of concern.

'So the cave-in was your doing?' Ina stated more than asked, giving herself time to answer his next question. 'This thing… it is calling to me, I think.' She paused and exhaled. 'It may be connected to Chaos magic, and if it is… I don't want the drow to have it. They would use it for nothing but destruction.'

Skarbnik nodded. 'You are right, and I made sure my unwelcome guests wouldn't get their hands on it.' He looked at Mar, whose posture radiated silent challenge, and said, 'Let me take you there. You should have what you came here for, no? Otherwise, your dragon may sink a dagger into my back for my help earlier.'

Ina looked up at Mar and rolled her eyes. 'Can you blame him? You just admitted to almost burying us alive. My dragon is slightly overprotective, but he has a good heart.' She saw Mar raise his eyebrows, and a mischievous smirk played over his lips, but he stayed quiet.

'Is that so?' The guardian laughed and rose from his makeshift throne, the stone instantly crumbling into the dust. 'Come, let me show you the reason for the call you feel inside.'

Ina took Skarbnik's outstretched hand, concealing her tiredness. Mar trailed behind them in silence, but she felt the comforting brush of his hand on the small of her back now and then. This time, they didn't have to squeeze through tight walls. It felt as if the mountains opened before the guardian, the walls flattening their surfaces as they passed, and after a short walk, they entered another much darker chamber covered in iridescent green crystals.

The air was stale, as though the cavern had been sealed for years. The moss on the walls glowed with a soft light, coating the chamber in an otherworldly green shimmer, but Ina didn't notice, clutching her chest as an overpowering pressure took her breath away. Mar's growl when he caught her collapsing and gasping for air broke the primordial silence of the cave.

'I knew she shouldn't trust you,' he said, sheltering Ina as she wrestled with her body's reaction. The old man studied them for a moment, then entombed Mar's legs in living stone with a dismissive wave of his hand.

'Of course she shouldn't. Only a fool trusts the old gods, but she belongs to my brother, and her strange resilience amuses me, making her special. Now let us see what this little one is worth. Follow me.'

Ina heard Mar ground his teeth, struggling to break free, and placed her hand on his cheek.

'It will be fine. We can't fight the mountain god in his domain. Please, trust me. I have to face whatever is there.' As Mar didn't budge, she added, 'Besides, you can't fight like this.'

'You wanna bet?' he said, but begrudgingly released her, the gold in his eyes deepening when she stood and followed Skarbnik.

The floor gently sloped down, and several small channels of water flowed into the centre, forming a small pool, in the middle of which was a large, crystal sarcophagus. It looked like they had found the mysterious tomb.

Why am I attracted to this tomb? Does he expect me to resurrect the dead to prove my worth? It was a stupid idea to come here. What if I fail? Will he keep us here forever or hurt Mar? she thought, rubbing her temple, suffocated by fear and worry.

'Here is the burial chamber you were trying to find. The location was a closely guarded secret until someone discovered its legend, and no, I will not hurt your dragon, at least not much. If that is what distracts you, I will free him. Now, come here.'

Of course, he can read my mind, fucking great, Ina thought, imagining some obscene gesture, and the widening smile on the old man's face told her she was right. Still, after hearing the crushing rocks behind her and muttering curses, she followed his command and approached the sarcophagus. It was made from a translucent green crystal, darker than the surrounding minerals. A faint glow emanated from one end of the coffin, illuminating the body of a female inside. As Ina came closer, the light grew brighter until it became clear the person encased in the crystal was likely a drow, as the green tint highlighted the greyness of her skin instead of hiding it.

The desire gripping Ina's chest seemed to pull her towards the glowing gem. Mounted in an intricate circlet resting on the woman's head, it glowed brighter as the witch reached out. Ina froze as she realised the gem's light pulsed, matching the beat of her heart. The visceral need to lay her hands on the stone resonated in her soul, and, trembling in desire, Ina clenched her fingers on the rim of the tomb to fight the urge to take the jewel.

'What is it? Why is it calling me?' she asked Skarbnik, only now noticing he was focused on her reaction the entire time.

'This circlet is a part of the Chaos regalia. One stone has already bonded with you. The other is on the finger of your enemy, causing his madness. That is why he came here, and that is why you are here. The stones want to unite.'

'And who was the woman?' she asked, looking at the beautiful features untouched by death and decay.

Skarbnik smiled. 'This is Sowenna Al'Ean, the last known Chaos archmage and empress of the drow dominium, who reshaped the world during mage wars.'

Mar's voice rang out in disbelief. 'The mage wars were over two thousand years ago. Are you trying to tell us this unblemished body is the infamous archmage who almost wiped out all life in the world?' The magic of the stone so enthralled Ina that she hadn't noticed Mar's approach, but it seemed he hadn't lost his ability to lose his temper at the wrong moment.

Skarbnik turned at the dragon's approach and smiled. 'Yes, that's the one. Now the woman you love will be the new Chaos archmage, and those idiots in the Mage Council were too blind to see it,' the old man said, and Mar started laughing while Ina looked at him, entirely at a loss as to what amused him so much. 'Will you take it, autumn girl? Sowenna made the regalia to unite the world under her rule. Now you can win this petty war for your king without even trying.'

His words didn't make sense, and it didn't help that she struggled to focus, fighting against the intense pressure imposed on her will when Ina felt she was losing this battle before she thought of reaching out to Mar.

'Hold my hand, please. No, hold both of them,' she told Mar, getting both men's attention before pleading with Skarbnik.

'Can you destroy it? Can you destroy both stones? I can't control their magic. Why the hell did you bring me here? You must have known how this would affect me, or do you want to create another archmage of Chaos and release me like a plague on the world? I don't want this power. It's not who I am!' she cried out in anguish. There was no, "let us talk like a civilised adult with a mountain god", just her infamous temper. Skarbnik's face lost all merriment, and the terrifying god of the mountain looked down at her, pinning her under his awful gaze.

'You are the Chaos archmage, unhappy, unwilling, afraid of your abilities, capable of terrible acts and wondrous miracles. The gods are watching to see which you choose, but I will tell you this: only you have the power to destroy the stones. To do that, you will need to possess each piece of the regalia, but once you lay your hands upon them, will you still want to? Now make your choice. Are you taking possession of the circlet?'

Ina looked at him for a long time. His words were equal parts horrifying and tempting, but it was the temptation that made her decision easy.

'I won't become a puppet to a maelstrom of magic I can not control. I can barely resist the seductive call of destruction as it is. Take my necklace, seal it in this chamber along with the circlet, and ensure no one gains access.' Ina felt her heart breaking when she said those words.

'You are an interesting human, little witch. Not only resisting the call of Chaos, but telling me what to do… I can see why Leshy chose you. I will seal the circlet within this chamber and guard it until you are ready to take it, but the necklace has bonded with you. Your body will wither and die if you are separated now. The old troll was right to bestow its magic upon you. I could almost forgive his other transgressions for the entertainment he has given me.' He approached her and placed his hands on her temples. The painful call from the sarcophagus subsided, but the image of a mirrored room appeared in her mind's eye.

Learn to block it, girl. You must learn to protect your mind from the people and objects that would influence you, but most importantly, from Chaos itself. Otherwise, you will go insane from its constant call.

The sudden voice in her head was so unexpected that she would have staggered back if not for Mar's body behind her.

Really, what are they teaching at the university now? Stop fussing and set the mirrors around your thoughts. Build the layers around it, make me see only what you want me to, and guard yourself against the call. Skarbnik kept speaking to her mind. It was so unnerving that Ina imagined the mental barrier she'd been taught in university, but tried to replace it with crystal mirrors this time.

Good, she heard. *Now, push out a few irrelevant thoughts you don't mind me seeing.* Ina smirked and imagined a kaleidoscope of images from shopping trips with Velka. She noticed Skarbnik grimace and pull his hands away.

'Yes, that will do,' he said aloud and backed away from her. 'Time for you to go, but remember, the stones accepted you, and the circlet will be waiting here till you're ready.'

With the call muffled to a slight buzzing, Ina bowed her head respectfully. 'No, it is too much for me. I came here not to take it, but to ensure the drow can never claim it. That's all I ever wanted.'

'It matters little what you want, my dear. You were born to bring the change, and that is what you are going to do.' The old man laughed and headed towards the solid wall, and his guests trotted behind him, unsure what to expect. The wall opened out, creating a passage and, led by the mountain god, they walked through the heart of the mountain, as if on an evening stroll, till they finally emerged into the valley they'd left the horses. Only their mounts weren't there, and a half-eaten saddle testified to the fact the orein had lost her patience with the valley's bounty.

Ina tried to hide how worried she was by this disappearance and courteously bid farewell to Skarbnik. When he left, disappearing into the solid granite cliff, she turned to Mar.

'I think we'll need to fly.'

CHAPTER NINETEEN

Rewan again looked at the letter from Liath and hid his face in his hands. The kobold raids had been bad enough, but he'd hoped it was nothing more than a grim winter and lack of supplies that provoked the attacks on the border, not an incursion by the drow. He hadn't expected this. Arknay was far away, and except for a few state visits and scattered trade deals, the drow country and Cornovii never stomped on each other's feet.

The letter was sent by Sa'Ren Gerel, not Ina or Lord Alleron himself, which was concerning, and Rewan would be offended if he cared for such things. They needed an army and military supplies, but there was a problem, Cornovii had none. Rewan rang a bell, and a servant immediately entered his office.

'Call for Lord Kaian. Tell him I need him at once.'

The servant nodded and rushed to fulfil his order while Rewan grabbed the treasury accounts and read the current balance. No matter how long he looked at them, the numbers didn't lie. Sophia, in her insanity, had stripped the kingdom bare. He could see countless requests from Liath for supplies, new recruitment, and anything to keep the army of Cornovii running, but all of them were maliciously denied. Now, they had the bare bones of a once mighty army consisting primarily of veteran soldiers, many old enough to be retired. Given a choice, he would authorise drafting new recruits, but it would take months to train them, and he didn't want to send unprepared youths to fight.

The doors opened, and Kaian walked in. One look and the assassin's jovial expression turned into a deep frown, and his steps sped up as he approached the king.

'What happened? You look like you've seen a ghost,' he said and gently cupped the king's head, lifting his chin to look into his eyes.

The concern on his face made Rewan sigh, and, covering Kaian's hand with his own, he pressed a small kiss to the man's wrist.

'I need advice, but most of all, I need to talk this through with someone I can trust. It's bad, my love, and I'm lost with what to do.' Rewan's voice was bitter. He'd been tired since he took the throne. There was never a moment free from problems. Refugees, supplies, the threat of rebellion in the south, not to mention the north that already did as they pleased, and now there might be an invasion in Liath.

'I can't advise you if I don't know the problem. But before you start, I have good news.' Kaian's soft smile always lifted his mood, and Rewan felt his burden eased just by having him near.

'Please, do tell. Gods know I need some good news.'

'Our indispensable Gruff and I, your handsome advisor, spent countless days searching the tunnels of Osterad. Between the horrifying experiments, a necromancer's lab, and some other unmentionable things, we found a vault that Sophia used to stockpile the money and treasures she had purloined from the citizens and the army. She likely planned to bribe them with it after she took the throne, which is an excellent strategy to silence the voice of discourse. And trust me, it looks like a dragon's hoard. She must have planned this coup for years, but safe to say, thanks to our discovery, you are the richest king on this continent.'

Rewan knew he should show enthusiasm for such a revelation, but all he felt was relief. 'Gold won't feed the army or train the soldiers,' he said, looking at Kaian as he pouted teasingly.

'I see you are cheerful as a teetotal tosspot today. Tell me what soured you so much that you can't even spare a smile for me after I crawled through the sewers to get you your gold.' Kaian's lips twitched when the king rolled his eyes.

'You and your metaphors. Anyone would think you and Ina had the same teachers.' Rewan couldn't help but smile. It lasted for a blink of an eye before the feeling of foreboding crept back again.

'War is coming, and we are as helpless as fish in a barrel. Sophia dismantled the army, and half the guards were killed in the palace battle. My only choice is to draft the common folks and send untrained youngsters armed with rusty swords to defend the country against well-trained warriors—' Rewan started, but Kaian's raised hand stopped him in his tracks.

'Or you could use your newly discovered gold, hire the free companies, and pay whoever is desperate enough to go to war to do it. My… associates can secure the palace, and you can use the guards to control and train the conscripted citizens.' Rewan's eyes lit up, and Kaian continued with a mischievous smile. 'Don't forget you have a dragon in your service if Ina has found him and didn't kill him on the spot, and the witch herself is a one-woman army.'

Kaian seemed ready to continue his rousing speech when the doors to the office slammed against the wall. The furious, grey-haired arch-healer of Cornovii entered the room, the mages, Arun and Jorge, trailing behind like nervous ducklings. Despite both now holding higher office than the formidable healer, neither man could stop the fearsome woman before Nerissa approached the king's desk, ratting ink bottles with her barely restrained magic.

'You will send an army and recover my niece from this disaster... Your Majesty,' she said, waving a letter in front of the king's face, her eyes boring into his soul as if she wanted to rip it from his body. Rewan pulled back because, knowing Nerissa, it wouldn't be much of a problem for her. She would also make sure he was alive and kicking during the procedure.

'Your Majesty, a particular artefact in those mountains must not be found. The safety of your kingdom and the continent depends on it.' Arun was much more diplomatic with his ominous warning.

Rewan looked up at Jorge, waiting for the mage's usual sensible advice, but the judicial mage only nodded in agreement.

'I assume you all received the same interesting information I did? I would wholeheartedly fulfil your demands, but the current problem is we don't have an army. I found...' he began, but the doors slammed open again, and an exasperated Daro entered the room.

'Your Majesty, I apolo—' He stopped as soon as Rewan's hand lifted, silencing him.

'Hopefully, this is the last time everybody treats my private office as a fish market,' the king said with slight annoyance. 'Now, let's get back to the point. We don't have any other army than the one already engaged in Liath, but here's my plan.'

As Rewan outlined his plan, including the recruitment of mercenaries and a draft of ordinary citizens, Nerissa cut him off, angrily telling him it was insufficient to stop an invasion of mages and battle-hardened veterans, proposing the need to strip the nobles of their defensive forces, pledging the soldiers of House Thorn, despite no longer having the authority to do so after being ousted from power by the current Duke.

Ever the political expert, the battlemage, Arun, shook his head, reminding the Healer those forces were needed in case the first battle was lost, adding that he would organise the mages into combat units and would harness alchemy masters, along with artefact makers, to produce weapons and magical protection for the army. Nerissa, not to be outdone, volunteered herself and any healers she could recruit to treat the injured.

The magical council was so often in opposition to the crown that seeing a group of powerful mages bickering like children in his office, and tripping over their feet to offer him help, was frankly very satisfying, even if it was due to the healer's missing niece and not his authority. Rewan's pessimism from earlier lifted as he saw a glimmer of hope emerging in this dire situation. With the eagerness of a puppy, Daro accepted the position of commander of the diverse army.

'Will your betrothed be happy with your decision?' Rewan asked politely, as he knew his new captain would have been wed in a week if not for this delay. 'Please tell her we will host the wedding in the palace once you return, and all expenses will be on me.'

'My king, if Velka knew about Ina's troubles, she would want to pack her bag and go with me. Somehow, she decided nature mages can be as deadly as those throwing fireballs, so if we can find some excuse for sending me away that does not involve Ina and war, I would be very grateful.'

Rewan chuckled. 'Well, she proved herself more than worthy during the palace battle. Still, I'm happy to help you protect your fiancée. I want you to set off as soon as we have a force large enough to be effective.' He acknowledged Daro's salute, amiably dismissing his new commander, and Arun, still arguing with Nerissa, followed. To his surprise, Jorge remained and insisted on talking to him alone. Kaian excused himself, and Rewan was left to face the judicial mage, who likely had alarming news to share.

'Just tell me,' Rewan said, simply expecting the worst, and he was not mistaken.

'How much are you willing to gamble on the witch this time?' the mage asked him, and Rewan pondered for a moment before he answered.

'I trust her. Ina does not crave power. She is loyal to me and so forthright that even Kaian respects her. As for the rest, it is a gamble, but why are you asking?'

'The divination was complicated and as unclear as usual when she is involved, but we may have a problem. Arun forgot to mention that the artefact is one of the Chaos regalia, and the drow prince is a strong psychic mage.' Jorge's lips narrowed to tight lines, and Rewan knew the mage was unhappy with uncertain predictions.

'How big is the problem, then?' he asked, simply hoping for a bit of explanation.

'Catastrophic, but I am unsure which side faces destruction. This girl drives me insane. All schemata get corrupted once I add her to the equation.' Jorge was visibly agitated when he turned to the king. 'She will be the deciding factor in this war. It is your decision how much you want to gamble.'

Rewan looked at the old mage and sighed. 'Do I have a choice? With the patchwork army we're assembling, my best bet is that, yet again, she will be the one who keeps me on the throne. I know what you're trying to say, but I will rule this country as a just king, and if I remove loyal people like Ina because I fear them, then I will renounce my crown as a failure and a fraud. Besides, I like her. Even when she's not here, her support gained me an army, and you can't say you don't like her too.'

'I do, but my role is to serve the kingdom. I hope Ina will prevail, but Chaos mages and the Chaos regalia are a volatile mix. Keep this in mind when making your decision. Now, please excuse me. It appears there are issues needing my attention.' The king could hear the issue Jorge wanted to deal with, the unmistakable voice of Archmage Nerissa, raised in anger, and the heaviness of magic in the air, so he swiftly dismissed Jorge and returned to his reading.

Rewan was left alone, looking through his letters, but this time, with a slight smile on his face instead of a frown. A cautious optimism grew, and he sat down to draft a decree for the new royal army. He had a plan, allies, money, and his royal witch, bringing all this together like a lucky charm.

❄❄❄

Ren walked along the castle walls to where Alleron stood, staring into the distance. The old lord acknowledged his presence with a quick nod, but continued staring at the shadowy Grey Mountains.

'Do you think they are well?' the duke asked. The question was casual, but the concern in his voice slipped through the calm façade of a military leader. Ren sighed, feeling the same worry inside, and took a moment to gather his thoughts before answering.

'I don't know, but Mar and Ina are formidable as individuals. Together? I wouldn't bet against them. The one thing I am sure of is that Ina is alive. I'd know if she wasn't.' He placed a hand over his heart. The sensation he'd felt since she healed him was still there, and he took comfort in the bond pulling at his soul.

Ren changed the subject to focus Lord Alleron's mind on the city. 'We've rebuilt the ballista and strengthened the walls. The veterans are training the common folk in simple defensive tactics, and Lady Lorraine is in the infirmary with those elders and citizens unable, or unwilling, to fight, preparing the medical supplies.' Alleron turned to the warrior as he finished his report. 'The shifter clans arrived today, not just warriors, but whole families. We need to accommodate them, my lord, and I feel it is a matter beyond my authority.'

'We have some abandoned houses in the city due to the recent raiding. Ask the quartermaster to give you the list and place the families there. As for the fighters, integrate them into the unit barracks. I've seen what shifter warriors can do in a rage. It would be good to have that strength in any potential battle.' Alleron turned back to the mountains, shaking his head. 'It's still not enough against a well-trained, veteran army, but Liath has weathered worse. We will endure.'

A half-frozen bird chose that precise moment to fall from the sky, barely avoiding the lord's head, landing lifeless on the stones. Alleron cursed loudly, startled by this unexpected missile, but Ren bent and picked it up. He looked at the dead bird until he spotted a small scrap of paper tied to one of his legs and unfolded it.

Hold on, Ghost, we are coming. Daro.

Alleron looked at him in surprise when Ren laughed and took the paper from his hands. His lips twitched when he once again read the note of possible salvation.

'I'll let the soldiers know. You make sure all our people are well looked after.' With the extra spring in his step, the Lord of Liath headed down, leaving Ren on the walls. The warrior raised his head and looked at the heavy, threatening clouds building over the castle. It would be many days till reinforcements arrived, but this message eased the heavy feeling in his heart. Now the primary concern was the absence of Ina and Mar. Ren closed his eyes and took a deep breath of fresh winter air, calming his thoughts. There was nothing he could do for now, and dwelling on things he couldn't change was pointless. He felt a snowflake landing on his cheek, and a female voice behind him asked.

'Is everything alright, Ren? Do you need my help with anything?' Ayni asked, standing next to him.

'Help? This is not your fight, Lady Ayni,' Ren said calmly, watching warily as her caring expression changed into anger.

'Yes, it is. I am a dragon. We do not turn tail and run. We protect those we care about.' Ren was surprised at the anger, but when Ayni's expression turned thoughtful, he found himself leaning towards her, captivated. 'I am old and tired, Ren, but here… with you, I feel alive again. I've lived so long without purpose and, sometimes… Well, it is different now. I will fight for Liath, for the blood that runs through their veins, and for the friends I made despite my foolishness, but most of all, I would stand with you, Sa'Ren, if you'd let me.'

The wind chose this exact moment to catch hold of her cloak, whipping it out and turning the heavy material into magnificent wings, and Ren stood speechless, spellbound by the ethereal beauty before him, this warrior woman; the peaceful but determined embodiment of winter. Lost in the moment, all he could do was reach up and reverently caress her cheek till reality slowly seeped back into place, and Ren remembered how to speak.

'My lady, your words humble me, but dragons are still feared here. Your appearance might cause widespread panic, and I don't want you being attacked like Mar.' Ren became puzzled when Ayni's eyes lit up with excitement.

'You could ride me into battle. The East was well known for its dragonriders in ancient times.' Ren's lips twitched in amusement at her words, and he answered with a light chuckle in his voice.

'Ayni, that is wrong in so many ways. You can't just tell a man to ride you in any circumstance.' As he'd never thought it possible to fly a dragon, all he could picture was the woman in entirely inappropriate ways. After a moment's struggle, Ren gave up and laughed. 'I don't even know how that would work. All I can see is a beautiful woman telling me to ride her into battle.'

Ayni's smile widened, and she grabbed his hand, pointing to the snowy garden below. 'I can show you. Come with me.' She dragged him down, and Ren didn't resist, amused and enticed by the prospect. Ayni led him deep into the garden until they disappeared from view before turning to him with a smile. She released his hand and moved a few meters away before the air shimmered around her, and a svelte, aquamarine dragon appeared in front of his eyes.

Ren stood in silence, admiring the beauty in front of him. When Ayni shifted uncomfortably under his gaze, he walked closer.

'You are magnificent, my lady,' he said, lifting a hand towards her. 'May I?' Ren asked, and when she nodded, he placed his hand on her dainty neck, trailing his fingers over the scales.

Soft shivers ran through the dragon's body as he stroked her, and Ayni's head turned. Her nostrils touched his neck, and she inhaled deeply. 'Please, sit on my back. I truly want this,' she said, and he heard surprise and a hint of confusion in her voice.

'Are you sure?' he asked. His hesitance equalled hers, but Ayni had already lowered herself to his level.

'I have never asked a human to fly with me, but… this feels right. You feel right,' she said, and a shiver once again ran through her body.

Ren climbed up and knelt in the space behind her shoulders. He was unsure what to do, but his legs naturally slipped into the gap between the joints and her body, and the skin moulded to his legs, holding him better than any harness. Ayni turned her long neck and looked at him with an unreadable expression.

'Are you ready?'

She leapt in the air when he nodded, and, with a few powerful strokes, they were high above the castle, leaving a rapidly disappearing world behind them. Ren gasped when dizziness swept over him, but soon he adjusted to the movement and the wind in his face.

Tell me if it's too much. Her voice in his head and the sudden intimacy that came with it almost caused him to fall at the shock of it.

'I will.'

Use your mind. I can hear your thoughts, as well as project mine to you. Mar didn't like it, but I hope you don't mind. It is easier this way. Now tell me what you want to see. Her thoughts were full of amusement, and as Ren got used to her presence in his mind, he also sensed Ayni's pleasure at having him as her rider, a sense of rightness that filled her soul.

Have many done this before? Flying together as partners?

In the past, yes. The Liath bloodline came from a dragon and his rider. He felt uncertainty in her thoughts before she added, *When dragons choose another race to mate with, they often become their riders. As far as I know, you are the first dragonrider in many centuries.* Her answer broke through his calm demeanour, and to break the awkward moment, he smiled before reaching out and stroking the base of her neck.

Could you fly around the castle? It might help to look for any weaknesses from above, he asked, changing the subject before his pleasure became too apparent. Ayni's feeling of anticipation when she mentioned the dragon and his rider was unsettling and touched the part of his soul he thought was reserved for Ina.

They circled the castle in silence as Ren focused on assessing the defences, cataloguing several points that required improvement. The feeling of freedom that accompanied the nearly effortless movement was new, but he already wanted it to last.

It can last.

The hope within those words went straight to his heart, but Ren didn't answer, feeling confused by the sudden warmth. After they landed and Ayni transformed, he embraced her slender frame. His lips found hers, and he lost himself in a long, passionate kiss that left the dragoness breathless long after he stopped and disappeared into the shadow.

CHAPTER TWENTY

Mar looked at Ina, confused and uncertain. *Did she just suggest we fly?* He still remembered her fear the first time she rode on Woron because of the horse's height, and now she wanted to fly? 'Are you sure? We can return to the village and try to get help from someone nearby.'

Ina shook her head. 'No, Liath needs to know what's coming as soon as possible, and your father will need all the help he can get.'

Mar knew Ina's reasoning was sound and, despite his doubts, trusted her judgement, knowing she wouldn't welcome an argument. As he turned away, a sudden chirp caught his attention, and there, on a branch over his head, was the strangest creature he'd ever seen.

It had the body of a bird, with dazzling, iridescent feathers shimmering against the sky and the head of a beautiful maiden, whose eyes were almost as captivating as the voice that began singing a peaceful, hypnotic song that lulled him into languorous indifference. The blinding pain that crashed through his face returned Mar to reality, but he couldn't understand why Ina was standing in front of him, shaking her hand and cursing.

'What are you doing? Wait, did you slap me?'

'You were lost in the Gamayun's song. Did you want to be enchanted forever?' she said and turned to the creature. 'No more tricks. Tell me why you're here.'

Mar frowned, listening to Ina confront the strange bird. She seemed more anxious than expected for someone who spent so much time berating every spirit or god she met, but Mar understood for once. The Gamayun was the prophet of the old gods, and only volkhves or zhrests received their portentous tidings. Despite the aching jaw, Mar was grateful for Ina's slap and listened intently, free of the enthrallment.

The Gamayun turned its head, oddly reminiscent of an owl, and answered.

'Mirror and crown in the raging fire,
Power or love which thy desire,
With loving gift and pain it brings,
The chained mind will shape the world.'

Mar now knew why the god's messenger talked only to volkhves, as he didn't understand a word of this prophecy.

Ina frowned and muttered to herself, 'Fucking riddles,' then, with a more pleasant smile, she addressed the Gamayun.

'Thank you for your words. I will reflect upon them.'

The creature's face didn't express any emotion as she preened her feathers until Ina spoke again.

'Also, I would like to kindly ask you to carry a message to the Stone Halls. Tell them that Lady Thorn calls upon the life debt of Vorberg Stonemeir and requests his aid for Liath.'

The old god's messenger puffed up its feathers in offence, disdainful arrogance clear on her face. 'Humans! Who do you think you are? I'm the divine messenger, not a servant to some upstart witch.' The screeching voice differed vastly from the peaceful song that enthralled him, and Mar struggled to master his shock at the difference, unable to do more than observe as Ina advanced upon the creature, hands on her hips and contempt in her words.

'Oh, get that stick out of your feathery arse. All you do is fly around spouting nonsense and shitting from trees. At least I try to help people. Now, I asked you nicely for help, so take your high and mighty rear end and fly to the Stone Halls. If the situation was important enough for a prophecy, I'm sure the gods want us to succeed.'

Mar winced and leapt forward to rescue his spitfire as Ina was on the verge of plucking some feathers. He was beside her in no time, covering her mouth with his hand and offering the Gamayun an apologetic smile.

'I apologise. My betrothed is not herself lately.'

The creature nodded before leaping up in the air. Its last words snapped out like a whip.

'Maybe the gods want you to succeed, or perhaps they are laughing as they watch you struggle. Only time will tell, autumn girl.'

When the gamayun disappeared, Mar released the struggling Ina, and she instantly turned on him like a feral cat.

'I could have handled that prissy crow,' she hissed, visibly angry, but the warrior reached for her again and pressed her body to his.

'I know you could, but I don't want to be hit by Perun's lightning on the top of the mountain because you fried his arrogant chicken. The prophecy worries me, and I want to return to Liath. Let's go down now.'

Ina grumbled something into his chest, but he felt her body relax, and with a tender kiss on the top of her head, he released her. He changed shape quickly and noticed with pleasure at how effortlessly he could do it now. It was almost like slipping into his old armour, comfortable and worn out in all the right places. Ina looked at him, and he revelled in the soft, dreamy smile blossoming on her lips. Mar lowered his head, and his forked tongue touched her exposed neck in a playful tickle, making her laugh and swatting him off before planting a playful kiss on his nuzzle. It was only then that Mar realised he'd made a mistake.

Desire shot through his body as soon as he tasted her skin. The visceral response, love, lust, and need for her to acknowledge their bond was hard to control. Just like the legends of dragons capturing blushing virgins to commit unspeakable acts, he craved to take her to a distant location where he could guard his treasure forever. Ina was by no means a virgin, nor was she blushing under his touch, but the dragon within him wanted more than her hesitant love. Ina must have noticed his struggle because she placed her hand on his neck, looking at him with concern in her eyes, and Mar felt more lost than ever.

'Get on, Ina, we need to get going.'

His abruptness clearly surprised her, but it wasn't the time or place to tell her how much he loved her and how being a dragon enhanced the possessiveness he knew she detested. Ina had made a point of saying she belonged to no man several times, but the only thought he had in his head now was, *I love you. You are mine.*

I will never give you up. He lowered himself, helping her climb onto his back, restraining his chuckle as the witch cursed every step of the way. Much to his surprise, his muscles tensed when she placed her legs between his shoulders and torso, instinctively holding her in place, and the bond between them flared to life, filling him with a profound sense of peace and completeness. Mar recalled the paintings from the Angrath Temple portraying the dragonrider. *Is it always like this? Or it is because of Ina's spell. I'll have to ask Ayni when we get to the castle.*

'Is this alright, Mar? I have no bloody idea what I'm doing, but this space feels right. Is it right?' She kept asking, shifting her bottom on the base of his neck. Not that he had any experience to answer her questions, but spreading his wings, he didn't feel any discomfort and barely felt her weight on his back. He was in the air with a few powerful beats of his wings, quickly catching a thermal. He felt Ina's hands gripping his spinal crest, quiet and shaking like a leaf. Flying at speed to gain enough height, the wind prevented them from talking, so Mar reached to her with his mind, expecting firm resistance, only to find none.

His brave spitfire was in a blind panic, not even aware enough to defend herself from his intrusion, and although Mar had planned to fly straight to the castle, he decided to make the flight as short as possible. The distance they'd already travelled would have saved them two days of marching over the rugged terrain, so Mar landed in a small clearing by the river at the base of the mountain they so arduously climbed. This would do, with horses, they would be in the castle within a day, but by foot, it would take longer. However, forcing Ina to endure such terror wasn't worth the time they would save.

He landed softly and turned to look at her.

'Ina, my love, we are on the ground. Open your eyes, please. We have landed,' he said, desperately worried as she slid to the ground and broke down sobbing. Mar transformed swiftly and gathered Ina into his arms, holding her trembling body until she slowly calmed down.

'I'm so sorry, and I've let you down. I wanted to do it, but I… I'm such a failure, so leave me here, go back and warn the city.'

Mar gently stroked the tears away from her swollen face with his thumb before lifting her head to face him.

'You are annoying, unruly, and a royal pain in the arse, but you are not a failure. We are all allowed to be scared, even monster-killing Chaos mages. Now, put some snow on that red nose before it gives away our position.' As he expected, his words annoyed her enough to stop crying. Ina, who mocked everything and everyone when she was in pain, wouldn't allow him to tease her without retorting. She looked at him with a challenge in her eyes and huffed.

'You are such an arse, Marcach. Best I sort myself in private to not offend your delicate sensibilities with my glowing complexion.' Despite her words, he saw the hint of a smile, and she collected herself, slipping from his embrace.

'I will wash my face, then we will go to Liath, and I will let Ren console me. He is much better at this,' she said, turning to walk to the river, and Mar had to smile at her paltry attempt at revenge.

Embarrassed by her weakness, Ina walked up the stream till Mar's figure disappeared behind the trees. Only then did she embrace a willow and lean her head against the rough bark.

'Well, that's the end of that. I was not born to be a dragon rider.' The memory of careening through the heavens made her stomach flip. Fighting her gag reflex, Ina knelt on the icy ground, plunged her hands into the babbling brook and splashed the bitterly cold water over herself, gasping in shock at the sensation. Still, it helped, and she continued until her fingers began feeling numb. Ina ignored the sudden sound of leaves rustling, but when she felt a presence behind her, she spoke without taking her eyes from the stream.

'I told you I would be back in a minute. You didn't have to sneak up on me. What if I was doing my private business?' She finished up, turning to face her dragon. Only to come face to face with an unfamiliar dark elf, arrogantly staring down at her. Ina gasped and stumbled backwards, tripping over an exposed root, her eyes widening in shock at his reaction. In a blur, he sprinted forward and wrapped his hand around her waist, preventing her from falling. Hard nails pierced her skin even through the leather clothes, and her mind was assaulted by the iron will of her attacker, immobilising her body. Ina, distracted by the flight and shocked by this sudden appearance, snapped her mental barriers in place a moment too late, and her psyche was ripped from her control, imprisoned within the magic of her assailant. Now helpless, she could only stand witness to her surroundings, unable to resist.

'I finally found you. I had hundreds of eyes looking for you on this side of the mountains since the mine collapsed, and finally, they spotted the dragon. Your Chaos called to me, even from above, but I almost missed your arrival.' She heard his soft, slimy voice as he pressed his face to her neck, inhaling her scent. She knew she'd heard it before, in the burnt-out village, issuing from the captured drow's lips. It was the voice of the scorned prince. Ina knew this should frighten her, but she felt nothing, not even disgust, at his touch instead, her eyes strayed to his ring. The drow smiled happily and brushed a stray hair off her face.

'You are delightful, little mage, and brimming with power and desire. Speak to me, my queen, but I want you to understand your new position. I'm Tar'eth Al'Ean, and you are mine.' He stroked her face gently as if he was afraid to break his new toy, and the pressure that held her mind in place diminished slightly. *What the… this lunatic… about? Dragon… mine… Mar… I have to warn Mar.* The thoughts flowed sluggishly, barely making sense, but the more she thought about the dragon, the more aware she became. Tar'eth examined her face as if he was looking for confirmation.

'Tell me you understand, Inanuan.' She could hear the tension in his voice, as if her agreement was important, despite already being under his control. Slowly, Ina began regaining the ability to focus on something other than the pulsating gem, only for her mind to thrash around, panicking in the cage it was trapped within. Her thoughts were finally her own, but her body and magic were under his control, and Ina felt her worst nightmare come true.

Bloody Chaos regalia! Come on, Ina. There must be something you can do. The burning anger that came with that thought sharpened her focus. She knew there was no way this mage came alone, and she needed to warn Mar. *You're not hurting my dragon, you treacherous bastard.* Tar'eth was still waiting for an answer, suddenly realising what she could do. Ina took a slow, deep breath and used the only thing he let her control—her voice—shouting at the top of her lungs.

'Mar! Run! It's a trap!'

The slap she got for her defiance stunned her. Still, despite the pulsing pain and iron claws of the drow's mind crushing her psyche again, she fought this unseen battle to free her mind with all she had whilst admiring the magnificent, charging dragon that burst through the trees.

What a beautiful idiot, Ina thought and shrieked as agony ripped through her body, strangling all resistance. Wisps of Chaos escaped her fists, wrapping around her captor as Tar'eth, hissing through clenched teeth, reached for it. Her magic protested, and she could see his muscles twitching in agony from his attempt to control it, but the echo of his thoughts transmitted not only the pain, but also the pleasure from this experience. *Why does Chaos never hurt me? What else do I have to learn about this bloody power?* she thought before the prince screamed, directing a deadly stream of Chaos towards Mar, barely missing. The ring on his finger crudely conducted the magic, but the malicious smile on the drow's face widened as he used Ina's body as a human shield, preventing the dragon from attacking and lashing out with a magical whip in a vicious attack. Ina watched, helpless, as the barely controlled Chaos tore at Mar's body as he tried to evade the ill-formed lash. The puppet master's control was far from complete, but still devastating.

'Neither of us wants Lady Thorn dead, dragon, but I will crush her mind before I let you take her. She is mine, and mine alone.' Tar'eth showed no mercy as he taunted Mar, his hands stroking her cheek possessively, and a single tear tracked its way down as Ina realised that, stripped of her free will, she became what she feared the most, a mindless tool of destruction. Still, the pain of wielding her magic took a toll on Tar'eth's control, and she could feel her bond with Mar seeping through the walls of her cage.

Run away, my love. Trust me, this once. He wants to use my magic, not kill me. I will be safe. Escape for me, please. She focused on the message, forcing her thoughts through the link that once again felt strong in her chest. Mar stumbled, and for a moment, she felt his surprise and anger but, most of all, an overwhelming sense of failure for not protecting her. Despite her plea, he pushed forward, and her magic created a lattice of cuts on his skin. *Get the fuck away from here, you idiot!*

Her command must have finally reached him as Mar shot into the air with a painful roar, followed by a drow's laugh echoing in the winter air. Tar'eth looked at his arms, covered by dendritic burns from wielding Chaos, and Ina managed to turn her head, but all she could do was look at the snow, covered with the golden red splashes of Mar's blood while pure hatred burned in her soul.

Tar'eth, I will destroy your dreams, your mind, and your body. You will live to suffer through every moment of your downfall, Ina thought, and Tar'eth turned, piercing eyes staring into hers, savouring her wrath. He laid a hand on her chest, playing with her necklace, before madness, hunger and bliss mixed on his face. *What is this bastard doing? Oh, gods, he wants to unite the stones through me,* she thought, trying to flinch away when, as if in a trance, he took the peridot ring off his finger and placed it on hers. Ina felt a thunderous tide of magic overwhelming her senses, causing her skin to writhe uncontrollably, covering her in goosebumps.

Tar'eth eyes widened, his breath quickened, and his lips crashed into hers, forcing a brutal kiss that sank his teeth into her flesh with a predatory growl. She could feel his arousal when her blood poured from the wound, and he licked it up, enthralled by the sensation.

'You taste of Chaos. You may hate me now, but I will teach you to love me. We will rule the realm just as Sowenna did. Mourn your dragon because you will never see him alive again once we are done with Liath.'

His words were abhorrent, but Ina focused on stabilising the stream of magic that flowed from the ring to her necklace, turning her body into a magical nova until the pulsing stones synchronised and settled into a quiet heartbeat. The green gem, dull on his finger, now looked and felt so alive, and Ina felt attuned to Chaos like never before. If Tar'eth had put the ring on her finger while he fought with Mar, her dragon would not have escaped alive. *Mar is safe, and I'm still me*, she tried to reassure herself, but the heaviness in her chest didn't lessen, and Ina congratulated herself that she left the circlet behind in fear-induced clarity.

A cold, soft hand on her cheek brought her back to reality, and she looked at her captor with hatred. He wasn't the only one who'd desired her magic, and she'd make sure his life ended the same as theirs. Her Chaos would never belong to anyone.

'Come, my lady, it's time to take you to meet your subjects. When our reinforcements arrive, we will go to Liath, and they will see for themselves what a treasure you are.' Tar'eth's joy irked her. When he moved, Ina felt her body jerk, compelled to follow him like a dog on a leash, but she still tried to resist. His assessing gaze fell on her, and Ina felt the restraints on her mind ease.

'You are right. A woman like you should not be dragged around like a slave, but don't test me, Inanuan, because I can do much more than take your magic.'

His voice was soft, but the electrifying pain that spread through her body, setting every nerve on fire, was not, and Ina ground her teeth, trying to remain conscious and not scream in agony. Soon the pain vanished, leaving her panting heavily, but she now had freedom of movement, despite his invasive presence in her head. *Excellent, he gave me a longer leash. What a merciful master*. Her thoughts were full of sarcasm and frustration as the witch touched her face, which still burned from the slap.

She gathered a handful of snow and pressed it to her cheek. This gesture caught his attention. The cruel man that tortured her mere moments ago, now looked at her with concern in his eyes. His hand pressed against her cheek, its coldness soothing the pain. She wished she could flinch away, but this could bring another punishment, and she had to stay conscious to plan an escape, so for the moment, playing submissive was her best shot. The healing magic saturated her skin as the drow repaired the damage, and even her torn lip healed under his touch.

'You shouldn't anger me. Look what you made me do. But all is forgiven now. You are mine now, my beautiful Chaos.' He pulled her against his body, his face pressed into the hollow of her throat, and inhaled her scent, trembling like a nervous lover. This sudden change in attitude and loving gentleness was more terrifying than his previous cruelty.

'Tell me you are mine. Tell me you understand. I will look after you, my beautiful treasure.' He pleaded with her like a mad man, but the more he craved her acceptance, the more she felt she could exploit this weakness and a plan formed in her mind. She would kill him with… kindness, but first, she needed him to trust her. Her hand drifted up, softly stroking his hair, and Ina answered, hammering her hatred into ironclad resolve.

'Yes, my Lord. Please forgive me.'

CHAPTER TWENTY-ONE

A short walk later, Ina found herself in a clearing, surrounded by drow hunters and their kobold helpers, all looking exhausted next to their foaming horses. One look at their leader, and they bowed their heads deeply. Not one person looked at her or questioned her presence.

'Back on the horses. We are returning to the stronghold, and don't forget to bow to your new mistress with the respect she deserves.'

One by one, each person knelt as she passed, and Ina was left unsettled by this unconditional obedience. After the show was over, everyone quickly mounted while Tar'eth led her to his stallion. The poor horse was barely standing, covered with whip lashes, and frotting from his mouth. Ina couldn't help but stroke the muzzle of the shivering animal, whose exhaustion was a clear sign of how Tar'eth overworked him chasing the dragon. With no magic to soothe his pain, Ina massaged the quivering muscles, whispering soothing words till Tar'eth lifted her to the saddle in front of him. The journey was a blur as the drow prince set a brutal pace, and soon, not only were the horses exhausted from the strenuous ride, but Ina was as well, especially since she did everything in her power to avoid touching his body.

The kobold stronghold looked too small for the army gathered inside. Horses and carts were everywhere, and mages' glittering robes mixed with drow knights' shiny plate armour. She'd landed in a hornet's nest, a perfect prison, but for the time being, Ina was too tired to care. She swayed on the horse and would have fallen, but Tar'eth's muscular arm caught her and carefully carried her inside.

'My lord, the reinforcements—' Ina heard a drow trying to catch his master's attention.

'Later! Bring refreshments to the lady's room and ensure the bath is ready. Any delay, and I will skin you all,' he said, carrying her deeper into the mountain lair.

Well, that is truly fucked up, Ina thought as her attentive new master gently lowered her to a chair in the room so dripping with gold décor it looked like a peasant's wet dream of wealthy decadence.

'How do you feel, my Lady Inanuan? The journey was harsh, I know, but I've arranged everything for you to recover,' he said, and to her surprise, he sounded genuine. If they'd met under different circumstances, she might be fooled into thinking he was gentle and caring.

'I'm fine, my lord, but I am exhausted,' she said, playing the role of a distressed princess and feeling as if with each act of compliance, he relaxed a little more in her presence. Ina didn't know whether ignorance or pride made him believe in her submission, but for the time being, it was her only advantage. While he focused on inspecting her room, completely forgetting her presence, Ina attempted the best passive pose she could muster. *Now I only need to rein in my temper till I find a way to bring this bloody mountain down on their heads.* The irony of this situation would make her laugh if the circumstances weren't that dire.

The doors slowly opened, and two people came inside. Initially, it was difficult to see in the darkened room, but the figure dressed in rich gold embossed armour must have been important because he addressed Tar'eth directly with only a brief bow.

'My lord, the reinforcements have arrived, and the crown prince is in command. He is demanding to see you immediately in the throne room. Sir, your brother is using his authority to take control of your forces.'

'I said later!' Tar'eth snapped, and Ina's hope rose slightly. She needed time to think. Getting him out of here would allow her to test the true constriction of his magic and whether the distance affected his control over her.

'My lord, your brother needs you. I should rest and attend to my female needs. Please, it would set my mind at ease if you welcomed your family to our new home.' She forced herself to stroke his cheek and even fluttered her eyelashes. Her soft and alluring voice captured his attention, and the mental pressure intensified.

Shit, I overdid it. He is not a simpleton. Ina's thoughts flashed through her mind, but she quickly suppressed them and tried her best to empty her consciousness of anything else but tiredness and hunger. She felt Tar'eth sieve through her thoughts while she sat there, completely still. Without warning, her stomach rumbled, and then again, startling the drow, and she felt Tar'eth withdraw. It looked like her chatty insides had saved the day.

'Fine,' the prince said and nodded towards the other figure. 'Serve your new lady. Her every wish is your command, understood?' He grabbed the servant by her throat, dragging her forward, and Ina gasped, pressing back into the chair. The witch watched as a porcelain mask turned to look at her. Its motionless features mirrored her own.

Tar'eth looked at Ina with a proud smile whilst stroking the mask, savouring her horror. Finally, he released the woman, who fell to her knees in front of the witch.

'There wasn't a day I didn't think of you, Inanuan. You and your magic enchanted me that night at the coronation ball.' He grasped the woman's face and tilted it to the light. 'I think I did well with this. She looks just like I remembered you, but she misses your spark. I need you, Ina. Give me your Chaos, my queen.' His voice was filled with an oily desire that seeped its tendrils deep into her magic, but without the ring, her Chaos didn't yield to his will. She felt his anger, and the pain that came with it crushed her lungs.

'Give it to me!' he shouted. She would be happy to oblige and burn him alive with her red flames if this could stop the pain.

'Unblock my magic… please… master,' she gasped, and when he let a trickle of her power slip through his block, the witch rotated her hand, and the red, visceral light of the pure Chaos shone on her palm.

Tar'eth eyes widened, and he licked his lips, looking at the physical manifestation of her power. Ina heard the others gasp, enthralled by the red flame, but even this didn't satisfy his anger. The prince grabbed the masked woman's hand and, before Ina could react, pushed it into the flames, laughing when the woman screamed and her skin bubbled angrily, consumed by the searing power.

She knew this amount of magic wasn't enough to fight her way out of this prison, and, stifling the retching caused by this perverted display, Ina closed her hand and looked at the prince, who now scowled, furious at the ending of his entertainment. 'Please, my lord, there are no windows here, and the smell of burnt skin is sickening,' she said, already feeling his oily magic spreading over her mind. Ina felt his anger and greed and prepared herself for his revenge when the seneschal spoke.

'My lord, your brother is waiting.'

Tar'eth stood motionless, his fist clenched tight, before turning without a word and leaving her cell. Overwhelmed with relief when the door closed behind him, Ina turned to the woman still kneeling in front of her.

'Who are you?'

'Your servant, my lady,' came the answer with a voice so bereft of emotion that Ina felt she was talking to a doll.

'What is your name?' she tried again, but the woman didn't even raise her head.

'Master calls me Volte. I have no other name.'

A mask. This fucker called her a mask. Ina wondered if this poor woman even knew what this drow word meant. The witch felt she had to see the servant's face and reached out, grabbing the straps and pulling them up. Volte screamed and held onto the mask as if her life depended on it. The reaction was so unnatural that Ina released her grip, letting the woman fall back into her pose.

'Take it off,' Ina ordered, but the woman only shook her head.

'Master told me to wear it. It is his wish,' she said, and the certainty of her conviction reminded Ina of the geas she tried to remove from the kobold.

'Bloody bastard!' she gasped, reaching for her magic, but the barrier Tar'eth left in her mind was still strong, allowing only a trickle to pass through.

'Don't say that. The master is kind. He loves us.' Volte's voice was full of haunted desperation, and Ina realised the woman's mind had been tortured until it shattered.

'Do you think the master loves you?'

'Oh yes, he does.' The confidence in Volte's voice was unmistakable.

'And… you love him?' Ina asked again, counting the bruises and bite marks on the woman's skin.

'Yes, I love him. You will love him too. He told me you will.'

There was no false note in Volte's voice, and Ina could not believe her ears. The eyes behind the mask shone with adoration for her tormentor, and the witch understood the gravity of the situation. What could he do to her if Tar'eth could make this woman love him, despite the torture he inflicted on her?

Ina quickly tore up the rich drapes to bandage Volte's injury and sent her for food. She needed a moment alone. Fear was a lousy advisor, and right now, she was scared, clueless, and in desperate need of some solution against mind magic. Ina needed a distraction and, seeing a brush on a nearby table, used the familiar routine to calm her mind. Looking into the mirror on the table, she could not believe her reflection appeared so peaceful when all she wanted to do was to scream.

Ina touched the stone on her chest. *Was it you that brought Tar'eth to me?* She remembered Skarbnik's words that the stones wanted to reunite, but she could not believe the will or magic of an inanimate object could cause so much grief. She thought of Volte's burn and flicked her hand again, looking at the weak, flickering flame that illuminated the room. It didn't burn her, yet any other who came in touch with it—maybe except Mar and Ren when she was in control to wield it—burned or collapsed into dust. Suddenly it hit her. She had her magic back. It was just a trickle, but Tar'eth's anger left a small slit open, and his control over her was not as absolute as he thought. The stray thought niggled at a memory until it blossomed into recognition.

'What can I do with you, my precious?' Ina whispered, looking at the flickering flame. 'I can't fight with it, not with a whole stronghold full of warriors and mages, but can I defend myself somehow?' *Skarbnik! That damn god had taught her to shield her mind. Did he know this was going to happen? Of course he did, why else would the Gamayun appear and prattle on about mirrors?* Ina's thoughts were racing. It sounded too easy, but she had to try. She focused and shaped the trickle of Chaos she felt inside into a smooth, reflective wall, stretching it around her inner thoughts. Just as she was about to seal the room around her psyche, Ina remembered Tar'eth searching her mind and quickly pushed out thoughts of fear, submission, and hints of contentment before sealing off the protective spell. If someone looked at it now, they would see nothing but a shallow noble lady ready to lie down and take it. *Now the hardest part, remember you are sweet and submissive till you find a way to get your magic back.* Ina snorted her amusement at that thought just as the door opened, and Volte entered, carrying a tray laden with food.

'Eat, my lady. We need to dress you appropriately. The master and the crown prince request your presence at your earliest convenience.'

Mar stayed in the air by sheer force of will, pushing his injured body to its limits, but the pain from his torn flesh was nothing compared to the torture of his mind. He'd failed again, and the woman he would happily die for was now alone and in trouble, and he didn't know how to fix it.

A half-delirious scan of the ground shocked Mar from his stupor as he saw Liath, its new defences and a ragtag army practising under his father's command. The dragon swooped down towards his father, landing in a tangle of limbs, gasping out a sob before reining in his emotions and standing up to face the crowd of unfamiliar faces, mixed with veterans he knew from his old campaigns. The wide-eyed stares reminded Mar he was a terrifying dragon, and he took a moment to transform, nearly collapsing as the toll from Ina's magic and blood loss made him dizzy. As a familiar hand grasped his arm and held him steady, Mar almost lost control at the relief of seeing his friend safe and sound.

'Where is Ina?' The tension in Ghost's voice was palpable, but the captain shook his head, looking around.

'Not here. Take me inside. There were… complications.'

As much as he wanted to shout out the call to arms, Mar knew his news would destroy morale and cause widespread panic. Ren looked at him as if he wanted his answers immediately, but much to Mar's relief, he finally nodded and supported Mar as they walked into the castle.

Someone must have informed his mother and Ayni of his arrival, as both women were at the entrance and started fussing over him as soon as he entered. Mar accepted it with grace, using the moment to collect his thoughts.

'Enough! Mar, where is Ina?' Ren shouted as the door snapped open, and Alleron entered the room.

'Where is the Chaos mage? Please tell me she is dead, not captured?'

Mar heard the quiet hiss of the unsheathed blade and stumbled between his father and Ren.

'Sa'Ren, no. He didn't mean that.'

Mar turned to his father, giving Alleron the scorn-filled glare. 'I never heard you wishing for anyone's death, let alone your future daughter-in-law.' He hobbled back to the chair, feeling defeated by the outburst, more than he was comfortable admitting.

'The drow prince captured Ina, and the bastard gained access to her magic.' Mar gestured to his wounds. 'We need to get her back so I can burn that fucker's smarmy grin to ash. I can lead the army to their fortress, but do we have enough provisions to lay siege to it?'

'If Ina wanted you dead, you would be talking to Veles right now.' Ren said this with absolute confidence, and Mar nodded in agreement.

'You are not taking the army. We don't have enough soldiers, and a siege in the mountains during the winter is suicide. Since they have her, I'm sure the drow army will attack here before long. We must defend the people of Liath, not throw them away for a single person, no matter how much she is loved.' Alleron looked at him, and Mar saw a leader who'd fought too many battles to believe in a happy ending.

'What have you heard?' Mar asked, knowing his father must have received some information about the invaders.

'The leaders of the Stone Halls sent a message that an army of drow and a contingent of mages entered the trade tunnel. With Ina captured, they now have a Chaos mage. How long do you expect we will last? Our reinforcements have yet to arrive, and even if they appear in time, I suspect they will be no better than serfs conscripted from the fields.' Alleron approached and placed a hand on his son's shoulder. 'I need a leader, Mar. So harden your heart, because if we can't free Ina, you're the only one with a chance of killing her.'

Mar watched his own fist crashing into his father's chest in slow-motion, launching the old lord a few metres backwards.

'What the fuck is wrong with you? Why do you want her gone so badly?' he asked, almost shouting his words, but while his father was still trying to catch his breath, Ayni answered.

'Because an unhinged Chaos mage controlled by a madman will be a catastrophe for everyone, not just Cornovii.'

The heavy impact of the door that followed Ren's departure merged with the sound of trumpets and a marching army's distant singing. Mar looked at his father angrily before breaking his silence.

'I will see to Ren. I know you are right, father, but I also know Ina, and she won't give up, so neither will I. She is stronger than you think.' His father gave him a quick nod, and Mar left the room, hoping he could catch up with Ghost before his friend embarked on a suicide mission.

It took him a moment before he found Ren. His friend had chosen the garden from all the places, and now he was sitting there looking at the frozen pond.

'This is my fault,' Ren said when Mar approached. 'I should have stayed with her.'

The sorrow in his voice was palpable and so familiar. 'No, Sa'Ren, I was the one who failed her. You not only warned Liath in time, but it appears you also recruited allies and arranged for reinforcements. Thanks to you, we have a chance of surviving the coming storm.' Mar's words, instead of helping, seemed to infuriate his companion.

'Yes, you failed her. She loves you so much, I would give my life for that love, and you left her at the mercy of the drow. Now your father wants to kill her for something you should have prevented. I won't let it happen, Mar. I will burn this place down before any of you lay a finger on her.' Ren stood up and faced his captain. The humble Ghost was gone, replaced by the man who would have been emperor of Yanwo if he hadn't forfeited his rights to his brother. 'She is the only family I have, and as long as I live, she will be safe.' Ren moved to walk past him, but Mar placed a hand on his shoulder, stopping him.

'You're a damn fool if you think I'd let them hurt Ina. Will you listen to my plan or stew in your anger at my incompetence and kill yourself trying to save her alone?'

Ren's intense gaze never wavered as Mar outlined his plan. They would wait in Liath, preparing for the drow attack, as it was unlikely the drow would hurt their most prized possession. When the enemy arrived, Ren would sneak into their camp and retrieve Ina. A sleeping agent would be used as the witch was under the drow's control. At the same time, Mar would attack from above as a diversion. For this to work, though, they would need to know the witch's position, and Ren suggested using the shifter clans to scout and infiltrate the camp as spies.

'Ren, if they capture you—' Mar tried to issue the warning, but Ren cut him off.

'No, that will not happen. I will succeed, or I will die,' he stated, and Mar shook his head.

'Then we'd best succeed, yes?' Now that the plan was set, Ren's voice sounded lighter, even happier, and Mar couldn't help but ask.

'I saw how Ayni looked at you, and I thought…' Mar shook his head and laughed, embarrassed by his own words. 'Forgive me, my friend. I hoped we would both find happiness, but now is not the time for that discussion.'

Ren looked at him, and Mar saw the understanding in his friend's eyes. 'Mar, Ina made it clear you are her only choice. I love her, and I will protect her with my life. It's not uncommon in Yanwo to love more than one person, but I know it is difficult for you to understand. As for Ayni, I know she has no loyalty to Ina, and I thought we shared something, but after her words today, I don't know… but I know I will not betray a friend to keep a lover.'

Mar nodded. 'Let's go back and brief my father on the plan and see what reinforcements our gracious king has gifted us. Perhaps it will be enough to save our worthless rears.' Mar started walking towards the castle. 'Oh, and Ren? Ina is not your only family, my brother,' he said, feeling those words were never more true than now.

CHAPTER TWENTY-TWO

The black dress she was asked to wear highlighted the paleness of her skin and left little to the imagination. Ina sighed deeply when Volte pinned up her hair and applied colourful makeup to her face. The witch looked at the mirror, and the face that looked back could easily belong in the brothels King Rewan's father enjoyed so much.

Ina closed her eyes and checked her spell. The only thoughts not hidden within the mirrored room were apprehension and the submissive attitude that would lower her captor's guard. Now, all she needed was to regain full control of her magic. The question was how she could coerce him to do this. Ina's kidnapper had mentioned first seeing her at the coronation ball, and she thought of giving him what he expected, her best version of the perfect lady of Cornovii, to see where it led. A knock at the door was the only warning she received as two guards walked into the room, and Ina stood gracefully, ready to fight for her freedom.

The guards didn't bother hiding their lecherous stares, but she pretended not to notice, her head held high, as she glided gracefully down the corridor, cataloguing each junction and turn on her route. Disappointingly, it seemed they were deep underground, and although she felt the brush of fresh air, she could not locate any exit points.

Ina looked around as she entered the throne room. It was reasonably large, but relatively sparse. Tar'eth stood arguing with another tall drow, who radiated condensed fury and disdain. Ina couldn't hear from so far away, and as she got closer, the stranger broke off his tirade to look at her lustfully, smirking.

'So you are the pet Chaos mage my brother was gushing about so much? Come here, woman, let me see you.' He tried to compel her, and Ina almost smirked at this weak attempt. This was a perfect opportunity to drive a wedge between the brothers, so Ina ignored the newcomer, and with a soft smile, she looked at Tar'eth and sank into a deep curtsey.

'My lord, you summoned me?'

Her devotion to Tar'eth made the new drow's eyes darken in anger, but her new master seemed pleased by her demeanour and gestured her closer.

'Come Inanuan, meet my brother, who came here to aid us in our endeavour. Ord'eth, show some manners. She is the first pure Chaos mage born in generations.' The prince raised her hand, pulling her closer and positioned her in front of him. Trapped between two drow, Ina felt suffocated as Ord'eth's hands trailed over her bare shoulders, toying with the peridot necklace.

'I see she's already bonded with two of the Chaos regalia. Did you find the circlet as well?' he asked, pressing closer, and Ina struggled to remain detached. With Tar'eth pressed to her back and Ord'eth taking liberties with her body, she felt soon she would have to lie down and take it or take a chance with this bit of power she had and kill at least one of them. Her rescue came from an unexpected saviour. Before this encounter ended in some sinister intimacy, Tar'eth pulled her back with a possessive snarl.

'No, I didn't find the circlet, and keep your hands to yourself, brother, or mother might find out what happened to your last wife.'

The grip on Ina's arm tightened as Tar'eth threatened his brother, and her blood ran cold when Ord'eth laughed. 'Fine, although you never used to mind sharing. So, show me, little brother, what is so special about her that you want to start a war?'

Tar'eth's smug smile sent a chill down her spine. He stroked her cheek with a single claw, and he said, his voice quivering in anticipation, 'Show him your Chaos, my lady, and we will march to Liath tomorrow.'

The barrier that held her magic fell, and Ina felt the commanding thought bouncing off the mirror wall, telling her to release her magic. The euphoria of being reunited with her power flooded her like a cleansing spring shower after a winter spent huddling near the fire to survive. With power came the thought of killing them on the spot. *I would have to kill them both, escape the fortress, and then hike to Liath.*

Ina hesitated. This building wasn't just a garrison for drows, but a place for common soldiers, servants, and kobold families, and she was not ready to sacrifice them all for her freedom. *We will march to Liath tomorrow, that's what he said.* Still wary of Tar'eth's control, Ina delved into her power, revelling in the moment's purity before offering the drow a serene smile and manifesting a ball of Chaos in her palm. The crimson flame danced over her fingers as she commanded its movements, and Ord'eths eyes widened in greed as he leaned in to inspect the magic.

'Show me what else you can do,' he said, and when Ina didn't move, the prince looked at his brother. 'Free her mind. You can subdue her later. I want to feel her fury.'

Ina felt the spectral shackles slide away, and Tar'eth looked at her, tense and ready to throw a net around her mind if she strayed. *Too late for this now*, Ina thought, but seeing him so prepared to enslave her again made the urge to collapse the mountain on his head nearly overwhelming. It was good they wanted to taste her anger as she had plenty to give, but it was not the time for this yet, so gritting her teeth to restrain herself, she reached for the Chaos and lit every torch in the room with her magic.

'Oh yes, little human, show me what you can do.' The sensual pleasure in Ord'eth's voice made her sick, and she turned towards him, but he just laughed at her obvious repulsion. *One dead drow doesn't make me evil*, she thought, blasting him with raw energy, but a translucent shield flashed around him seconds before impact, and much to her regret, her spell was deflected, smashing into a wall.

The granite melted, and cold fresh air and sunlight flooded the room. Suddenly blinded by the daylight, the princes covered their eyes, and Ina approached the opening. The round hole she created gave her a good view of the snowy tops of the surrounding peaks, and Ina's heart sank at how far down the ground was. For the first time in her life, she regretted not having wings.

A hearty laugh shook the room, and Tar'eth's magic again flooded her mind, safely reflected by the mirror's surface. The witch took a deep breath, slipping into the role of an obedient captive. When she turned, Ord'eth was patting his brother on the shoulder.

'She made you a window in solid granite. Not even dragon fire can melt the rock like this. You won, my brother. As you stated, we will march to Liath tomorrow,' he said and approached her, grabbing her chin and forcing her head up. Ina let her hatred escape the mirror room, and Ord'eth smiled. 'So feisty, but nothing a good whipping can't fix. I'm the Shield of the Queen. Your magic can't hurt me. You should have chosen Tar'eth as your target when you had the chance. Did you know women rule in Arknay, Inanuan? We do their bidding, and even I must listen to my mother, but you are not a drow, my little morsel, and I'm looking forward to taming you.'

Fuck this. Shield or not, I'd rather die than let you have me, Ina thought and reached for her Chaos when the drow leaned forward to kiss her. Suddenly, a powerful arm pulled the man away. Tar'eth held his brother tight, violent madness shining in his eyes.

'She is mine. You will not touch her. And when we move to Liath, you will follow my command, just as our mother instructed. Yes, I read the letter, so I know you are mine to command.' Tar'eth pushed his brother aside, and the unbridled hatred in the crown prince's eyes promised vengeance for this moment. *He wants to kill Tar'eth, so I need to find a way to use it*, Ina thought and suppressed her happiness. It was a long way to go, but her freedom and the discord between brothers were an excellent place to start her personal war.

'I hope he didn't hurt you, my lady,' Tar'eth murmured, and Ina couldn't stop thinking something was wrong in his head if he treated her with the courtesy of a fated lover while happily imprisoning and torturing her.

'No, my lord, he didn't. Thank you for your protection.'

Her submission and flat voice pleased him, and Tar'eth called the guards to escort his prize to her room. As Ina was about to leave, he grabbed a handful of her hair, bent her head to one side and pressed his face to her neck, breathing in her scent, his hands trembling in excitement.

'My brother is a fool, but I will not disrespect your power by treating you like a whore.' He grazed his teeth over her skin, and his grasp strengthened before he pushed her towards the door. 'Go now before my resolve breaks.'

Ina walked as fast as possible whilst trying to look dignified. This man was a mess, and she swore she would never complain about her overprotective dragon after this experience. She needed a quiet night to think about the situation. Ord'eth's abilities posed a problem. Hopefully, nothing a good blade or dragon fire couldn't sort out, but she had to be careful and tread lightly around him for now. The witch sat on the bed and pressed her hands to the peridot on her chest. *Mar, if you can hear me. I'm well, and I'm coming, and I promise I will sort this out, somehow.* She sent the words into the connection she felt in her chest. It was only a slight chance, but she hoped the message reached her dragon.

The day dragged on, and Mar wondered if anyone would notice if he beat his head against the wall till he passed out. The turmoil in his mind was driving him insane. With all his heart, he wanted to fly to the kobold fortress and tear it stone from stone till Ina was safe in his arms. The captain's tactician mind held him back by the thinnest of threads. Only the prospect of incinerating that smug drow and humbling his army kept Mar from ruining their best chance of winning.

Mar staggered towards the stables, regretting the previous night's overindulgence, ignoring his father's disapproving stare. *You try taming this raging inferno without a drink, old man.* The thought was petty, but eased some of the pain in his head. A recent memory helped even more. When the stable boy ran up earlier, bouncing excitedly, telling him Woron and the witch's strange mount had appeared at the castle gates, he nearly broke down and cried.

The stable welcomed him with the musky smell of horses and leather, and despite the dire situation, Mar started to relax. Woron's head hit his chest playfully, and he patted the horse's muscular neck.

'I failed you too, old boy. I shouldn't have left you there alone,' Mar mumbled, petting the affectionate horse before reaching for the brush. The slow rhythm of grooming his warhorse centred Mar's thoughts, the familiar soldier's work reminding him of the tasks ahead. He had to assess their reinforcements, as his father decided he would lead the regular soldiers to secure the city gates and walls. Ren would lead the skirmishers with a mismatched army of shifters, mercenaries, and those men and women of Liath able to fight. Alleron, as a military commander, would take overall command and deal with the mages who were supposed to arrive from the capital. Mar smirked, feeling Nerissa's hand in all this. The magical academy never allowed its battlemages to be under the army's authority. Still, there was nothing the old healer couldn't arrange for Ina's protection, and Mar was grateful for all the help he could get.

Thoughts of the witch rekindled his shame at failing to keep her safe, and his growing worry for her safety. Mar tightened his fist on the brush, feeling helpless like never before. A sudden searing heat in his chest brought him to his knees. Since his transformation, Mar could occasionally feel Ina's emotions through the link, but this connection hit him like a hammer. His consciousness was flooded with reassurance and love. That crazy, untamed witch was calling to him, and as usual, Ina didn't do anything in half measures, giving him the full blast of her power. Mar gasped. *Her power!* A dragon's joyous roar shook the stable walls as he realised Ina had regained control of her magic.

'So, what is so enjoyable about rolling around in horse shit? Oh, and aren't you supposed to be a scary dragon or something?' asked a deep baritone that could only belong to one person.

'Daro! Haven't they locked you up yet?' Mar raised his head to see his two friends looking at him with amusement. A glance down, and Mar laughed ruefully. His hands and knees were deep in horse manure, and he was grateful Ina's magic hadn't landed him face first in the damn stuff. He got up and rushed to Daro with a malicious grin, arms reaching to embrace his comrade.

'Oh no, you don't, you scaly fucker.' Orc backed up, waving his hands in front of him. 'Wash first, I'm now a respectable captain of the guards, and I refuse to smell like a stable boy.'

Mar laughed harder and went to the trough to wash himself off. While passing Ren, he heard a soft inquiry. 'Ina?'

'Safe and sound, and if I'm not wrong, in control.'

Ren nodded. 'I felt it too, but it looks like you were her primary target. I should be grateful for once because, gods, you stink.'

After washing, the three men went to the training grounds, where Mar looked over the reinforcements from the capital. Palace guards, delicate and shiny, next to battle-hardened veterans and bold and rowdy mercenaries, like debutants before their first ball. Mar couldn't help but punch Daro in the head.

'Oh, mighty captain, I'm so happy you got this job. I'm not qualified to keep those gods of war safe,' he jested, pointing to the young nobles barely grown enough to hold a sword, but Daro only turned to him, flashing a toothy grin.

'Oh, but I forgot to tell you. The king wants his dragon back. Quoting his majesty, *"I haven't dismissed him from my service".*'

Mar rolled his eyes and looked at the motley crowd before him. With a roguish grin, he roared, startling his friends but grabbing the attention of everyone on the field.

'I am Marcach of Liath, and you have three minutes to form ranks and ready yourselves for inspection.' He waited for them to follow his command before speaking again. 'From now on, I will be your commander, and, as some of you may already know, I am also a dragon, so look carefully, and don't crap your pants when you see me in battle.' His words were met with a nervous chuckle before he continued to issue their orders.

'As the Lord Commander decreed, I will lead the standing army. Those already conscripted, free companies and veterans who previously fought here will stay on the training ground. We will practise defensive formations and anti-siege techniques, as you will likely be the first to face the combined kobold and drow forces.' Mar pointed to Ren, who stepped forward as if on command.

'This is Sa'Ren Gerel. He will take command of the shifter clans and hunters. I know you are keen to fight, but your skills lie elsewhere. You must be shadows, destroying their provisions and causing havoc from the sidelines. For this task, there is none better than the Ghost of Yanwo himself.' Mar looked at Ren, who nodded, flashed him a mischievous smile, and stepped to the side, exposing Daro. Mar approached and placed a hand on the orc's shoulder.

'Our captain of the king's guards and his regiment will secure the civilians and operate the defensive machinery. The city will be under his control. Remember, behind those walls are everyone who is too old, too young, or ill-equipped to fight. The walls are the only thing that defends them from death. Don't forget, war is no excuse for criminal behaviour, and anyone caught by the guards will be punished according to martial law.' Mar grimaced and added after a moment, 'The mages will go to the walls as well, but don't be deceived by our bejewelled colleague's appearance. They can rain fire on your head, so don't provoke them and ensure their wrath is aimed at the enemy.'

Mar observed as the men and women divided themselves into groups. He'd never had such a mismatched bunch to lead. Suddenly, a messenger caught his attention.

'Sir, your father wishes to see you immediately, and your companions as well.'

That could only mean one thing: trouble was coming, and his father was calling for his war council. Mar turned on his heel and walked to the main castle, gesturing for Ren and Daro to follow.

The map room was buzzing. Mar noticed his father sitting stiffly on his chair, his fingers picking at the armrest, and the old woman sat next to him. The captain's eyes narrowed warily. The arch healer of Cornovii had a habit of scolding him like a schoolboy.

'Mar, I'm glad you're here. Lady Nerissa has some questions before we can plan the defence of Liath.' He smiled through pursed lips, ruthlessly throwing his firstborn under this runaway carriage.

'Where is my niece?' Nerissa turned to him, pinning him down with her baleful gaze. Mar almost shrank back, remembering just how formidable this mage was, knowing any falsehood would end in pain and humiliation. Mar dutifully briefed her on their adventures, including their parting from Ren to the moment Ina was captured. The more he talked, the more Nerissa paled, and when he came to the last moments of his tale, the old woman looked bereft and frightened

'I know she is alive. I can feel it.' Mar was trying to reassure her, but when Nerissa looked at him, he saw the depths of her despair.

'I know she is alive, no drow would dare kill a Chaos mage, but do you know how they treat women of other races? This is not my first war, and I've treated those who lived to tell the tale of their encounters. Drow men like pain. It excites them, and they are inventive in finding ways to inflict it. I know Ina has value to them, but they will enjoy trying to break her.'

Mar felt his blood turn to ice and rushed to the door, but his father's voice stopped him.

'It is too late now, and I called you all here because the latest refugees tell of a black army heading this way. As much as I wish Ina were safe and with us, can we focus on the matter at hand? She will be here soon anyway, and this city is in danger.'

Mar squeezed his fist and moved back to the table. His father was right, but it didn't make it any easier for him, and judging by Ren's grim face, they both shared the same desire to destroy their enemy.

They finished late at night, and Mar went to his room, unsuccessfully trying to catch some sleep. The soft knock on the door surprised him, but what was even stranger was that Ayni had visited him at such an hour.

'What can I do for you?' He could only hope whatever brought her here was a trivial problem, but her determined expression didn't suggest anything good.

'Can I come in, Mar? We need to talk.'

Too tired to argue, he opened the door wider, letting the dragoness inside.

'I'm sorry,' she started, but Mar waved her off.

'Ayni, I'm tired, worried, and need some sleep. Whatever you want to apologise for, it can wait till tomorrow.'

'No, it can't. I neglected to teach you for long enough and look at the consequences. Tell me what happened. Why you landed next to the river, not straight in Liath?'

'I told you already. We just needed to land quickly. Ina is not used to flying, that's all.'

'That tells me she panicked, and you didn't know about projecting.' Ayni looked at him, and Mar felt it was more to reassure herself than expecting his answer. She sighed and averted her eyes when he shook his head before explaining.

'Projecting helps the wingless ones who, due to various circumstances, have to ride a dragon. For them, being on top of the beast in the clouds is a terrifying experience, and you can help by projecting your thoughts and feelings. Just think about the peace you feel inside when you glide through the clouds. It will help, and she will feel safe on your back despite her fear.'

Her words shocked him. He had already instinctively connected to Ina during the flight, but didn't even think of calming her down that way. If he only knew it back then. Now, looking at Ayni and remembering how comfortable he felt with

Ina on his back, he asked, 'So there is a chance she could be a dragon rider?'

'No, you and Ina have a bond like no other, but for the dragon to unite with the rider… it is special in a different way. First, you feel that you have found your companion, and the bond that connects you during your first flight ensures you never have to project for them because they already have the heart of the dragon. Sometimes it transfers into a mating bond, or they become the closest of brethren.'

Mar noticed the soft blush on her cheeks and couldn't resist asking, 'You and Ren?'

'Yes…'

Before Mar could enquire more, the dragoness walked to the door, but before she left, she turned around and looked directly at him.

'For what it's worth, you can count on me. Whatever trouble is heading this way.'

CHAPTER TWENTY-THREE

The following two days were hectic. Mar trained his troops day and night, trying to form a coherent fighting force from so many independent units. If he'd had more time, he could've created an army that any commander would be proud to lead, one that could protect their borders and prevent these predatory attacks. As the captain of the palace guards, Mar often felt more like a babysitter to dissolute nobles than a military leader, so despite the circumstances, he felt more like a soldier than he had in years.

After finishing for the day, the proud but weary leader scraped mud off the parts of his body he could reach and headed into the bathhouse, soon followed by a very tense Ren. After letting the heat relax overworked muscles, Mar turned to his friend and asked, 'Any news from your reconnaissance missions?'

'They will be here tomorrow, and Ina is with them. Two drow nobles are parading her around like a puppet,' Ren said, and Mar frowned at his thoughts.

'Is she… aware?' he asked, trying to calm the fast beating of his heart.

Ren sighed heavily and ran his hand through his long, raven hair. 'I can't be sure, but I think she is. The drow forced her to change the river's course, and Ina arranged it so the settlement below would still have access to fresh water, all without causing damage to the forest. She also seemed to notice the shifters, even in their animal shape, or at least that's what they told me.'

I will see you tomorrow, and let's pray you are there to come back to me, my spitfire, Mar thought as he closed his eyes to enjoy the last peaceful night before facing the harsh reality of the morning. A sudden blast of icy air caused a rash of goosebumps on his skin when Daro stormed in.

'Fucking hell, Mar. I have to deal with your father, Nerissa, and the hellion leading the birdbrained mages, and you're here relaxing. Oh… Ren,' the orc stuttered before looking around. 'Did I miss the announcement? Or was I not invited?'

Mar barely opened his eyes, but his lips twitched in amusement at the orc's outburst.

'As you are the only one dressed here, get out and come back with some mead and more appropriate attire. It may be the last night I see you both alive, so let's make it worth remembering.'

Daro stood there for a moment before storming off. When he returned dressed only in a towel with three sizable jugs of mead, his massive body filled the remaining space in the bath chamber. He passed the alcohol to his friends and raised his drink for a toast.

'For our ladies and our friendship, may it never grow old.' When they'd all finished, Daro's smile widened.

'And now you will tell me why Mar isn't a dragon and why the women are gossiping over how his "wife" can't take her eyes off Ren. How much trouble did you get into without me?'

'We'll need a lot more mead for this discussion,' Mar said, and Ren smirked at those words. But pressured by his friends, the dragon recounted the story that made Daro's eyes widen, cursing the turn of events.

'I can't wait to tell Velka,' he finally laughed. 'So just to be clear, you're with Ina, despite this woman, Ayni, claiming to be your wife, and now Ayni is into Ren because you wouldn't agree to be her husband?' Daro couldn't stop laughing when he turned to Ren. 'And what do you have to say about it? You were all over Ina like a rash, and now you are not?'

'Ina made her choice and asked me to move on, so I am.' Ren's calm answer even provoked a reaction from Mar.

'You make it sound so easy. What about Ayni? Does she know she wasn't your first choice?'

'Is she my choice, Mar?' Ren asked, but Mar knew his friend was teasing him. 'Ina and I were not fated to be together, and these feelings will always be a part of me. As for Ayni... she is much older than you think, and despite having such poor taste in potential husbands, I like her company. Hopefully, she also likes mine. For now, we both decided to enjoy it while it lasts.'

Mar wished he knew how to express his gratitude and respect for his friend. Out of them all, the Ghost was the wisest, and he brought peace to this troublesome matter with his simple answer.

Daro looked between them and hit his palm into the wet wood. 'Bloody bones, you two know how to complicate things. This calls for another drink.' His blunt comment eased the tension in the air. The conversation drifted into barracks humour, battle preparation, and mutual appreciation of manly muscles and perky pecks. The mead flowed freely, and the comments became more ribald as the jugs emptied.

It was well past midnight when servants were called to escort the three staggering men to their chambers, alerting Alleron that his three commanders were temporarily indisposed.

Ina swayed on the horse, wishing she rode her orein. Zjawa's steps were smooth and relaxing, but after a whole day of riding on this gnarly little donkey, Ina felt every bone on his back, and her face ached from holding the plain emotionless face of a doll.

Now that the drow army had descended from the mountain, it was clear their numbers would be a significant threat to the castle looming before them. Ina noticed the new ballistae and lots of soldiers on the walls. *Ren, you are a miracle worker*, she thought with relief.

The drow princes commanded their troops to set up camp, each glaring at the other for daring to take control, and the witch hoped she would get to rest and stretch her legs in her tent. The sun had already set, and an early night was upon them when Ina pondered over her next move. Initially, she intended to sneak out as soon as they set up camp, but after hearing more of their battle plans, she resolved to stay with the drow army and give them a nasty surprise once the siege began.

She must have played her role well, as the princes ignored her to continually snipe at each other, trying to outdo their rival with bigger and better magical plans. Thanks to their rivalry, Ina learned about blood magic, the sacrifices they needed, and the control it gave them over the oath-bound kobolds to use as fodder for their battles and spells. She had to be rested and well-fed to deal with whatever power would be used tomorrow, as she would face several highly skilled mages. As soon as she sent a servant for some food, Ina heard a ripping sound from the side of the tent, and a small knife appeared in the gap, followed by a black-clad figure.

The figure was too short to be a drow, and Ina wished she had the hunting knives Ren had given her at the beginning of their journey. Instead, she reached for Chaos, and blazing vipers wrapped around her forearms, ready to strike. At the last moment, she hesitated. There was something familiar about how her visitor moved, so she waited, poised to attack, as he removed his mask, and Ina recognised a familiar face.

'Ren! What are... Thank the gods. I'm so happy to see you,' she said, falling into his embrace.

The warrior pressed her to his chest, inhaling in her scent, reassuring himself that it wasn't a dream before he pulled back and grabbed her hand.

'We have to go. Use your bond to send a signal to Mar. He will create a distraction, but it won't take long for the drow to secure you,' he said, pulling her towards the cut in the fabric, only stopping when she resisted.

'No, I need to stay. Tar'eth plans to attack soon, and he has mages who can manipulate Chaos. Not as well as me,' she said, rolling her eyes before resuming her explanation. 'But they plan to use blood magic to fuel their spells and rain magical fire on Liath. I have to stop it.'

Ina tried to release Ren's hand, but he held on tight.

'It is too dangerous. You can do it from the castle. Please, let's go. I know you think this is what you need to do, but you are a weapon they can use against us, not just your magic. You think Mar wouldn't do anything they asked to keep you safe?' Ren's plea for Mar told her how desperate her friend was, but she held firm to her resolve.

'No. Go back and tell him I… that I will do my best, and I'm of sound mind. Also, the kobolds are innocent and are being forced to fight by unnatural means. Maybe they can help if they're freed from it. From what I've seen in the stronghold, they are also victims. Now, go. I will be fine. I promise.'

Ina watched as Ren struggled with her decision, but the sound of someone approaching caused him to curse in his native language before disappearing from the tent. Ina only had a moment to cast a simple illusion on the ripped fabric before Volte entered, carrying a tray of food and offering the meal to Ina with a respectful bow. The witch ate slowly, examining her options.

Despite her confidence when talking to Ren, she was still unsure how to stop the drow without killing all the innocent victims of their magic. As for using her Chaos, the force was not fussy in picking up the targets, and the destruction of the battlefield always threatened her control, combining it with drow spells… No! Blood magic was forbidden for good reason, and her knowledge from her university education indicated that the only way to disrupt that power was to break their link to the sacrificial victims. There was another problem. She didn't know what spells they had prepared in advance, but she knew even with two items of the Chaos regalia, she didn't have enough of her magic to face a sect of powerful mages supported by an army and two drow princes unless she siphoned the life of their victims.

I'm just as bad as these monsters, using death and destruction as fuel. Bitterness darkened her thoughts as she accepted the need to wait until the battle started and used the deaths of the soldiers to give a needed boost. It was tempting to attack now, sparing the soldiers' lives even at the cost of her own, but common sense prevailed. Even if she killed Tar'eth and some of the mages, there was still Ord'eth with his unnerving shield, and she doubted she could stop them all because, despite the picture portrayed in tavern ballads, she knew the true extent of her power.

Still, somehow, she would have to destroy the corrupted mages or disrupt their ritual before it could be completed. *Small task for a witch,* Ina thought, biting her lip, trying to find the best way to stop the ceremony when her thoughts were interrupted by a new arrival. She looked up and saw the prince before her, dressed in armour so black it seemed to absorb the surrounding light, and ice slid down her spine at how intimidating he looked.

Tar'eth approached her. He passed a bundle to Volte, and the woman in the porcelain mask came to him, taking it with reverence.

'Prepare your lady. She must look like a drow queen, and you have half an hour before we leave to introduce ourselves.'

When the servant unpacked the bundle, Ina saw black leather armour, dark as the night itself. Tar'eth stroked her face and smiled. 'You will see your dragon soon, likely for the last time, alive at least. We need to make sure you look your best.'

Ina felt him probing her mind again, but she showed him only what he wanted to see, her thoughts hidden behind the mirror wall. They were almost alone in the tent, and the idea of blasting him with Chaos was so tempting. If only there weren't a second leader. *If you had the circlet, you could control them all.* The dark whisper in her mind giggled maniacally, and Ina pushed it away, focusing on the problem of Ord'eth. The crown prince seemed more stable and tactically minded, and even without his abilities, this made him a significant threat. Ina, feigning indifference, raised her arms, letting Volte help her with her outfit. Unfortunately, Tar'eth was still there as she changed into the revealing black armour.

Who the fuck exposes their tits and thighs when heading to battle? Ina thought, looking at the strips of leather and silk more fitting to the brothels of the southern kingdoms than a wintry battlefield in Liath. She had little time to think about it, feeling Tar'eth's scorching gaze as his eyes devoured her body from the corner. Soon he was not just gazing at her with desire, but it took all of her strength not to shudder when his fingernails trailed down her back and his breath moved over her neck.

Her captor restrained himself from inflicting further indignities before taking Ina from the tent to his brother and mounting his horse, lifting her onto the saddle before him, aiming a smirk at the crown prince.

The army was already marching, and it surprised her how such a sizeable force moved so quietly. Then she realised the drow mages had cast a silencing spell that muffled even the snorting of the horses. Ina gasped at how, without sound, the black army was almost invisible as it moved in the middle of the long winter night. She glanced at Tar'eth, but luck was on her side. The drow prince was too busy supervising his army to pay attention to her display of independence.

With Tar'eth and Ord'eth preoccupied with relocating the forces, Ina had time to observe each placement. The kobold infantry and enthralled humans were the first line of attack, set to roll siege towers to the walls, their ranks supported by archers and flanked by heavy cavalry. The drow mages organised themselves at the back of the army, pulling along massive crosses.

At this precise moment, Ina realised this attack wouldn't be a mere skirmish, but a full-blown battle. Under cover of the night, the drow army was marching to attack Liath, and she was stuck there without a plan or preparation. The infantry moved forward, and she sent a desperate call to Mar, hoping he would be awake to hear her.

If he heard or not, torches burst into flame along the walls, bells began ringing, and the defenders roared their welcome, followed by a volley of arrows.

She heard Tar'eth curse and shout out commands while the silencing spell fell apart, filling the air with the pandemonium of battle as warriors ran towards the walls to meet their doom. As people began dying, Ina felt the first wisps of Chaos caress her skin like an affectionate cat, rubbing itself on her, begging to be let in. Screams filled the air, but not from the battlefield. These came from behind, surprising her, and the witch snapped her head around. The horror she saw stunned her. In her innocence, she thought the drow mages would use the blood link to take their power from the soldiers' deaths in battle, but now she witnessed the true purpose of the crosses.

Each one held a victim splayed out over the makeshift altars, as dark mages slowly flayed the skin from their bodies, harvesting the pain and death to create Chaos. The mages frantically siphoned off a fraction of the power into spells that they used to attack the gates of Liath, but the majority crashed into Ina, drawn by the regalia she wore, almost bringing the witch to her knees.

The suffering of the victims overwhelmed her mind. That anyone could do such a thing horrified Ina in a way she had never experienced. Even the deaths on the battlefield hardly registered as she stood there, transfixed by the sight before her.

Ina's indifference to the battle was noticed, and Tar'eth moved in front of her, barking out a command to destroy the walls, but with his power no longer controlling her mind, the witch didn't notice until, screaming in her face, he struck her so hard that she crashed to the ground.

Suddenly, the world snapped back into focus, and the sounds and smells of battle assaulted her senses. The drow prince was already upon her, and his face was a mask of rage when Tar'eth lifted her by the throat and, like a doll, turned her towards the city.

'I said, destroy the walls.' He snarled with a raging fury. Chaos swirled around her, burning his skin, but the drow didn't care, and on the edge of blacking out, Ina saw a dragon soar into the night sky.

'Destroy those fucking walls!'

He shook her violently, demanding obedience before realising she was no longer under his control. An inhuman screech tore from the drow's throat as Tar'eth attacked her psyche with the full power of his will, indifferent to the possibility of destroying it. Ina resisted, but Skarbnik's spell crumbled when he smashed her defences and reached for her magic. Before he could take hold of her again, Ina felt a cold, dark knot in her heart explode, and a crimson wave burst out, craving the death of her tormentor. A grimace of pure fury distorted her face as Tar'eth screamed, his skin melting from the torrent of Chaos. Driven by instinct, the witch reached into her hair and, in one smooth movement, pulled out Mar's gift of love, the viper hairpin, and sank it deep into Tar'eth's eye.

Shock and horror burned in the drow's remaining eye when she pushed harder, cackling gleefully till the sharp stick struck the back of his skull, splintering inside his brain.

Tar'eth collapsed to the ground, pulling her with him. Her actions went unnoticed as the screams of the victims and chants from the mages continued unabated, but lost in her magic, Ina didn't care. She stood up slowly and raised her head, calling Chaos to her like a precious, obedient puppy. War raged around her, and the witch savoured the destruction. Suddenly, she saw a volley of fire rolling in her direction, and Ina dispersed it with a casual flick of her wrist. The culprit, one of the blood mages, was preparing another volley with the victim's blood still dripping from his fingers.

Abominations, one and all. Vile creatures unworthy of living, Ina thought, seeing more mages turn in her direction. As these new threats assaulted her mind, she screamed, slamming both hands into the hard, frozen earth and channelling all the death and destruction of the battle into one monstrous, Chaos-fueled curse.

'Let the earth beneath us take your souls, you pig-fucking whoresons.'

The condensed magical energy burst out, blasting apart the ground beneath her feet. The earth shrieked in pain, splitting open into a deep chasm, swallowing the mages and their dying victims. At one with the Chaos, Ina rejoiced in the destruction as the earth beneath her crumbled, and she fell into the crevasse, smiling as she searched the heavens, hoping for one last glimpse of her dragon. *All monsters will die now. The rest is up to you, my love. Win this war for me,* she thought, closing her eyes, accepting her fate as she fell into the endless darkness of the violated earth.

CHAPTER TWENTY-FOUR

It took three burly men and a blow to the head to stop Mar from flying off to retrieve Ina after Ren told him she'd stayed in the camp. Even when he woke up, his eyes still shone with the dragon's golden glow.

'Tell me again why I shouldn't tear you apart for leaving her there?' Mar asked, pacing around the map room like a caged animal. Ren rolled his eyes as he witnessed Mar's over-protective nature return full force, realising that the enraged dragon would be useless if not calmed down, and quickly.

'She decided to stay in order to disrupt their magic. Mar, you know Ina. She has her own ideas on how to do things. We can't do anything about it now, so please focus on the task and think like a leader.' Ren approached him and placed a hand on Mar's shoulder. 'I saw the preparations, and I'm sure the army will make a move tonight. After all, both drow and kobolds prefer to fight in the dark.'

Mar looked up, teeth bared in a ferocious grimace, common sense fighting with his heart, but his years of soldiering and the trust in Ren's judgement eventually won. Mar placed a clawed, trembling hand on the map.

'Tell Daro to set up mages and archers on the walls. Prepare for a frontal attack, but don't let them light up the torches. I want the infantry alongside—'

'Mar,' Ren quietly stopped him. 'Ina said they have Chaos mages but mentioned they were weaker than her, so I think they will focus on the gates. Or maybe it's that Chaos mages just hate doors, but we must strengthen them.'

Mar nodded and scratched his beard, noticing how long it had grown.

'Post a force of infantry and cavalry by the gates. If they fall, the only option will be to charge forward before those vermin pour into the streets and start slaughtering civilians.' Mar looked at Ren. 'Did Ayni agree to help? I would love to have a pair of eyes above the battlefield to ensure we don't face any nasty surprises.'

Ren snorted a short laugh, and Mar looked at him, raising his eyebrow.

'Not only does she agree, but she also wants me to be her rider.'

Mar's heart quickened, and he looked at his friend with a mix of joy and concern. 'Ren, for the dragon, this is… you don't ask anybody to be your rider.'

'I know, as I said in the bathhouse, we both are aware of the situation and want to see where it leads. Now, don't you have a war to win?' he finished with a reassuring smile. Suddenly the door burst open, and an errand boy's tousled head appeared in the gap.

'My lord, the scouts reported the black army is on the move!' he shouted at the top of his lungs and ran to alert the other commanders.

Mar sighed heavily, stripped off his clothes, and used his magic to create a complete set of armour. Ren approached and poked it with his finger. Hard, overlapping dragon scales covered Mar's body; formidable protection for the upcoming battle. The captain had recreated the golden dragon crest of Liath on his chest so well that it almost appeared alive, making Ren shake his head.

'That's handy. Now shift your arse, pretty boy, or we'll miss the battle.'

The walls were quiet but well-manned. Mar watched as Ren discussed something with the leader of the shifters, and his friend came back to him with a grim expression on his face.

'His pack reports hundreds of soldiers approaching our walls, but I can't see or hear anything from here. Still, the werewolf swears on his life his scouts saw them, that he can smell the army, and that the scent intensifies with every passing minute.'

Mar nodded. 'Then we will trust his judgement. Light up the fires. We should welcome our guests with full honours.'

One by one, torches and fire baskets were lit on the walls, and their light revealed a sea of black armoured soldiers almost under their walls.

'Tell the mages to increase the light,' Mar commanded, cursing under his breath when the gravity of the situation hit him. He had allowed the enemy army to sneak up to the city walls.

Beams of light cut through the darkness, fully revealing the army's size at the castle walls. A wall of sound crashed against Mar's ears as the enemy mages released their hold on the spell of silence, and the screaming army charged forwards to attack. Mar snapped out orders to his sergeants, and, with instant obedience, they turned, shouting to their men. The launching of rocks and arrows swiftly followed, the screams as they landed sickeningly vile. As the kobold soldiers pushed onwards, the first few reached the walls, and with a nod from the captain, boiling oil was poured onto the helpless soldiers.

I need to find out what metal the kobolds used to craft their armour if we survive this, Mar thought, seeing how the arrows harmlessly bounced off the dark metal plates.

Soon Mar came face to face with the first attacker who breasted the rampart and drew his sword, screaming his battle cry before punching out with the hilt, forcing the surprised soldier back over the parapet to his death. The taste of ozone and sickly red light told the captain that the mages had joined the battle. Fireballs blazed a trail over his head into the town, destroying several buildings, and soon the fire spread, causing panic to those hiding within. Just as Mar turned to order their own mages to help, a young man in garish robes screamed an incantation, and water erupted from the sceptre clutched in his shaking hands to douse the flames.

Stood on the battlements, his sword deflecting a blow from his latest assailant, Mar staggered as an unseen force slammed into the castle gates and walls, killing scores of climbing soldiers. As he looked down, the captain shuddered at the sight of the crushed warriors before several fireballs struck the gates below. It seemed the enemy had finally focused on the weakest part of the defences, and Mar had a feeling they wouldn't last long.

'Ren, ready the soldiers. We must open the gates and attack before they turn the entrance into rubble!' he shouted, trying to make himself heard over the noise of warfare when something yanked on his chest. A quick glance revealed it wasn't physical, and Mar looked out, following the direction of the pull. A flash of red hair caught his eye, and the sight of the male grappling with her caused his dragon to erupt.

The next thing he knew, Mar was airborne, his eyes fixed on Ina, her magic an incandescent halo as she fought, falling to the ground with her assailant. His roar shook the sky, but even his massive wings couldn't get him there before another drow attacked her with magic, and Ina plunged her fists into the ground, releasing vast amounts of power.

The strain on his wings was immense as Mar forced himself to fly faster than ever before. Watching, helpless, anguish tearing apart his heart at the sight of Ina screaming and staring at the entire sect of drow mages as they disappeared into the collapsing ground. The chasm that formed swallowed them as if they'd never existed, but then, to his horror, the earth crumbled beneath his spitfire's feet, and she fell into the abyss, smiling serenely, her face turned up to the sky.

Mar dived in without a second thought, and the smell of lava soon replaced the musky aroma of dirt as his claws closed on Ina's torso. Thrusting out his wings, the dragon screamed in defiance as he fought to fly out of the molten crevasse, magma rising and closing the unnatural gap just below his tail before, with one more agonising beat, Mar's body smashed through the ridge of the chasm. Curling up to protect his precious cargo, Mar rolled, crashing to a halt in front of a shocked drow army.

Heart hammering in his chest, Mar gathered his courage to look. What if he came too late? He slowly raised his wing and sighed with relief at the sight before him. Ina knelt on the ground, coughing out the dust and fumes, but it was the most beautiful tableau for the exhausted dragon. His witch was alive, and that was all that mattered.

'Will you get off me, you overgrown lizard! And why the hell did you risk your life like this?' she said between bouts of coughing, and relief flooded him. Mar forced his body to move, but as soon as she stood up and he noticed the ruin of her clothing, he wanted to cover her up again and take her somewhere far away. If her magic wouldn't win this war for them, her arse would.

'Err… I… who…? Ina, if you want some armour, I promise I will buy you the best, but this? Please save it for our bedroom.'

As the surrounding soldiers began shaking off their surprise and drew their weapons, the dragon casually swept his armoured tail out and crushed the closest ranks. Unsure whether he should laugh or lock her in the vault, Mar blatantly ogled Ina's body without a hint of shame. The black leather chest plate and a few strips of black silk left very little to the imagination and were useless for protecting her against attack.

'Really, Mar? Like it was my choice,' Ina said, and her chin went up, challenging him, but Mar pointed to the heart of the battle that, in the meantime, had turned into a chaotic mess.

'I need to go back. You eliminated the enemy's magic, but people are still dying here.' He could see the counterattack from Liath after he took to the air had tipped the scales in their favour, but at what cost? The remaining drow prince had regained control after the initial setback caused by Ina's intervention. Mar looked down when Ina patted his neck.

'I have an idea that can stop it. I just need to get to higher ground. Would you let me fly with you again?' Mar was taken aback by her request. Their previous flying experience didn't end well for his spitfire. Still, Ina looked determined, and she was already climbing on his back.

'I can help, but I will have to link to your mind when we are airborne.' He noticed her nod and added, 'Where do you want me to go?'

'I trust you, do whatever is needed to get me up over there.'

Mar didn't question why. Ina's ideas were often unusual and challenging to execute, but they saved the day more often than not, so he nodded when she pointed to the centre of the battlefield. Mar leapt into the sky, wincing at his damaged muscles, and felt her body shiver and her thighs squeeze painfully at the base of his neck. Still, if she could endure this, so could he, and, steadying his flight, Mar headed towards the centre of the battlefield. He felt the power of Chaos gathering around her. The sensation was strange, but not unpleasant. Their arrival didn't go unnoticed, and Mar had to evade several arrows aimed in their direction.

'Stay here.'

He hovered over the centre, following her command. He felt Ina stretch out her arms, and raw Chaos from the slaughtered on the battlefield condensed around her. It felt like the weight of the fallen souls on his back. Suddenly, Ina released the magic with a single word that lit the sky and shook the earth, beating down like the hammer of the gods.

'KNEEL!'

Mar felt himself falling, and he could hear the snapping of the bones of those who attempted to resist.

'Ina!' he roared when his wings collapsed against his will, falling from the night sky.

'Fuck! I'm sorry, I'm so sorry!' the witch shouted in utter panic. Mar felt the link between them flare up, giving him enough strength to resist the compulsion, slowing their descent till he landed heavily between kneeling soldiers.

'You could have warned me.' Mar was not happy about the situation. Yes, she stopped the fight, but now enemies and allies alike were bound to the ground under her spell. And Ina, as usual, paid no attention to his words, only patted his neck like an overgrown horse. Still, he felt her hand tremble, and he shook his head. 'How long can you hold them like this?'

'I don't know,' Ina answered before adding, 'I can see Ord'eth. Please take me to him. We will end this now.'

Ina looked around the battlefield from the top of the massive dragon as they approached the kneeling drow.

'Ord'eth Al'Ean, it is a pleasure to see you again, this time in a more appropriate position. Still, I can't hold talks with a slave, so stand up.'

From the height of Mar's back, she watched him struggle to his feet and approach them. His eyes were bloodshot from the effort and rage, but Ina sensed something else: fear and reverence.

'Come on then, witch. Kill me. That's what you want. After I humiliated you in the keep, I should have ignored my feeble brother and beat you till you begged to serve at my feet.' He spat the last words out, and Ina was sure he was goading her, but she'd had enough killing for today.

'That would make me very much like you, don't you think?' Ina said and slid from Mar's back. The faint trembling in the peridot at her throat told her that the power harvested from the battle was waning, and if she continued to use magic, more death and destruction would be required to sustain it. 'I will give you a choice, Ord'eth. You can negotiate with me to return to your homeland with the remnants of your army and your pride only slightly dented. Or you can die here, and I will ensure every bard on the continent will sing of your humiliation and destruction. I can also promise that if you choose death, I will use it as a lesson to the world, and it won't be quick or clean. When I'm finished, everything you are, or could be, will forever be mine.' Tendrils of Chaos attached themselves to the drow's chest, and Ina pulled gently, barely tugging on his life's energy. Yet, the drow's face twisted in torment.

'I'll negotiate!' he shouted in an anguished voice, and Ina nodded.

'Then command your people to retreat to the far side of the field,' she said and looked at Mar. 'Please tell your army to go back behind the wall.'

'Yes, my liege,' Mar said, and his eyes shone with amusement when Ina closed her eyes and released her magic, letting it return to the aether. The energy tethering both armies to the ground dissipated into the air. Only Ina knew how close she was to losing control over it. The soldiers slowly climbed to their feet, shaking in fear, and left, following their superior's commands. Soon after, Alleron, accompanied by Ren and Daro, galloped over, halting in a flurry of mud and cursing, in front of Ina and the dragon.

'What the hell just happened here? One moment I was fighting on the wall, and the next, we were all on our knees and struggling to lift a finger,' asked the orc, but Ina didn't listen, focusing on fending off Zjawa, who had followed the trio and kept biting her armour.

'I know, I know, I shouldn't have left you there. Just stop it, girl. I said I'm sorry.' Ina pushed the horse's head away and stroked her with tenderness while the orein continued nibbling her clothes. Alleron coughed a little to get her attention, and when it didn't work, he grasped her shoulder.

'Inanuan Thornsen, stop playing with your orein and tell us what happened here and why this drow is still alive?'

His voice, but more his touch, made her look at the group of men. She didn't even notice Mar had changed and was now standing nearby, holding Woron.

'We will negotiate.' She saw Alleron's desire to protest and raised her hand. 'Lord Commander of Liath, I'm not asking. As a judicial mage and agent of His Majesty, King Rewan of Cornovii, I am telling you we will negotiate with the drow and kobolds.'

Ina didn't miss Mar's smirk, and she couldn't help but add, 'I've had just about enough of this fucking war.'

'Then please, my Lady Thorn, I bow to your authority. You have my castle at your disposal.' Alleron bowed slightly, gesturing for his men to chain Ord'eth, but Ina cut them off and sent them to search for anyone willing to stand as the kobold leader.

As soon as they complied, she jumped onto the orein and said, 'Daro, please ensure everyone gathers in the map room in about an hour. If the lord commander of Liath agrees, of course.' Mar's father nodded, and she turned her horse to head towards the castle, trying hard to pretend she didn't hear Daro's remark when he turned to Mar.

'What happened to Ina? When did she suddenly become the god of war, and what the fuck is she nearly wearing?'

From the corner of her eye, she saw Mar slap the orc's head and answer him. Gesturing obscenely, Daro snorted and went to look for the kobold representative. All seemed to go smoothly, and Ina hoped she could get out of sight before the urge to cough bent her in half. She couldn't risk showing weakness so soon after stopping the warring armies. A few minutes with a healer should do the trick, and then she could see to the negotiations. The thunder of a galloping horse behind her made her look behind. While Mar and his father escorted Ord'eth and a few drow nobles to the castle, Ren chased behind her, only to stop when their horses came alongside.

'Care to tell me why are you trying to disappear from the battlefield as soon as possible?' he asked, and when she didn't respond, Ren sighed and reached for her reins, provoking a mean snap of the orein's teeth. 'What happened there? I felt your magic forcing my submission, and you almost broke Ayni when she fell from the sky.'

'I stopped the fighting. There was enough Chaos to destroy the mountain, but I only channelled it into one command. Just like in the legends. Isn't it hilarious?' Ina said and barked a short laugh that soon turned into a bout of coughing. 'Just get me to the healer. The fumes cooked my lungs because I forgot the rule of not screaming when falling into a pit of fire.' The city gates were looming closer, and Ina saw Ren's eyes widen at hearing her statement, reaching for her in concern, but she shook her head.

'No, not where they can see me. The Chaos mage must leave the battlefield strong and victorious, or they will use my weakness to start fighting again like rabid dogs.' Much to her relief, Ren withdrew, but the vertical line between his eyebrows and the tightening of his lips told her he was not happy with this arrangement.

As soon as they entered the city, Ina's rigid posture sagged, and she collapsed against the orein's back. Ghost kicked his horse into a gallop, and Zjawa followed closely. Ina was grateful for her unusual mount as the witch didn't feel the speed at all, almost like she glided through a dream, and the witch idly wondered if she should worry about that, which caused a giggling fit that quickly turned into more coughing.

They arrived at the castle in no time, especially since the citizens were too busy assessing the damage the magical fire did to their households to pay attention to the insane pair galloping through the streets. Ren stopped the horses before the grey building and helped Ina off her mount. In the heat of battle, she hadn't felt the damage, but now all the injuries, tension, and exhaustion overwhelmed her with a vengeance and Ren's gentleness made her cry.

'It will be fine. You are safe now, and whatever is broken, Nerissa can fix it.' His reassurance caused a small moan from her lips.

'What is she doing here? Please don't let her see me like this,' she whined, wiping her tears.

'You're not suggesting I'm not allowed to see my most frequent patient?' The icy voice from behind cut as deep as a dagger. 'I allowed you to search for your dragon, not get nearly killed in another war. Gods, give me patience with this girl.' Ina turned and tried to smile under the hawklike regard of her aunt. Finally, the old healer started issuing orders, taking a bag from the shelves.

'Fill up the bath and add this to it. Ina, come here.' When servants rushed to fulfil her order, and Ina obediently staggered to her aunt, she was grabbed by the scruff of her neck, and her face was pushed over the surface of a steaming bowl.

'Breathe in. It will clear your lungs, then we will strip you of… whichever prostitutes clothes you stole, and you will take a bath.' Nerissa looked at Ren. 'Why are you still here? Don't you have a job to do?'

Ina saw Ren salute and march out of the healing house with a rueful smile. The steam from the bowl eased the painful knot in her chest, and she felt her breathing ease. Servants quickly stripped her of the hideous leather armour before leading the witch to the bath chamber where, to the witch's horror, she saw a bath filled with something that she could only describe as rotting grass. Nerissa didn't give her a chance to voice her doubts and forced her into the water. Ina shouldn't have been surprised by the almost instant feeling of relief. After all, her aunt was the arch-healer, but the bliss she felt when her bruises and tiredness melted away was unreal.

'Thank you for always being there for me, auntie,' Ina said, smiling at her relative and earning a small head pat.

'Someone has to, my child. You are such a troublemaker. Now soak for a while. Your body is exhausted and what you did on the battlefield was… unprecedented. A word of power? You shouldn't even know such magic exists.' Through heavy eyelids, Ina saw her aunt shake her head. 'Your creative ways of using magic continue to catch everyone's attention, and the council will want to scrutinise your every move. So rest while you can.'

Ina felt cool, soothing magic seep into her body. Her eyelids closed reluctantly as exhaustion took over, and she drifted to sleep.

CHAPTER TWENTY-FIVE

The sound of raised voices penetrated the warm darkness that cradled her mind. Ina tried to ignore the grating noise, but the sound of a familiar arrogant, angry voice cleared the fog from her thoughts, and she slowly opened her eyes, a wry smile lifting the corner of her mouth.

'I will see my betrothed whenever I please. Now, get out of my way, woman, before I pick you up and move you myself.'

She heard a woman's shriek, and the door opened to reveal a cursing Mar, fending off servants with one hand and struggling to hold the door with the other. Ina couldn't help but chuckle.

'Let the hairy oaf inside. He will come in anyway, so there's no need to get hurt trying to stop him.'

When the door finally closed behind him, Mar pressed his back to the solid oak, blocking the only exit. His eyes scanned her body, immersed in the green goo that had become crusted on the surface.

'Why didn't you tell me you'd been injured? I would have taken you to the castle immediately.'

'Mar, I had to use all my power to stop the fighting. Do you think they wouldn't have killed me the moment they sensed weakness? Besides, Nerissa already had the pleasure of punishing me for getting hurt. Why else do you think I'm sitting in this swamp?' The smile meant to reassure him left him tugging at his beard before almost launching himself to bury his face in her neck.

'I know, you're right. No, the soldier in me knows you are right. What you did out there was magnificent. You were a queen commanding her unruly subjects. But love, I can't lose you. Being forced to leave you in the hands of the enemy, only to see you nearly die in the battle, tore the heart from my chest. Whenever you are in danger, I fail to keep you safe or even realise you are injured. Maybe I should step back and let Ren be with you. He is a far better man.'

Ina rolled her eyes so hard she was surprised they didn't pop out of her skull and go for a walk. She placed a wet, slimy palm on Mar's cheek and grabbed a handful of his beard, forcing him to look at her.

'For an intelligent man, you can be a top-notch idiot. First, I was not in control when he captured me and charbroiled your sorry arse before forcing you to fly away. Second, my injuries weren't bad enough to fuss over. And the most important thing? I chose you. If I wanted to be with Ren, I would be, and neither you nor any other man except him would have any say in the matter. So stop brooding about it and help me get out of this rancid sludge. I believe we have some negotiations to attend.' Ina attempted to stand up with comedic results as her feet slipped on the slippery mess. She almost cracked her head on the bath, but Mar, muscular arms at the ready, lifted her out and, stealing a kiss, set Ina's feet gently on the ground. He pressed her naked body to his chest for much longer than needed and leaned down, giving her ear a gentle bite.

'Stay there. I will call the servants,' he said and turned to walk to the door, happy to leave the rest of the work to the maids.

A short while later, Ina emerged, clean and smelling of winter apples, only to notice him frowning again.

'What now?'

'We need to fatten you up. I miss thc curves I saw in the hut,' he said, and Ina raised her eyebrow.

'Well then, how about we start now? I'm starving. Also, when you have time, do something with your beard. You look like a crazy, oversized dwarf, all bushy and wild.'

'My father ordered some food for the negotiations, and you are right. I let myself go a little. I was worried about my woman being trapped in drow dungeons, but I will tidy my beard as soon as you promise me you'll never wear that parody of armour in public.' He offered her his forearm, and they walked off towards their next battle.

'Marcach of Liath, are you blackmailing me? Especially since I noticed how much you appreciated the view.' Ina could not resist teasing him. She would never wear those leather rags even if they paid her, but Mar didn't have to know.

Mar raised her hand to his lips and kissed it gently. 'I would never do such a thing, but as I'm not the only one who appreciated the view, I find myself a very unsettled dragon.'

Ina shook her head, laughing. 'So, you are jealous and overprotective. You will have a hard life if you decide to be with me.'

Mar stopped and turned to face her before cupping her face in his large, callous hands. 'I told you, I'm here to stay, and I'm learning to be less of an ass. I didn't storm the kobold stronghold or stop you when you cheated Morana of her tribute. All I'm asking is a bit of patience. It is difficult to change overnight.'

Ina wished she knew what was going on in his head, but for the time being, she wrapped her arms around his muscular torso and cuddled him. They stood like this for a moment as passing servants, and other castle residents gave them amused looks. Finally, Mar eased Ina away.

'Everybody is waiting for us, my love. Let's go before my father comes here himself to get you. We will talk later in the evening. By the way, I'm sleeping in your bed tonight.'

'Are you indeed? What if I don't allow you to join me? You do have a track record of displeasing me.' Ina's annoyed tone was enough to let him know her thoughts on men who invited themselves into her bed.

'Then I will sleep next to your bed or guard your doors. After all, dragons must protect their treasures.' He winked and scooped her up, effortlessly jogging towards the map room, as they were already late.

When they arrived, the map room was crowded, and Ina regretted suggesting this location for the meeting. The long table was cleared of the provincial map, and now everyone was seated in front of an impressive meat platter, their late arrival welcomed by the angry stares of the assembled men, salivating over the meat. Ord'eth and two other drow nobles were sitting on the table's far side, guarded by Daro and his men. A kobold with one lone associate sat next to the drow, and, to Ina's surprise, a delegation of dwarves sat opposite the kobolds.

'What are they doing here?' she whispered to Mar, but not quietly enough to prevent the dwarves from hearing.

'You asked for our help, and we have come. Two hundred of our best infantry. Sadly, we missed the battle due to a little tussle in the trade tunnel,' he grumbled and looked at her, chin raised defiantly, expecting her to challenge his presence.

Ina only waved her hand. 'We are grateful for your arrival. We will likely need your services after this meeting.' She cast a pointed look at the drow and took her seat on the remaining chair between Alleron and Marcach, Ren positioning himself behind her.

'I asked you here to negotiate a peaceful end to this pointless war.' She looked at the drow nobles. 'Your initial goal of gathering the Chaos regalia will never be achieved. It drove Tar'eth insane just wearing the ring, and I can assure you the empress and her remaining legacy are now sufficiently guarded. No one, not even a Chaos mage, can retrieve it now.'

Ina looked at them, waiting for Ord'eth to acknowledge her words. When he nodded, she continued, addressing the drow and kobolds together.

'You came here to wage war, but I don't hold this against you. Kingdoms rise and fall, and every fool may try their luck. However, for better or worse, this is my home, and I will defend Cornovii until my dying breath. I will stop at nothing, leaving scorched earth and wailing widows in my wake as I visit your lands to repay your kindness. This is the moment to make your decision, so ask yourself: do you want to be my enemy, or accept that you have lost?'

Ina smiled and relaxed her hold on the Chaos magic, letting its tendrils gather around her, coating her skin in a bloody red hue and waited till the gasps at the table went quiet before addressing the kobolds. 'You lost your leaders and many of your kin in this war, but you also broke the oath given to Marcach of Liath.'

Her words hung in the air, and the kobold stood up. 'As you said, our leaders are dead. We were forced into servitude and had to follow the orders of those who held our families hostage, but we do not offer that as an excuse for our broken oath. Our lives are yours to command.'

Ina's words were heavily coated with sarcasm when she spoke. 'Dying is easy and so noble for your kind, but I have no use for your death. Nevertheless, the current status quo can not continue. You will swear allegiance to the house of Liath. You will keep your mines, your stronghold, and choose the one who will represent you in front of your lord and king. You will be part of Cornovii.'

'Inanuan, that is not within your authority. What do you think you are doing?' Alleron's outburst broke the dead silence that followed her words.

'I'm negotiating.'

'Negotiation means you let those involved decide, not make the decision for them,' the old lord said in frustration.

Ina smiled as she rose from her chair, dominating the room despite her small frame. She exhaled slowly, and a tremor ran through the stone walls of Liath, shivering the glass in its casements, leaving the gathered people exchanging worried looks. *They think I am lost to the madness.* This thought amused her, but Ina decided there would be no half measures today.

'My lord, I respect you as a ruler of your domain, but let me clarify something for you. I, Lady Inanuan of Thorn, judicial mage of Cornovii and the emissary of His Majesty, King Rewan, will make my ruling today, and I will make peace. Everyone here can take my terms and follow the king's orders, or reject them and see how far I will go to end this conflict. Cornovii has had enough of this constant warfare on the borderlands. We need a peace that will last generations, not pretty words that can be ignored by a greedy-minded mage with a fancy ring.'

Alleron looked at Mar, searching for support, but his son only shook his head. 'We tried it our way, and we ended up fighting yet another battle, so I'd say it's time to try another way.'

Defeated, the Lord of Liath sat straighter and looked at the kobolds through narrowed eyes. 'I will accept your service. You will send me fifty of your youngsters to train amongst my men. After two years, they will come back home. They will stand on the front line of Liath's defences if you break the peace. In return, we will help you re-establish your home and send supplies to help you survive the harsh winter. Will you accept these terms?'

The silent exchange between the kobolds lasted only a moment before, as one, they knelt in front of Alleron and offered him their blood oath.

The ceremony completed, the kobold leader turned to Ina.

'Lady Inanuan, our people are starving. Our granaries and stores are often empty for the winter. We are no farmers, and this oath has stripped us of any way to provide for the keep. We have ore and gems, but that doesn't feed the cubs.'

Ina's smile brightened the room. 'I don't think you understood Lord Alleron's offer. You are part of Cornovii. You will receive help and food to survive the winter. I'm sure someone will see the benefits of trade with your people and negotiate with you for your metals and gems.'

'Khmm…'

Ina looked at the dwarves and their elder, who'd interrupted her speech, and he bowed to her. 'My lady, forgive the intrusion, but if we're talking about trade. While we have an extensive mining operation in the Stone Halls, some minerals can be found only on this side of the Grey Mountains. Stonehall would like to participate in any trading agreement that may be negotiated in this region. With the trade tunnel safe from attack, we can offer our assistance with the markets of Zaron and Warenna.'

The elder looked at her, and Ina saw the promise of golden coins flashing in his eyes when he listed the benefits of trade with the Stone Halls and took her silence as disagreement. Suddenly, he slammed his hands on the table.

'Damn it, fine. We will equip the army of Liath. Our smiths and weapon masters will offer a twenty per cent discount, and we will send artisans to Liath. What else do you want, child, my blood?'

Ina bit her lip, trying not to laugh when the stoic elder bounced on his chair like an impatient toddler, fearing the deal of his life would escape his grasp.

Ina looked at Alleron and Mar, both men gritting their teeth, waiting for her decision. She could see the same greed in Alleron's eyes, but this time for swords and armour crafted by dwarven masters.

'I will leave this decision to the Lord of Liath, but I believe such a trading agreement would benefit everyone—' She couldn't finish because Alleron reached toward the elder, grasping his hand.

'I accept.'

The eagerness of his action made her smirk, and Ina didn't want to let this opportunity pass.

'I'm pleased to hear we have an agreement, esteemed elder. As you are here with your infantry, I will ask you to escort our guests back to their side of the mountain. I'm sure Arknay is missing its sons and husbands greatly.'

'We are not a package you can dispose of.' Ord'eth's entire posture radiated offence and disdain, and when his nobles started muttering in agreement, Ina approached them. Despite him trying to flinch away, her hand landed on the prince's shoulder, and she let her magic seep into his skin. He tried to shield, but it wasn't a direct attack he could deflect, and he was soon whimpering under her touch. However, Ina was unsure whether it was in pain or pleasure, but when he opened his eyes, she saw it was a mix of both.

'I haven't forgotten you and what you tried to do to me in the keep. So please, go ahead and give me one more reason to send you after your brother, but before I do, which do you think I should do? Keep your head above my fireplace as a souvenir, or send it to your mother as a memorial?'

More magic seeped into him, and she saw her touch tearing his arrogance apart and a lifetime of conditioning to female dominance resurface. She sank her nails into the soft skin of his throat. 'You will do as I say, and you will never step foot in Cornovii unless you are called by his majesty or beg for his permission.'

He nodded eagerly, grabbing her hand as Ina stepped back. This act of submission was both satisfying and repulsive. It took only a slight lift of her eyebrow for him to let her go. Ina moved back to her chair, feeling exhaustion stealing over her mind. Even the rejuvenating bath couldn't restore the energy lost from so much magic use, but there was one last item on her agenda.

'Lord Alleron, the shifter clans fought and died under your banner. I would appreciate your support in offering them full citizenship of Cornovii. It is only fair they enjoy your protection after their sacrifice in your service.'

'My lady, I would do that even without being asked. Now, can we continue to negotiate a trade agreement?' Alleron was eager to bargain with the dwarves, and Ina felt she had nothing more to add.

'Thank you, but I would ask you to continue without me. I know nothing of trade and wish to meet the mages from the capital now. Unless my presence is indispensable, I will leave you to it.'

Ina stood, every inch the noble lady, and left the room. The demonstration of magic brought about the desired effect, but left her body on the verge of collapse, and she headed straight for her room. Dizziness swept over her as she ascended the stairs, the world a spinning blur, and the rapidly approaching floor was the last thing the witch remembered.

'My lady, it is time to wake up, please. They are all waiting.' A distressed servant's voice broke through her dreams, and Ina sat up on the bed, rubbing sticky eyes.

'Calm down, girl. Who is waiting?' Ina asked, wishing whoever was waiting for her would contract some particularly virulent disease and let her sleep.

'Everybody. They're ready to depart, and Lord Marcach is finally allowing us to wake you. You have been resting for two whole days. Please let us help you dress.'

Ina looked around, confused. A bath was steaming in the corner, and her bed stank of sweat and healing salve. She stretched her body, but her exhaustion and injuries were gone. *Mar must have gone insane when I fainted*, she thought, smiling wickedly, and moved to the bath, letting the servants do their jobs and listening to their gossip.

Ina learned Mar had taken control in his usual overbearing manner, cracking heads and growling in displeasure. With his father gleefully neck deep in trade negotiations, the protective dragon became a terror in the barracks. Soon the soldiers learned that no protesting would spare them from training alongside kobolds and shifters, and the worried dragon had the temper of a toddler with a sore tooth. Ren, it seemed, would often escape his friend's tantrums by flying patrols on the back of Ayni, and thanks to this, both were becoming closer and happier, spending the time terrorising the retreating drow army to keep them true to their word. People returned to their homes, and Alleron granted ownership rights of any empty houses to those who chose to stay in Liath.

Ina found the servant's gossip reassuring, so she relaxed as they braided her long, damp hair into intricate braids. All seemed to be going in the right direction.

'So why are we suddenly in such a rush?' she asked the senior maid and noticed the woman bite her lip.

'I'm not sure, my lady, but on the day you held this… negotiation, Lord Alleron sent a message to the king, and we received an answer this morning. The young master called for a meeting and told us to wake you up as they needed to return to Osterad.' The maid rubbed her nose, and Ina waited, hoping she would add something to explain the need for rushing around. With a nervous bite of her lip and a twinkle in her eye, the old servant leaned in close to add, 'Maybe it's because you are famous now. There is a ballad the tavern bards composed after the battle. Let me sing it for you.'

Ina moaned and waved her hand to stop it, but it was too late, and the maid started singing.

Commanding the earth and fire,
Called by soldier's death,
The vision of last desire,
Whispered in a dying breath,
Morana's tribute taken,
By the lady of the crimson veil,
Kneel to her power and live,
To taste her sweetest ale.

'At least they didn't mention my whorish armour,' she whispered. The servants laughed at her crimson cheeks, and Ina considered asking the king to ban every bard who sang about her exploits from Cornovii. A knock on the door interrupted her musing, and Ren's head appeared in the gap.

'Ina, are you ready? We must go if we want to get to the ferry before dark,' he said, and a slight frown creased his forehead when he noticed her pained expression and giggling servants. 'Is everything all right?' he asked, and Ina smiled sadly.

'I heard the new song.' She saw Ren's lips twitch as he fought hard not to join the giggling crowd, but eventually, he lost, and his quiet laughter joined the others.

'Wait till you hear your new nickname. But unfortunately, we have to go. If you would join me, my lady?'

When they finally headed out, their little cavalcade was cheered by the citizens of Liath to the city gates. There were paintings of dragons on many of the city's buildings, almost as if the last battle revived the heritage of Liath, and now the people were proud to show it. Mar moved Woron closer to Ina and reached for her hand.

'Hope you had a nice rest. I'm sorry if we disturbed you, but Nerissa told me it was safe.'

'You spoke with my aunt?'

'Yes, and she wasn't happy. If that woman's tongue were any sharper, she would have flailed the skin from my body for not caring for you properly. I was informed, very firmly, that you required two days of full bed rest and that if anyone disturbed you, there would be a new head mounted over her mantle.' Mar looked at her as if she were made of spun sugar, ready to break at the slightest bump, and Ina returned his look with a scowl, snapping him out of whatever mistaken ideas he might have.

'Anyway, today we received a letter from the king, urging us to return to the capital, making sure we dress for the occasion. I didn't have a choice.' Mar continued explaining his actions, and Ina closed her eyes for a moment, breathing in the crisp winter air.

'It will be good to return home. I miss Boruta, Velka, and my bed,' she said, stretching till her bones creaked. 'But what is the occasion we are supposed to dress for?' she asked, noticing Ren and Daro wore their dress uniforms, and Ayni looked divine in an aquamarine dress with a fur-lined cloak to match.

'I don't know, but the king emphasised it in his letter, and my father pestered us to polish our armour till it shined,' Mar said, and Ina looked at her simple, high-quality grey dress and fur coat.

'So why am I dressed like this?'

'Because, my love, none of us had enough courage to dress you in something you didn't choose without your consent. I know you don't like the pretence of pageantry. Ren told me how you refused the king's orders after the last battle, but we packed you a gown worthy of your beauty and status, which even my mother admired.' Mar was visibly amused, and Ina couldn't stop thinking about Lady Lorraine's impeccable fashion sense. The witch straightened up her dress and answered with dignity.

'No, you are right. This will do. This will definitely do.'

CHAPTER TWENTY-SIX

The journey to the capital went quicker than Ina expected. The weather was pleasant, and their small group travelled along the main road without mishap, stopping only for one night's rest. Daro set a gruelling pace, and the men couldn't stop teasing him, saying he was rushing to return to Velka's warm bed. More often than not, Ren trailed behind them, engaged in a conversation with Ayni, and Ina felt quite conflicted about them. She loved to see him happy and relaxed beside the dragoness, but her relationship with Ayni was complicated. Deep down, Ina was worried about what would happen if the capricious female moved her attention to yet another man.

'If you don't stop, this frown will stay with you forever.' Mar's voice made her turn her head around.

'What?'

'Each time you look at Ren, your scowl gets deeper than the chasm from the battle. I thought you were happy for him,' Mar said, reaching out to tuck a stray curl behind her ear.

'I am. I just need to get used to this,' Ina said and stood in the stirrups to rub her backside. The journey would be short, but her tailbone was paying the price of this speed, and she wasn't looking forward to sitting down after the ride. Mar looked at her and called for the riders to stop.

Daro's horse danced under him when the orc turned back to Mar.

'We are so close, just an hour or two, and we will be in the city. Why do you want to stop now?' He didn't even dismount as the rest of the company leapt to the ground, happy to stretch their legs.

'I know, but we are tired. Do you want Rewan to meet Ina with a foul mood and a sore arse?' Mar's words were enough for Daro to dismount the horse, and Ina rolled her eyes.

'Stop making me into a monster. I'm not that bad.'

The witch huffed a little and sat on a tree stump, trying to sort out her wind-blown hair, while her cursing and swearing left a wide space around the frustrated woman as her comb got stuck in the tangled mess. Soon she felt Ren's slender fingers on her head and his amused voice.

'Let me help you before the recruits wet themselves in fear.'

His touch felt right and so familiar, melting the tension in her neck. She sighed with pleasure as he detangled her hair, plaiting it back in intricate braids, and Ina regretted losing the viper hairpin Mar made for her. *I know it made Mar happy that I used it to kill that bastard, but even so, it was special to me*, she thought, and the memories of the battle filled her mind.

'What keeps your thoughts occupied?' asked Ren.

'The casualties of the fighting. I wonder if we could have stopped it earlier or avoided the whole damn mess in the first place if I knew more about Chaos,' she said with a bitter smile and felt Ren's hands still for a moment.

'We did what we could with the resources and information we had. And ultimately, we won a war and went a long way to uniting the races in Liath. Despite what you did during the battle, you are not a god, so stop blaming yourself for things beyond your control.' His scolding tone was so sharp that Ina couldn't help but laugh.

'You are impossible, Sa'Ren, but thank you for reminding me who I am.' She cuddled her cheek to his hand and paused before her soft, quiet voice stopped his hands. 'The link we share, I think it helps to ward off the Chaos madness. Even in the darkest moments, its light helps me find the right path. Thank you for being my friend, my moonlight guardian.'

❄❄❄

Mar stopped by Ayni, who was grooming the horse with unnecessary force.

'He still loves her,' she murmured when Mar came closer.

'I know.'

'And this doesn't bother you? She seems to love him too.' The dragon's tone was bitter, and Mar placed his hand over hers and turned her to face him.

'No, I'm not. Ren will always love her, and Ina will always see him as a friend who might have been more if not for her love for me. They made their choices, and they never crossed the line. How can I blame Ren when I feel the same? I can only tell you he handles this much better than I would.'

'But I wanted—' Ayni started, but Mar stopped her.

'I know, and trust me when I say Ren has a deep affection for you. You have earned the trust of a man who has fewer friends than Daro has tusks. So give him time. Love grows slowly when magic isn't involved, and don't underestimate our Ghost when he chooses his path, or you will miss out on something truly wonderful.'

Ayni looked at him with growing understanding, and a tentative smile lit her face. 'I hope what you say is true. I want to get to know him better. All this time, I thought I wanted a dragon to soar in the skies with, but his presence affected me more than any dragon ever did. I want to give that feeling a chance.'

Before she could say more, Ina and Ren joined them. The witch looked beautiful with frost-blushed cheeks and a crown of copper hair wrapped around her head.

'Shall we go? I would like the chance to sleep in my bed tonight,' Ina said, and Mar nodded without taking his eyes from her face, and when she approached the orein, he grabbed her by the waist and lifted her onto her mount in one smooth movement, taking a moment to kiss the soft, warm skin of her wrist.

'I hope I will be welcomed in this bed of yours tonight. I can even share it with your cat.' The playfulness in his voice made her chuckle.

'Ah, but the question is, will he want to share it with you?'

Mar replied with a twinkle in his eye and a snap of his fingers. 'Then the deal is set. I will prostrate myself before the furry god, hoping he will grant me the maiden's love for the night.'

She couldn't believe this man, teasing and joking around, was the hairy oaf who made her life so difficult when they investigated the monsters of Osterad. She patted the orein good-naturedly on the neck and pointed to the road. Zjawa snorted loudly and gave Mar a distrustful glance before heading down the road. The rest of the company followed, and soon they were travelling at a brisk trot, enjoying the midday sun. As they approached the capital, more and more people lined the route, cheering and waving at their company till Ina was left squirming in the saddle.

Eventually, they stopped at the city gates, the king's herald blocking their way as he struck an imperious pose. With a flourish worthy of the finest playhouse, the pretentious emissary bowed, flashing a wide smile before launching his proclamation.

'His Majesty welcomes the saviours of Cornovii, the mighty Chaos mage, Lady Inanuan of Thorn, and the king's dragon, Lord Marcach of Liath, on their return to Osterad, and is pleased to grant an audience to such august personages at the palace at their earliest convenience. If you would please follow me?'

Ina sighed, feeling the likelihood of a bath, bed, and rest vanish into thin air. She could feel Jorge's hand, or rather, his predictions were to blame for their timely welcome and urged the orein forward. Zjawa, sensing her mood, snapped the feather off the herald's hat with visible pleasure, but before the witch could tell him where he could stuff his audience, Mar placed a hand on Zjawa's reins and nodded.

'It will be our pleasure to accept the sovereign's gracious invitation.'

Two rows of trumpeters launched into an enthusiastic victory fanfare as they entered the capital, and a large crowd, cheering and waving, parted before them as they headed off to the palace. Ina was surprised by the public's reaction. The citizens of Osterad rarely showed ostentatious emotions, but now clapping and cheering followed them, and she realised the king was using their small group for political gain.

'Ina, this is important. Please don't be… yourself,' she heard from Daro as he brought his horse abreast of Zjawa.

'What is important?' she asked as the partially restored palace gates appeared at the end of the street, gasping at the sight before them. 'Oh fuck, what is this? Are we here for a public execution?'

Even Mar looked surprised by the welcoming committee. On a makeshift platform, looming over a crowd of gathered nobles, sat Rewan and what appeared to be the new royal council. Everyone was dressed to impress and visibly upset at the situation.

I will kick this royal bastard's crown jewels so hard his progeny will feel it. Ina's temper was about to boil over when King Rewan reached up and elegantly offered his hand to help her to the platform.

'Nobles and citizens of Osterad, please welcome the heroes of Cornovii. Inanuan Zoria Thornsen, Lady of Thorn, and Captain Marcach, scion of House of Liath.'

Rewan raised his hands, and the crowd on both sides roared their approval. Ina saw Nerissa and Arun on the council chairs and felt envy bite her pride. Her great-aunt must have used a relocation spell, a high-level Order spell, to get here so quickly. A sharp kick to her shin reminded Ina to smile and wave to the welcoming crowd, even if the look she gave Mar promised violence later.

'Thanks to the effort of the two ducal houses, a terrible threat to our country has been defeated. When the rogue drow prince defeated the kobolds and forced them to renege on their vow never to raid our kingdom, they made the fatal mistake of threatening the house of Liath. With Lady Inanuan, the dragon of Cornovii defeated the evil forces of Arknay, expanded our borders, and created a trade agreement that will strengthen our country for years to come.'

The cheer that greeted these words forced the king to pause in his speech and wait till the crowd quietened before continuing.

'To celebrate this victory, we will provide twenty gold coins and a full cart of supplies to all who decide to return to Liath to help develop a lasting peace there.'

Rewan's words finally made sense to her. The refugees. The capital had looked more crowded than she remembered. She looked at Rewan, and he shrugged under her scrutiny. Once again, the cunning monarch was riding the wave of their success, but she could not fault his intentions. Still, Rewan looked at her as if he expected her to say something, and Ina rolled her eyes as she lowered herself into a deep curtsy before replying, keeping the sarcasm to the lowest level she could manage.

'Thank you for your kind words, Your Majesty. I am happy to have assisted the Dragon of Liath in his endeavours. Our country has gained powerful new allies, and the magic of the Grey Mountain shall stay free from evil for as long as I live.' She rose slowly, and Rewan seized the opportunity to speak.

'Our land is safe thanks to these heroes. To honour them and all those who fought in the Winter war, I, Rewan Mavolo, Sovereign of this great country, grant every soldier, human or not, and the families of the fallen a lifelong pension with full protection of the state. Captain Marcach, a warrior and leader who fought valiantly and proved that the heritage of Liath will always live on in her sons, shall now be known as the Royal Dragon of Cornovii. As he has proven his leadership, honouring his courage, from today onward, he shall lead the army of

Cornovii. Hail all Lord Marshall Marcach of Liath, the Royal Dragon of Cornovii!'

Ina heard Mar muttering curses as he bowed his head for the king and accepted a massive steel sigil with an embossed, rampant dragon. Her hopes that Rewan would stop at this were destroyed when he spoke again.

'Before we celebrate and allow our tired heroes time to rest, I have one last announcement. For her accomplishments and unquestionable moral strength, Lady Inanuan of Thorn will receive the title of Royal Witch and a seat in the Royal Council. Her unique magic and forthright manner shall benefit all of Cornovii, and its king shall endeavour to accept such honest counsel.'

Covert laughter ran through the crowd as people remembered the songs of her antics with the late king. As soon as Rewan finished his speech, servants with platters full of food and drinks appeared from behind the platform. With an enthusiastic cheer, the crowd threw itself on the feast while the nobles and council disappeared inside the palace.

'I'll show him. Royal witch. He'll soon find out how big of a b—*witch*, I can be,' Ina said, almost spitting the words and marching towards the palace. She had barely stepped through the gates from his latest task, and he now wanted to saddle her with the royal council and additional responsibilities?

Kaian slipped out of an alcove, intercepting her. 'Mar, Ina, Rewan would like to see you both in private. I would ask you to remain calm, please, it's been a difficult time here as well, and he didn't have much choice.'

'Where is he?'

'In his office,' answered the master assassin with a quirk of his lips. 'You know the way. I'll join you there soon, so please don't break anything expensive.'

The office was messier than Ina expected, with stacks of paper and reports strewn across the desk. Rewan stood by the window, looking out, lost in thought. As soon as he heard them enter, he turned, running in her direction, and locking her in a tight embrace. This sudden gesture caught her off-guard, and Ina awkwardly returned the hug.

'Thank you, my friend. Thank you so much,' he said, cuddling his cheek to her head. 'You have no idea how incredible you are.' The tiredness and genuine affection in his voice cooled her anger, and Ina sighed, feeling there would be many things to discuss later. For now, she let him embrace her as something inside her told her even kings needed a little comfort on occasion.

'Your Majesty, would you mind explaining what's going on?' Mar's dry voice broke the moment, and Ina turned around to see the newly appointed Lord Marshall standing by the door, fists clenched and attempting to restrain the anger flashing in his golden eyes. Rewan laughed as he released Ina and gestured to the chairs set out in readiness. The doors opened as soon as they sat down, and Kaian walked in, heading towards the king.

'Did I miss anything fun?' he asked in a cheerful voice, and Ina felt a tingle of mischief run through her veins.

'Nothing much, just Rewan fondling me, Mar getting jealous… the usual,' she answered, and the master assassin exploded into laughter before planting a soft kiss on the king's lips.

'Did you really fondle our Ina, my love?'

Mar gasped and looked at the couple, completely bewildered. As for Ina, she'd heard the rumours that Rewan shared his father's taste for all genders and watched them with a knowing smirk that turned into a genuine smile when she noticed the budding hope in Rewan's eyes, but she still couldn't help herself.

'Since we are all happily fondled now, would you care to explain the ridiculous pageantry at the gates, and I'm definitely still mad at the title. Royal Witch? Couldn't you think of a title that makes me sound less like a crone?'

Mar finally regained his composure and nodded. 'Congratulations on finding someone worthy of your love, Your Majesty, but I second Ina. These titles will cause nothing but trouble for everyone involved.'

'So you don't mind, Lord Marcach?' asked Kaian, and Mar rolled his eyes.

'I'm a soldier, remember?' he said as if this explained everything, and Ina caught the king's chuckle before his face turned serious again.

'Since the war started, we've had countless refugees coming to the capital, and not just from the west. Initially, we managed, but we quickly ran out of space to house them, and people started dying from the cold and disease. As you can imagine, after the recent troubles with monsters, we had to find a solution before there was any rioting. I needed to convince those of Liath it's safe to return home, and those from southern provinces we have a remedy for their troubles,' Rewan said, and Ina nodded as he confirmed what she already suspected.

'What troubles, and why the titles? We don't need or want them.'

'There is more brewing in the south than we could cover in this brief meeting. The lords of the south have been using the situation in Liath to foment a rebellion, and my spies are sure that as soon as the snow melts, they will implement their plans. The peasants whisper of Marzanna stalling the spring and rotting the crops. There is also a rogue volkhv who seems to have the power to do miracles. So I am using you. The stories from the battlefield are already spreading across the land, thanks, in part, to Kaian, but that means as soon as the nobles see I have your loyalty, they will think twice about starting another war, and whatever mage is stirring the pot down there will be deterred by Ina's power.' Rewan turned to Mar before continuing. 'I apologise for emphasising you being a dragon and tying you so close to the monarchy. The threat of both a Chaos mage and a dragon was too good not to use. That is why I made you Lord Marshall. I understand if you choose never to fight on a battlefield again, but I would ask you to rebuild the army of Cornovii. Thank's to my sister's greed, all we have now is gold. Use it to build and train our army. You have a free hand to do as you please.'

'As you say, I am a dragon. How do you know I still care about the problems of Cornovii?' Mar asked quietly, and Ina saw how deeply disturbed he was by this recent revelation.

Rewan smiled, covering the hand resting on his shoulder with his own, looking up into Kaian's eyes. 'Sometimes, you have to trust your instincts. Now go, rest and think about it. Oh, and don't forget about the wedding.'

'Yours?' asked Ina, blinking rapidly, and when Rewan shook his head, she stomped her foot. 'I am not getting married.'

When both men burst into laughter, she gave them an evil look. Kaian stopped first.

'Velka and Daro's. I don't think they want to wait any longer. Your friend stormed in here as soon as Daro put his foot inside the city walls, demanding the ceremony be held in three days.'

The thud of the slammed door shook the palace walls as Ina ran out to the king's office, one thought in her mind. She had nothing to wear, three days to prepare, and hadn't even been home yet.

It took some searching to find her orein, till Ina thought to head for whoever was cursing the loudest in the stables. After following the sound of shouting, she arrived at a surprising scene. Two groups of stable hands were arguing, one armed with whips and crops, the other with carrots and apples, both bickering over who could best save the winter hay from this crazy animal. The animal in question was lying in a pile of broken hay bales, happily munching on what appeared to be the remains of several rats, the tail of one hanging from Zjawa's teeth.

'Zjawa, we are going home,' Ina called, and the orein leapt up, happily prancing over to her rider, to the collective relief of everyone involved.

The journey through the town took much longer, and Ina was close to losing her patience several times after trying to avoid all the people reaching out to touch the "magical horse."

Her townhouse was quiet and dark, and Ina felt her heart tremble. An almost forgotten guilt resurfaced, and she took a deep breath, hoping her unfortunate servant was still alive. After all, she hadn't seen her after the palace battle, despite knowing she'd been injured. Delaying the inevitable, Ina removed Zjawa's saddle and tack and led her to the small stable.

'There, this is our home. I hope you like it. If not, I want you to know you are free to leave.' Ina pressed her head to the orein's long neck until the mare playfully snorted in her hair and nudged her towards the house. Slowly dragging her feet, Ina walked up to the door.

Much to her relief, there was no musty smell typical of abandoned houses. After lighting a few candles, Ina noticed her small abode was pristine and clean, but before she could see more, a bolt of black fur hit her chest, sending her crashing to the floor.

'Boruta, my love.' Ina embraced her cat and pushed her face into the soft fur, inhaling deeply. The familiar forest scent brought tears to her eyes. She had survived and returned home safe and sound.

'What have you done this time, you Leshy spawn? I told you she will be home soon.' The surly, dry voice could belong to only one person.

'Marika, I'm so glad you are alive.' Ina choked on tears, seeing her scarred face and arm hanging limply to the side, but her housekeeper didn't seem to notice.

'So you are finally back? Did you bring anything from the palace, or should I cook some soup?' she asked as if nothing had happened, and Ina hadn't been away since the beginning of winter.

'Some soup would be wonderful.' The witch got herself off the floor and embraced the girl. 'I mean it. I'm sorry for leaving you alone, and I'm happy you are alive and here with me.'

'Yeah, I'm happy too, and I'm more pleased that you are alive as you owe me almost two months wages.' The werecat patted Ina's shoulder and went to the kitchen, leaving her baffled in the middle of the room.

Ina picked up the cat and went upstairs. Later, after a bath, some soup, and not getting a single answer from Marika about her injuries, she went back to bed and slowly closed her eyes. Just as her mind began to slip into the land of dreams, the bedroom door slowly opened, and a tall masculine shape slid into the room. She heard the bed creak under his weight, and a large arm grabbed her waist, pulling her close to his body.

'Mar…?'

'Hmm…?' he murmured in her ear.

'You have your own house with a very nice bed. What are you doing in mine?' she asked out of curiosity, enjoying his warm hairy chest pressed to her back.

'I don't have a home anymore, and unless some good-hearted witch gives me shelter, I am a homeless man,' he said, and Ina jolted upright on the bed.

'What the hell are you saying now? You are not living here.' She'd barely gotten used to the idea of being in a relationship, and he already wanted to move in with her? 'And where is Boruta? He always sleeps with me,' Ina finished as if the feline could fix any problem.

'Your cat is nose-deep in the finest steamed partridge from the king's table. So unless you want me to kick Ren back to the barracks and Ayni onto the street, I will have to impose upon your hospitality,' said Mar, unphased by her outburst.

Ina eyed him for a moment, muttering something about cat traitors and brainless men, but finally lay back down. Mar wrapped the blankets around her and embraced her from behind. It felt impossibly good, and Ina sighed in resignation.

'Only for tonight. Or maybe a day or two till you find a place to live,' she said, basking in the masculine scent with the hint of freshly washed dragon.

I will give him a week, but only because I'm a kind and reasonable person, she thought, unable to see Mar's mischievous smile and the golden light of his eyes glowing in the room.

Rurik looked at the dark clouds that hung above Osterad, promising more snow. The Winter War, as peasants had started calling events in Liath, didn't go as planned, and much to his surprise, Cornovii had emerged stronger than ever, but that only reinforced his belief Ina was the person they needed. However, his hope that Ina would voluntarily follow the path he laid out for her faded when she returned from the mountains without the circlet, but at least that fool of a drow gave her the ring. Giving him such a precious artefact had been a gamble, and although it didn't go as planned, the witch now possessed two pieces of the regalia. Today, as Rurik observed the welcoming heroes, he couldn't help but smile. *Such inelegant titles. She could be so much more. No, she will be so much more*, he thought, pondering over their plans.

The Osterad scheme went well. Ina was removed from the Leshy's protection, and once he waved the necklace in front of the troll's face, Gruff had leapt at the chance to pass it to Ina, but the Liath was almost a total failure. *It looks like our future archmage will need more substantial encouragement to reach for her power.* It was time to go to the south. The seeds of discord were already there, and his mother had helped to fan the flames. Not that he liked her idea, but revolutionary ideas required an iron will, and if that's what it took to force Ina's hand, he would sacrifice everything to complete her conversion.

Afterword

Dear Reader,

We hope you enjoyed our book and would love to hear about your experience. We would kindly ask you to leave a review on your chosen website.

If you are interested in following Ina's adventures third book in the series called SPRING BLIGHT will be released at the end of April, and pre-orders will soon be available on Amazon

For more information about our books and giveaways, please sign-up for our newsletter http://eepurl.com/hZhWcT.

To keep in touch via the website or social media, please check our all-in-one link: https://linktr.ee/olenanikitinauthor

Once again, we very kindly ask you to review and rate our book

Olga&Mark (aka Olena Nikitin)

Glossary

Baba Yaga – (Slavic mythology) is, in Slavic folklore, the wild old woman, the witch; the mistress of magic and a mythical creature.

Bi chamd khairtai - I love you (Yanwo dialect)

Botchling – a lesser monster, a small creature resembling a highly deformed fetus - created from the improper burial of unwanted, stillborn infants - preys on pregnant women.

Boruta – (Slavic mythology), a forest demon, is often considered an avatar of Leshy.

Chaos – the life itself. In our books, it represents the primary source of magic and life. The primitive, brutal force of unrefined magical energy that can change the very structure of living beings and inanimate objects.

Chram - (Slavic mythology) – the most sacred place, a temple for the Slavic deity associated with specific rituals, prophecies and miracles. Chram could be a building but also a forest, swamp or any natural setting.

Cornovii – Merchant kingdom between the Black Forest and Grey Mountains. Because of the geographical position multiracial centre of trading.

Daro – "dark power" Steppe Ork, the rebellious son of tribe thane drafted into the King's Guards, known womaniser.

Gruff – "the rock" Rock troll, owner of Drunken Wizard and spymaster of Osterad.

Hela - also referred to as the "Two-Faced Terror", is a goddess of the dead, especially those who drown in the sea.

Imp – a lesser demon. Imps are often shown as small and not very attractive creatures. Their behaviour is described as being wild and uncontrollable. Imps were fond of pranks and misleading people.

Inanuan – "beautiful destruction." Also known as Ina or Inanuan Zoria Thornsen. High-born lady of the principal ducal house of Cornovii and the first pure Chaos mage born in a generation.

Jarylo/Jaryło - god of vegetation, fertility and springtime.

Jorge – "supreme knowledge". Arche-mage of pure Order. He can foresee the future by applying his order magic to reality patterns.

Kaian – "strong warrior". Scion of the primal ducal house of Cornovii, the House of the Water Horse. Also head of the Assasin Guild.

Kings's guards – also called the second son's company. Unit designed strictly to guard the palace and investigate issues related to high-born nobles or state affairs.

Kobold – member of the kobold race. Cruel and proficient warriors and metalworkers living in the mines and tunnels in the Gray Mountains. Shorter than humans, often seen in bulky black metal armour. Their race has zealous adherence to oaths, pacts or customs.

Lada/Łada - a goddess of love and Nature's rebirth in the spring, patron of weddings and matriarchy, and protector of families and ancestors who passed away.

Lady Midday/Południca – a mid-class demon who makes herself evident in the middle of hot summer days, takes the form of whirling dust clouds and carries a scythe, sickle or shears. She may appear as an old hag, a beautiful woman, or a 12-year-old girl. It is dangerous at midday when she can attack workers, cut their heads off, or send sudden illness.

Leshy – (Slavic mythology) a God of wild animals and forests. He protects the animals and birds in the forest and tells them when to migrate. He is a shapeshifter who can appear in many forms and sizes but is usually a tree, wolf, cat, or hairy man. His fickle Nature causes him to help one he deems worthy and punish those who mean wrong to the forest.

Liander – "flower of pride". Half-elve, the strongest psychic mage of his time. Also, the court mage after Ina's departure.

Liath - dukedom of Cornovii associated with the House of Liath. It is a mountain region on the west defending the Grey Mountains and is known for its military power.

Litha or Kupala night - a midsummer solstice celebration dedicated to love, fertility, and water. Young people jump over the flames of bonfires in a ritual test of bravery and faith. The failure of a couple in love to complete the jump while holding hands signifies their destined separation.

Marcach – "wind rider." Also known as Mar or the Scion of Liath. The oldest son of the principal dukedom house of Cornovii. A war veteran and current Captain of the King's Guards.

Marika –"kitten" Were-cat from Grey Mountain clan and Inanuan housekeeper.

Morena/Marzanna - She is a personification of the repetitive cycles regulating life on earth, the changing seasons, and a master of both life and death. As Morena symbolises death on the battlefield,

Marzanna symbolises Winter Death, the starvation period that happens at the end of the winter when supplies are low.

Morganatic marriage – a marriage where a high-born woman marries the commoner losing her status.

Meridian -The meridian system is a concept in traditional Chinese medicine adapted for this series. Meridians are paths through which the life energy is known as "qi" or chaos flows. In the book, meridians are energetic highway that distributes life energy/raw Chaos along the body.

Nawia – (Slavic mythology) is also used as a name for an underworld over which Veles exercises custody. Although slavs knew no concept of hell in our books, we associate Nawia with the unpleasant part of the underworld.

Nerissa – grand -duches of house of Thorn. Arch-healer of Cornovii and Inanuan grand-aunt.

Osterad – The capital of Cornovii. Started as a simple river port with time, grew in riches and became the centre of human magic on the continent.

Phoenix – (Greek mythology)Immortal bird, a good omen, that dies in flame to rise from the ashes

Rewan – "the cunning one". Hair apparent, and later ruler of Cornovii.

Roda – "the nest", womaniser and drunkard. King of Cornovii, also known under "Limp Dick" moniker after Ina's outburst.

Sa'Ren Gerel – "son of a moonlight". The native name of Ren, one of the King's guards. He is also known as the Ghost for his exceptional sword master skills and otherwordly cold demeanour.

Senad – the bastard child of a high house, lesser noble. Second in command of King's guard and Marcach friend.

Sophia – "the white gem". – Princess of Cornovii, sister of King Rewan, renowned for her beauty.

Striga/Strzyga (Slavic mythology) – is a female creature who feeds on human blood. Their origins are connected to the belief in the duality of souls. A common explanation was that a human born with two souls could become a *strzyga* after death. Such people were easy to recognise, born with two rows of teeth, two hearts, or other similar anomalies. They could die only partially – one of the souls is leaving for the outer world, but the second one is getting trapped inside the dead body, losing many aspects of humanity. *Strzyga*'s appearance can resemble an average person with a mean character. The longer they live as a *strzyga*, the more they change. They are often presented with bird-like features: claws, eyes, and feathers growing off the back.

Swaróg/Swarożyc- god of fire, blacksmithing and creation, pictured as an old but powerful man with white hair and a hammer. Often believed to be the creator of the world.

Truthseeker – a branch of mind magic associated with Order. A psychic mage who connects with another person's brain to trace patterns of lies and, if needed, dissect memories looking for the truth.

Tomb hag/ Grave hag are territorial creatures. Their lairs resemble caricatures of human homes and are built near burial sites. They venture out at night to hunt, stalking straggling travellers or mourners too lost in their grief to notice the sun's setting.

University of High Magical Arts/ The Magica Council – School and the highest authority for practising mages, witches and warlocks that has supreme jurisdiction over the magic of Cornovii

Volkhv – high-rank priest of pagan religion

Veles – (Slavic mythology) a major Slavic god of earth, waters, livestock, and the underworld. A shepherd and the judge of the dead that rules Nawia. Associated with swamps, oxes and magic.

Velka – lesser noble. Gifted Nature with a strong association with trees and flowers. Also, Ina's best friend.

Vyvern - was a large winged lizard, distantly related to the dragon, with a poisonous stinging tail and sharp teeth.

Shifter tribes – shapeshifters with the ability to change into three forms, human, animal and shifter form, that contain both aspects of their soul.

Wyraj – (Slavic mythology) part of Nawia, an equivalent of heaven

Yanwo – far east land, ruled by the Dragon emperor and famous for trading silks, spices and gems with Cornovii.

Zhrets – low rank preist in slavic religion. A man who performs the sacrifices.

Acknowledgements

This writing journey would be much more bumpy and difficult without the people who helped us create this book. We would like to give our special thanks to

- **Maxine Meyer** - our excellent editor, who brought the book to shine and helped me to imporve my skils.
- **Germancreative** - I can't emphasize enough how we love her covers and how well it portrays the spirit of my books.
- **Najlakay** – for drawing an impressive map of Warenga
- **Fukamihb** – for illustrations that bring a smile to my face each time I see them
- **Daianav** – for excellent typesetting skills and for making my book pleasing to the eye.
- Our wonderful beta readers, who pointed out all the bigger and smaller plot holes and let us plug them all before the book reached you.

Andronia001, Sasha_pj, Monicam1001, Michaelpcoetzee, Bawrites and Rachel Sanders

About the Author

Olena Nikitin is our pseudonym. We are life partners and an enthusiastic couple of writers fascinated by fantasy/paranormal romance. We love humour with a down-to-earth approach to life, and all of this with a bit of steam and spice you can find in our books.

Hidden behind the pen name:

Olga is Polish, armed with a wicked and often inappropriate sense of humour and typical Slavic pessimism. She has written stories since childhood, initially mostly about her work. As an emergency physician, she always has a story to tell and often does not have much time to write. Also known as The Crazy Cat Lady, and proud to be one.

Mark is a typical English gentleman whose charm, refined taste and undeniable sex appeal tempted Olga to fly across the sea. Don't tease him too much; this man has an impressive sword collection and knows how to use it. He also can fix everything, including Polish syntax in English writing. He got shot in the Gulf War, and if you give him good whiskey, he will tell you this story.

For more, check: https://www.olenanikitin.uk

For updates and Newsletter, sign in: http://eepurl.com/hZhWcT

Also By:

All I ever wanted was the freedom to live as I chose… but I am the Harbinger of Chaos, and that sealed my fate.

When my temper got the better of me in front of the entire court, I ended up in the Black Forest, exiled and forgotten. If not for the Leshy, God and Guardian of the glades, I would have perished here, but chose me, and I lived.

Then everything changed with Marcach and Sa'Ren, both on the brink of death, with only me to save them. Not being a healer, I resorted to the only thing I knew and performed a forbidden spell that forever entangled our souls.

The monsters that brought them to me are still on the rampage. The kingdom is in peril, and my past returned to haunt my future. Dragged back into court affairs to face unseen enemies and a spellbound love I never wanted I have to fight for who I am and who I want to be.

I am lady Inanuan of Thorn, Chaos incarnate and the bearer of change... but I want to be known as Ina.

Yes, THAT Ina, the untamable witch that told the world of the king's limp dick.

Immerse yourself in Season's War series and learn about the kingdom of Cornovii, where passion is mixed with cruelty, and the unwilling hero with world-shattering power has to make impossible choices. Dark Fantasy with mature themes - reader caution advised.

Available on Amazon: https://www.amazon.com/dp/B0B1Z1P47P

A LITTLE ACCIDENT,
Season's War Prequel

"PRIDE AND CHAOS SHOULDN'T BE MIXED IN ONE CAULDRON."
Nerissa the Arch Healer of Cornovii

Life is complicated enough when you are the scorn Chaos mage and the lady of the noble house. However, Ina took the art of misfortune to new heights, the day she decided to save the life of the common frog.

There is a reason the common folk say "no good deeds go unpunished," and Ina's moment of weakness can bring catastrophic consequences.

Available on Amazon: https://www.amazon.co.uk/dp/B09XLM1CWG

Printed in Great Britain
by Amazon

10975344R00221